Praise for *Cowkind: A Novel*

"Cowabunga, what a first novel! . . . Petersen is a master of difficult tricks: he creates complex characters with few words and minimizes his animal characters' cuteness, instead using them to explore the human psyche. Comparable to Richard Adams's *Watership Down* or *The Plague Dogs*."

— *Library Journal*

". . . a fascinating book . . . With wit and wisdom, insight and invention, Ray Petersen has written about cows that converse, speculate, and have an innocent interest in the world around them . . . quite an interesting tale by a skilled author."

— Denver *Rocky Mountain News*

"Give first-time novelist Petersen credit: Not many would have thought of exploring the hard lives of a farm family through the eyes of a dairy herd. And even fewer could have sustained the conceit as successfully as Petersen does . . . Petersen's fabulistic evocation of cows is wonderfully detailed and moving: Their rituals, beliefs, troubled grasp of the world are all vivid and convincing . . . this is one of the most original and promising of recent debuts."

— *Kirkus Reviews*

The Middle of Everywhere

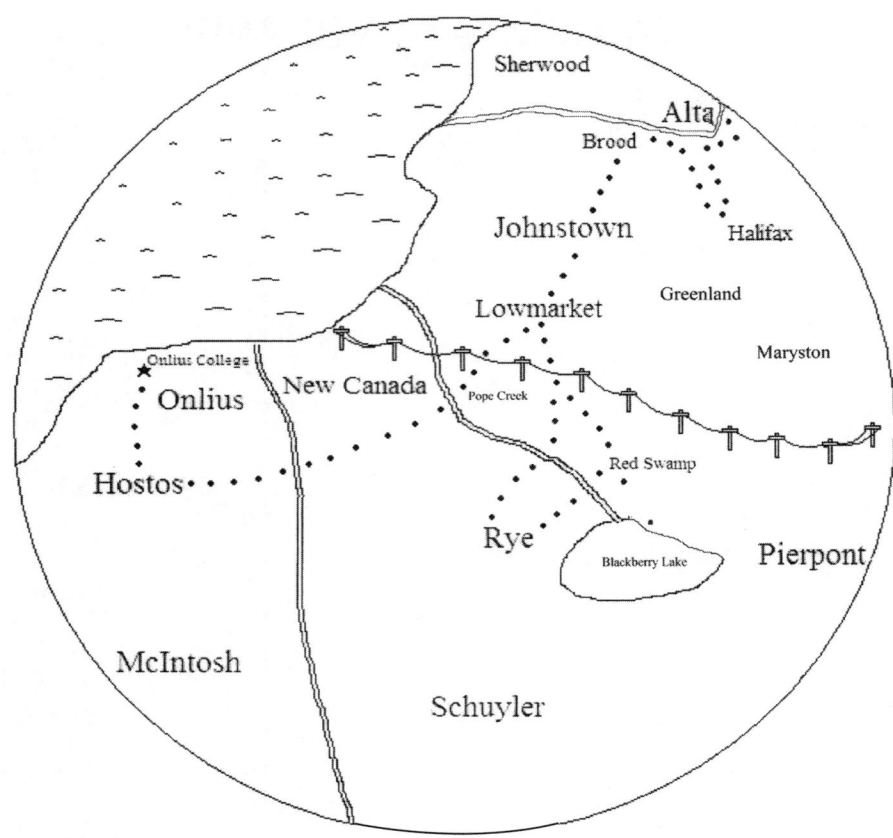

Map designed by Joel DiCaprio

The Middle of Everywhere

A Novel

Ray Petersen

excelsior editions
State University of New York Press
Albany, New York

This is a work of fiction. Names, characters, businesses, places, events, and incidents are either the products of the author's imagination or, in the case of "real" public or political figures, are used in a fictitious manner. They do not denote or pretend to be based on any private information about actual persons, living or dead.

Cover photo: Paul Cowan / Dreamstime.com

Published by State University of New York Press, Albany

© 2012 Ray Petersen

All rights reserved

Printed in the United States of America

No part of this book may be used or reproduced in any manner whatsoever without written permission. No part of this book may be stored in a retrieval system or transmitted in any form or by any means including electronic, electrostatic, magnetic tape, mechanical, photocopying, recording, or otherwise without the prior permission in writing of the publisher.

For information, contact State University of New York Press, Albany, NY
www.sunypress.edu

Excelsior Editions is an imprint of State University of New York Press

Production by Diane Ganeles
Marketing by Kate McDonnell

Library of Congress Cataloging-in-Publication Data

Petersen, Ray.
  The middle of everywhere : a novel / Ray Petersen.
    p. cm. — (Excelsior editions.)
  ISBN 978-1-4384-4470-3 (pbk. : alk. paper)
  1. New York (N.Y.)—Fiction. I. Title.

PS3566.E7638M53 2012
813'.54—dc23   2012001541

10 9 8 7 6 5 4 3 2 1

For all of those who survived the Eighties (and the Aughts),
and especially for those who didn't.
For Luke, we miss you

Contents

Acknowledgments / ix

Cast of Characters / xi

Chapter One
A Mile in Kenny's Shoes / 1

Chapter Two
Strange Bedfellows / 25

Chapter Three
Getting to True / 49

Chapter Four
Kenny Goes to School / 75

Chapter Five
The Middle of Nowhere / 103

Chapter Six
Kenny Takes His Shot / 139

Chapter Seven
The Inside Track / 175

Chapter Eight
Burning Love / 213

Chapter Nine
True North / 257

Acknowledgments

I'll do my best to keep the acknowledgments shorter than the book. All of the following people have been important in giving Kenny direction.

Early readers of the manuscript who provided helpful insights begin with Corin See and our first writers' group (Karen Lizon, Rob Morrow, Laurie Lind Petersen and Dean Anthony). I'm also grateful to Corin for plucking my query letter out of hundreds and recommending my first novel to Bob Wyatt, who published it at St. Martin's Press.

James Peltz and Diane Ganeles at SUNY Press have demonstrated both enthusiasm and patience while working with me to get this book into print for Excelsior Editions, for which I cannot thank them enough.

Paul Slansky's book *The Clothes Have No Emperor* was wonderful in capturing the atmosphere of the Reagan years. Thanks to John Koelle for recommending it, and to Debbie Sperry for her Eighties research.

Profound thanks to Peter Corodimas for his generosity with time and stylistic comments; Todd Davis and Kenyon Wells for their great advice, meta-encouragement and for being sounding boards; and all my students and colleagues at Jefferson Community College, especially Ron Palmer and Rebecca Riehm for arranging teaching schedules allowing me to write.

Thanks to Gene at the Disc Connection for help with musical references; to Don Martin and Ernie Prievo for technical details about the paper mill; and to Peter Landesman, Jane Wilcox, Marty Fleisher, Ann Clark, Fred and Lynda Feldman, Kimberley Reiser, Diana Zimmer, Tom Barthel, and Tom Sims for their inspiration at critical junctures.

Tom Kriger, Brian Waddell, Ingrid Overacker, Lynn Sprott, Glenn Miller, George Davis, and Jim and Polly Shaud kept me grounded through many revisions.

Thanks to my stepson, Joel DiCaprio, for taking the roughest of ideas and translating them into a map of Kenny's travels. Those assisting me with design ideas and tech support include Dreamer Schwartz, Ross Robinson, and Jeremy Moench. Special thanks go to David Bowhall for the final design of the compass points and the Onlius County map.

Erin Begel, Jeremy and Joel DiCaprio, and Luke and Zane Petersen helped me in more ways than I could recount, including typing, design, and character names. Alice and Lee Booth helped with baby-sitting, and Keitha Petersen kept the faith.

Laurie Lind Petersen did all of the above, as well as being my muse, typist-in-chief, editor-in-chief, morale-booster, proofreader, and hyphen advocate. I cannot imagine being able to accomplish this without her.

Cast of Characters

These people are points on the compass of this story

Kenny and Aurelia Hopewell—the man-child wanderer sent to save the Alta paper mill; his sister, left to take care of him

John Harlan and Robin—untenured college professor struggling to maintain his integrity; his student and love interest

Janie and Billy Nicmond—millworker/college student/single parent; her son (AKA Cujo)

Cough Niclay and Horace Patell—Kenny's father's best friend; the mill foreman/company man

Zola and Lyle Lester—Politics Department secretary; her millworker husband

McAdam, Wispen, Koemover, The Judge—the Onlius College president; the college's V.P. for Administration/Younger Brother; an Abstract Empiricist; a puppet-master

Celeste and Ernest Guppy—a graduate-school dropout and faculty wife; her court-jester-wannabe husband

Georgette Casimir—matriarch of the outlaw Casimir family

Charles Darcardt—retiring professor looking to pass the mantle

Johnny Percy—a disabled Vietnam vet, protector of the family farm

Stosh and Prett Casimir—the elder and younger brothers Casimir

Alfonzo and Tilia Aligheri—an Old World couple in the Town of Brood

Carrie Casimir—Georgette's daughter and Joanie Prwanzas's former best friend

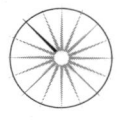 Carmen; Emilio Aguinaldo—McDonald's worker and struggling college student; homeless namesake of a Filipino insurrectionist

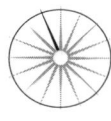 Gerry Scott—lonely farmer who takes in Kenny: not the Happiest Man In the World

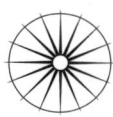 Gunnar Molshoc—well dowser and driller, Vietnam veteran

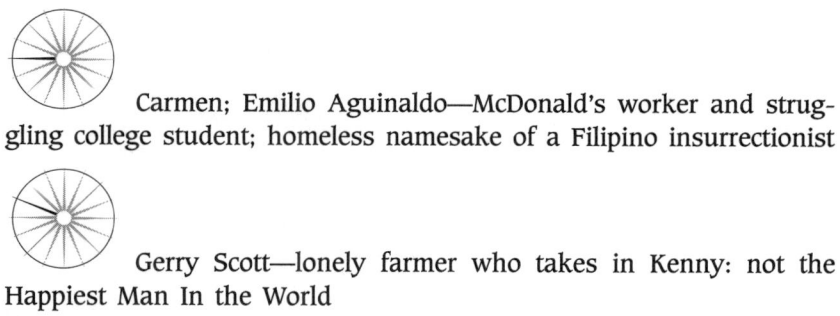 Marie Earhart—Celeste's port in a storm

A state of mind

Chapter One

A Mile in Kenny's Shoes

 On the fly

In dreams Kenny Hopewell always knew where he was, and where he was supposed to be. That's why the first two times his sister Aurelia called up the stairs to wake him he had trouble shaking off the sleep. The third time he was struggling to figure out where he was. After a few moments he remembered he was in his own room. As far as he could tell.

He sat up with a start, a fleeting memory fragment that he had something to do, then settled back in bed a while studying the room, his feet hanging off the end of the mattress. The ceiling was dull white. Shadow tails like anti-comets stretched out from flecks of sand paint in the muted morning light.

He turned on his side toward warm sunlight splayed across the top of his dresser. For early May it was very warm, past expectation. Not that Kenny would know that this spring was much milder than normal. If you asked him, he would say it was summer already.

Four and a half steps from the bed to the dresser, underwear in the top drawer on the right, socks on the left. This was the one he was keeping the baby snakes in, the ones he'd found two days ago. Shirts next drawer down, pants below them. Seven steps to the door of the closet, comic books on the bottom shelf. Around the corner, four steps to the hallway door, then downstairs to the right into the kitchen.

Kenny gobbled down three bowls of Sunny Square Frosted Flakes and four pieces of toasted white bread before saying a word.

"Was I s'posed to go someplace today?" he asked Aurelia.

"You said Cough wanted to talk to you Friday," Aurelia said, as she wiped crumbs from the table.

"What day is it?"

"Friday."

"Ohh, man." Kenny bounced up from his chair and ran out the front door.

"Kenny, check your fly!" Kenny paused on the top step of the porch, tugged the fabric of his pants out past the bulge of his belly to get a good look at the zipper. It was closed, mostly.

He shook his head, disgusted.

He was on a mission, and she wasn't taking him seriously. Just because he hadn't been able to hold a job, even trying hard. He didn't get her.

"Criminy, 'Relia. Cough don't care nothin' about my fly, we got business."

He made it by a quarter to eight, fifteen minutes late, but found Cough still sitting on the peeling plank bench on the mill side of the school, combing his fingers through his oiled black hair. The crowd of workers going into the mill was getting thick.

"You're late, Kenny. What's the matter?"

"Aurelia took too long for breakfast, Cough. Wasn't my fault," Kenny said, looking down at his sneakers.

"That's okay, Bud. No harm done. I just wasn't sure you were goin' to show, and this is important. You know that, right, Kenny?" He slid his hands behind his knees to steady them, like he'd had to do the last couple of years.

"Yes, sir," Kenny said solemnly. He had heard it in his father's friend's voice yesterday afternoon, when Cough said he needed him. This was no regular errand.

"Listen, Kenny, my shift's startin' pretty quick. Remember your cousin we talked about before? And the message about the mill? Well, get it to him, pronto. We need help in a hurry." Then Cough glanced nervously in the direction of the mill gate, "And don't tell nobody what you're doin'. It'll likely only screw things up."

Kenny made a zipper motion across his lips.

"You know Janie Nicmond, right? Got a little boy Billy?"

2 / The Middle of Everywhere

"Yeah." Kenny remembered a skinny, freckled kid who wouldn't eat the cereal dust when Aurelia baby-sat him.

"Okay. Janie is waiting to take you to the college. Let me tell you how to get to her house, okay?"

Kenny nodded calmly, as if he was used to getting directions to go to new places, as if he went on missions all the time.

"You've gotta go across the bridge," Cough began. "Do you think you can find your way to the bridge?"

Kenny's head swam with images of streets, alleys, and bridges. He tried to listen to every word Cough was saying, but was distracted by the falling water that ran the paper mill. He wiped his right palm against his pants. Heat flushed his cheeks and forehead.

Cough grimaced.

Kenny got quieter, trying to follow the details. He heard Lark and Bridge and Right and Left and Bud's Hardware. Like always, the sequence was fluid; the directional points shifted and danced.

Cough asked again if he understood.

Kenny nodded yes, thinking the question was whether he had been paying attention.

Cough glanced over his shoulder at Horace, the tour boss, who was smirking as he pushed the gate slowly toward where it would lock him out.

"Ya know where you're goin'?"

"Yeah," Kenny said. He was supposed to find Janie's house.

"Don't tell no one what you're doin'. Not even Aurelia. It'll spoil it," Cough hissed, then hurried across the street.

"Okay."

Kenny watched the mill gate swallow his dead father's best friend. He choked down the lump in his throat, tugged up again on his zipper, and began.

 John Harlan at work

Harlan could not stop himself from looking. She was about forty-five, yet seemed older, the corners of her mouth pulled downward by the weight of her life.

Carmen's paper was really bad, a few good passages tossed into word salad, full of grammatical and spelling errors, no thesis. It looked like she was still using a typewriter, with the ribbon worn down to nothing, the print was so light. Harlan suspected she had lifted much of it directly from one or two encyclopedias and a technical journal. All the telltale signs were there—awkward transitions, passages with syntax problems, some vocabulary so specialized and sophisticated that even Harlan was not sure what it meant.

She didn't belong in college. Not this one, nor a better one, nor a community college, nor an ag & tech. She just didn't have it. She was going to find her way to some gas-mart job, or probably two clerk jobs, together about fifty hours a week with no health insurance: stuck at minimum wage.

It was more than he could bear to do, telling her she was in over her head. The only thing in his power was to give her another chance, talk her through the plagiarism so she could get a D in his class. Then she'd go back to plagiarizing. Let someone else be the one to say she couldn't cut it.

And Bobo back there, the lacrosse player from Long Island. If there were standards any more, he'd have a negative grade-point average. But he would be in school as long as he wanted; maybe not this one, but somewhere, because his old man would pay for it.

Bobo looked up and stared back at Harlan, his bloodshot eyes straining to focus. Harlan looked away. Too much eye contact might be trouble.

He couldn't afford that on his student evaluations.

 On a lark

Straight up River Street a block and a half to the intersection with Main. Left past the bowling alley and across the bridge, first right onto Lark. Not quite three blocks down on the north side of the street. Janie's place was next to Bud's Hardware and Lumber. The directions were that simple.

Kenny was fine walking up River Street, remembered Bridge well enough to get himself across the river, then turned slowly on the southwestern corner of Main and Lark, clockwise and counterclockwise, looking for a clue. He cycled Cough's words through his mind, recalling Lark, one Left and one Right.

Had he taken a left or a right already?

Bud's son Carly drove up Main with the delivery truck and took a left onto Lark, the *Bud's Hardware and Lumber* lettering on the driver's door catching Kenny's eye and pulling him in pursuit.

By the time Janie Nicmond gave up on waiting and left for college, Kenny was five and a half blocks west on Lark, nearly in tears from losing sight of the delivery truck, having completely forgotten where he was going.

 Janie learns significance

"And is that a significant statistical difference?" Dr. Koemover queried, tapping his foot four times before looking up from the floor tiles for a hand in the air. There were none, though most of his customers still seemed to be working on it.

"Ms. Dovinger? Is that a significant statistical difference?" Ariana Dovinger nodded her head three times. The other students watched her carefully to make sure she was nodding yes, and not just caught in her reflexive spasm.

Koemover smiled quickly, his thin upper lip raising evenly. "Very good, Ms. Dovinger. Barely significant. I thought the sampling error might trip you up. Very good." Ariana's head bobbed more rapidly in reply.

The computer lab door opened gently, almost silently. Janie slipped in, trying to get to her seat unnoticed.

Koemover glared, following every step with his eyes. His followers glared, too, Ariana's head bobbing to add emphasis.

"Ms. Nicmond, the other customers and I were discussing whether there was a significant statistical difference in the behavior of Jewish voters in New York State's last two gubernatorial elections. We were all wondering what you thought."

Janie was burning in her seat. First arguing with her mother-in-law about watching her son while she was at work, then waiting so long to give someone she didn't even know a ride to college that it made her late for class. And now this corn-hole. He knew she was late, she knew she was late, everybody knew. What was the point? If there had been any other eight o'clock classes left that she could use for her distribution requirements when she finally got her Pell grant, she wouldn't even be here.

"Ms. Nicmond?"

She studied him: pinched nose, pinched mouth, pinched eyes, pinched everything. "I don't know, Doctor Koemover."

"Well, how would you find out, Ms. Nicmond?" he asked, as he took the transparency that contained the formula off the overhead projector.

Jennifer Kudrow also was stuck in the class because it had been the only open one that fit her schedule. She was a theater major, not a favorite of any of the faculty directors. She was so bored with college, thinking about either dropping out of school, transferring, or having an affair with a professor. She swiveled in her upholstered computer chair so her back was to Koemover and scratched YES in big letters on her notebook, holding it so Janie could see.

"I guess I would have to have the formula and the data to find out," Janie said.

"Do you have that information?"

"No."

"Would it be helpful for you to have that information?"

"Yes."

"Then I would suggest that unless you are an extremely gifted psychic, you make an effort to get here on time." The Koemover crowd snickered in sync.

"Perhaps you'd like to try guessing, Ms. Nicmond."

Janie started to shake her head, then noticed Jennifer's sign. "Uh, I could try, I guess."

Koemover reddened. "Then let's have it. Is there a statistically significant difference in Jewish voting behavior from 1982 to 1986?"

Janie looked away from Jennifer, toward the bulletin board covered with credit-card application brochures in the back of the room. She'd already seen the cue. "Yes."

"Why, that's wonderful. She guessed correctly, with only a fifty-fifty probability of success. Isn't that amazing, everyone?" Ariana's head bobbed thoughtfully.

"What degree of significance, Ms. Nicmond? By a large margin?"

Jennifer crossed her legs, dropped her notebook flat on her lap. When Janie swiveled her head back in her direction, she saw Jennifer holding her thumb and forefinger about half an inch apart. Janie rolled her eyes to the ceiling for a few seconds.

"I would say it's statistically significant by only a very small margin."

"You'd have to explain your methodology to me, Ms. Nicmond. Perhaps you were listening outside the door before you came in. It doesn't matter, however, because I do not believe you could reproduce the result with fresh data with any degree of accuracy, could you?"

She shook her head. "Probably not."

Koemover harrumphed and set a new transparency on the overhead. Janie looked both ways, then mouthed a "thank you" to Jennifer. Jennifer gave her a bored smile.

 Cough at someone's mill

Cough was in the break room with the other tenders, temporarily freed from their paper machine, having a cigarette, listening to the latest story about who was buying out the mill, worrying about Kenny.

He picked at the ashes trapped in the gummy gray surface of the table with his left thumb, the one not split so badly the quick had never healed.

"I tell ya, it's Germans," Red Winston, the fourth hand, was saying.

"Shit, yeah," Lyle Lester, the back tender, weighed in. "They're buyin' up everything. Them and the Air'bs."

Cough wished there were a way to find out if Kenny had made it to Janie's. But she was at college, and he couldn't see calling Aurelia. All she could say was whether Kenny was home. If he wasn't, it still didn't mean he'd made it.

"How d'ya know it ain't the Air'bs?" Charlie Ayles asked.

Lyle smiled a disgusted, knowing smile. "That's why yer a fifth hand, Charlie. Whadda they know 'bout makin' paper? They ain't even got no trees in them countries." He tipped his head back and drained the last of his Coke.

"They don't need to know nothin' if they got the money," Charlie insisted.

Red nodded forlornly. "Horace knows, I'll betcha, but he ain't tellin'."

Charlie, Red, and Lyle all craned to look at Horace through the small window to the shop floor.

Lyle dented his Coke can inside and out. "Yeah, he looks pretty smug lately. You know he's cut in."

Red snorted. "Course he's cut in. Ain't nothin' they could ask him to do he wouldn't do. Give 'em his left nut, he would, an' say thanks for givin' me the opportunity to contribute. Right, Cough?"

"Um, yeah," he answered. "You guys got it all figured. It's the Germans."

"Where you been, Cough," Charlie laughed. "We're onto Horace now."

"No place. Just thinkin'." He pressed tobacco-stained fingers on the table. Cough was uneasy talking any more. He was wishing he could have trusted Aurelia and Janie enough to tell them about his plan. Then he wouldn't have to worry about Kenny.

He thought about that for another minute before deciding he'd done the best he could.

It wasn't his fault Aurelia and Janie were women. No one could help that.

 Zola Brooks, code-cracker

Everyone in the politics department was distracted by Zola's impending marriage. She had always been devoted to her job—working overtime without pay, taking lunch at her desk, never complaining about last-minute typing, being courteous even when the faculty seemed to have forgotten how. Now a fear was spreading that she might stop being so accommodating. President McAdam was especially afraid, because lately he had been bringing certain papers across the Commons for her to type, away from the surveillance of the vice president of administration, Herman Wispen.

Once she's married she might not be as loyal to the college as to her husband, or some other stupid thing, McAdam fretted. But still he slid the papers between pages of *The Chronicle of Higher Education*, folded and tucked it under his elbow, and strolled as unselfconsciously as he could past Ms. Axe's desk and Wispen's office door, then on over to the Research Center. Once safely ensconced in the MEN FACULTY bathroom, he assembled the papers in an interoffice mailer.

"How are you doing, Ms. Brooks?" he asked, minutes later.

"Afternoon, Dr. McAdam," she replied. "I've got this ready. Hope they're all right."

"Uh, yes, I'm sure they are, Zola. Sure they are. I have something else for you that needs to go out today."

"Today?"

"Yes, I'm sure it'll be okay. Ms. Axe, you know, is very busy." He stopped surveying the dots on the ceiling tiles to focus grimly into Zola's eyes. "Very important, very busy. Sure it will be fine."

Zola looked at the four legal pages of scrawling and fought back an urge to glance at the wall clock.

"President McAdam, Harold usually comes by for the mail at about a quarter to four, and I'm afraid I might not have them perfectly ready by then."

"They won't be mailed, Zola, not mailed. I'll pick them up myself, when they're done. Here till six, at least, you know. Very busy. Just go ahead, get started. Sure it'll be all right."

Zola saw Koemover slip behind his office door a few seconds before McAdam retreated past it. She glanced at the clock, 3:16 p.m., and waited for Koemover to emerge and start circling. She was only halfway through the directions for his 150-question exam, not needed until next fall, and she was supposed to leave by 4:30—her usual time—to get to her wedding rehearsal and dinner.

He'll just have to wait, she thought, shutting down the file for the directions for Koemover's test. They were long enough to be a test in themselves. No wonder his students were afraid of his methods class. She fished an unmarked computer disk from the back of a drawer behind her copier-toner refills.

"H-U-M-P-T-Y," she typed in for the password, then O-V-E-R-L-O-R-D at the first password file prompt. She tapped her fingers twice while the computer set up the final invisible prompt.

"W-H-I-T-E-W" she entered before Koemover appeared in her peripheral vision. *Is he close enough to see?*

Koemover sensed he had been detected, aborted the stealth approach. "Hello, Zola," he tested.

"Hello, Dr. Koemover," Zola replied, punching the Escape key. Her hope of leaving on time shut down with the file.

"That's not my test you're doing, is it?"

Not unless you've started writing on legal pads, in Swahili. "No, it isn't, Dr. Koemover. But I've been working on it. I'll be able to finish it Monday."

"Monday? But won't you be on your honeymoon?"

"Not yet. I'll be in next week."

"Oh, well, then, I guess it's okay. It can wait until next week, I guess. Don't you think?"

I think it could wait until Thanksgiving. "Yes, there's plenty of time, Dr. Koemover." Then she gambled, "There's a high-priority item I need to take care of, right now, if I could."

"Is it for the president? Dr. McAdam? I saw him at your desk."

"Ye . . . yes, he was here." *Should I?* she thought. "Uh, he noticed you weren't at your desk."

Koemover turned a whiter shade of pale. He darted off to his office.

As she rebooted the file, Zola reflected on potential interruptions. *Earhart? No, not on a Friday afternoon. Guppy? No, I think he's gone, too. Let's see. Harlan? If it's anybody, it'll be Harlan, Last-Minute Man.*

She peered at the legal pages. Even if she could read them, she wouldn't finish before four-thirty.

"Due to the e-x-p . . . What? Due to the e-x-p- of the framline . . . What's a framline?"

Harlan opened the door to the office suite, trundling in with an armload of US Foreign Policy essays in white essay booklets. Zola tunneled her vision into the legal pad.

"E-x-p . . . ion. Expression? expiration? expansion? That's got to be it, expansion." She heard the door to Harlan's office close gently. She might have a chance after all.

"College could o-p-t-a-r-r assistance through a study . . . optarr? What the? college could optarr assistance? Let's see, optar, optic, often, offer. Offer. That's it."

"Zola?" Harlan interrupted. "Zola, don't let me interrupt, but aren't you supposed to be gone by now? Don't you have a rehearsal or something?"

Zola sighed under her breath. *He's so sweet. But now I've got no chance.* "It's this last thing I have to do, John, but I'm almost finished," she lied.

"Is there anything I can do?"

Do you know hieroglyphics? "No, you just have a good weekend. You're coming tomorrow, aren't you?"

"Sure, Zola, with bells on. Wouldn't miss it."

"Great, see you then."

"Okay. Don't sweat that memo, or whatever it is. It'll have to wait until you get back."

"I'm almost done, really. Just a sentence or two."

"Okay, I'll get out of your hair. See you."

"Bye. See you tomorrow." *Oh, well,* she thought. *Nice guy, too bad about all the tenure pressure.*

She looked at the clock, five minutes to four, and at the bottom of the first page of McAdam's secret memo. *I'll never make it.*

Harlan stuck his head back in the office. "Zola, there's no way you can finish that today. Especially with your screen frozen."

"But the screen's not . . . See you tomorrow, John?"

Harlan nodded and turned to leave as she picked up the phone receiver.

"Fred? This is Zola . . . Yes, I know. I was supposed to be out of here already . . . You're way ahead of me . . . You sure it wouldn't hurt anything?" Zola punched the key to save what she had on the file, then shut it down.

"Okay, we're even now . . . Oh, that's nothing, I'd do that anyway . . . Thanks, Fred. See you tomorrow? Great. Mm-bye."

She eased the receiver back onto its base and watched the dummy file empty from her screen. 10-9-8-7-6-5-4-3-2-1. Better leave a message with Axe.

Zola dialed McAdam's administrative assistant, waiting through nine rings for her to pick up.

"Hello, President McAdam's office," Marla breathed into the phone.

"Marla? This is Zola Brooks. Listen, I have an item for Dr. McAdam, but my computer screen just froze up. I'm afraid I won't be able to finish it today. Could you leave him that message, please?"

A pronounced, agonizing pause was punctuated by three huffing sighs. Finally Zola heard, "I suppose so." She said "Thanks" quickly and hung up, grabbed her purse and ran out of the office. She couldn't tell whether the sound of the ringing phone was in her imagination.

Marla huffed three more times, making sure the polish on her nails had jelled before she called McAdam.

"Mis-ter McAdam?" There was a pause, during which Marla snickered to herself. She could almost see McAdam turning red in the face from being called Mister.

"Yes, Ms. Axe?"

"Uh, yeah. Zola Brooks just called. Her computer's down and she can't get that thing done today."

"What?" He was nearly shouting.

"Her computer screen's frozen, she said."

"Well, is it?"

"Uh, let me see." Marla swiveled in her chair, dialed Fred, and got no answer. "Nobody's at the computer center."

"Thank you, Ms. Axe." McAdam replied quietly to cover his panic. At the very least he had to get those papers back in his own hands right away.

Though leaving the office again was sure to tip off Admin VP Wispen that something was up.

 Janie, home with Billy

Janie pulled into her driveway ten minutes after her son got off the bus. He was waiting for her, on the porch, sitting on the grimy linoleum playing with a naked armless doll he'd dragged off from a garage sale. She was glad he was at least a little out of sight, better than that time when she'd put a house key on a string around his neck, and his father had taken it, made his own copy, and cleaned her out.

She hated it so bad. She was always afraid. A lot could happen in ten minutes.

"Wha'cha doin', punkin?"

"Puttin' my marbles away," he said, not looking up, blowing his spiky bangs back from his eyes.

"Whaddaya mean, putting your marbles away? You didn't have them in school with you, did you?"

"No, but, guess what? The marbles go inside Dolly."

"Let Mommy see, honey, I'm not sure what you mean."

"Okay, but just a minute," he said, concentrating, his back still turned toward her. "I'm not done yet."

Janie unlocked the door, swung her backpack across the threshold, fought the urge to sit down on the floor.

"Billy, Honey, can you bring Dolly inside? Mom's gotta start supper."

"I will in a minute, Mom. I'm almost done." She watched him fumble marbles into the armholes of the doll, his lower lip disappearing under his teeth. His arms were so thin.

"Honey, please, Mom needs you to come inside, right now."

She couldn't take the looks from old lady Boyar in the next apartment, or the reproach of the landlord if he spotted Billy alone on the porch. Not again.

Finally he looked up, clutching the marble-filled doll like a prize.

"Here it is. It's ready now."

"I see. Can I take it for a minute?"

"Sure, it's okay."

She hefted the doll in one hand, taking his elbow in the other to lead him inside.

"Naw, Mommy, Justin's gonna be outside."

"I know, Honey, but I want you to stay in. Isn't there some good show on TV, some cartoon? Wait a minute," she added with false enthusiasm. "Isn't Sesame on?"

He frowned and sighed. *Oh, God,* she thought. *He doesn't like Sesame Street any more. I know that. What's wrong with me?*

Billy stood rooted just inside the doorway, waiting for his mother to demonstrate she knew anything about him.

What's wrong with my kid? Everybody else's kid is glued to the TV and he wants to play outside. When am I ever gonna catch a break?

Billy's lower lip puffed out in ever greater measure of pouting.

"Hey, soldier, you did a real good job putting these in here," Janie started out. Billy shifted his weight on his left foot. "Are you thinking about keeping your marbles in Dolly all the time?"

"Can't take 'em to school that way," Billy muttered.

"Uh-huh. That's right. But you're not supposed to take them to school anyway. Right?" She cocked her head to one side, the signal that he should let her be the Mommy.

"I remember."

"Well, of course you do. I knew that. Would you like to help me get supper?"

"Oh all right. I guess so." After the macaroni elbows were boiled and the tomato sauce was almost warmed up, Billy's grandmother arrived to watch him while Janie went off to work the second shift.

"Come give Mommy a hug," she called twice. She gave up when she realized he couldn't hear her over the television.

 Kenny on the edge of town

Kenny had passed the mill and the school and Rudrick's Bar and Grille. His backpack was loaded with everything he figured he needed to complete the mission. Three cans of fruit cocktail, saltines, a sweater, his old Cub Scout book, and a ball of string.

It was five o'clock, and this was as far as he had gone. After Carly had given him a ride back home from Outer Lark Street in the hardware truck, he got caught up watching TV. Then Aurelia made him lunch—tomato soup with crackers and a tuna-fish sandwich—and he'd started reading a comic book. The second-shift mill whistle brought him back to his mission. The only way not to let Cough down was to get to the college on his own. He packed and got out of the house before Aurelia could start supper. Nothing stopping him now.

"Hullo, Kenny. Wha'cha doin'?" Kenny looked both ways up and down the road, up into the maple trees along the highway, then turned a full circle, twice.

"Kenny. Over here. Under the car.'

Kenny stopped spinning, waited for his head to clear, and peered across the highway. WAGNER'S AUTO GARAGE & GROCERY. He didn't know any Wagner.

"Kenny. Under the car."

Kenny squatted on his haunches, scanned under the car parked by the gas pump, saw nothing, then began to lie down on the side of the road.

"Kenny. Under the Ford, the red car."

"Red, white and blue. Red," Kenny recited as he located the car in the garage, over the repair pit. After looking both ways twice, he crossed the highway and walked toward the repair bay.

"Wha'cha up to, Kenny?" the more familiar voice said.

"N . . . nothin'. I wasn't doin' nothin'." When he rounded the fender of the Ford he saw Chauncey, the man who pumped gas into Aurelia's Rambler and sometimes gave him a cream drop. Kenny liked

14 / The Middle of Everywhere

root beer barrels and black licorice a lot more than cream drops, but he always said, "Thank you, Chauncey" or "Thank you, Mr. W" if Aurelia was right there staring at him.

"Hi, Chauncey. What're you doin'?"

"Working on this car, Kenny. Hey, ya heard about the mill?"

"Yeah, 'bout them maybe closin' it?"

"Yes, yes. That would be terr'ble, terr'ble," Chauncey said.

"I know. That's what Cough said. He said we gotta fix it."

"Well, sure. But how?"

"Uh, uh, I dunno. How'm I s'posed to know?" Kenny replied, suddenly remembering Cough's warning.

"Hey, Kenny, I was just talkin', ya know."

"Yeah, I'm okay, Chauncey. I'm not doin' nothin'."

"Say, I bet you'd like a cream drop, wouldn'tcha? They're the best, right, Kenny?"

"Yes. Thank you, Chauncey."

Kenny climbed the two wooden steps up into the store, leaning heavily to the left to compensate for their rightward tilt. Chauncey was one step behind him. He handed Kenny a cream drop.

"So where's Aurelia? Where's the Rambler?" Chauncey asked. Kenny was examining the glass jar filled with root beer barrels on the shelf behind Chauncey, tugging on his left sideburn, the one longer than the other since Aurelia had last cut his hair too short.

"I . . . uh . . . I . . . uh . . . don't know, Chauncey." As panicked as he was, Kenny's eyes remained focused on the root beer barrels.

"So you're on your own, huh, Kenny? Havin' an adventure?" Chauncey asked.

"Yeah, no, yeah, Chaun-zey, I guess." A thick glob of sugary cream stuck to the roof of his mouth. He savored it, his gaze still fixed on the root beer barrels.

"Are you sure you're okay, Kenny? How's that cream drop, huh?"

"Idss good, Chaun-zey."

"Then why are ya always starin' at them root beer barrels?" Chauncey's daughter Connie asked. She'd come in from pumping gas while Chauncey was working on the Ford.

"I wasn't starin'," Kenny said, reddening.

"Is this true, Kenny?" Chauncey asked. Kenny wanted to resist his eyes, but could not.

"Ye-yes, Chauncey. Root beer barrels are my favorite, and black licorice."

"Then it's a good thing Aurelia wasn't with you today. All this time I thought it was cream drops."

Kenny was silent, the full import of Chauncey's statement slowly sinking in. He waited, hoping against hope that it was okay for him to like what he liked.

"Here ya go, Kenny," Connie said, handing him a fresh root beer barrel she had just plucked from the jar.

Chauncey grinned at Kenny's concentration. "Kenny's on an adventure, Connie."

"I thought so, Pa. Ya know it, I thought so, as soon as I seen that Aurelia wasn't here."

"Doin' somethin' for Cough," Kenny mumbled, embarrassed.

"What? Are you on an errand, Kenny?" Connie asked in a humoring tone.

"Uh, kinda. It's no big thing, just somethin' for Cough."

"Yes, Connie. They've got a plan to keep the mill open, ya know," Chauncey added solemnly.

Kenny felt even more embarrassed. "Well, I guess I gotta go, now. Thanks, Connie. Thank you, Chauncey."

"Here, take these," Connie said, putting a handful each of root beer barrels and licorice into a small brown paper bag. "If you're gonna save the mill, you'll need somethin' to tide ya through." Chauncey's eyebrows raised, surprised at her generosity.

"You say hello to Aurelia for us, now, Kenny. An' tell her not to be afraid to bring the Rambler in again."

"Okay, Chauncey, thanks." Kenny felt suddenly more confident than he could ever remember feeling before. He was back on task.

By sheer luck Kenny headed in the right direction out of town, hiking toward the setting sun. He made the first quarter-mile on his sense of adventure, then began to hunger after Connie's CARE package.

The taste of the root beer barrel still faintly on his tongue, he chose a twist of licorice to chew as he plodded along. He sucked thoughtfully. The anise filtering into his nostrils fired a synapse.

"Here, Kenny, you can have a piece of this," his father, Wiley had told him, handing him a twist of black licorice. They were driving in the old Rambler, on their way to see Kenny's mother in the hospital. Wiley drove carefully because his knuckles were so cramped that his hands were like claws.

Martha Hopewell had gone for a drive two days prior, alone in her car, until the paved town road had turned to gravel a mile and a half before the turn onto Route 93. She was overcome, drove off the road to walk into the brush. Her clothes were all wrong. She left them behind, and climbed naked into the briars, a blackberry patch. Her long black hair caught in the briars. Each cut of her flesh was a gift, a sign that she was on the right path.

Martha's best friend, Grindel Molshoc, had been telling her that she needed to get right with the Lord. Grindel's husband sure worked at it. It was all he ever talked about. Helmut had very definite ideas about God. God was vain and jealous.

But Wiley was too easygoing in the Ways, at least that was what Grindel always said. "A man cannot be lax in the Ways. Either his heart's got to have the fire for the Lord, or he'll be in it."

Martha had tried through gentle persuasion, but Wiley just snuggled up to her, pressing up behind, misinterpreting her intention. He was such a loving man.

Grindel assured her this was even more wrong. "You've got to tell him. He has to hear the Word plain and simple, and answer it himself, or not. You can help him to hear. But you can only save yourself."

Martha couldn't get him to have the fire. She withdrew more into the world of Grindel's church. It had been the only place where Grindel felt some measure of control.

Martha got out of the hospital in Wiley's custody. He took over the cooking and got Aurelia to do the dishes and pick up around the house. That left Martha more time to thumb through the Bible, and to stare blankly out her bedroom window at the willow by the river.

Kenny couldn't recall now whether he'd seen her at the hospital, or why she had gone back.

He just knew it had been a long time, years now, that he'd missed her.

 ## McAdam in the bunker

He was back at the office, sitting in Ms. Axe's chair, the bent-necked lamp over the desk where his secret papers were spread out. There were no windows to the outside from Axe's work area, not like McAdam's office, where it was too easy to see in.

"Tic, tic, tic . . . tic, tic . . . tic . . . tic, tic." The keyboard sounded like an anemic Geiger counter. McAdam was a two-finger, one-thumb typist, all on his right hand. The nails of his left hand were being gnawed away, in raw bitter bites.

"Zola could have finished typing this if she'd wanted to," he pouted. "So selfish of her."

He really hated this business. The need for subterfuge. But no one understood. It came with the job. It had to be done, and it had to be quiet.

Baxter McAdam was tall and despite occasional fits of dieting and working out, heavy-set. His once reddish-brown hair was graying and it would be wavy if he ever let it grow that long. But what defined him more than his size, and the cut of his business suits, the imploring and solicitous tenor voice, what now shaped his facial features into a mask of gregarious worry, was his role. He was a pitchman for an endangered species—the public university—one that could only be saved by becoming what it was not.

He was always having to determine exactly how to go about destroying the village in order to save it.

McAdam was only halfway through the second page, squinting at his own handwriting in the strangled light, when Wispen got the call at home that it looked like something was going on in the Bunker, near his office.

 John Harlan, submerged

Files were stacked up to window level along three walls of the tiny den, one trail of them from the desk, to the door, through the hallway, into the bathroom. Yellow legal-pad pages and yellowing photocopies spilling out of worn manila folders sought their own level of disarray.

Once home, John Harlan had gone straight to the tub, and was now submerged, trying for sensory deprivation. It was like this every weekend, had been for two years, while he tried to write his dissertation. He was feeling stronger about this one, his third topic.

> The United States military has undergone a sea change in the postwar world, not only in its relations with the rest of the world, but also in how it treats its own soldiers. The deliberate

exposure of soldiers to radiation from atom-bomb explosions at Ground Zero exemplifies this change.

This was not news; it was all true. The depression slowed him even more.

Breaking through the surface of the tub water, Harlan gasped and shook his head from side to side, water spraying from his dark curls. He swiped the back of his hand across his face to clear the water from his eyes, and grabbed the legal pad on the floor next to the tub.

The use of Agent Orange, involving massive exposure of soldiers during the Vietnam War, indicates a growing callousness, a rise in the perception of the soldier as the Other.

Harlan wanted to take a break, grab some dinner, catch up on grading, call his officemate Guppy to shoot the shit.

Instead, he plunged himself back down, below the surface.

 Ernest Guppy at rest

Guppy was in his chair in the living room, combing through the *New York Times*. He scratched his beard along the jawline. "Celeste, did you see this about Tammy Faye Bakker?"

"See what?" Celeste knew her husband couldn't control his addiction to the news. But she couldn't see why he had to drag her away from whatever she was doing, in this case making dinner, to hear it.

"It's really juicy."

"Can it wait?"

"This is too good to wait."

"Then come in here, Ernie. Don't you want to eat?"

"Sure. Of course." She waited for the telltale rustle of the paper, indicating that he was not going to move.

The paper rattled. She started slicing carrots again.

"Celeste!"

"What?"

"Would you *please* . . . are you still cooking?"

"Yes."

"Sorry. I'll leave you alone." She counted backward from twenty. He was seated at the kitchen counter before she reached three.

"Listen to this. Jim and Tammy Faye Bakker denying claims about his sexual indiscretions."

"Which indiscretions would those be?"

"Well, let's see. He said he's never been involved in wife-swapping, nor in homosexuality, and he's never been to a prostitute."

"What's that leave? Bestiality?"

"Or some unthinkable fetish," Guppy agreed. "Necrophilia, maybe. He would've been better off with the hooker, don't you think?"

"Mmm." She turned over the rice in the cooker, pressing a few grains against the sides with the edge of a wooden spoon to see if they were done.

"And it gets better. Tammy Faye wants to work in a doctor's office. Can you imagine coming out of anesthesia, and the first thing you see is Tammy Faye?

"Would that count as mercy killing?"

"Perfect. Assistance without physical evidence. They could clean up."

Celeste studied the batwing eyelashes in the photo, from across the countertop. "Cruel and unusual punishment," she muttered.

"You're right. The Supreme Court will have to make a ruling. The majority probably in favor of Death by Lethal Reflection; Thurgood Marshall, Brennan, and White dissenting."

"What's this, Ernie?" Celeste said, pointing to a front-page headline.

"Didn't you know? The Iran-Contra trial is beginning."

"I wasn't paying attention."

"You weren't? This could be bigger than Watergate."

"It could, but I don't think it will." She turned from the counter to spoon the green beans around in the steamer.

"Well, you are awfully cynical, sweetheart. Didn't you follow Watergate either?" He tried to pluck some crisp beans from the steamer basket. Celeste shooed his knuckles away with the spoon.

"Actually," she replied, "I was riveted. I used to talk about it with my friends all the time. They said I was driving them crazy."

"If you . . . then why aren't you into it now? Why this attitude?" Guppy was slipping into graduate-school mode, contesting whatever she said.

She rolled her eyes. "I don't think I have an attitude."

"Not paying attention is certainly an attitude."

"Dinner's almost done. Could you set the table?"

"Sure, but don't change the subject."

"Who's changing the subject?" She pointed him toward the dining-room table.

"You are."

"Fine, then, I have an attitude. I just don't expect anything to come of this."

"How can you say that?"

"How can I not? Look at what's happening. Everyone's losing their memory. That isn't a cover-up? It's like the whole administration is an Alzheimer's ward." Celeste opened the cupboard and began ferrying dishes to the table.

"But Celeste, don't you think everyone should stay engaged?"

She drew in a deep breath, released it, then said quietly, "Do you want me to be engaged?"

"I think so, yes."

"Okay, Deaver, the influence peddler," she said over her shoulder. "What happened to him?"

"Sweetheart?"

"And Stockman. The man lied to Congress, told the press and went back to lie to Congress again. And they just swallowed it." She snapped the oven dials back to OFF, then jammed her hands into the back pockets of her jeans.

"Uh, Celeste," Guppy said, unwilling to lose the reins of the conversation.

"And Watt selling off national forests, because Jesus is coming soon. And Burford or Gorsuch, or whatever her name was, at the EPA. What was that?"

"Celeste, I get the . . ."

She spun around. "You *know* Reagan had them all take the Fifth during the EPA scandal. You *know* that."

"Yes."

"And you were the one who told me about the ketchup. You remember, don't you? Ketchup in school lunches. Instead of real vegetables. You told *me* that." She was punctuating with the spoon, grains of rice flying at Guppy's chest.

"But I don't see . . ."

"You don't see what?" she said. "What the problem is? I'll tell you. Why do *I* have to have an attitude? Why don't *you* have an attitude?"

"What good does it do?"

"Exactly."

"What do you mean?" Guppy's voice was rising.

"I mean what you mean. What good does it do?"

She turned back to the oven, opened the door, put on oven mitts to pull out the baked fish.

"Celeste? Relax. I was just joking."

"Yeah," she said tiredly, setting the pan down on a wicker coaster. "I know."

Aurelia waits

Aurelia gazed out the window of the front door. *It's got to be because of his special gift,* she was thinking, flicking the light switch off and on with their secret signal. Kenny's special gift was the way his mother had described his inability to distinguish left from right, up from down, any direction on the compass. She was worried that her own special gift would be someday to go crazy, like her mother.

Wherever he is, I hope he's warm.

"I wish he'd stop doing this to me," she said out loud, embarrassing herself.

The baby snakes lay curled up in Kenny's sock drawer, fat and happy from the flies Kenny left for them. They'd have no need to move for a while yet.

Kenny under the stars

He'd walked as far as the licorice and root beer barrels could take him. It was near dark when Kenny reached Percy's Corners, and he was instantly puzzled. One man driving a Honda Accord slowed and stared, with that *Are you a retard?* look on his face. Kenny looked down and let him pass.

He stood motionless while seventeen cars swept by, through the sunset and moonrise. He was even more confused.

Across the ditch and up the bank past the stone wall, he found a comfortable place under a maple.

Stars shone familiarly. He tried to sort out their patterns. Kenny only recognized the Big Dipper. There was some star in it or near it that he'd been told a lot of times would help him find his way, but he couldn't remember which one.

Maybe he would have a better idea how to go on in the morning.

Imelda Marcos*on Zola Brooks

I cannot see why she has to be bothered with wedding details. I do not understand it.

I told Ferdinand what was needed and it was done, except for my shoes, and the man who made that mistake will never make another one.

Her shoes. They are so important, and I would not be surprised if they are all wrong. Perhaps I should tell Ferdinand to take care of it. It is good for him now to have things to do.

---

*When Ferdinand Marcos was deposed as dictator of the Philippines in 1986, his wife Imelda had to leave behind three thousand pairs of shoes.

Chapter Two

Strange Bedfellows

Kenny in a fog

The ceiling of his room looked milkier, blurry. Kenny blinked, rubbed his eyes, tried to focus. It faded and drifted. *Why is it so cold?*

He shivered, fumbled for the covers, clawed up dirt and crumbs of last autumn's dead leaves. *Where is this?*

He raised himself up on one elbow, looked around, figured out he was not in his room. Fog was slowly rising from the ground.

Kenny's first impulse was to cry. Aurelia was nowhere, and he was hungry and cold.

He climbed to his feet, turned all the way round, searching for a fragment of memory. Pale green buds of maple leaves peeked out from the fog in the early morning stillness.

How did I get here? Aurelia probably would have given him a ride out to this spot. Kenny decided to wait for her to come get him. He picked at the sleep in the corners of his eyes and stared at the aging asphalt.

Percy's Corners was now an abandoned crossroads of the Old Halifax Road and County Route 17. There hadn't been any Percy's there since the '68 milk strike, when Old John Percy disappeared after someone took a shot at a bulk-tank truck, and the state police came looking around. Everyone believed it was really Young Johnny, just home from Vietnam, longhaired and looking kind of wild. The state police had had to talk to Young Johnny. Young Johnny had sat there on the porch steps, cleaning his deer rifle, slowly and carefully, even though it wasn't close to deer season. Then he himself disappeared a few days later.

Only one plank step hadn't caved in, the porch-swing chairs hanging free, the swing on the front lawn turned toward the house so kids could sit while shooting out the last pieces of window glass. Samantha used to paint the swing every year around this time, early May, so she could sit out to listen to the peepers on warm, rainy nights. When she passed away, Old John gave up on dairying, turned to raising calves for veal. All of Samantha's gardens, vegetable and flowers, had surrendered to wild growth before Young Johnny showed up after Khe Sanh.

The barns still had roofs, shakes loose and listless, but they leaned so that no one dared go inside. Nothing was left but mildewed hay and pieces of cracked horse harness, unused since Young Johnny's big brother Eugene was caught hitting their sister Rose during a fight over a bicycle. Old Johnny wouldn't stand for anyone hitting a woman.

Kenny waited for Aurelia at the corner for close to half an hour. Then an approaching blue Ford slowed and turned left, the driver oblivious to Kenny. The sticker in the rear window said Onlius State College. Recognition washed over him.

He crossed the street kitty-corner to hitch a ride in the Ford's direction, toward where the sticker said the college was. Four cars later a yellow-haired woman with a station-wagonload of kids pulled over, the kids staring at him as if to say, *You don't want to get into this car.* Kenny didn't pick up on it, squeezing into the middle next to the toddler car-seat.

Its occupant was sitting atop the buckled crossbar, picking at the dirt under her toenails. She wore a faded Alf shirt she had mostly outgrown, and a Sunny Square brand blue plastic disposable diaper, strained at the fastener tabs. Tea green eyes under dark curls.

"Where ya headed?" the woman asked. She had a pretty face, even though her eyebrows were painted too high.

Kenny panicked. "This way, as far as you're goin'," he replied.

"Into town?"

"Yeah." It's gotta be in town.

"Okay, we live just on the other side. I'll drop you off."

"Thanks." *Great, I'll get there and be done by this afternoon.*

Zola before her wedding

Zola woke in sweaty sheets, the list of things she needed to do before the wedding reeling in her mind. Making sure the fire hall was set up for the reception, and that people would clean up after. Getting Lyle's family to the church and fire hall. Trying to do it all without seeing Lyle before the ceremony.

Zola was superstitious.

It was a good thing her mother and sisters were making most of the food, or she'd have had to do that, too. *The flowers!* No, she didn't have to worry. Lyle had put a stop to that. "It's foolish to spend a lotta money on somethin' like that," he had said. *"Sure, nothing special about this day,"* she had stopped herself from saying. It was easier to give up than to agree with Lyle's mother about getting lilies. *My God, lilies!*

There was fog all over when she got up, pretty thick, she couldn't see to the other end of the yard for it. It was supposed to be a nice spring day, that's what the weatherman had said, but you couldn't trust them. She didn't need it to be sunny and beautiful, just so it wasn't raining. Raining and lilies and Lyle's mother, and probably having to clean up the fire hall after, that would be too much. She couldn't handle that. She also worried that her recently-dyed hair might streak brown. She was sick of people making assumptions about her red hair meaning that she had a temper. Sometimes she thought people were tiptoeing around her.

The phone rang.

"Hello."

"Well, good morning, darlin'. How are you on this fine day?"

"Good, Mom. I'm fine." She'd been hoping so hard it was Lyle.

"Good, good, honey. Don't you worry about a thing. Your sisters and I have all the food taken care of. There's plenty of Grandma Brown's Beans, macaroni salad, potato salad, sandwiches, everything. Ellen will do the punch."

Oh, great. Kool-Aid wedding punch.

"You'll see, everything'll be fine," her mother continued.

Zola worried that the people from the college would turn their noses up at the homemade reception food, her sister's un-spiked punch. She tried to imagine what could stop it from being a disaster.

McAdam operates

"Grrrnnnnn - nnrr - ronn - nnrr." One piece of toast was stuck in the toaster. President McAdam frowned, pulled the silverware drawer open, plucked a fork from its molded slot and unplugged the toaster.

There should not be any of these irregularly-shaped pieces of bread. She knows that. McAdam lifted the toaster with one hand onto its side, deftly pried out the jammed piece with the fork, like a surgeon. The entire rescue of the damaged toast had taken about half a minute, putting him not too far behind schedule.

Natalie was still in bed, pretending she didn't know something was amiss. Her husband turned in to bed much later than normal last night, after an hour of pecking at the computer downstairs in his office. *He's got a secretary,* she thought, *why should he be doing this himself? Baxter really is just so dedicated, it's like he's half-man, half-college.*

She couldn't see why all the secrecy on a Saturday morning.

He couldn't tell her.

McAdam swiped the toast with margarine, twice downward, twice from left to right. He ate each piece in the usual way, taking even-sized bites from left to right, alternating with measured sips of frozen concentrate orange juice, no pulp.

Seven twenty-three. The paper should be on the front porch step. "What is going on today?" he said, through clenched teeth. The paper was not there, not on the top step, nor on the second step, but behind the first of the juniper shrubs, on the edge of the walk. McAdam stormed down the steps, snatching up the newspaper, and then spotted a bright yellow dandelion growing between the stones dividing the lawn from the shrubs. "And I suppose you think you'll grow back," he admonished, clawing at the dirt to get the rest. He dug and scratched up as much as he could, almost forgetting he was supposed to meet people downtown.

He did not get down to the roots.

Harlan percs up

Harlan woke nervous, anxious, angry, his bed cold and hard. If it weren't for how horrible graduate school had been, he'd be completely paralyzed by now. But it wouldn't let him go. It was so horrid that he had to keep fighting back through. Two years of feeling like shit, the tacit initiation rites into academia, the systematic attack on his self-esteem.

Coffee, Harlan thought, stumbling along the hallway, left shoulder brushing, then bouncing off the wall. His head pounded from the wine the night before.

Today I could get the rest of this chapter done, he thought, feeling the tightness begin in his chest. *Oh damn, Zola's wedding.* He would blow most of the day at the wedding and reception, get home too tired to write, then have to work all day Sunday for the next week at college. He'd already spun his wheels too much on the writing.

Harlan ran water into the percolator, swished yesterday's coffee around, tipped it out into the sink. He peered into the percolator, considered scrubbing it clean, then sighed and filled it to 5. He dumped the grounds into a metal trashcan, thumping the excess on the side. A layer of caked-on grounds rimmed the coffee holder. He searched the sink filled with dirty coffee cups and cereal bowls for something to scrape it with, found nothing.

"Oh, well," he sighed, wiping most of it out with his finger before refilling it. By the time the coffee was percolated, he had written three sentences on the Army's LSD tests, and in frustration crossed out an entire page on Agent Orange. As he kicked aside a pile of books to get out the door, he debated with himself whether to take a pad and some photocopies in case he got a chance to work during the reception.

"This is sick," he said out loud, and closed the door. Then he cursed himself for deciding against bringing his work.

Mrs. Casimir's wild ride

"You look like you been out all night," the woman driving said pleasantly. She glanced over her shoulder at Kenny, the car angling toward the center line.

"Uh, yeah, camping," Kenny replied.

"Mom, Claude is lookin' at me," a daughter said from behind Kenny's ear. She was skinny, had streaked blonde hair and freckles. "He's lookin' at me again."

"Well, it's awful early to be campin' out, don'tcha think? Catch your death o' cold." She veered back to the right, the front passenger tire skimming the shoulder of the highway.

"I guess so."

"Mama, make him stop," Emmy insisted.

"I ain't doin' nothin'," Claude grumbled from the far side of the third seat.

"Honey, don't pick at that," the mother said to the boy next to her. He was lifting a scab halfway from his elbow.

"But it's itchin' me."

"That's because it's gettin' better, Chester. It itches when it's gettin' better."

"Mo-om, he's doin' it again." Emmy swung her arm back to take a slap at Claude, hitting Kenny's ear with her elbow.

"I hope you're not travelin' a long ways, are ya?"

"Uhm, uh, I don't think so."

"Ya don't think so. Ya mean you don't know where you're goin'?"

"Uh, yeah, sure I do." The toddler was astride his shoulder now, sticky fingers in his hair. Kenny wasn't sure what the dampness on his shirt was from. It wasn't warm enough to be sweat.

"Chester, I told ya to leave that be."

"It's *itchin' me*," Chester yelled back.

"It won't heal that way. You'll have a scar. It'll leave a mark on ya."

"Chester's gonna look like *Joa-nee*," little sister Marie chanted.

"What're you talkin' about, Marie? Not Joanie Prwanzas, I'll tell you. You better *not* be."

"Ole Meltie Face, Joanie Prwanzas," Claude crooned.

Suddenly a person appeared on the driver's side of the middle seat. Carrie had been invisible before, pug nose under plastic rim glasses now withdrawn from the book. The shocked look behind her glasses and red blotches in her cheeks betrayed her friendship with Joanie.

Carrie had been withdrawn ever since the fire, more so even than Joanie, her mother thought, because now her best friend had completely cut her off. Joanie wouldn't return Carrie's calls, and when her mother finally told her to just go over there and see her face to face,

Carrie had come home quiet, and wouldn't talk to anyone. But she'd stopped trying to call Joanie.

"All of you just quit it," the mother warned.

Carrie retreated behind the cover of her book. "Meltie, meltie, meltie," Claude whispered behind her ear.

"Claude, honey," his mother said, matter-of-factly, "I'm thinkin' that the dogs need to be cleaned out when we get back."

"You baby. You just wait," Claude hissed.

"Oh, and Claude? There was something else I wanted you to do, but I can't remember what it was." Claude said nothing more.

"Son, ya don't have any place to go now, do ya?" the mother asked Kenny.

He sat silently, blushing, for half a minute. "Uh, no ma'am."

"Then you're comin' in an' eatin' with us."

"Naw, that's okay."

"That wasn't just an invitation, it's a statement of fact. It's a Casimir family rule. You *are* eatin' dinner with us."

The toddler looked into his eyes meaningfully, then grabbed at his hair, jerking his head forward and back.

"Ow. Why'd you do that?"

"Din-din," the child answered. "Yew ah stay-yin."

Guppy theorizes

Guppy had just returned with the *New York Times*, some croissants and heavy cream for coffee. But before he could settle into his high-backed *New York Times* chair, Celeste called him to help her get ready for Zola's wedding.

"I don't see why I need to," he called back.

"Why you should help?"

"Yes."

Celeste appeared in the hallway entrance to the kitchen, her short blonde hair mussed from just having pulled on the clingy green dress she wore at weddings. Guppy was instantly aroused at how it set off her green eyes, full lips, and white teeth, but was unwilling to concede the argument.

"Would you care," she spoke evenly, "to enlighten me about why you shouldn't help?"

"It's a cultural thing, Celeste."

"What is?"

"The reason it's difficult for me to get involved in this project."

"This project," Celeste repeated. "By this project, you mean getting ready for the wedding?"

"Yes." Guppy settled into his leather armchair.

"Ernest?"

"Yes." He felt tingly when she used his full first name, like when he had his mother's full attention.

"How is this a cultural phenomenon?"

"Well, in a market society, with a history of a male-dominated workforce, the onus is on the breadwinner—more typically the male—to be thrust into the competitive arena."

"And," she prompted, sinking onto an ottoman.

"And, being out in the market, in the constant competition, jockeying for position, is so draining . . . "

Celeste thought of the parties she had put together, doing almost all of the cleaning, the cooking, the entertaining of other faculty wives and students, becoming increasingly invisible in the presence of Guppy's female colleagues. *The problem is the college.*

". . . that I have to decompress when I'm not in public."

And this big rationalization. Celeste wanted to believe it was mostly the college's fault, because the alternative was just too much. "Don't you want to go to this?"

"Well, I guess I do," he replied, with a hurt look.

"Then how could it be draining?"

Guppy squirmed in his armchair. "Part of me kind of doesn't want to go."

Celeste snorted softly, then rose to her feet. "Well, the part of you that has the energy to go might consider helping out, okay?"

"Okay," Guppy said. He laughed. "Don't you ever tire of putting up with me?"

"Now that you mention it, it's frightfully draining." He smiled. She smiled back, wondering why she still humored him.

All her children

Kenny rode with the Casimir family through the heart of Halifax Center, a crossroads of County Route 33 and the Old Halifax Road, last eastbound stop sign in Onlius County before the Adirondacks. Halifax Center had one of everything—grocery store, post office, gas station, church, library, diner—in two buildings kitty-corner across the intersection from each other. It had no bar, and no beer or wine in the grocery store, since before Sorley's added the gas pump to the general store. The Temperance Society of Alta and Halifax had pushed through a dry law in 1887, repealed by the Alta town fathers the day after Prohibition ended, but still in effect in Halifax. People generally drove into Johnstown or Alta to buy alcohol. An inability to wait until he got home to start drinking had done in Mrs. Casimir's husband, Little Prett, on the Old Halifax Road, a half-mile east of Bunny's Pizza Oven and Cold Beer, a quarter-mile west of the Halifax Town Line.

Little Prett had driven log trucks for a living since fourteen, legally on the road six weeks shy of his twenty-first birthday. He got the license at his Uncle Stosh's insistence. His father, Big Prett, complained to Stosh that it would be nothing but trouble for the boy to get his license, that it would only increase the chances they'd have to pay taxes. The family had already been forced to send the kids to school.

The logging business survived Little Prett getting his license, and his death, but his family kept pushing further and further outside the law.

People in Halifax counted out to each other the four years between Little Prett's death and the birth of Georgette Casimir's youngest. Most of the time she took the kids with her when she went out line-dancing. At least one time she hadn't.

Stosh and Big Prett had never said a word to her about it. They knew how Little Prett could be. They knew better.

Zola pledges her troth

"I dunno, I guess so," Lyle had said, when the minister asked if he would promise to take Zola's hand, for richer and poorer, in sickness and in health, till death did they part. That had been her nightmare, every night for almost three weeks running. But when the actual moment came, he did not hesitate.

"I will," he'd said, in the bemused way of all Lester men. It was Zola who had stumbled at the moment of truth. From the instant she had seen him in his rented tuxedo at the front of the church she'd been in an excited daydream, a glow of warmth enveloping her from the memory of that hug by the river, when they had stolen away from the rest of the Lester's at the picnic. An energy she could not describe had crept outward from her heart, through her whole body. And now it was filling her again. She had barely heard the minister calling those assembled to witness this union, had not noticed how stern the minister was whenever he was addressing Lyle—especially when he was saying that matrimony was a state one should not enter into lightly. She had not seen Lyle glare back at the minister.

She believed that this was the moment she had been looking for all her life. It would make up for everything else, being the oldest, having to be the mom when her mother's nerves gave out, dealing with the incompetence and arrogance at work. When she looked into Lyle's beige eyes, she saw her own glow reflected back to her.

"Do you, Zola May, take this man to be your lawfully wedded husband, do you pledge your troth, for richer, for poorer, in sickness and in health, till death do you part?"

Lyle's eyes gleamed. Zola felt there were sparks of white light shooting outward from her. She felt everyone watching her, waiting through the pause for her to respond. Rastin leaned to the right, behind Lyle's shoulder, leering at her.

The glint of self-absorbed covetousness in Rastin's beige eyes caught her, washed away the glow, replacing it with the memory after the hug by the river. As she had let go of her fear, she had felt the heel of Lyle's work shoe tucking behind the bend of her knee, felt him gently then urgently pressing himself into her hip.

Lyle's eyes were questioning, Rastin's just this side of lust.

"I'll do it," she gasped, the witnesses slumping back into the pews.

McAdam at the heart of it

McAdam coasted his wife's LeBaron down the last block before the warehouse. Even though he rarely drove anything but the college car, he still was careful not to be recognized. He looked around furtively before crossing the street, not sensing Wispen on the radar he had developed.

The warehouse once had been the heart of the industrial base of Onlius, a mammoth lumberyard from which railroad timbers were shipped out all over the Northeast. It had been empty for almost thirty years after World War Two, when it was torn down for conversion into a strip mall. The new mall on the east side, now two years old, ensured there wouldn't be many people around early on a Saturday to recognize the principals at this breakfast meeting in the Koffee Shoppe.

"I'd like the last cup, no cream, no sugar," McAdam barked at the waitress. *Good, still one empty seat. I'm not the last one here.* He saluted Gordon hello.

Peter Starling flinched. *What's that last-cup bullshit?* McAdam had the sternest—yet most earnest—expression he'd ever worn to one of the sessions. *Oh, man, does this stink. He's really into it.* He noted again how McAdam's duck-footed gait made it look like he was always heading your way.

"Well, we may all be here," Gordon offered.

"The Judge had another engagement this morning, Francoise said. I believe we should handle this without him, don't you, Peter?"

Starling smiled the thin smile that meant he saw no reason to disagree, then tilted his sugar packet another ninety degrees clockwise, feeling the granules slide down to a new center of gravity. *I really oughtta tune into this, if they're starting without the Judge.* McAdam looked exceptionally agitated, and that comforted Peter. Gordon was going on in his oily, distinctive tone, laying out the options the way he saw them. Unsurprisingly, it turned out there were only two: one, to do nothing, and two, to do what Gordon wanted.

"Of course, Henry, no question about it," McAdam said to Gordon. "But do you think we should even mention turning over the franchise to the new owners of the mill? Why not just handle this quietly, let them gradually shrink the workforce on their own?"

"Why, Baxter, this isn't about shrinking the workforce. It's about getting the nose of government out of where it doesn't belong."

No one paid attention to Starling during the meeting. That was okay with him, because he tuned out as soon as he gathered that he was just there to smile, perhaps nod when it got really tense, when Gordon, McAdam, or the others were unsure of themselves.

He couldn't help smiling a little, on the inside, that these movers and shakers would look for his approval, need him there. He wondered if it was what he'd done back in high school, on the football team, and in semi-pro afterward, or the hunting and fishing guide business he'd had since he dropped out of Onlius State after one week. But it couldn't be the business; that was small potatoes compared to what these other guys did, the numbers of people they employed, the way they could get the word out if they wanted something to happen. He tilted the sugar packet again.

McAdam had not calmed down through the entire meeting. Maybe it was the three "last cup, no cream, no sugar" refills, but he seemed more wound up now than when they started. McAdam was the one Peter trusted the least of this crowd, always winking at him in that way that startled him so, when trying to sway the group away from Gordon. Plus, he suspected McAdam somehow had found out he'd only gone to college for a week. That'd be just like him.

Gordon was winding up; the real business of the meeting had been over for twenty minutes. They were going to intercede. It had to be done. McAdam looked out of the corner of his eye at Peter Starling, sitting there with that same vacant, idiotic smile. Every time he tipped that damn sugar packet it was like hearing nails on a blackboard. *This is ticklish business, I don't understand why he's here.*

Peter had been daydreaming about being out on the boat, opening day.

He was wondering the same thing.

Janie knows

Janie got home late, went right to bed, and woke with a headache. She called her ex-mother-in-law Barb first thing after the Tylenol, to ask for more sleep before she came to get Billy.

"I got things to do, ya know."

"Yeah, I know, Barb. I just need another hour maybe."

"Today's my grocery day, ya know."

"Yeah, I know. I've taken you lots of times, remember?"

"Of course I remember. I just gotta get my groceries today. All the stuff is usually gone by Sunday after church."

"I know, Barb. I'll only be maybe an hour. I just gotta try to shake this headache. How's Billy, anyway?"

"He's fine. He's a good little boy. Eatin' some cereal, which I'm almost out of, ya know."

"I know, Barb, I know. I'm on my way over. Hope I don't get sick." She pressed the receiver hard against her right eyebrow and let the wave of nausea wash over her. She couldn't remember feeling this sick since she was pregnant with Billy, and picked up so much weight on her thin frame that Earl decided to take off.

Billy would just have to watch cartoons until she could catch up.

Wispen on patrol

Administrative Vice President Wispen swung by McAdam's house on his way to the college. *Hmmm. College car's there, but the LeBaron's gone. Let's just see who's really at home.* He idled to his stakeout point.

McAdam on the case

"Can't tell if he's there or not. Car could be in the garage," President McAdam muttered to himself. "If he's not home, where would he be?" Alarming thoughts flashed through his mind—of Wispen on the loose in McAdam's office files, Wispen sorting his household refuse for the stray piece of damning debris. That was why McAdam never rented a videotape—because of the record left behind.

That hedge along the southeast will provide cover most of the way. Then that pine. If I can see through the side-door window, I'll know whether his car is in there.

His special sense for Wispen was not alerted, so McAdam decided to gamble on the reconnaissance mission. He scampered along the edge of the hedgerow to the open stretch of back lawn, dropped to all fours, then duck-ran to the pine tree. For five minutes he stared at the back windows of Wispen's house, detecting no movement within. Then he sprinted the last fifteen yards to the back corner of the garage, circled behind it, walked quickly to the side door and peered through the window.

Empty! He's probably at the college already. Better get right over there.

Five minutes earlier Wispen had gunned his car down the street from McAdam's house, having observed McAdam's wife Natalie come out to pick up the mail—knowing that McAdam had been out for some time now, undetected.

Kenny tests his wings

Mrs. Casimir was in her glory. A new chick in the nest. "Now tell me, son, why is it that you're goin' somewhere but you don't know where it is?"

"Uh, I . . . I know where it is," Kenny stammered. "It's just that I'm not s'posed to tell anybody."

"What do you mean, not tell anybody? What's the big secret?" Mrs. Casimir was sitting on the back porch step with Kenny, watching the toddler scoop dirt out of a freshly dug hole in the yard.

"I've got somethin' to do that I'm not s'posed to tell anybody about. It's real important." Kenny was still worried about Cough's warning, yet he sensed Mrs. Casimir was not a threat.

"So you know what you're supposed to do?"

Kenny nodded.

"And you know where you're goin'?"

"Yeah," Kenny lied, fingers crossed on the hand he'd sneaked out of sight.

"And how to get there?"

A double lie was tricky. She had caught him off guard. Just because he had to find his cousin at the college, he wasn't going to start taking chances. He uncrossed his fingers.

"I sorta know." This was true. Cough had told him it was on the other side of the county.

"Stop that now, darlin'. You leave that dog alone," Mrs. Casimir told the baby. "He don't need none of that dirt in his ears.

"Well, Kenny, it's your business. You can stay here if you like, at least have supper with us. Can you do that?"

Kenny reflected, not feeling pressed to say something right away. He watched the baby sprinkle dirt down the front of her diaper, considering what he should do.

"I think I oughtta go," he finally decided, feeling a tingle in his feet. "Thanks, ma-am, for the ride and the food and everything."

"That's okay, son. Happy to do it. Listen," she said, her plump hand on his arm. "If you need to, you can always come back. You'll know how to get here, just ask anybody if you get lost. Promise?"

"Promise."

"And you're takin' some food with you, for supper at least."

It hadn't even occurred to Kenny to refuse. He'd been thinking about an apple pie cooling on Mrs. Casimir's sideboard in the kitchen, hoping she'd give him a slice to sweeten his mission.

Darcardt gets sentimental

"God, why does it have to be so hot? It's only May." Zola could feel herself soaking into her wedding dress, making it stick to her waist. Lyle looked uncomfortable in his polyester tux, still hung over from the party his brothers threw for him. His face was bright red, the collar a half size tight. He stood hunched into the gray jacket, his unusually long arms dangling from the sleeves. Zola shuddered at how it made him look that much taller.

Lyle and his brother Rastin seemed to share an inside joke, probably from the bachelor party. This was the third time today she had caught him pointing semi-discreetly at the bridesmaids. Rastin's third marriage had just ended from too much interest in Patty's girlfriends. The first two marriages ended for the same reason, at exactly the same moment, when his wives discovered each other at a bowling banquet. The first, Belinda, was the angriest when she found out that the Margie for whom she'd been subbing during the winter was also married to her husband. They had broken the second-place trophy in half during the fight.

Guppy eyed Lyle's family's table. "Would you take a look at that? It's uncanny."

"Oh, yeah," Harlan agreed, trying not to look. The men all wore the same expression—bemused smiles, eyes glinting, mouths opening and closing slightly, taking in the humid air.

Darcardt sidled over to his seat next to Harlan and Guppy. "Isn't this what Jim Jones served his guests in Guyana?" he said, tasting the Kool-Aid punch. He fingered one of his long white sideburns, up to where his fringe of hair stopped.

Harlan suppressed a smile. "I doubt this Kool-Aid is laced with cyanide."

"I'm not so sure," Guppy said dryly, eyeing Lyle's family. "And besides, you know what I heard? Once they'd gotten everybody used to drinking the Kool-Aid, they gradually took the cyanide out. And that's what killed them."

Darcardt grinned. "As the titular leader of the college contingent, I would like to propose a toast," he bellowed, rising from his seat. His almond-shaped gray eyes shone.

With all eyes upon him, Darcardt addressed the head table. Harlan, Guppy, Celeste, and Marie Earhart shifted in their chairs.

"The lovely bride and her, uh, equally lovely husband are entering into the most wondrous and challenging time of their lives, forging a bond that will last forever." Lyle was frowning, Zola smiling appreciatively.

"And this happy state of mind is arrived at by being absolutely faithful, completely loving, no matter what comes along . . . Fire, disease, pestilence, war . . . You will grow ever closer together through these experiences and ever more in love."

The tinkling of glasses and applause began fitfully at the end of Darcardt's call to battle.

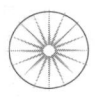

Kenny backtracks

Kenny walked out of Halifax Center back toward Percy's Corners. The only guidance he had was that he was already in town, so if he wanted something bigger he'd have to go north or west. He'd come close to asking Mrs. Casimir how to get to the college, but he figured her family probably didn't know much about Onlius State, or any college for that matter. Aurelia's friend Patty from high school had taken secretarial at the community college at Mohawk Valley while her boyfriend studied automotive technology, and then she'd gotten out of touch with Aurelia after she married that Rastin Lester. She never said much about Patty, but one time Kenny had heard her talk to one of the cashiers at the Grandy Market about "college snobs" like she knew something about it. Mrs. Casimir didn't know about being a snob from beans, that much Kenny could tell.

Timothy, orchard grass, and dandelions were almost a foot high, unusual for this early in May. It had been a much sunnier and warmer spring than normal, everything getting early growth. Peepers were also out ahead of schedule, including those doomed to be run over on warm, wet late-April nights. Kenny stooped down to examine one dried-out eyeless carcass. It was squashed so flat, he wondered if he could toss it like a Frisbee. He reached out for it, fingertips moving idly over the smoothness of its back.

From within the dried flesh he felt a car speeding, its driver anxious, in too much of a hurry to get where he didn't really need to be. He knew the need to mate was the only reason to be in that kind of rush, lost in that much passion.

There was only that much left of the frog's consciousness, but it made him sit down in the grass, a memory washing over him.

Ninth grade. Susan Fermi with dark hair and dark eyes, more shy than he. Weeks of his best attempts to concentrate focused on how to talk to her, ask her to a basketball game. He'd been in Level Three since third grade, but now in high school they thought he might be dangerous in BOCES or shop, so there was no choice but local diploma classes.

They shared a lab table in general science. She wore plaid skirts and grayish-yellow white blouses, the same clothes her older sister had worn in the same class last year, even though she was taller than Bonnie so the skirts revealed more of her skinny legs.

Kenny was interested in legs and hair and eyes and breasts, but mostly by shyness, loneliness, vulnerability, need. It was December and she was the only person in his grade who had not called him stupid.

Mr. Tracy walked the attendance rosters down to the office right after lunch every day when they resumed the split period. Kenny had been unable to eat all his sloppy joe, he was so distracted. By the time he got to his seat the chocolate-milk residue hung in his mouth like ashes. While the rest of the class played with Bunsen burners and went through the motions of copying Mr. Tracy's dissected-frog drawing from the board, he tried to calm his heart.

"Susan," he squeaked, his pubescent voice soaring, "uh, do you like to go to the basketball games?"

She was frozen in her seat, pencil stub gripped awkwardly in her hand, left elbow clamping the notebook to the table. She didn't answer, didn't look up, didn't breathe.

"Su-san," he whispered, afraid of the rest of the class listening to his moment of shame. It was no use. He had to lift his eyes from the book and look at her, speak directly to her.

"Susan," he whispered a shade louder. "I asked if you liked to go to the basketball games." He focused on the fine hair along the edge of her jaw, afraid to look into her eyes.

She wouldn't look up. She had heard everything he said, but could not respond.

Kenny noticed the red in her cheeks, spreading across her jaw into blotches on her throat. Her face was turned slightly to the right, nose pointing to the center of her notebook, eyes shut.

His mouth puckered closed. Chill settled over him. She doesn't like me either. Then he saw the color in her face empty to the palest white. She was trembling, a tear curling along the edge of her nostril.

Kenny felt the clammy darkness of panic swimming before his eyes, that burning, freezing feeling of everyone's eyes upon you, not knowing the answer, wearing hand-me-down clothes, being called stupid, having no one stick up for you.

"I'm sorry, Susan," he whispered, and began to make it look like he was copying down the notes.

She hadn't lifted her eyes from her notebook, or stopped shivering, for the rest of the class.

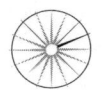

Lester mating rituals

"Is that another shirt?" Guppy asked. "He must have an extra set of sweat glands." Lyle had not stopped dancing since the deejay started, except to change out of sweat-soaked shirts during slow songs, to hit the dance floor again during the fast ones.

"Zola's enjoying herself," Harlan observed to Earhart. Zola's face was flushed, eyes bright and wild. She seemed to have forgotten the college people were there.

Guppy watched Marie Earhart smirk as she observed the Lester men strut on the dance floor. It did not become her. He studied her fine features, pale skin, how her walnut-brown hair complemented the brown, soulful eyes.

She took one dance with Harlan, and one odd slow dance with Darcardt, her willowy frame eyed all the while by the Lester clan. She returned their leering with a model's disinterest, which only got them hotter. After Rastin had sidled by, giving her the most blatant, lingering once-over, she sat with Harlan, Guppy, and Celeste to study the Lesters more systematically.

"Do you think it's learned, or hereditary?" Guppy asked Earhart.

"What exactly do you mean, Ernest?" She always used his full first name when she wanted to pull him up.

Guppy twitched, then resumed. "Their behavior, of course. For instance," he paused, weighing the words, "are they practicing some . . . some mating rite that has allowed them . . . hmm, hmmm, hmm . . . allowed them to parallel the development of their species with ours?"

Harlan suppressed a smile before he offered, "You're such a snob, Ernie. If I thought you listened to yourself, I'd never hang with you."

Guppy knit his eyebrows in mock concern.

"I don't think you're at all funny," Earhart said evenly, all the while glaring at Rastin. "If only for the sake of Zola's feelings, you shouldn't talk that way about those people."

"Those people . . . those people. You see, you have the same fascination as I. It's the social scientist in you. Now what is it that makes them that way?"

"If you insist on my indulging you, genetics enters in with the Y chromosome. And the rest is an oppressive patriarchal mindset imposed in the cultural vacuum of an isolated rural environment."

Earhart turned to look Guppy in the eye. "Unfortunately, it's not as unique as you seem to think."

Celeste shifted on her seat, suddenly tuned in to Marie.

Guppy quickly searched his table for a receptive face, and fixed a serious, nodding gaze upon Harlan. "I suspected that would be the thrust of your analysis. I was merely concerned that our good friend Zola may be about to swim in the dangerous end of the gene pool." Earhart scowled, as much at Guppy as at Lyle's father, who had just given her a lewd wink.

Gimme shelter

Kenny was hungry again, despite downing a double piece of pie with the sandwiches Mrs. Casimir had given him for the walk back. He had eaten all the food in his backpack, except the fruit cocktail, which he couldn't figure how to get out of the cans. Food had helped steady him after the flashback from school. It always helped when he was hurt or confused.

He stuffed the waxed-paper wrappers into his backpack, nestled the frog carcass in the front pocket, and started to walk again, red sun setting behind his left shoulder.

Too early for berries or fruit, no nut trees near the highway, the only food he could find was shafts of orchard grass that he unsheathed and chewed on for their milk.

He was really hungry.

The moon had risen before sunset, providing clear silvery light. Kenny had no idea where he was headed, or where he could settle for the night, so he just kept going, the chirping of peepers his only company.

Back away from the road, in meadow growth near the edge of woods, he could pick out the faint reflections of moonlight in the eyes of browsing deer.

It comforted him to travel at night, feeling that without light, other creatures might be as directionless as he.

That house looks empty. I could stay in there, Kenny thought. There was no light anywhere, no glass in the windows, some ragged furniture on the lawn. Moonlight glinted off broken glass as he picked his way through the grass to the front porch. The only remaining plank step crumbled under his feet. He heaved himself from the ground onto the porch, which creaked and felt as if it were going to lurch. He crawled across the threshold inside.

All he wanted was some place with a floor and a roof for the night, but he found couch cushions already arranged into a kind of mattress just inside the door. Kenny struggled out of his backpack, kicked off his sneakers, and stretched out. Just as he was about to drop off to sleep he heard a ca-chuck sound from upstairs, like a credit-card machine, or a rifle bolt being worked into firing position.

No's for news

"Oh, please, John," Celeste pleaded with Harlan. "Don't let Ernie do this. It's truly awful."

"I don't know. It sounds okay."

"That's right, you don't know. It's a sickness. He can't stop himself," she implored.

"Come now, dear. You're making too much of this," Guppy said. He motioned for the waitress to refill his coffee.

Harlan looked torn. Celeste couldn't bear to add to his suffering. "All right, Ernie, lay it on him. But," she told Harlan with a weak smile, "don't say I didn't warn you."

"Well, to begin," Guppy said, "there's something from yesterday's paper I couldn't pass up. Did you see the story about the country-and-western songs that make fun of the televangelists? No?"

Harlan shook his head, embarrassed.

"I believe it was front page."

Harlan looked down at the checkered tablecloth.

"Well, you have to keep up with the news of the day, John. That's one of the expectations here, you know. Let me bring you up to speed. It seems that country and western singers, like that Ray Stevens, are making fun of fundamentalists, on southern radio stations. Can you believe it?"

Harlan was nodding, but his thoughts were far distant. *The 1980s version of the military-industrial complex,* he was thinking, *is being challenged in a fundamental way by the workings of Gorbachev's perestroika.* He was wishing he could just go home and write some of this down. *To the extent that the Soviet Union and the Eastern Bloc are serious about a rapprochement and actually achieve a restructuring of their economies, the United States will have to develop an entirely new rationale for its military spending.*

"But you cannot believe, Ernie," Celeste was arguing, "this means anything in the long term."

"Of course it does. It's an awakening of consciousness."

"Those same people will be writing love ballads for Oliver North before you know it."

"This is an opening, a window," Guppy insisted.

"Jerry Falwell already has taken over the PTL. And as for Ray Stevens being enlightened. Didn't he do *A-hab the A-rab*?"

"You just can't bring yourself to admit . . ."

. . . but perhaps the greatest legacy of the nuclear arms race is its self-fulfilling capacity for expansion to meet our self-induced threat . . .

Kenny's flashback to Nam

Kenny was shaking.

"I'm sorry, Kenny. Try to relax, okay," Johnny Percy said, leaning the rifle back against the stairs. "I remember you, Kenny. You were okay." He lit a cigarette, keeping his hand cupped around the end to keep the light from escaping.

Kenny still was frightened from seeing the rifle pointed at his face, Johnny whispering harshly, calling him a fucking gook. "I didn't recognize you at first, Kenny. But you prob'ly don't remember me from school. You couldn'ta only been in first grade, maybe kindergarten. D'you remember me?"

"Ya don't? Wow. *Think,* man. The playground. Teeter-totter, man. Them kids pickin' on ya. Hittin' ya in the ass with the teeter-totter. Ya gotta remember that."

It was hard for Kenny to remember any one incident of abuse at school.

"Jesus, I remember it just like yesterday. I came over and kicked their asses 'cause you were so tough. You didn't cry or nothin'. I thought, 'That's cool.'"

Johnny seemed to relax a little, took the cupped hand away from the cigarette end for a moment. "Yeah, I remember you, Kenny. You were all right." He snuffed out the cigarette on the butt of the rifle, then pushed himself up to his feet with it.

"Don't worry, man, you just get some sleep here. Go ahead. I'll take this watch."

Kenny lay back down obediently. *So that was Johnny Percy.* He felt really bad now that he had wet one of Johnny's cushions.

Ronald Reagan* on Kenny Hopewell

Kenny Hopewell? Hopewell? Yes. Mommy, that's the man who goes around with Frank, right, the bodyguard? No . . .

Well, sometimes not being able to remember is a good thing.

It's saved me a few times, like when I was lost once on the Pacific Coast Highway. You remember that, Mommy? That was in a picture, right?

Now, who were we talking about?

---

*During his 1984 reelection campaign, President Reagan became visibly disoriented during the concluding remarks of his televised debate with Walter Mondale, his anecdote trailing off to nowhere.

Chapter Three

Getting to True

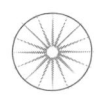

❋ Not at home

One plaster patch looked like the Batmobile. Another hole in the ceiling was shaped like Big Bird. The walls didn't look familiar at all. They were grimy.

"Uh-oh. Aurelia's going to be mad. I got my bed all wet." Kenny couldn't recall why he brought these cushions in, or why he had slept with his pants on instead of pajamas. He was having trouble remembering this part of their house.

"Mornin', Sport. I think it's your turn for the watch," the man said. He looked sort of familiar. He had long, scraggly blond hair, was wiry, with big feet for someone shorter than Kenny. His bloodshot blue eyes jumped from focus to focus, refusing to remain in anything approaching eye contact, as if they were looking for his ears, which stuck straight out through his hair.

Why'd I wet myself? I haven't done that in so long. Where am I?
"Hey, have you got anything to eat?" the man said. "I'm starvin'."
Kenny remembered his backpack. "I might have some stuff."

He pawed through the wax paper, found the string and the fruit cocktail, checked in the front pocket and pulled out the squashed frog.

"Oh, hey, somethin' from the meat group, too. Y'know somethin' Kenny, I don't think that guy's gonna help much on the mission."

My mission! That's what I'm doing. Yesterday's memories flooded his mind—the ride with the Casimirs, finding the frog, being scared to death by Johnny Percy, telling him about the mission.

"Yeah, guess you're right, Johnny." He gently packed the frog back into place and then rolled a can of fruit cocktail across the floor to Johnny. "I don't know how to open it."

"No problem. Got a can opener on my knife." Johnny got the cans open quickly; they each drained one.

"You're definitely gonna hafta take the watch, bud. I'm crashin'." Johnny's eyes were burnt red. He was propped up on one elbow, ready to fall asleep flat on the worn linoleum.

"Yeah, sure, I guess." Kenny was frightened. He didn't like to have anything to do with guns. "Uh, anybody special I'm s'posed to look for?"

"Anybody," Johnny said wearily. "Especially cops . . . or gooks . . . or the CO. If you get a shot at him, take it. We'll win the pool."

Kenny flipped the cushions over, hoping that the wet and smell hadn't gone all the way through. Johnny was asleep in less than a minute.

Kenny thought about staying, but Cough's voice was filling his head. He quietly leaned the rifle against the stair banister, slid across the porch, and set out looking for the college.

Zola's honeymoon

Lyle, sleeping, wore a satisfied, almost innocent look. His pompadour was slicked back by sweat from the reception, and after. Zola still felt weak.

She went into the bathroom. Were her red hair roots showing already? Had Lyle noticed the wrinkles in the corners of her eyes, the puffiness below them? She was seven years older than him, why had he wanted to marry her? She worried her way into the kitchen, through the search for eggs to scramble and bacon to fry.

Lyle wandered down the hall into the kitchen, attracted by the aroma of coffee brewing. He knotted his hands together around Zola's waist, nuzzled the back of her neck.

"How much bacon should I make?" Zola asked.

"Make all of it," he replied, his eyes smoky. "We gotta keep our strength up."

Zola flinched.

Harlan at rest

Everything was wrong. Harlan's headache was hanging on this morning, a dull knot of pain behind his right eye. He had not done dishes for three days. There was a smell in the sink. It was becoming unbearable. He'd have to wash the dishes even before he got breakfast. And after that he had a ton of things to do before Monday morning—two sets of papers to grade, three final exams to make up.

The dissertation would have to wait again.

And a side of worms

Janie flipped her pillow over to bring the cool side next to her cheek, and tucked the sheet between her bare legs. She couldn't believe how hot it was for the beginning of May.

Bam! Something crashed against the door. Bam! "Oh my gawd," Janie moaned. "What is it now?"

Billy was trying to wake her up, because there was a commercial on TV. He was bouncing his kickball off the door of Janie's bedroom, wanting her to come out and pour him a bowl of Froot Rings. He was tired of eating them dry from the box. He was bo-ored.

"You do that . . ." Bam!

"You do that one more . . ." Bam!

"Bil-*lee*," she screamed. "Stop it!"

Silence.

Janie waited a minute, then turned on her side to get settled for more sleep. Billy was engrossed in a Teenage Mutant Ninja Turtles commercial.

Bam! The Ninja Turtles ad was over. Rainbow Brite was on. Bam!

"Billy, get in here. Right now!"

He opened the door matter-of-factly and walked straight over to the side of her bed, a blaming look fixed on his face.

It made Janie even hotter. "You know you're supposed to be *quiet* until I get up on the weekends. You *know* I don't get much time to sleep in." He started to turn his head away.

"Don't you turn away from *me*," she yelled. "I have to wash clothes today, get groceries, study for my *finals*."

Billy's lower lip formed a ledge for his anger.

"And you just had to keep pushing, trying to wake me up."

The lip curled downward, pulsed in and out, the prelude to tears.

"Oh, don't you do that to me. Don't!"

He had to turn away. She grabbed his arms to pull him back, fought his twisting away from her. "You are going to listen to me," she insisted. "Why are you being so bad?"

"I'm *not* being bad," he shouted. "You don't *never* wanna play with me. *Never*." He twisted to the floor, stomped two steps toward the door, then crumbled, his back to Janie.

"Well, I guess I better fix you some breakfast, bad boy," she said, in her lightest teasing tone.

Billy didn't budge.

"What would you like? Let's see. Froot Rings, or pancakes, maybe. I know," she gambled, "I'm gonna dig up some worms for you, and put some bugs in it, and spit. How's that sound?"

He turned his head partway around, just enough for her to see a glimpse of dimple.

"And wait, I almost forgot. We've got some gopher guts. And dog poop."

He giggled and turned back toward the door, but the trembling of his shoulders tipped her off.

"Come on over here, bad boy."

He wiggled his fanny backward on the rug toward Janie, close enough for her to grab him, toss him on the bed and tickle him, while he giggled helplessly.

"Are you gonna let Mommy get some sleep?"

He shook his head, still gasping for air.

"Are you gonna help Mommy with the house?"

"No," he squealed, smile in full dimple.

"Are you gonna let Mommy do her homework?"

His smile dissolved into a frown. He pushed himself off the bed and stomped out of her bedroom, slamming the door behind him.

"Honey! Aw, c'mon, Billy. Don't . . ."

Bam!

McAdam keeps the faith

President McAdam always attended the earliest service at the Presbyterian church, knowing that Gordon and the others went to the later one. He'd gotten the minister to agree not to tell anyone that he went to both. It made him feel more secure to know what the sermon was about, so he could be seen reacting appropriately to it. He usually took notes early on, and if he did not have to concentrate entirely on the sermon, prepared his calendar for the next week. He sang hymns in a flat buzzing monotone.

Leonard Koemover was not a member of this church, had never before attended a service, but today he showed up and sat three seats away from him. Strange, he'd seemed to McAdam too wrapped up in statistical analysis to be interested in matters of faith.

"Hello, President McAdam," Koemover said, leaning over the end of the pew. "Good to see you."

"And you, Doctor, and you," McAdam replied, putting an edge in his voice to see if he could make Koemover jumpy. He had to lose him before people started gathering for the second service.

"I especially enjoyed the message about Christ being a model administrator. I always enjoy learning those kinds of things."

"Yes, yes. My favorite part as well. The line and staff delineations for the Apostles. Brilliant."

"Yes, brilliant, that's exactly what I was going to say." An awkward pause followed, during which Koemover attempted to think of further conversation while McAdam looked past him to acknowledge the lesser movers and shakers as they filed out.

"And Judas would equate to whom, do you think?" Koemover finally asked.

"Judas? Well, obviously that's where the analogy breaks down," McAdam snapped, cutting him off. Koemover began to slink away.

Judas? Judas would have been a vice president or a dean, or one of his accomplices, McAdam thought, watching Koemover disappear.

The Casimir's trespassing

". . . Hallow-head be Thy name, Thy kingdom come, Thy will be done . . ." Mrs. Casimir felt it envelop her. This was the one part of the service when the kids knew they had to sit absolutely still, stop pinching and poking each other, let nothing disturb the moment for their mother. Georgette loved the way everyone's voices and energy seemed to swell in one thick prayer. It was always the best moment of her week.

". . . forgive us our trespasses . . ." Carrie sneaked a look across the aisle at Joanie's twin brothers, sitting with their mother. Before the fire Joanie and Carrie always used to sit together in church, "practic'ly on top of each other," Claude complained, but ever since, Joanie hadn't come to church at all.

Mrs. Casimir squeezed Carrie's hand. Carrie let her hand go limp, staring across the aisle.

Celeste seeking solace

Vertical blinds. They were the first thing she had gotten rid of when they moved into the Bacon Street house. Gray and cold. Slices of sunlight that worked their way through, hollowly. Celeste had known she couldn't stand to stay at home with those blinds in the kitchen window.

Lately she had been thinking about retrieving them from the attic, to put them back up.

"Is there more coffee?" Guppy called from the den.

Celeste poured him a cup, placed a coaster on the end-table next to Guppy's chair, tried to retreat back to the kitchen.

"Celeste, have you seen this?"

"What?" she sighed.

"The latest on Ollie and the boys. You won't believe it. *I* hardly believe it."

Something inside her slumped.

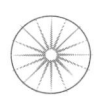

Kenny's plague of frogs

Kenny felt kind of bad about leaving Johnny alone in his house asleep, especially since he was so upset, but he knew he had to get to Onlius, and it seemed like Johnny wouldn't want to leave his house to help him.

It didn't look good for getting rides today, but he didn't mind. After his visit to Johnny's, he was okay being alone for a while.

Dew caught the light. The tops of the tag alders and locust trees on the horizon shone pinkish-gray. Maple tree leaves had not yet emerged in that fierce overnight blossoming only noticed after the fact.

Kenny had kept track of the road back from Halifax Center, eliminating it first from his possible choices. He headed toward the sun until he saw a nice spot under a maple, suddenly recognizing it as his shelter the first night out. Confusion settled over him for a while, building until anxiety made him bend his head down between his knees.

"Oh, I hate this," he whimpered. A half-minute of blood flowing back into this head calmed him enough to straighten up and look around again. "Let's see, this was the first road I walked on," he said in what he wanted to be his calm voice. "An' I was on that road over there," he said, waving his hand in the direction of the intersection. But at that moment he couldn't remember exactly which other road. He turned around, walked back to the center of the crossroads, looked in all four directions. Dark clouds swam before his eyes. His chest felt as if it were filled with some thick liquid, like cold molasses. He couldn't catch his breath. He lost every memory from the past two days.

Where is Aurelia? his mind screamed. *How could she let me be lost here?*

He sat down in the middle of the road, tore at his shirt and pants in a frenzy. "I can't . . . stand it."

And nightmares of being lost reeled through his mind—at school, in town, *at his house, in his room.* Kenny felt as if the earth were opening up to swallow him. "I get lost in my own house," he sobbed. "I can't remember where I am, or what I'm s'posed to be doing, aw . . . aw . . . all I can remember is forgetting all the time. I'm . . . *lost.*"

He started to tear at his shirt again, felt the backpack slap into his shoulder blades, then paused, reason coming through dark panic. Slipping out of the backpack, he began to unload it around him. String, wax paper, candy wrappers, his Cub Scout manual, and in the front pocket, a frog carcass.

He held it for a few seconds in his palm. Nothing clicked. Then a rush of terror. A car was bearing down on him. He was sitting in the middle of the road! Kenny tucked and rolled with what was left in his backpack all the way to the gravel shoulder.

Wait, there's no car. Whaddami doin'? He slowly opened his palm again and stared at the crushed remains of a dried-out frog.

There was no voice left in it, nothing to help him get his bearings.

It had no legs—that was it. He had saved it to remind him of his father, the time he'd lectured Kenny about being cruel to the frogs he and Barry Whistleknot had found in the swamp behind Barry's house. Kenny had wanted to keep them at first, was filling his pockets with them, until Barry told him not to be such a weenie. Barry had a shiny new jackknife his father had just given him for his eighth birthday, freshly sharpened by his dad on his grinder. "Just right for some frawg-stickin'," Barry'd said. He took one of the frogs from Kenny and sliced off its legs, then hurled it against a rock. That made Kenny woozy, but he was afraid to let Barry see, so he turned away from him, scattering as many of them back out of his pockets as he could.

"Hey, whaddaya doin'?" Barry protested.

"N-nothin'. Hey, they're gettin' away," Kenny said, pretending concern.

"You wuz lettin' 'em go, Kenny," Barry said, a menacing grin spreading across his face.

"No, I wasn't."

"Yeah you wuz." Barry grinned and nodded his head, figuring out what Kenny's punishment should be. "C'mover here," he said, still nodding, still grinning.

"What? Whu-ut?" Kenny squatted down to search for more frogs, ready to feed Barry's blood hunger.

"Whatcha doin' now, catchin' 'em? You can do that inna minute. First you gotta c'mover here." There was no question what was going to happen next.

"Okay, okay," Kenny whimpered. Barry dug his nails into Kenny's right arm, squeezing the biceps until he was hopping from one foot to the other in pain.

"There ya go, Kenny. You know you had it comin'."

Kenny nodded his head quickly and sniffed.

"Now get back ta work. Get me some more frogs."

Kenny was already on his knees at the edge of the water, leaning into the cattails.

"I wanna big one this time," Barry said.

"Here's one. It's not real big, but it's okay." Kenny tried to work the charley horse out of his arm. "It's kinda big, ya know."

Barry clutched the frog in his left hand, worked its legs out between his fingers and slashed them off.

"Haw, haw, haw," he laughed as the blood spurted. He hurled it against a rock.

Kenny was searching for the next victim, being sure not to look in Barry's direction, or at the blood. He reached the next one out behind him, still peering into the cattails, when he felt Barry hurriedly shoving the handle of the jackknife into his palm.

"Okay, there ya go," Barry was saying. "Take it back. I don't wanna use it anyway."

"What?" Kenny asked, still searching.

"You wanted it. Here, take it." Kenny was still grasping the knife when he turned around to look, and saw his father staring at the blood on his hands. He looked very upset.

"I was tellin' him he shouldn't do that," Barry was saying.

"No, you wasn't," Kenny said. "You was . . ."

"Kenny, I want you to go back home. Right now! You understand?"

"Yeah, Dad. I . . . I'm goin'. But . . ."

"No buts. Just git!"

Kenny threw down Barry's knife and tore off. He had run a quarter of a mile before he realized he had no idea where he was. He wandered for almost an hour before Cough found him near the back of the mill, his face streaked with tears and frog blood.

"Where you been, Kenneth?" Cough said, in the same authoritative tone his father would have used. "You were s'posed to be home an hour ago."

"I know, Cough," Kenny sniffled. "I was tryin', I just couldn't find it." He stared at the ground, tracing a half-circle in the gravel with the toe of his sneaker.

"Kenny, ya can't find your way around anywheres, can ya?"

"No," he said softly. He felt like his ribs were squeezing in from both sides, crushing his heart. He wasn't supposed to tell.

"I knew it," Cough said, shaking his head. "Y'ain't never been able to get yourself to true, have you? Well, that don't mean you're dumb, Kenny, or slow. If ya can't help it, then it ain't nothin' to be ashamed about."

Now Kenny was confused. What Cough had told him went against everything people had been telling him at school, that he was stupid. The people at his mother's church didn't say anything. They just stared out of the corners of their eyes, nodding when the minister talked about God punishing the wicked. The Hopewells must have had it coming. The congregation only wished it knew all the details.

Once he'd gotten home, Kenny's father asked if he'd really been the one cutting the frogs' legs off. Kenny told him no. "Guess I knew that," his father said. "Did you tell Cough about your problem? That you can't find yer way around anywheres?"

"Yeah, Dad."

"Guess I knew that too."

"I'm real sorry."

"Don't be sorry, Kenny. We shouldn'ta been tellin' you to keep quiet about it all this time. It's my fault about that."

Kenny sat perfectly still, drawing shallow breaths, expecting to get spanked.

"I was scared when you were lost," Wiley said. "Really scared. We've gotta find some way for you to get around, at least around here."

They tried. Wiley, Martha, and Aurelia would make up phrases and songs for Kenny to say to himself as he walked anywhere. "The mechanic went to school before the mill," repeated over and over, would get Kenny from his house to meetings with Cough. At least it got him around town.

Now Kenny started to cry, for the frogs. He clasped his hands around his knees, rocking back and forth in the dry ditch, unable to get his father's face out of his mind.

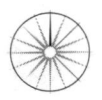

Harlan & the communistics

The domino theory as a cause for the US in Vietnam. The domino theory was definitely a cause for the US in Vietnam.

> It was the idea that countries like the Viet Cong would take over other countries like the South Vietnam and make it communistic. Then the other ones like Tailand and China will go communist too.

"Oh well, at least it's got a thesis statement," Harlan groaned. I wonder if this guy even shows for class? The country of Viet Cong? Bet he doesn't know anything about Diem or the National Liberation Front.

Harlan had circled "Tailand" and "communistic," and put a huge red question mark after his brackets surrounding "China will go communist."

> The US got into the war because it wanted to help the South Vietnams from being taken over by the North Vietnam's and the communistics.

He couldn't take this anymore. He had some fantastic students, but more that seemed just to be going through the motions.

Harlan counted the essay booklets left in the pile for his eight o'clock class. Seventeen. He had only read through eleven the first time, and there was another whole set from the ten o'clock class that he'd promised to give back tomorrow.

Did he have to pee again? Yeah, he thought so. It was his third vist to the bathroom in the last two hours, his reward for getting through every block of five essays. When he wasn't grading papers, Harlan could wait for hours between bathroom visits.

The remote distracted him on the way back to the office. He grabbed it and settled into a worn overstuffed chair in the living room. Maybe a little Bugs Bunny would help him clear his head so he could get back to work.

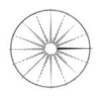

Another Sunday stakeout

Administrative V.P. Wispen was having his usual brunch at one of the tiny tables in the bakery near the Presbyterian church. He dunked a doughnut with his long, elegant fingers, chewed it with his gray teeth. His car was parked around the corner of the next block.

From his seat by the window he had a clear view of Brisbane Avenue and the intersection with Church Street. It was the one route available to McAdam to get from his church either to the college or his home undetected—or so McAdam thought. Wispen had told his operatives to use all of the other parallel streets that fed onto Brisbane Avenue at this time of day, and he was sure for weeks now, since February, that McAdam had been scared off of them.

Wispen figured he had only seven minutes more to wait, to be certain McAdam was staying for the second service, and then he would have at least fifty minutes to look around in Zola May's work area.

Johnny takes the point

Johnny had come within a couple of inches of shooting himself in the foot. The mouse that had brushed his big toe, looking for crumbs, had skittered off under the stairs.

"Jesus freaking Christ! Who's got the fucking watch? I did my watch."

He crouched with his rifle poised above his knees and quickly checked the back and front doors. Nothing was moving. There was no sound he could pick up above his own racing heart.

Where's the kid? Where's Kenny? His eyes narrowed. He scanned the hallway for any sign of Kenny, lay on his stomach just inside the door to recon the front porch. Nothing was missing.

But Kenny knew how to get to the house, and he knew that Johnny was there, and Johnny didn't know if Kenny could be trusted. Johnny had to leave again to get more cigarettes and food anyway, but now he didn't feel safe going into town. Where to go, where to go?

"Well, I don't know if he was being straight about his mission, but I'm gonna find out. And if he was settin' a trap," he whispered to himself, "that's gonna be one sorry gook." Johnny laced up his boots and reloaded his rifle. He decided to try to get to the woods behind the house, and parallel the road to Halifax Center.

Kenny goes west

The gunshot that missed the mouse snapped Kenny out of the frog nightmare. He snatched his backpack and took off toward the west as fast as he could, wetting himself again as he ran.

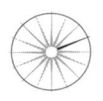

Lyle on honeymoon

Lyle was sleeping quietly again, lying on his stomach. It was only her second morning as a newlywed, but Zola May was thinking about how far behind she was at work. *What was this new project of McAdam's? Why couldn't Marla do it?*

She eyed Lyle's shoulders and the back of his neck. There was so much hair, so thick and coarse. His weathered neck was long and the hair had not been shaved, like shaggy bark on a cedar fencepost.

She leaned farther on her side to reach over and touch it, but pulled her hand back, not yet wanting to wake him for another round of love.

McAdam makes a friend

"President McAdam," Darcardt said. "It is such a pleasure to meet with you. Thank you for agreeing to this luncheon."

"Not at all. Happy to do it. Delighted," McAdam said. Charles Darcardt made him nervous. He was one among a legion of faculty at the college of whom McAdam was suspicious, who made him feel like they were putting him on. McAdam couldn't stop himself from slicing the lettuce in his salad into ever finer, perfectly symmetrical squares.

"Oh, I'm so glad. I've been looking forward to this," Darcardt continued, an almost-sincere gleam in his eye.

McAdam sipped his iced tea, wiped the condensation from the bottom of his glass before he replaced it on the table. He looked up just in time to see Darcardt's bemused expression.

"So what is it that I may help you with?" McAdam asked, the left corner of his mouth pinching reflexively.

"How remarkably direct. That's refreshing." Darcardt's eyes clouded. "The help I was interested in was not for me, you understand. It's a matter regarding a colleague."

McAdam raised an eyebrow. "Oh, I see. Someone in your department?"

"Yes."

"A recent addition to the faculty?"

"Relatively, yes."

McAdam leaned in closer, elbows on the table. "Would it be best if this individual's name was not stated directly in conversation?"

"Well . . . I suppose that could be useful." Darcardt looked confused again. Then it hit McAdam. This man is good! To appear to be confused while leaking information about a colleague was pure genius. It could cover them both.

"Is this really more of a hypothetical problem?" McAdam said, with the suggestion of a wink.

Darcardt appeared genuinely lost. McAdam felt more and more comfortable. *This man is a treasure.*

"Uhm . . ." Darcardt tried. "Am I . . . uh . . . to understand that you feel no names need to be mentioned?"

Collaboration! McAdam's senses quickened. Finally he had found someone who could work with him.

"I think it could help us to speak more freely," McAdam said.

"Uh, I suppose it could."

"Oh, of course. Well now, what can you tell me about this non-problem?"

Darcardt began carefully, starting with rumors he had been hearing about Harlan's deficiencies. Each detail made McAdam feel more at ease.

"I am afraid you may be misunderstanding my intentions, President McAdam," Darcardt confided. His brow was furrowed, his steel-gray eyes doubtful.

McAdam could barely suppress his admiration. *What a performance!* "I don't believe there is any misunderstanding, Dr. Darcardt. You've done an admirable job on behalf of this individual, and of the college. Please feel free to speak with me whenever you have something on your mind."

"But I don't believe any of this is true . . ."

"Of course you don't." McAdam smiled, reached for the check, perused it, and left just enough to cover his meal, no tip.

At the zoo

Kenny ran for nearly a mile before he slowed to a jog, and then a fast walk. Since he hadn't heard anything after the gunshot, he started to relax.

How am I gonna get my pants clean? he worried. *I think I'm startin' to stink.* He thought he could wash his pants in a pond or stream if he could find one.

The sun was drying him, but he could tell he smelled. It brought him back to third grade.

His dad hadn't wanted him to be in Level Three. He said he would rather move first, enroll Kenny in a different school, but Martha had just gone into the hospital, and he didn't want to leave her. The principal and school counselor said it was for the best, that Kenny couldn't perform with the other kids in regular classes.

It was a zoo. For the first seven weeks he sat at his desk humming loudly to drown out the noise. After a few days he noticed there were five other hummers. At least nine of the kids on most days, and sometimes four more, constantly were getting out of their seats and roaming around. Only two of them tried fairly regularly to set their desks on fire.

Kenny was even more frightened of the quiet ones. Anything could be happening with them—shyness, withdrawal, over-medication—but you never knew what it was unless something bad happened, like Roger Beery cutting himself on his arms with a piece of razor he had broken out of a plastic pencil sharpener. It wasn't the blood so much as the look in his eyes, like each new cut made him feel better.

Roger didn't come back to Kenny's school after that day.

Skeeter Dobbins was the one who peed herself. Not on a regular schedule, but whenever she got too worked up. Kenny hated those days because his teacher was distracted, and the screechers got even louder. Besides, word spread like wildfire around the elementary school that there were wetters in his class, so after a while it didn't make a difference who you were, the rest of the kids called you a peepants.

Kenny kept moving, far off the road in the ditch, looking for some place to wash.

Harlan tries to forget

At midafternoon Harlan was still sitting in his living room, skipping through the channels. He was flipping back and forth between two baseball games and MTV. While he was watching a Crowded House video, "Don't Dream It's Over," the national debt topped two trillion dollars.

In the old country

Kenny sat in the stream in his underwear. The water was freezing cold, but clear. He pounded and pounded his jeans against the rocks until he was certain they were okay, then put them back on to dry as he walked.

It had been a short climb down the bank to Steelhead Creek and back up to the highway. The air was warm and dry, with a light breeze that was keeping the black flies and mosquitoes away. Almost two miles outside of the village of Bent, in the town of Brood, Kenny came upon five older men playing bocce in a close-cropped sheep pasture behind a solid peg-and-mortise barn.

"Aw, dat's a salami," one of the men said as his toss rolled to a stop far short of the pallino. His shirt was buttoned up to his throat, a few generous folds of flesh sagging over the collar.

"You leavin' me wit' almos' no shot, Benjie," a taller, thinner man said, obviously Benjie's partner. "They got t'ree balls left, an' I on'y got this one."

"Then move the pallino, Giorgio. Find a place nex' to those two of ours in de basin."

Giorgio rolled his ball on a gentle arc to the left of Benjie's, with a sideways spin to bring it back to the right. It came in on the left of the pallino, like a Brooklyn strike, carrying it over the rim of the basin that had been left when a Dutch-diseased elm had blown over in a windstorm. When it came to rest, the pallino was nestled between Giorgio's two bocce balls and Benjie's first shot.

"You up, Alfonzo," his partner said. "You gotta move it again."

"Too close to the rose bush. Damn you guys. I'm not gonna mess with Tilia's roses." Alfonzo launched his ball, the red plaid, bouncing it almost dead a foot before the rim. It turned over twice, appeared to stop, then eased over the rim down the gravel bank of the basin, taking a slight leftward carom off a root, nudging Giorgio's ball away from the pallino.

"Who's closer?" Alfonzo's partner Gregor asked, as soon as the ball had come to rest.

"Don' you move," Benjie barked at the spotter. "It don' make no difference who's closer. We're all outta balls."

"I wan' him to check." Alfonzo pulled out a handkerchief, and blew his nose with gusto. He picked the larger left nostril with it.

"But we're all outta balls."

"Well, I ain' gonna shoot my ball 'less I know who's closer," Gregor insisted.

"Shoot," Benjie said, pushing Gregor's elbow just enough to make him drop a bocce ball.

"Dat's your shot, Gregor," Benjie said with a straight face. "You shoot, Alfonzo."

"Is not my shot," Gregor shouted.

"Is so," Giorgio said.

"That is not his shot," Alfonzo said.

"I think it is. What you think, Nick?"

The spotter shook his head from side to side slowly, bored with the routine.

"I guess you're right, Nick," Giorgio said. "That shot's too close for Gregor." Giorgio and Alfonzo laughed heartily at that, while Gregor bent down to pick up the ball he'd dropped.

"Too close," Alfonzo said, laughing. Gregor took aim and rolled the ball, much too fast, careening over the rim of the basin, bouncing hard to the right off Alfonzo's root and knocking over a rose.

"Arrivederci!" Giorgio said, smiling and waving at Gregor's ball as it kept rolling.

"Basta!" Alfonzo shouted. "Nick, you check who's closer!"

"No, no! He shot his ball. You canna check now," Benjie said. They all looked at Nick, who nodded his head sadly.

"You're not gonna check?" Alfonzo asked Nick. Nick shook his head.

Alfonzo sucked in a deep breath, hunched over into position, took a step off his right foot, and released his last ball. It dropped in exactly the same spot as his first ball, turned over twice again with just a bit more speed, thunked to the left off the root toward his first ball. Giorgio and Benjie were on their tiptoes, trying to follow the trajectory.

Kuk, Alfonzo's ball said as it hit Giorgio's just to the right of center, nudging it farther away from the pallino. *K-kek*, they heard as it ricocheted off Benjie's ball and back to rest next to the pallino.

"Bello!" Giorgio cheered admiringly, smiling at Alfonzo. Benjie coughed sharply as Gregor was releasing his ball, causing it to sail through the cluster around the pallino, scattering them. When they had come to rest, Benjie's was closest, and Tilia had lost another rose.

"Damn you, Benjie."

Arms in plaid shirts and ancient tweed jackets began to flail, leathery hands scarred by splinters and steel flicked back and forth in anger, putting emphasis on Polish and Italian curses.

The bells for 5:15 Mass at St. Theresa's began to ring, instantly stopping the commotion. They listened until the bells stopped tolling, crossed themselves and began to argue again. Nick was gathering the balls, because the game was over. Benjie and Giorgio had won.

"Play again! That was a cheat!"

"No! We won. It's over."

"Go home, cheater!" Gregor said to Benjie. "Nick's turn to play."

"I'm going wit' Benjie," Giorgio huffed. "Poor losers," he said over his shoulder as he walked off. "Poor losers."

Gregor looked at Alfonzo and Nick, all still shaking their heads. Nick motioned his head toward Kenny on the side of the road. "You wanna ask the kid to play?"

Harlan finds a focus

Sunlight streamed in the window of Harlan's study, seductively. He had three essays left for the eight o'clock class, all of the essays for the ten o'clock class, and two more final exams to prepare. He got up to sharpen his pencil, went to the bathroom again, was distracted anew by the remote. He settled, surfed through the channels, caught an MTV rerun of the Motown Anniversary special.

Harlan wondered why he was bothering to keep up the pace. The prospects of getting tenure without completing his dissertation were slim; if he didn't do a good job teaching, nonexistent. Koemover had asked him last week how many committees he was planning to serve on next year.

He wished he could just let himself be a hack, tackle a microquestion as if it were worth investigating and knock out a quick manuscript. What difference could his work possibly make, anyway?

Michael Jackson was singing "Billy Jean," dancing backward as he appeared to be moving forward.

Harlan jumped up in his chair. "Wow! It's the Reagan administration." He ran for his pad, suddenly full of dissertation ideas.

Aurelia starts the search

Aurelia was too anxious to go to St. Theresa's, too much in need of help not to go. As she heard the service bells ring, she ran the big-toothed pink comb through her limp mousy hair, trying to give it the appearance of having been washed in the past couple of days.

She tried to put on brown eye shadow to cover the redness, but got it smudged. Wiped it off. Smudged it again. She looked at the clock, saw she was already late, and started a fresh cry. Then she realized that she had not missed church since the first Sunday after her mother went into the hospital.

She cleaned all the makeup from her face, pulled on a shapeless yellow print dress, and rehearsed an excuse for the puffiness of her eyes. She had already decided to call everyone she could think of after the service to ask if they'd seen Kenny that day. People wouldn't be surprised to hear Kenny was lost. She hoped no one would ask for how long.

When she got back, she tried Cough first, letting his phone ring eleven times before giving up. He was at a meeting with the people from his shift, trying to puzzle out ways to keep the mill open.

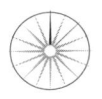

Harlan adrift

Harlan kept plastic bags of sliced meats, cheese, radishes, celery, and green beans within arm's reach among the stacks of essay booklets, notepads, transcripts, and photocopied articles. Whenever he was writing, he munched incessantly, though he had no hunger. Already it was dark, and he'd barely begun grading the essays from the ten o'clock class. He wished he were as zealous as Koemover about short-answer exams. Koemover had not read a student paper since the Carter Administration, his last semester before tenure.

The television had been on for hours now, for background noise. Whenever a commercial came on and distracted him, he changed the station. For a moment he thought about watching *60 Minutes*, then guiltily turned to a *Star Trek* rerun. He couldn't stand the thought of grading more papers before he had finished this section of the Vietnam chapter.

> The My Lai massacre set in motion a threefold reexamination of military practice, involving the responsibility of soldiers to obey orders which they believed to be immoral; the use of free-fire zones in areas occupied by noncombatants; and the handling of media coverage of military actions. Soldiers in the Post-Calley era

He had been staring at the last three words on the legal pad for close to twenty minutes. "Shit," he muttered after another fifteen minutes. He dropped the pad and picked up the stack of essays to begin grading again, two paragraphs into the first essay wanting another bathroom break.

The sports page

"Why don't you follow sports anymore?" Celeste asked. Guppy was engrossed in the "Week In Review," gearing up for his routine. She was trying to distract him.

"What, Celeste?" he sighed.

"I said," she sighed back, "why aren't you reading the sports page any longer?"

"Why would you want me to read the sports page?"

"I didn't say I wanted you to read it. I just want to know why you've stopped."

Guppy crossed his legs, folded the newspaper section three times neatly, assumed an exasperated face. "Why should you care?"

"I don't. I told you. But it was something you used to enjoy."

"Oh." He began to unfold the "Week In Review" again. "I stopped enjoying it."

She raised her eyebrows.

"You really want me to do this?"

Celeste smiled and pulled the end off a croissant. This would have to be more interesting than the news routine.

"Let's see. I used to watch baseball, the Mets. And the Dodgers when I was a kid. Everybody in my neighborhood did, and then they moved to Los Angeles. Even though that broke my heart, how could I stop rooting for Duke Snider? Jackie Robinson wouldn't go, and Campy had the accident and was paralyzed. And Sandy Koufax, was I supposed to hate him? I loved those guys, but it wasn't our team any more.

"And the Mets . . . It was strange when they were first in the Polo Grounds, then even stranger at Shea. But, you had to love the Mets." He tugged at his earlobe.

"You know what it is, Celeste? What is there to root for anymore? The teams move to follow the money, the players too. I used to laugh at the TV announcers, especially for football games. 'Dallas takes on New York,' in those harsh voices, like it was war. And it was, still is for some people, I guess. It's the American version of feudalism, territories at war. But now it's not even tied to territory, and our heroes, our mythic heroes, have changed sides. 'Now pinch-hitting for the Grendels: Beowulf.' Benedict Arnold was just ahead of his time. The first American free agent."

Celeste was restless. Actually, this was worse than the news. Guppy was biting off each word. Celeste twisted the pieces off her croissant, swallowed them dryly.

He kept it up. "There's too much business in it. If you pick up the sports page, there are more articles about money than about games. And it's affected the players. Hitters who can't bunt, basketball players who can only dunk, third-down specialists." Guppy was working up spittle in the corner of his mouth. Celeste started to retreat to the kitchen.

"And football's just violence for its own sake," he continued, following her. "It's reinforcing our aggressive tendencies without the redeeming quality of championing something, because there's no community or team loyalty anymore. You know what it's doing, it's conditioning us to corporate loyalty instead of to communities. It won't be long before there're conglomerate teams, and then team names will take a back seat to the corporate logos. The Chicago Reeboks, Dallas Pepsis, the New York Merrill Lynchs. Then whatever they do anywhere in the world—support South African apartheid, whatever—we'll just applaud it.

"But do you know what's even worse?" Celeste felt too badgered to shake her head. Guppy had cornered her behind the counter. "It's this proliferation of sports coverage in the newspapers, sporting magazines, radio call-in shows. It created *USA Today*. There's more on network TV, and my God, cable TV. Twenty-four-hour-a-day sports. Australian-rules football. Tough-man contests. Cliff diving. Not once a year on *Wide World of Sports*, but all day, every night." He began pacing.

"These are the models for kids, because they're the models for parents. More and more organized leagues. Kids five years old in leagues. You know what leagues mean? Organized pressure from parents, earlier peer pressure, five-year-olds who will grow into terminal adolescents without ever being their own referees. We're into our second generation of people never having to be fair, never having to be good sports so kids will come back for the next pick-up game. End zone dances. Showing people up. Trash talk. As if . . .

"And the absolute worst of it is . . . with too much sports coverage, there are so few universally shared experiences any more. You don't have to skip school or work to catch a World Series game, so that's not special. So many games in so many places on so many channels. It divides us." Guppy had a new sort of gleam in his eye now. Celeste made a break for their bedroom.

"It's pluralism, Celeste," he said, following her. "Madison's pluralism, splitting us apart by the sports culture. Divide and conquer. Sports are now more important to us than is human suffering. How can we expect people to get engaged in public life when everyone's numbed by pre-game shows?"

"Ernie?" she said, finally out of room to run.

"Artificial turf. Professionals in the Olympics."

"Ernie?"

"What?!" He was clenching his hands, pacing with greater intensity. "Prime-time professional wrestling. Designated hitters. Brokerage ads during football games."

"*Ernest!*"

"What?!"

"Please tell me about what's happening in the news."

He paused, drawing in a deep breath.

"Well," he said. "Oh, man, this Iran-Contra stuff."

Janie called in

When she left him, Billy was curled up in bed, knees beneath him and bottom up in the air, his mouth open, breathing in a soft angelic way. The laundry and dishes were done, and Janie had just settled in at the kitchen table to do her homework.

"All right," she said to herself. "Should I do history first or stats?" She got a glass of Pepsi and cracked open the text for Koemover's class.

The phone rang. Horace wanted her to come in for the third shift. No, she couldn't get out of it, somebody was sick.

She called Billy's grandmother to come over, got dressed for work. She'd have no time to study for finals that night.

Kenny taken in

"Haf some more, Sonny Boy," Alfonzo told Kenny, who was finishing his second plate of linguine. "The sauce is special, ya know. Tilia made it with her own tomatoes. Don' let it go to waste."

Kenny couldn't believe how good the food was. This sauce looked like it had other stuff in it. Aurelia's sauce was thinner, just plain red, and didn't have little bitty leaves and things. One of those little leaves got caught in the back of his throat and made his eyes water. Alfonzo gave him some more red wine to wash it down, which seemed to make it swell up. He clamped his mouth shut, snorting blasts of air through his nostrils, eyes full of tears.

Tilia came in from the kitchen, carrying a tall glass of water for him. He gulped it down and panted a few times. Then he piled back into the linguine. Alfonzo smiled at Kenny's appetite, while Tilia went back to the kitchen for more bread.

"You don' have to hurt yourself, Sonny Boy," Alfonzo told him. Sonny Boy was what he'd been calling Kenny since they were teamed up as bocce partners. They had played three points before Kenny rolled one ball seventy feet past the pallino, across the road and down into the ditch on the other side. Alfonzo decided to call the game so Kenny wouldn't lose any of the balls.

"Nuh, I won't," Kenny said, through a mouthful of bread. Tilia brought pastry for dessert, quietly nodding as she watched him eat. The jowls under her puffy cheeks jiggled.

"That's okay, you chust eat." She lifted her arms. The flesh sagged from them. "Mangia," she said.

Kenny ate the rest of the linguine, bread, and two pastries before he moved from the table. They all went out to the porch so Alfonzo could smoke with his coffee, his hands so large that the cigar looked more like a cigarette. He kept refilling Kenny's glass with wine, until Kenny was sagging into his chair. He hadn't had so much to drink since he'd been caught downing beers in the tool shed with his cousin Denny in tenth grade. He was no good at holding his liquor.

Kenny fell asleep on a recliner lawn chair on the screened-in porch, with Tilia's afghan over him. Alfonzo was looking at him as if he were a stray puppy.

Tilia told him not to get his hopes up. Just to wait. See what the boy would do.

Tammy Faye Bakker[*] on Aurelia Hopewell

She is a good Christian girl, that's for sure. You can tell by the way she stands by her man. That's her brother, I mean. Kenny. That's what I mean by her man. Her brother. She's takin' care of him. You can tell, you know what I'm sayin'?

But it's not right she hasn't got a husband, someone to take care of her and love her in a Christian way.

She needs to get rid of those dresses. Lord, they're so dowdy, and her hair. Do something with it. Looks to me like it's got plenty of body, if she just got to a hairdresser once.

And makeup, she doesn't do anything special, nothing to let out her spiritual glow. Nothing to make her jump right out at you, you know. You can barely see her eyelashes . . .

---

[*]Wife of discredited PTL pastor/magnate Jim Bakker, Tammy Faye Bakker got a divorce and confessed an aspiration to become a medical secretary.

Chapter Four

Kenny Goes to School

In the closet

"Chick-a-dee-dee-dee. Chick-a-dee-dee." Sunlight was streaming in through the storm windows of the porch into Kenny's face. He shifted on the lounge chair and fell back to sleep, dreaming he saw a flashlight shining at him. He couldn't make out who was holding it.

"Better come on outta there." Kenny was hiding in a storage closet with someone he couldn't see.

"Come on, I mean now," the voice said. The flashlight pulled back just enough for Kenny to see a man's face, round, with a fleshy nose and close-set eyes. He looked like some kind of policeman. Kenny's first impulse was to move behind the white uniforms in the closet. When he did, the policeman reached in through the door and pulled Kenny's mother from the closet. Martha was dressed in a drab gray housecoat and Wiley's work windbreaker, the one Aurelia had brought to the hospital after he died.

"What were you doing in there?" the policeman asked.

"The same thing."

"What same thing?"

"Waiting for Jesus. I'm waiting for Jesus."

"Well, lady, I really don't think he's in here." He led her down the hallway back to the nurse's station, cursing under his breath. Kenny stayed hidden behind the white coats, quaking with fear and shame, *trying to figure out how to get his mother back. He had missed her so much, for so long now.*

He woke up missing her.

Harlan makes the grade

Up at six to grade more papers, Harlan rubbed one bony knuckle into the ridge of his eyebrow, trying to squeeze out the knot of early-morning tension. He made a pot of coffee out of reflex, drank half a cup. The ache turned to a throb.

"Damn. I've gotta stop doing this." For months he had been convinced his headaches were a reaction to coffee and eating fast food, not getting enough sleep, eyestrain from bad handwriting. Plus he thought it was the stress, from teaching, writing, trying to keep up with committee assignments, trying to make a favorable impression on McAdam and now Koemover.

But there was part of him—a part he rarely allowed to surface—that knew what it was. He'd started noticing the headaches last December, around the time he'd first begun having a drink, then two, so he could get to sleep after grading papers, and reading the horror stories that were his dissertation.

Darcardt in '42

Darcardt dreamed that his wife Judy came to talk with him. She told him their daughter Bonnie was fine, the baby looked beautiful. He smiled at her, because she looked just like she had when they met, auburn hair up like Katherine Hepburn. It used to make him uneasy when she appeared that way—Bonnie was fifteen years older now than Judy was in 1942—but last night he was at peace with it.

Darcardt awoke in the middle of a twisted pile of blankets, chilled even on this unusually warm night. The radio hummed "Chattanooga Choo Choo." He wandered around the house in his pajamas, looking for Judy, not finding her except in a few framed photographs.

At Grandma's house

Alfonzo woke Kenny from his dream. "C'mon, Sonny Boy, Tilia's got breakfast for us. Come eat." There was bread with thick crust, and cheese; eggs, scrambled with diced tomatoes and peppers, garlic, and dill. Tilia poured him thick dark coffee in a small porcelain cup decorated with a rose pattern. The coffee was so strong it made Kenny shake his head. He reached for more cream and sugar from the pitcher and bowl with the same rose pattern.

"Howja sleep, Sonny Boy? I hope okay. Tilia said to leave you on the porch, and I said not to worry. He's gonna be all right." Alfonzo pushed another helping of eggs onto his plate, clicking his tongue when Kenny politely lied that he was full.

"So how did you sleeping?" Tilia asked. Kenny felt a catch in his shoulder-blade, and in his lower back from the lounge chair, but said nothing. He started eating again, as if he had never seen food. Alfonzo smiled at first, then looked worried when the feeding frenzy didn't let up.

"Do you think he'll stay?" Alfonzo whispered to Tilia. She watched him eat, so unassuming and guileless, a young man without a care. Still she thought she could see some shadow over him.

Kenny took another drink of coffee, stirred in more cream and sugar, sipped it again, stirred in even more. It needed honey instead of sugar, and nonpareil candy and raspberry Jell-o with fruit cocktail inside. He was remembering the Jell-o and nonpareils, salads with Italian dressing over Hershey Kisses, cocoa made with scalded milk, the milk skin in a teaspoon on the saucer for Kenny to eat so he could grow big and strong. The creamier and sweeter the coffee, the more Kenny drifted into the memory of visiting his grandmother after school. The smile of a nine-year-old spread across his face.

Tilia watched him, feeling sad without knowing why.

This worm's life

McAdam put a new blade in his razor for Monday morning, though the old one was still sharp. If he failed to change it on Monday, he could lose track. That could throw off his entire schedule.

He also kept a spare razor, which he had never used, in the washroom in his office. But he changed the blade every Monday anyway. The spare clean and pressed white shirts, the suit, ties, socks and shoes had come in handy once, after a Chamber of Commerce ham steak-lunch gravy left a spot on his shirt.

This morning his toast was a shade lighter than he liked it, but it was the only way to keep the toaster from sticking. Chew, sip, chew, sip, chew, sip. His thoughts drifted to the dream he'd had, the huge metal-beaked bird trying to pull him from the ground where he'd been busy turning vegetable mass into humus.

The worm symbolism made sense to him. He was used to dealing with stuff no one else would touch. Sure it could get messy, but it simply had to be done. Anyone in his position would have done the same things.

McAdam wished he could figure out what the bird symbolized, with its gleaming beak and metal camouflage feathers, laser-beam eyes. It did the same thing every time in the dream, soaring over once before diving down upon him. It planted its legs on each side of his wormhole, beak probing until it snapped over his head and shoulders, tugging him out of the earth.

Just as the thing tipped its beak back to swallow him whole, he'd thrashed enough to wake his wife, so she could shake him out of it.

He didn't deserve this. Didn't he have enough to think about, with everything at the college and Wispen constantly looking over his shoulder?

He sealed his second cup of coffee in a traveling mug and clutched the Alta file folder in his free hand. He might have enough time to swing by Koemover's office and throw a scare into him, then still slip into his own office ahead of Wispen and Ms. Axe.

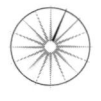

Horace makes eye contact

"I'll be needin' ya again tonight, y' realize?" Janie's tour boss Horace was telling her. She regretted stopping in the break room before going home.

"Can't do it, Horace. Got too much to do, to work a double."

"'Fraid there ain't no choice, babe. Melissa's gonna be out for a coupla days."

"Aw, come on. Can't you get somebody else? I'm not the only person in this mill who could cover for her. Christ, Horace, I got finals."

"It's breakin' my heart, babe, it really is. Look, if I could help ya, I would, but I'll be damned if I'm gonna bring in somebody who doesn't know their ass from a forklift when I could get somebody experienced." Horace sucked on the little hole in the plastic lid of his coffee cup, then licked the cold bitter stuff from his lips.

"Can you try, Horace? You can at least try, right? There's gotta be someone else. I know I can't afford it."

"What makes ya think you can afford not to work?" Horace snapped, his watery blue eyes turning icy.

"Oh, don't say shit like that, Horace. You know you're not gonna threaten my job. Not if you want me to do a double."

"I'm not sayin' it's up to me, babe." Horace looked at her squarely, his nine fingers folded together on the scarred cafeteria table in the break room.

"What's that s'posed to mean?"

"It means you gotta do this, babe."

"But my kid. I gotta watch my kid. I can't stay over another night." Janie looked at the floor. She could feel the heat leave her face. She had options. Not work the double, maybe lose her job. Work the double while Billy slept at home alone, hoping he would be okay and she wouldn't get caught. Ask Billy's grandmother to watch him while she worked the Number Three shift, taking the chance that she wouldn't call Billy's father and give him a reason to try to take Billy away.

She saw Horace staring at her chest. She slowly straightened her back, gauging the movement of his eyes a few inches upward. Earl used to say her smooth honey-colored hair and overbite were sexy. Now she was no longer sure how to look attractive.

"Horace. There's gotta be a way you can give me a break." She didn't move, made no attempt at eye contact. He shifted a little, away from her, so that he was still looking at her breasts without being as obvious.

She tried to get her body to tell him, *You know this isn't fair.* She couldn't figure out how.

"Don't know that I can help ya," he muttered.

"Well, what's the matter with Melissa, anyway?"

Horace flinched. "She's, uh, sick. I dunno."

"So, you're telling me that you don't know what's wrong with Melissa, but you know she's too sick to work her shift tonight. That's what you're tellin' me," Janie pressed.

He flinched again. His nine fingers twitched, the last of his coffee spilling onto the break table.

"Said she couldn't come in."

"So you're threatenin' me with a double, or I lose my job." Janie's voice was rising.

Horace looked away. "It's no big deal."

"You can go fuck yourself. I'll tell the steward," Janie said.

"Forget it."

"Forget it? Whaddaya mean, forget it?"

"I mean forget it. So don't do the double." Horace's tone was mean, his voice low.

"I'm not doin' it," Janie said gamely.

Horace said nothing.

"I'll see you this afternoon," she said.

He still was quiet.

Oh God, I'm so late. I gotta get Billy home for the bus to pick him up, she thought as she left. *I can't believe this bullshit.* She started to tremble, not sure she'd be coming back to work.

Harlan's thirst

". . . When you were givin' those guys a piece, you were givin' me . . . miles an' miles of . . . misery."

"Da-doom da-doom da-doom." Harlan was trying to get himself to wake up, cranking the radio alarm. Sammy Llanas's screaming adenoids kept him from falling asleep again, but he still was far from being awake. He'd conked out sometime after three, with an essay booklet in his hand, hallucinating that it said something about Bob Dylan and the Star Wars defense system. It was supposed to be about Lebanon.

He shaved, showered, found some clothes to iron for school. An ink stain on the pants pocket set him back; he had to find and press a second pair of pants. That pair was too tight because he'd been overeating while writing and grading papers.

He was getting ready as fast as he could. *How am I going to finish these papers in time for class?* The more he thought about it, the more keyed-up he got. The more keyed-up he got, the more he wanted a drink.

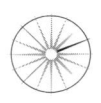

The honeymooners, Part II

Zola May lingered in bed next to Lyle, pressed up against his back, her hand in the curve of his hip. Work was the farthest thing from her mind. It was already after seven. She'd have a tough time getting to the college without being late. *I haven't been late once, in eleven years. They can cut me some slack for one day.* Zola kissed Lyle's shoulder blades, just below the downward slope, where there wasn't quite so much wiry hair. He stiffened for a moment, then relaxed, letting her tease him into readiness.

"You got enough time for one before work?" Lyle asked, beige eyes dreamy.

"Maybe," she said, "for two."

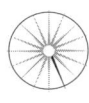

If a tree falls in the forest . . .

Darcardt liked eight o'clock classes. His early morning students were always quiet and sleepy, allowing him to go off on grand soliloquies. He liked to imagine they agreed with him, and signed up for his courses because of his spectacular insights. And he was right, about four of them. The others were late signing up for classes.

"So we've arrived at the Reagan presidency. How are the Iran-Contra investigations likely to affect the administration?" He surveyed the room for a glimmer of understanding, or consciousness. Only two of the seventeen present looked to be asleep, but the other fifteen could be jungle-sleeping for all he could tell.

"Well, does anyone believe the hearings will have any impact on the administration?"

Eyes glazed over, jaws set. None of Darcardt's Gang of Four, as they called themselves, had shown up.

"Isn't there a critical mass for these scandals? Some point past which the public won't accept any more?" Darcardt pressed. Tim Kilgore seemed to be the only one still listening. He squinted his eyes, the corners of his mouth upturned condescendingly.

"I don't see why people should even care about this thing. It seems to me that Reagan and North did the right thing, getting the hostages out." Kilgore was holding his jaw in his pudgy right hand. It was helping him hide his smirk.

"Of course freeing hostages is good, if that's what it accomplishes. But there was a net increase of hostages taken. Was it okay to break their own laws? Sell arms secretly to Iran? And divert money to the Contras?"

"Hey, whatever it takes," Kilgore said. "We don't want communists in this hemisphere." He looked around for support, nodding and grinning at the zombie class.

Darcardt thought about describing again how bad the Somoza dictatorship was that the Sandinistas had overthrown, how the Reagan policy was designed to frustrate alternative paths to development so that Nicaragua would remain dependent on the US, how Reagan's defiance of the World Court case against the US would undermine international law. A quick glance around the room convinced him not to bother.

"Let's see if we can get back to the original question. What will be the Reagan legacy? Let's start with foreign policy. The revival of the Cold War? Supporting the regime that uses death squads in El Salvador? Are these actions by President Reagan signaling a return to Schlesinger's imperial presidency?" Darcardt asked.

"Yeah, if you want. Imperial presidency. Okay, but what difference does that make?"

"Do you agree that the Reagan administration is loading too much government authority into the executive branch?" Darcardt said.

Kilgore was stuck. "Too much government authority" had penetrated his conservative skull. It made his knee want to jerk. "I wouldn't say Reagan did too much," he replied, confused, retreating.

Darcardt understood Kilgore's dilemma. It was the paradox for all conservatives. How can you advocate the free market and hands off of business, yet get into people's lives so deeply elsewhere? Kilgore's problem was his attempt to be a consistent conservative—he hadn't learned it was impossible. Hands off guns, war against drugs. Don't allow abortions, but look the other way with toxic dumping that kills babies. No wonder kids were so confused. Maybe it would help if the contradictions were more clear.

"Tim, do you get any financial aid for college?"

"A little. They say my parents make too much."

"Yeah, I thought so. But the bright side is, the less financial aid, the fewer government employees, right?"

Kilgore shot a hateful look at him.

The rest of the class sat in silence.

Mrs. Lester loses it

Zola May was at her desk, depressed because now she was married—a new woman—and still stuck in the same routine. She booted up her computer, and felt under the rack of file folders in her second file drawer for the McAdam stuff she had left on Friday. It wasn't there. She checked the same place again, front and back, looked through all the hanging files, searched in all her other file drawers, the storage closet, and the departmental file cabinets. *If I can't find this file, he'll have me fired.*

She was sitting at her desk with her eyes closed, trying to breathe slowly and evenly, to think carefully.

When she opened her eyes, McAdam was staring at her.

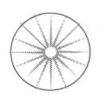

Kenny forgets himself

"Come on down," the announcer was saying, as hysterical people hugged each other, danced around, and ran down the aisle to stand behind podia with flashing lights. The Price is Right was Alfonzo's favorite show between ten and eleven. He only clicked over to the Home Shopping Network during the commercials. Alfonzo liked to complain about the stupid people who didn't know the value of things, and about how much things cost. Tilia was frequently wondering out loud what kind of people would buy those things anyway.

Kenny had watched The Price is Right before, but it was not one of his favorite shows. The part he liked best was when the models were running their slender fingers along the edges of the items up for bid.

Today he wasn't watching the program so much as he was watching Alfonzo and Tilia. Alfonzo had thick, wavy hair, gray and brown, and an arch in his nose like Kenny's uncle Royal. Tilia's hair was salt and pepper frizz. She was short and heavy, but always on the move. He didn't think they were relatives of his—at least he had no memory of them—but they seemed to like him, and they'd been treating him like family. He thought they actually were feeding him better than Aurelia did.

He lay on the oval rag rug Tilia had made for her son when he was a boy. Kenny was much taller and heavier than Michael had been, but he bent his legs at the knee, back and forth, like Michael had when he was little.

Kenny looked over his shoulder at them on the couch, studying their wrinkled faces. If there was something he was forgetting, he was pretty sure they'd have told him.

Celeste in the mirror

"You know you're going to make me late. You know how much I hate that," Guppy complained. Celeste was getting his lunch. Part of her did hold him up intentionally, and another part of her couldn't wait for him to be out of the house in the morning. She stirred heavy cream into his coffee thermos, twisted the cover, and set it into his metal lunchbox. It was a sturdy relic he had picked up at an antiques auction, an inexplicable part of the estate of a New York Central railway executive. Guppy was attached to it for the same reason the railway executive had been: it had belonged to a worker. Carrying it across the campus, having other people see him carry it, made him feel he was dramatizing his claim that the college was turning into just another factory.

Celeste moved the breakfast dishes off the table, hesitating in front of the dishwasher on each pass to the counter. She finally decided to wash them by hand. She ran the water in the sink until steam rose to fog her glasses. Somehow the scalding water was soothing to her nerves. For a long time now she had not run the microwave, or read a book the whole way through. Whenever she tried, her heart pounded so fast, so much blood throbbed in her ears and behind her eyes that she would lose her eyesight, her hearing, every sense save her equilibrium. The last time it had happened, she was in the kitchen, making hors d'oeuvres for some of Guppy's colleagues. He'd lifted her from around her waist and sat her onto a stool at the counter, without her feeling anything. After excusing herself, she had lain in bed, wide-eyed, listening to Guppy hold court about the Reagan visit to Bitburg, anticipating his witticisms. That had been the worst episode since her breakdown during the comprehensive exams.

"I don't know, I can't tell you," she repeated. "I just can't tell you any more." The conference table was stained mahogany, polished by papers from application files, sweaty palms, an occasional brush from the sleeve of a tweed jacket. She had been noticing the circular stains of coffee cups in the soft light while she avoided eye contact with the exam committee. She still could breathe and hear, but as soon as she tried to untangle a question, dark clouds traveled across her vision, settled over her mind. All she could manage at first were halting statements, and as it worsened, simple clauses and fragments of thoughts. Followed by the apologetic refrain, "I can't say any more. It's the best I can do."

Years later now she could not even remember all the people on the committee, nor any question, nor a single halting response. She could only remember how many times she had wanted to say, "Let's stop this. Let's stop." She also could remember how painfully relieved she was when her advisor ended the questioning early. She left the campus without waiting to hear the results of her oral exam, went home and collapsed into bed. When the letter arrived three days later from the committee chair she did not open it for nearly a month. Although it stated that she had passed her comprehensives and had advanced to doctoral candidacy, she stopped going to campus. She had failed, she told herself, and anyone who asked. She knew that.

Ernie never talked about his own graduate-school experience, so she assumed he hadn't suffered. She thought the savage undermining of her self-confidence had been reserved for her, the academic in-club's equivalent of hazing.

It wasn't even nine-thirty yet when she dumped the dishwater and scooped the greasy bits of food from the sink trap to toss into the compost bucket. Monday was her day to mop and wax the hardwood floors in the kitchen, dining room, and Guppy's study.

She felt she might enjoy doing the floors on her hands and knees again, with rags.

McAdam's safe house

"If I could be certain she's telling the truth about losing those papers, I'd have her fired," McAdam muttered under his breath. He was sitting on the toilet in his office bathroom, flushing repeatedly as the sink faucets blasted water, covering—he hoped—his dialogue with himself about the Zola May matter. The bathroom was in the farthest corner of his office away from Wispen's office and Ms. Axe's desk. He checked it thoroughly every morning for listening devices, including the airspace above the ceiling panels.

"It's not like they have the whole file. I've got all the memos from the Judge and Gordon here. How much could they know?" He flushed again, rose to pace the three steps back and forth as he thought. "She might be telling the truth, and we'll find that memo, so I can always fire her later. But," he pushed the toilet handle again, "if she's lying, she could be expecting to get fired, and wants to use it for evidence against me. I just wish I knew for whom she is working. Yes!" he exclaimed, sitting down on the bowl again. "I might be able to use Zola May to flush out the rest of Wispen's accomplices."

"So we'll just let her keep her job. For now."

In Zola's daydream

Zola's panic about the lost file had passed after McAdam left. He'd urged her to redouble her efforts to find it immediately. She could tell how upset he was, a combination of anger and fear, but that only left her more confused about why she felt a tenderness and protectiveness toward him. Zola's early morning daydreams about Lyle had given way to images of McAdam curled up safely in her arms.

Johnny in the open

The sky was too bright today, cloudless. No morning fog, even, for cover. Johnny had to strike well into the woods to keep from being detected by road patrols. He'd had no luck finding Kenny in Halifax, so he'd decided to scout along town roads in the direction of Brood to intercept him. At least the sun had made the ground dry, so once he found a place with cover—a forgotten '49 Pontiac rusting on its rims on the east bank of Steelhead Creek—he climbed in to sleep until the sun went down.

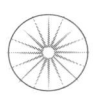

Not a little kid anymore

Finally, the mail came. Aurelia had been up and ready to go searching for Kenny since 5:30, but she'd had to wait until the Social Security disability check came in with the afternoon mail so she could get some cash for gas. Now she only had a few hours to search, before she had to go clerk at the Kwik Mart.

Cough had told her that Kenny was heading to Janie's for a ride to the college, but now, of course, he could be anywhere.

"I dunno what I was thinkin', Reel," he'd said. "I'm sorry. We was just gettin' so panicked about losin' the mill, an' I only made him promise to not tell nobody 'cause we been dicked around so much by the plant, tellin' us one thing an' then the total opposite."

Aurelia let Cough know she was furious he'd sent Kenny without telling her. It was the first time she'd ever spoken that way to one of her father's friends. She couldn't believe herself.

Cough had slumped into one of his kitchen chairs, shaky right hand running through his oiled hair, whispering, "Damn, damn, damn." He saw she'd been crying, and let himself think about all the things that might have happened to Kenny in three days.

"I'm sorry, Cough, I shouldn't have said that. Kenny surprises me every once in a while, too. Sometimes it makes me wonder if he needs me as much as I think he does."

"You done a good job, 'Relia, don't fault yourself for nothin'. He's a real good boy, an' you done it alone. Don't fault yourself." He'd said it to the tabletop, pine painted white. "I don't think we oughtta tell nobody else, like you said about Social Services an' all. But I can look tomorrow afternoon, after my shift, an' then again after the meetin'."

Aurelia shot a look at him.

"I gotta go, 'Relia. A lotta people are countin' on me."

"I understand," Aurelia said. "Let me know if you find out anything."

"Sure."

When she left he was chewing on the half of a thumbnail on his left hand. After a few minutes of pondering, Cough got the strongest feeling that Kenny was surely lost, but alive, unharmed. He had the same certainty about it that he'd had when Kenny's father Wiley had told him that he was sick, and Cough knew instantly he was dying.

Casimir geopolitics

"No, you don't unnerstan'. Commonism is good," Stosh was shouting over the roar of his chainsaw.

"What you talkin' about, commonism is good? Yer crazy," Big Prett yelled back. They were deep in the woods in East Halifax, cutting cherry, beech, and ash illegally off public land.

"Yes, I'm tellin' ya, commonism is good fer the 'conomy."

"Yer tellin' me we got commonism in America?"

"No, no. That's not it. It's good fer us when other countries got commonism."

Prett made a face, sliced off another limb from the fallen cherry tree. Stosh had finished his end, thick shoulders and arms working rhythmically, and was getting ready to cut it into log lengths. He could see that Prett was still troubled, by the way he held his head sideways, cocked at an angle, and because he glanced back Stosh's way with those fierce black eyes every once in a while, like Stosh was doing him harm by making him think.

Finally Prett hit the kill button and strode back to Stosh. He stood as upright as he could, the McCulloch saw handle balanced in his right hand, left hand hanging at the ready to fire up the saw again, instantly.

"Stosh, you gotta tell me. We commonists?"

"Thttp, thttp, thttp," Stosh spat quickly, a chunk of oily sawdust finally hurtling from his mouth to the ground. He rubbed his scarred hands together while he pondered, taking much too long for Prett's sense of well-being.

Stosh finally answered, "We aren't commonists, we are Republicans," and glared at Prett with his narrow-set eyes.

"Then why you saying commonism is good?"

"'Cause when commonism is big, the president always spends big money. When commonism goes away, he don't spend no more."

"How 'bout Ree-gan?"

"Ree-gan's spending a lot to get rid of the commonists. But like I said, if he gets rid of 'em all, the economy's goin' to be bad."

Prett puzzled on that for a moment.

"So it's best when the president tries to get rid of the commonists, but they don't go away?"

"Yeah, that's it. Like when Eisenhowitzer was president."

Prett appeared to be totally confused. "If it's good to have commonists, then why's the president wanna get rid of 'em?"

"He don' want to get rid of 'em. He only wan' to spend money tryin' to get rid of 'em."

"Then why don' he give 'em the money?"

Stosh looked up at Prett in utter disbelief, like he had been caught jacking deer. Before Stosh could try another way to explain, Prett's face lit up.

"An' then we could be commonists?"

Wispen rightsizes

Wispen glided down the corridor toward the Student Services offices, feeling refreshed every time he made eye contact with a member of the college staff who looked down or away. Marty Obermeier was on a stepladder lifting out ceiling panels to hand to Fred Watson. They were trying to find the source of a leak that had shorted out some wiring in the registrar's office. Marty did not understand why Fred tapped him on the shin, so he failed to look down and acknowledge by deference Wispen's tour through his work area.

Wispen made a mental note:
Catch Obermeier in some indiscretion.
Fire him.
Add another person to security staff.

McAdam gets new orders

"Yes, sir. Yes, Judge. I'll be right over." McAdam knew this was about the mill and the hydropower rights. This was a deal he definitely wanted, but having to leave in the middle of the day to go see Sumner Hayslee—otherwise known as the Judge—made him very nervous.

Should I check with Axe? McAdam thought he'd better. If the president left campus without some kind of appointment, it would be noticed.

"Ms. Axe?"

"Yeah." Marla was breaking in a fresh stick of Juicy Fruit.

"Do I have any appointments right now?"

"Gimme a minute."

She scanned the calendar, reported that he was free until 3:30.

Now how do I get out of the building? McAdam thought Wispen was still on his afternoon tour of inspection, so if he could distract Ms. Axe, he should be able to duck out behind her divider to the side door facing the Student Union. A quick dash across the parking lot, and he'd be safe in his car.

"Ms. Axe?"

"Yeah."

"I hate to bother you again, and I realize this is short notice, but I need you to set aside whatever you're working on, to get something else for me."

Marla snapped her gum.

"Could you please go over to Institutional Research and have them pull the admission figures by degree program for the last five years? Oh, and when you have them, put them in my box outside. I don't wish to be disturbed at the moment."

McAdam rolled on a new layer of deodorant and turned the switch to alternate the lamp lighting. He counted to five after hearing the last klic, klic, klic of Axe's high heels fade away, then crept out and closed his office door noiselessly.

In Michael's shoes

"Tilia. You think maybe Sonny Boy can fit in Michael's clothes?"

"Michael's? You wan' we give him Michael's clothes?" Tilia's arms were bent in the air just above the armrests, her shoulders hunched over her torso like she'd been punched in the solar plexus.

"You got some of Michael's clothes. Give them to Sonny Boy." The way Alfonzo said this to the television screen made it look like it was a message from the Home Shopping Network.

Tilia held the fingers of her right hand against her breast, to gauge the racing of her heart. Michael had left the house fresh out of high school, enlisted in the army and gone to Vietnam. He'd been MIA since 1967.

Alfonzo had not gone into Michael's room since the night he'd left home. Since the fight. Alfonzo had wanted his son to work at the mill, live with them until he got married, make grandchildren for them, take his place on the bowling team after Alfonzo passed. But Michael had wanted to see something of the world before settling down.

Alfonzo forbade anyone else to go into Michael's room. Once he had caught Tilia getting some things to send to him at boot camp, and afterward put a padlock on the door, keeping the key on a chain that fastened to his belt loop.

When they got the word that Michael was missing in action, he took the padlock off the door, but never again entered, himself. Sometimes Tilia went in there to be alone, more frequently after Alfonzo retired.

Tilia was still waiting for the word from Alfonzo. He was apparently absorbed by the television.

"It don' make no diff'rence no more, Tilia," he said. "He's gone." His voice trailed off to a whisper.

Kenny was back on the braid rug, watching the clock wind down on the special-offer cubic zirconium necklace. Tilia, looking at him flex his legs to the floor and up again, thought about how lost he seemed, yet not uncomfortable or afraid. It was obvious he'd had on the same shirt and pants for at least a few days. "Come on, Mister," she said. "Let's fin' more clothes for you."

Kenny followed her up the stairs and down the hall to a door with cobwebs on the upper corners of the frame. Tilia crossed the linoleum floor to the one dresser, opened the top drawer and stepped back for Kenny to take a look. He checked her face to be sure it was all right for him to touch these clothes. She couldn't return his look, could only mutter "Go ahead" before she left Michael's room. As many times as she had gone in there—to sit on Michael's bed, wash and refold his clothes into the dresser, just stand alone and cry—she was unprepared to see another young man in there. She pulled the door closed behind her and went downstairs to the kitchen, to chop onions for the supper sauce.

Kenny had a feeling that some of these clothes, like the coveralls, had been handed down from Alfonzo to his son. They looked like Alfonzo could put them on right now and fit him fine. But the clothes that were clearly Michael's, pegged pants and dress shirts, had the feel of someone who was trying hard to make an impression, to fit in. They were all too small for Kenny's belly. The only clothes he might be able to fit into were the coveralls, so he put them on. A little short, but otherwise okay. Kenny hooked his thumb in one of the large loops by his pocket.

The shirt drawer held mostly horizontal striped knit shirts and a few starched white dress shirts, and in the back left-hand corner, a baseball that had been signed To Mike, Dom DiMaggio.

He was starting to feel restless and out-of-sorts, like there was supposed to be something here for him, but he couldn't see what it was. Kenny was feeling more and more uncomfortable, so he went back downstairs. When Alfonzo saw him in the handed-down coveralls, he had to get up and go out of the house.

He was there outside when the phone rang, when Tilia told him it was Cough.

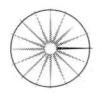

McAdam forgets his place

McAdam checked the soles of his shoes three times while gathering the courage to knock. With as much importance as he could muster, he said, "Francoise, the Judge said he has some papers for me."

"Could you follow me please?" she said. "He's been expecting you."

I'm late, McAdam fretted.

"Mister McAdam, from the college," Francoise intoned.

"Yes, good to see you, Baxter," the Judge said dismissively, as he closed the door behind them.

"My pleasure, Judge."

"Well, Baxter. Matters are proceeding apace, just as planned. We'll still need your help to put this arrangement in the appropriate light, of course."

"Understood. But people might not realize it's good for the long run to privatize the hydro site. They might think the college is selling out."

"Baxter, relax. There are always shortsighted people. There always have been, and there always will be, people who just don't see the big picture." The Judge tugged his vest, leaned back in his leather swivel chair, waved McAdam into a velvet armchair. McAdam paced a few steps, realized that he was panicking, tried to sit. He could not be at rest.

The Judge said, "I thought you people worked all this out on Saturday. Gordon told me you had reservations, but he didn't say you weren't prepared to back us up." He paused and looked over the top of his glasses at McAdam, squeezing the bulge of his lower lip between his thumb and forefinger.

"It's not that, Judge. Not at all. I see the logic in all this. I'm just uncomfortable with the idea of the college playing such a prominent role in a situation that will, uh, you know, temporarily, uh, inconvenience a few people."

"Doctor McAdam," the Judge said, swiveling toward the window, "you are a relative newcomer to the area."

Third generation, McAdam thought. He squeezed his hands between his knees.

"If one puts this hydro lease into its proper context, one realizes it is long overdue. Local governments, here as everywhere, are necessarily provincial and backward-looking. They cling," he said, his attention now focusing on his cat stalking birds at a feeder, "to the past. Past glories, past attainments, outdated status. The village in question, here, has held onto that dam for over a century now, doling out power for industry only after it takes care of the school first, and its tiny village offices, and the Christmas-light display and all their other little projects. The mill has not been able to expand, automate, and keep up with the times because it has to go to those local officials, hat in hand, to get every little increment of power. And this is public power? Since when did the public do anything right, except for when it got out of the way of the entrepreneur? Why, that mill would have expanded its share of the market and been integrated into the larger economy ages ago, if it had been able to get as much power as it wanted. Don't you see that, Doctor?"

McAdam lunged at the bait. "Well, I cannot disagree that you have a much more firm, uh, grasp of the situation than I. It's just that the college's, uh, mission, as I'm certain you realize, is limited to education. That's what we do, educate." The president knew why towns like Alta held onto their publicly owned resources. He remembered advocating that once himself, in his first teaching job, long before he went into administration.

The Judge sighed heavily, his back still turned to McAdam. "Then educate. No one is asking you to do more." He swiveled around to face McAdam. "But make no mistake, we need you behind us on this. The message needs to be delivered that the sale of this hydro facility to the new owners of the mill is a positive, a major contribution to the economic development of this area. You are with us on this, aren't you?" The Judge leaned back again, tilting his head in the direction of the framed Certificate of Recognition hanging on the wall, which thanked him for his efforts on behalf of the college fund.

"Yes. Yes, of course. Absolutely."

"I knew it. There was never any question."

Francoise had appeared out of nowhere to show him to the door. The Judge rose from his chair and padded over to the wall safe inset in the bookcase shelf. He eased a thin gray envelope from it, and extended it to McAdam. "This is the prospectus for the research grant from the new owners to the college. Feel free to ensure that it's mentioned at some point during the ceremony on Saturday, won't you?"

McAdam swallowed and nodded.

"We do need to get together more often, Baxter. You must bring Natalie over some evening for dinner. Let's do it soon, shall we?"

"Yes, I'd like to," McAdam managed to say over his shoulder as Francoise led him away.

"Francoise," the Judge called, hearing the front door close. "Francoise?"

"Yes, Judge?"

"You handled that well. Thank you. This project is a rather tricky affair. Perhaps," he mused, "you can be more gracious in the future if he shows us sufficient nerve."

"Yes, sir," Francoise replied, already on her way back to the dusting.

"Oh, and Francoise, after that session, I feel that I may be needing a relaxation session."

Inside she cringed, and thought, *Oh, wonderful.*

As the Judge climbed the stairs to his room, Francoise retreated into the kitchen to slice up the cucumbers. She heard herself grinding her teeth, decided she'd better get it out of her system before going upstairs.

He nodded imperiously when she entered his bedroom and then lay back in bed so she could distribute the cucumbers in the usual arrangement on him. Almost immediately after they were laid against his temples he could feel himself relaxing. He sighed when she reached his nipples.

Francoise hesitated after applying the rounded end in his navel. "Judge?" she asked, because he could not bear to be called by any other name than Judge during the cucumber ritual, "Will we be in need of another?"

"Yes, I believe so. Thank you, Francoise."

She retreated to the kitchen for the vegetable pruning as he concentrated on releasing all his remaining muscle tension. *They keep jacking up the Social Security age*, Francoise thought, as she hollowed out one end of the cucumber.

The Judge was fast asleep long before she had finished inserting the last small slices between his toes.

Returning to base

"I don't like this," McAdam was repeating to himself on his drive back to campus. "I wasn't supposed to be out front. Not when the shit was about to hit the fan."

Harlan in a haze

Harlan felt sick by 2:45, with three more hours before his last class of the day. Two students were in his office complaining about grades, and three more waiting outside. It would be easier to explain why they'd gotten those grades if he could just focus. He kept thinking it would be easier if he could just have a drink.

Janie in a daze

There were three problems she hadn't even looked at when Janie handed in the math test. Rivers had smiled at her and whispered, "This feels like an A" when she gave him the papers. It had been her best shot at an A all semester, lost because she had to get home early to try to talk Barbara into watching Billy all night, so she could go to work for the double shift. She wasn't even letting herself think about when she would get some sleep.

Johnny in a '49

Spec 3 Percy couldn't chase away the fly that was buzzing around, trying to wake him up. The jeep seat seemed larger than normal, with extra padding, but also smelling of mildew more than jungle and diesel. The noise of chainsaws in the distance faded in and out of his dream, transforming from annoying insects into a cruising motorcycle and finally a helicopter in trouble, twisting back at an impossible angle, rotor blade sheared, angling into a jungle hillside. He awoke, heart slamming, hiding again from the VC, the only guy from his unit to make it back alive.

He'd relived those three days of hiding, hiking back to base, for almost twenty years, through the rest of that tour and another, in several hospitals, on his father's relocated farm, at the old house, and now in the backseat of an abandoned car on the edge of the Adirondacks.

Johnny climbed out through the glassless window and looked for the angle of the sun. There still were at least three hours before dark, but he was worried about the people with the chainsaws.

He figured he should stay along the creek until it crossed the road running into Johnstown. Then he could parallel it in the dark, and probably pick up Kenny's trail again.

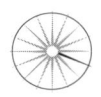

Noise in the attic

"Celeste? Celeste? Have you seen the news today?" Guppy called through the entire house. The Gary Hart and Donna Rice scandal was in its second day of coverage—a definite item—and he was champing at the bit.

Car's here. Has she taken the bike out? He checked in the garage. Her bicycle was hanging in the same spot where it had been for years. This is really odd. Is she out with someone?

Guppy searched his memory for mention of an appointment, and could not come up with anything.

He walked through the house again, calling her. "This is . . . it's not like her to just disappear," he said to himself.

The doors into the garage and house weren't locked. "She must be in here somewhere." He realized he hadn't looked in the attic. When he climbed the narrow wooden steps of the trap door ladder he found her sitting on the floor, staring vacantly at a cardboard box loaded with file folders, deep in thought.

"Celeste? Are you okay?"

"Oh. You scared me." She quickly covered the box and got up from the floor. "I was just . . . I got sidetracked."

"By what?"

"Nothing. Old things. From school."

Guppy started to ask again, but she was drifting. He decided it would be best to get her mind off whatever was bothering her.

"Could we go downstairs? Are you finished up here?" he pleaded, taking her arm.

"What? Yes. Oh, sure," she laughed nervously.

"I've been wanting to share this with you all day," Guppy grinned. "That story about Gary Hart is big time now. Can you believe it?"

Celeste shook her head.

"It looks like this could put him out of the race next year."

"Uh huh," she said, already lost in the memory of her parents' last visit when she was in graduate school, after the nervous breakdown.

Michael leaves again

Cough had called to let Alfonzo know about the big meeting to discuss saving the mill. Even though Alfonzo was retired, the mill's closing would threaten his health insurance. Cough was saying, yes, Alfonzo, you should come to the meeting.

As soon as Kenny heard Cough's name, when Tilia handed Alfonzo the phone receiver, he got agitated. It had been the first surge of memory about his mission.

"Uh, M-mama. . . I've gotta go. There's somethin' I gotta do. I'm sorry."

"Is it trouble, Sonny Boy? Do you got trouble?"

"N-no, Mama. It's not trouble. It's something I hafta do, that's all." It had bothered him, ever since they'd told him to call them Mama and Papa. There was something about it that made his cheeks and ears burn.

"You will come back?"

"I'll try."

Tilia's hands fluttered like mourning doves around her head, brushing along the hips of her housedress, trying to come to rest gripping the edge of the table top.

"Can you haf someting to eat, Sonny Boy, before you go?"

"Yeah, I guess so."

She hugged him, once, quickly, before she could talk herself out of it. It was the difference between when Kenny was leaving now, and when Michael had left twenty-one years ago.

"Now while you eat, I will pack more food for you, an' your clothes." Tilia went out to get Kenny's corduroy pants off the line, and found the largest work jacket Alfonzo owned to put in his backpack along with it. She jammed in hard cheese, bread and a hunk of salami so the pack was bulging, then went back to sit with Kenny, to supervise his eating. He only needed to glance in the direction of the coffee and fried dough to be served more. By the time Alfonzo was off the phone, he was stuffed.

"Papa. Sonny Boy needs to go, but he says he gonna try to come back when he's done. He been eating an' he got some more food with him for when he goes. Shake his han', Papa."

Kenny was hulking over Alfonzo, in Alfonzo's retired overalls, politely extending his hand.

"Why you gotta go?" Alfonzo said. Tilia frowned at him.

"He got something to do, Papa."

"What thing?"

"I can't say what," Kenny answered, looking down. Tilia watched the blood rise in Alfonzo's face. "I'm s'posed to do something, to help with the mill. I forgot before. I'm not s'posed to tell it."

Alfonzo exhaled deeply, years of anger flowing from him. He leaned against the doorframe for support.

"Shake his han', Papa," Tilia urged. "Tell him he's a good boy."

Kenny's hand was still outstretched, like a dog offering a paw on command.

"Sonny Boy, we gonna miss you," Alfonzo said, in a broken voice.

"I miss you, too," Kenny answered, in a voice that came from the room upstairs.

Celeste by a thread

"It's way back on page 16 of the Times," Guppy was saying. "But it's in there. It's front page in all the other papers, I'll bet."

"That wouldn't be surprising." Celeste kept looking up at the corners of the room, where the walls met the ceiling, checking for webs.

"I can't believe that a presidential candidate would be so stupid. Why would you challenge reporters to follow you around if there was a chance they could find something? It doesn't make sense."

"Yeah." Celeste rose from the rocker and climbed onto the back of the divan, waving at a tiny thread of spider filament.

"You don't think it was a set-up, do you?" Guppy was speaking louder, trying to draw her back. She had been like this for hours now.

"What?"

"Do you think it could be a set-up?"

She looked directly at him, confused. "What could?"

"The, uh, deal with Gary Hart and that Rice woman." He waited for a sign of recognition. "It's, uh, in the papers . . ." Guppy slowly chewed on the inside of his lip, watching her glare at the ceiling corners. "Hon?"

She had splayed her fingers out, was holding herself rigid between the divan and ceiling, like a primate testing its cage.

"Celeste!" Guppy shouted. She shot him a look. "This conversation isn't helping, is it?"

She blinked. "What conversation?"

"Uh . . . the stuff in the paper?"

She jumped down, sat on the carpet, hugging her knees to her chest. "I'm okay now, Ernie. I can listen. Please."

"Sure. Sure. Well, there's this Gary Hart and Donna Rice thing, right? But you know what else is happening? Nancy Reagan said she was going to tackle the US–Soviet intermediate nuclear-missile question, but decided she'd clean out Ronnie's sock drawer instead. Is that supposed to be cute?"

It's about time. It needed cleaning.

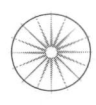

Kenny in the open

Kenny had walked almost three miles on the highway toward Johnstown before he realized he had no place to sleep for the night. It had taken him longer to leave Tilia's house, because she kept hugging him and Alfonzo was working his hand like a water-pump handle. Only when he promised four times to come back would they let him go. He thought Tilia was crying.

With dark approaching, whitetail deer were appearing in meadows near the edges of woods, browsing as dew settled. Kenny could feel the dampness settle into his shoulders. He searched in earnest for shelter.

Johnny back on track

Johnny had reached the overpass for Route 94, and felt there was sufficient night cover to parallel the road again. He would have to find a way to get through, or around, the village of Bent. But he figured he'd be catching up to Kenny pretty soon, now that he was rested and could travel faster.

Kenny goes to school

From a distance it looked to Kenny like a dog lying on the side of the road, but when he got up close he found a young male deer. Too old for fawn's spotting, not old enough to have more than nubs for antlers. Its head was wrenched back over its front leg, like it had been trying to run off the road when it was hit. There was still a fading light in its eyes. Blood trickled from its smashed insides.

Kenny kneeled down and stroked its fur along its side, down to the margin where the brown met the white underbelly. He held his hand on the deer's neck, felt it stiffening. The life left so slowly from its eyes, with such gentleness. There was not even a trace of anger for the driver, just remorse for not following quickly enough across the road. The eyes dimmed completely, and Kenny felt nothing else from it, but kept his hand on the deer's neck. *Be at peace,* he felt it saying, *be at peace*. When the voice stilled, he pulled the body farther away from the road until it was resting on grass, so it could go back to the earth.

He began trudging along the roadside again, thinking. He was still trying to understand when he spotted the abandoned one-room schoolhouse at the crossroads where the highway met the Johnstown-Lowmarket road.

Once inside, he decided to sleep in the cloakroom in the back, since that was where he'd spent so much of his time in grade school. It felt the most familiar.

George H. W. Bush*on the Judge

The Judge. That's what they call ol' Sumner up there, isn't it? Well, he deserves it, he's a deserving man, of it, he deserves it.

He's a good man. Did a lot for us up in that part of the country back in '84 and in '80. You know, in the campaign thing. Good man. Knows his people up there, because he is one of the people up there.

Yessir, he's the kind of man they need, we need, because he knows the people and he knows the whole building the economy thing and he is one of the people.

The Judge. He is our man up there.

---

*Vice President George Bush, Sr., was known for his mangled syntax and was often parodied long before his son, George W. Bush, took it to another level.

Chapter Five

The Middle of Nowhere

Kenny cloaked

Kenny was convinced Miss Montrage had forgotten him. That was the only thing it could be. And Mom and Dad were too scared of Miss Montrage to come and get him, so he'd have to stay here, forever and ever. What would happen on weekends and when it got to be summer and school was closed? Would the janitors feed him or would he just starve to death in the cloakroom?

Maybe it was already summer, because it smelled so musty, like no one had been here for quite a while. There were no boots or coats, not even his, so it probably wasn't winter. He couldn't believe no one had missed him at home, at least enough to send his pillow and blanket.

Whatever it was he had done this time, it must have been bad. He was sort of relieved he couldn't remember it.

Kenny fell back into a fitful sleep, full of dreams of Miss Montrage making him sit in a corner by himself, Miss Montrage saying, "No, no, Kenneth" and "I don't believe you" and "Keep your hands and feet to yourself."

He curled into a tighter ball, and kept sleeping.

Janie, becoming shiftless

Janie's mouth tasted bitter, like alum she had smeared on canker sores. She ran her tongue along the front of her teeth and thought she tasted yellow stains from cigarettes and coffee that had gotten her through the double shift. She figured one more cup would help her pick up Billy from Barbara's house and get him ready for school, before she went in to college. There was an hour between when Billy left and when she'd have to leave, but she was afraid to chance that much sleep. She knew she wouldn't get up in time for exams.

Horace was waving her over to his post by the loading dock. She tried to ignore him but he started to shout "Hey, hey," so she walked over.

"Melissa called in sick again," he said, giving her the trust-me look with his watery blue eyes.

"Don't even think about makin' me do another double."

"Somebody's gotta do it. An' you've got the most experience." He touched his wisps of blond hair just above the part.

"That's because you're too lazy to get off your ass an' call somebody else in an' train 'em."

"You better just calm yourself down, missy." Horace looked her in the eye.

Janie leaned against the handle of a freight dolly, waiting for the white stars crossing her eyes to fade away. "Horace, it is Tuesday morning. I haven't had any sleep since Saturday night. If you try to make me work another double, you'll have to fill out an accident report, and change that Days Without Lost Time Accident sign you're so proud of."

He spat a combination of tobacco juice and something else he had hemphed up. It landed inside the cement step on the right side of the loading dock. That seemed to be all he had to say.

He was bluffing, she knew it. She had got him thinking about accidents.

"I'll tell you, Horace. I'll work Melissa's shift for you tonight, if you want. But," she hissed, "you have to find somebody to work my shift. Deal?"

It would be easier for Horace to get someone for second shift than for the graveyard shift. "I guess I'll give you a call on that, later. I gotta make sure I can get somebody for the Number Two."

"Not good enough. Take it or leave it. I work the Number Three for ya, or my regular shift. Make up your mind."

The only question now was how Horace was going to show he was still in charge. She could see him working on it, rolling the chewed-up plug of Red Man in his mouth. Then his eyes narrowed, and he spat another stream.

"All right. But you gotta promise somethin' else, got it?"

"What's that?"

"Yer done with school, when, next week?"

"Week after," she lied.

"Perfect. There's a little detail in a coupla weeks."

"What detail? An extra load of pulp? Maintenance?" He shook his head. "Wait a minute," Janie continued, "are you puttin' together some crew to do a load of them dirty books?"

"Naw, I wish," Horace replied. He turned away from her and muttered, "I'm not s'posed ta tell."

"What?"

"I'm not s'posed ta tell," he said, a little louder, as if he wanted her to keep asking.

"Look, Horace, I wanna get goin', so I can see my kid for five minutes before I go to school. Why don't you just tell me so you can get the second shift filled an' go home yourself?"

"All right, but it's your fault if there's trouble. All I can say is, it's a packin' detail." He studied her face to make sure she understood the significance. The last vestige of color left her face. She reached with her other hand for the dolly handle.

"Don't ask me no more," Horace said, confidingly. "I'm already in enough trouble. I'll see ya on Number Three." He walked away, to get another cup of coffee, before calling in a sub to work Janie's spot.

When he looked back over his shoulder she was still doubled over, trying to catch her breath. *It's true,* she thought.

They're shutting down the mill.

Wispen gets inside

Today was a college-wide assembly day, the last meeting of the school year. McAdam was going over his notes again, getting worked up about what the Judge wanted. Should he say something today about the mill? If he didn't, would the Judge find out? Then what?

Marla buzzed him on the intercom.

"What is it?"

"Admin Veep Wispen wants to know if you're busy."

"Uh, yes, I am." *What could he want? He knows.*

"Could he disturb you for a moment?"

If only for a moment, that would be a godsend. It's that man's life's work. "Uhm, not right at this moment, Ms. Axe. Tell him I'll call him in a few minutes, when I'm done with this important matter."

Pause. "Okay, but he says it's urgent." McAdam slapped the file closed and shoved it into the desk drawer.

"All right, then, send him in." The doorknob turned before McAdam said "in." Wispen made eye contact with McAdam's desktop, as if thinking, *So that's where he put it.*

"What can I do for you, Herman?" McAdam asked.

"It's this budget report, Doctor. As I was looking it over," Wispen said, scanning the baseboards, "I had the feeling there may be items that would give some people the wrong impression, about our development plans."

"What kind of impression?" McAdam's lip crinkled and spasmed ever so slightly. Wispen had pushed the right button.

"President McAdam," he answered calmly, "responsible people have no objection to any part of our budget. You know that."

McAdam took in a breath, forced it whistling out of his nose.

"It's just that the in-house consumers of this information always try to read things in, things that you and I and responsible people, quite frankly, know aren't there."

"What kinds of things?"

Wispen wore the we're-in-this-together look he'd been practicing for this conversation. "Oh, instructional technology, information systems automation, signage, security personnel. Those items we've worked so hard to educate our stakeholders about."

Wispen's list hit McAdam like a Sugar Ray Leonard combination—left jab, right to the body, left hook, uppercut. The first three were his pet projects. Wispen shared his enthusiasm for those, even though his special province was security. McAdam hated to lose any political capital on that one, but he needed Wispen to push his agenda.

"So what do we do?"

"We could be honest with the faculty and staff," Wispen began, "and explain that this is merely our, uh, a national trend. Or," he paused, gauging McAdam's reaction to the honest approach, "we could frame the report in a context that would encourage people not to examine it too critically."

"Let me be clear on this context approach. What are you suggesting?"

"Well, let's think about this. Hmmm. What do you think of emphasizing the fight for state support? People right here on campus don't know how hard that's been."

"Already part of my report," McAdam replied stiffly.

"Good, good. But is it enough?"

McAdam shrugged. "Well, what else would there be?" He said it as if he had no idea what Wispen was trying to get at.

"Good point. What would get their minds off the signage, and temporization?" McAdam shot him a look. Temporization was the most obscure euphemism they had come up with to explain moving the office clerical staff to part-time, no-benefits status.

"I know," Wispen offered. "If there was some context in the community for this kind of, uh, change."

He does know! The weasel, McAdam thought. *It's unavoidable now. I've got to say something about the mill.*

Grrnnnt. Marla was buzzing again.

Right on cue, Wispen thought.

"Ms. Axe, I'm in conference right now, with Vice President Wispen. Can't be disturbed."

"O-kaay," she sang back.

"Now what were you saying?" McAdam asked.

"I was saying that if we only had some other, uh, distraction to occupy the people who are so quick to look for fault . . ."

Grrnnnt.

"Ms. Axe?"

"Yes."

"Is this something very important?"

"I guess so."

"You guess so?"

"I thought you might wanna know what somebody said."

"What who said?"

"Uh, one of the security guys." Wispen looked pained, like he was suffering along with McAdam.

"Well, what was it?"

"Someone said he saw that Judge guy on campus, over by the Research Center."

"I've got to go," McAdam shouted. "I'll talk with you later." He shooed Wispen toward the door with his hands as he ran out.

"Okay, I'll be in my office," Wispen answered, the doorknob to McAdam's office in his hand. He watched McAdam hurry around the corner to the front door. Axe rolled her eyes and swiveled 180 degrees in her chair, her back now turned to him.

Wispen gently nudged McAdam's door open. Another quarter of an inch and the spring latch would have locked it. He smiled as he slipped into the office.

Darcardt on the rise

He was stretched out on his bed, quilted covers pulled up to his chin, sock feet sticking out from under the covers. He was naked except for the socks, which he had put on in the middle of the night. It was nine thirty-seven, over two hours past his normal rising time. He'd tried to get up earlier, worried about being ready for his eleven o'clock class, but he had a terrible headache and didn't seem able to move.

Carrie Casimir gets out

Dodgeball again. Mr. Tornatore usually had the boys play dodgeball in June, on days so rainy they couldn't go out. Now with budget cuts, he had boys' and girls' classes during the same gym period, and since he was retiring he let the boys talk him into dodgeball every day, even when it was sunny.

Carrie Casimir hated dodgeball, most of the girls did, but now it was even worse. Before, she'd been able to get on Joanie Prwanzas' team most of the time. She could hang back by the bleachers giggling and screaming with Joanie until they had been hit by balls and were out of the game.

Joanie was actually one of the most athletic girls, because she'd played softball, touch football, and hockey with her brothers since she was little. The fire had no effect on her agility, strength, and coordination, but she had sat on the bleachers during gym class from her first day back at school. Whenever Carrie tried to sit by her, Joanie would turn away.

"Kwitcha hidin', Carrie," Joanie's brother Jacob shouted. "Git out into the open where I can smash you."

Carrie was weaving back and forth behind Roberta Burndy, the largest player on her team. Sammy Trumble, Jacob's best buddy, caught a ball at shin level and held it, waiting for the signal to nail down Carrie in a crossfire.

"Now yer gonna get it, Carrie," Jacob taunted. "Quit tryin' ta hide."

Carrie blinked back tears, tried to make herself an even skinnier target.

"Cut it out, Cash-meer," Sammy yelled. "Hey, Snout," he shouted at Roberta, "move back by the bleachers, so the baby calf can't hide behind you no more."

"The baby calf," Jacob snorted.

Roberta scrunched her nose and stuck her tongue out.

"C'mon, Snout, move!" Sammy yelled.

"Roberta, c'mon!" Jacob shouted. Because Roberta was his cousin, and his mother had warned him not to call her names, he would not say Snout.

"You make him stop callin' me that," Roberta yelled back. "I ain't doin' nothin' for that pinhead."

"Throw the balls!" the other kids were screaming. "Just throw the balls an' get Snout out!"

"Ya wanna get Snout out?"

"But what if we don't get the balls back? I want Cash-meer."

"*Move*, Snout. Get your big butt outta the way," Sammy screamed.

"Mister Tornatore," Carrie called. "Mister Tornatore. They're not playing right."

Mr. Tornatore looked up from his desk chair, where he'd been leafing through golf-resort brochures. He looked up at her. Because of her thick glasses, he couldn't see in. Carrie held her breath.

The other kids were still screeching at Jacob and Sammy. If Mr. Tornatore got mad and called off dodgeball, they'd be spending the rest of gym running laps.

"Prwanzas! Trumble! Quit holding onto those balls! Throw 'em!"

"I'll give the ball back to you if I get it," Ricky Sizemore told Jacob.

"Yeah, I will, too," other kids were shouting.

Roberta retreated until her backside was pressed against the bleachers. Carrie wanted to tell Mr. Tornatore she was sick, but then they'd just gang up on her in the next class. She took two quick hitches to the right until Sammy stepped up and hurled his ball at her knees. She jumped and cleared it, but was slammed by Jacob's sidearm ball just to the left and under her shoulder blade. It knocked her down, leaving a three-inch floor burn on both knees. The balls caromed back to Sammy and Ricky, who surrendered his to Jacob. They and the rest of his team pelted her three more times as she retreated to the bench with the other "outs."

Carrie sneaked a look at Joanie, on the other end of the bench. She was looking straight ahead, her face expressionless.

Koemover goes global

Dr. Koemover surveyed his International Trade class, those with alert, adoring expressions, the few who had started out hostile but now seemed sleepy, the smug ones, and those still trying to discipline their anxiety. He was proud of them—most of them—proud of their effort, proud of his work. Everyone had made the attempt, he believed, to understand the most powerful transformative force on the planet, the fountain from which all human civilization flowed, the Idea behind all history: the market.

At the moment a smug one was coaxing a normally sleepy one.

"You've got to be kidding," Christon sneered. "Foreign corporations investing in South Africa is the only reason South Africa is worth anything. I don't think they'd have any economy if we weren't there."

Bobo tried that idea out in his head. South Africans twenty thousand years ago squatting on their haunches, waiting for the USA to be founded, for industrialization, for the development of Standard Oil, and then the globalization of corporations. *"Shouldn't we get something to eat?" one says to the other.*

"No, can't do it, there's no USA yet."

"Oh."

He thought about saying something to the guy, but he knew Koemover would jump in and steer the discussion so he would end up looking foolish. Because of that, he let the guy drone on and let his own eyes go out of focus. Koemover would think he wasn't paying attention, but that was okay. Much better than feeling stupid again.

"It's the wonder of the Market, individuals all over the world making free, private choices, and as they do they are changing the way people live on other continents," Koemover was saying now.

Sarah had been sitting quietly through the entire class. Koemover had sneaked a glance over in her direction every once in a while because she had shown talent as a market indicator in the past, but today she seemed resistant to logic. She'd only been able to listen to part of it. Her mind kept drifting to what she was going to do for a job now that the Coconuts movie video store was being closed and moved to the mall on the other side of Onlius. Her three years at the Cayuga Street store and her sixty-five-cent an hour raise had put her in a vulnerable position, especially when the new scanner registers would require retraining anyway. Coconuts could offer better discounts with more minimum-wage employees.

Sarah was having a hard time reconciling her last work assignment—packing the stock to be moved—with Koemover's notion of the final solution, the march of the market to its triumph over ignorance:

The Global Shopping Center.

It made her wonder if he would ever consider letting go of tenure, or the step increases in salary the faculty union negotiated while he refused to pay dues. She had a feeling the answer was probably no.

Darcardt down the stretch

Five minutes it felt like, for Darcardt to drag himself out of bed, the pounding in his head was so bad. Good thing he had instant coffee in the cupboard.

It wasn't supposed to be like this, not on your last day in front of a class. Darcardt couldn't remember anyone describing a last day like this, so sick you could barely move. Brown had gone out the same way he'd come in; crusty, abrupt, condescending. Onguey had delivered a master lecture on the politics of the spirit in liberation theology. Christa Morre had listened to student presentations in her trademark calm, encouraging style, punctuating each with a statement about how they could take their work further in graduate school.

She had looked as relaxed, and professional, after class as anyone he'd ever seen.

Darcardt had hoped to take a route similar to Onguey's, though focused more on global political economy, US national identity. It was a disturbing theme, so filled with realities his students resisted that he'd thought several times about ditching it. Why not go out with something upbeat, like Buddhist economics, or even the Long View of History, where he could point out how industrial workers really did have more freedom than peasants under feudalism?

But he knew he would be tempted to bring up how industrial capitalism brought along other freedoms, like the freedom to starve, the freedom of unemployment.

And the more he thought about lightening up, the more memories flooded him about friends who had paid the price. Mentors who had supported the Spanish Loyalists against the Fascists in the late thirties, then had been passed over for tenure or, if they already had it, denied promotion time and again as their compromising colleagues climbed the ladder over them. Friends who had marched for civil rights, or to end the war, or to keep open admissions. And now this thing with Harlan.

He had met C. Wright Mills once, on a visit to Columbia for a conference. Mills, who had written *The Power Elite*, who had scored his colleagues for shirking their duty to defend democracy in *A Sociological Imagination*, then later would write *The Causes of World War Three*, was alone in the cafeteria drinking coffee from a cardboard cup.

Darcardt remembered thinking at the time that Mills looked like a Negro sitting at a Woolworth's lunch counter. The cafeteria was fairly crowded, but tables around him were empty. It did not surprise Darcardt when he heard a few years later that Mills had left the country, having published *Listen Yankee* a year before the Bay of Pigs invasion.

If he had not died young, what would Mills be doing now?

He certainly wouldn't be a partner in Jerry Rubin's brokerage. Would he have twisted in the same political breeze that had blown Moynihan into Nixon's administration? Would he have gotten cynical passing into old age, like Dos Passos and Steinbeck?

Not likely.

Darcardt pictured Mills writing a piece about the 1984 Olympics in Los Angeles, a Gold Medal binge for the US because of the Soviet boycott. Mills would have turned it on its head. *The Great Celebration*

II. Rocky Balboa Fights the Enemy Within, on pay-per-view. Ronald Reagan laying a wreath on the graves of SS officers at Bitburg. Mills would have lost it on that. What would he have titled it? *The Great American Indifference?*

The first sips of coffee had intensified his headache, then it throttled down. By the time he'd finished breakfast and was ready to drive to school, it had settled just above his temples.

He'd be relieved when he could get the class over with. Every time he tried to concentrate on the lecture, it felt like voltage snapping down along his skull.

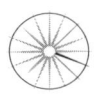

Celeste in hot water

Celeste plunged her hands into the steaming water, held them there until she could feel all the nerve endings from her fingertips up through her shoulders. *There,* she thought, as she moved her blistering hands over the dried egg yolk on the plates from breakfast, *that ought to be hot enough to make a difference.*

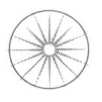

Kenny uncloaked

He closed his arms in around the dog, nuzzling his cheek against it, until he felt in his sideburns the pull of teeth from a zipper. Kenny flailed awake, jerked the backpack away from his face, the clump of deer fur falling the rest of the way out of the pocket.

From where he was sitting, he could see only within the wedge of light from under the bottom of the door. Kenny moved into it, dragging the backpack by its strap. He waved his hand through the dust particles that drifted in the sunbeam, tried to pull a handful of sun up to his eyes. It made him sneeze, made the dust swirl in the light triangle surrounding him.

"Sneee," he tried to cover his nose. Lingering anxiety from the dream made him frantic to quiet the sneezing. Miss Montrage might make him stay in from recess again to mop and dust the cloakroom.

He pinched his nose and held his breath until his lungs burned, then let go and gasped as quietly as he could. *Wait a minute, I don't hear anything.* This time he breathed shallowly and listened. There were no sounds from the classroom, only faint birdsong outside.

Kenny cracked the door, peeked out, then eased it open. The large room was warmer from the sunlight splashing in through those windows not yet boarded up. Glancing around, he saw the heavy front-row desks still bolted down, black paint peeling from them, slivers of glass scattered over the floor. Nothing was familiar about this room. *This isn't my school.*

He gathered up his backpack, placing the tuft of deer fur back in the pouch, and went out the door. He didn't need to glance around to check for Miss Montrage.

Zola passes an exam

87. The main impact of mass media on political opinion is to

    a. encourage citizens to think in more ideological ways.

    b. reinforce preexisting biases.

    c. impose a more liberal perspective.

    d. impose a more conservative perspective.

Now, that's an interesting one, Zola May thought. *I'll bet it's C,* she guessed wrongly. She stopped typing, arched her neck, swaying her head side to side, tried to shake the soreness out of her shoulders and wrists. *More than halfway, but if I know Koemover, he'll be expecting it today.* The date on the exam, December 15, 1987 tormented her. *This is a final exam. For next semester.* The thought kept rolling through her mind. *What an asshole.*

Zola May stretched again, this time squaring her shoulders back so that her chest thrust out. She caught a glimpse of Guppy looking at her. She jerked her head back to the screen.

I wonder what she sees in that Lyle, Guppy wondered as he watched her breathe in and out.

I'll bet she likes it rough.

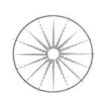

Aurelia on the edge

"So what did he have with him?"

"I dunno. Not for sure, Aurelia," Chauncey answered. "Connie, do you remember what Kenny had with him?"

"His backpack was all I saw, but you got me for whatever was inside it." Connie's right hand was on her hip, the fingernails of her left were scraping at a spot of dried coffee on the countertop.

Aurelia's mouth lifted, then sagged, tugging her cheekbones down, threatening a new flood from the corners of her eyes. Chauncey could not look at her. He kept wiping at his hands with the gasoline-soaked end of a greasy rag.

"He was okay, Aurelia. We gave him some candy."

Aurelia smiled a little. "Cream drops."

"No. It was root-beer barrels," Connie said. "And licorice."

The panic sweeping across Aurelia's face was too much for Chauncey. "We could help you look for him."

Licorice? Root-beer barrels? Aurelia was frightened of all the things she didn't know about Kenny. She still couldn't believe he would leave to go clear across the county, into Onlius, on his own. She was still angry with Cough for sending him. The thought of looking for him in the city terrified her.

"I'll let you know," Aurelia managed to reply. "I don't want for you to have to be away from the garage," she added, thinking that the more people who were searching for Kenny, the more likely Social Services would find out.

"It's no trouble," Chauncey lied. "I don't have too much to do."

Connie scratched more loudly at the countertop.

"Well, you let me know if I can help," he said, wiping the back of his hand. It left a film of grease on his knuckles, thinned the smudge on his wrist.

"Okay, thanks." Aurelia turned for the door.

"Eight in gas?" Connie asked.

"What?"

"Did you have eight dollars worth?"

"Uh, yes. Yes, I did." Aurelia pulled a black vinyl wallet from her pocketbook, counted out seven ones from the bills compartment, and zipped it closed on the few tens and twenties. Her mother had taught her that singles spend slower than bigger bills. She squeezed the ends of a red gummy change purse between the fingers and heel of her right hand, plucking out three quarters, four nickels, five pennies. "I almost forgot."

"That's okay, you had stuff on your mind."

After Aurelia fired up the Rambler, headed out of town, Connie wandered into the garage to squat at the edge of the pit where her father was working a wrench under a Ford pickup.

"If the mill stayin' open depends on Kenny, we better be gettin' some videos and lottery tickets in here to keep the store goin'."

Carmen at the golden arches

Carmen mixed up the third order in a row at the drive-thru. Her mind kept drifting to the paper she was reworking for Professor Harlan's class. Everybody at work loved to give her grief about college.

"Yessir, Golden Arches U," Sump laughed. "Dr. McCheese. How much you got out in loans? Five grand? Ten?"

"Not ten," Carmen said under her breath.

"What? Whatcha say?"

"Not ten," she said again, same volume.

"*Wha-cha say?*" Sump shouted, grinning. "*Ya say you're a public-speaking major?*"

"I said *not ten*, you bastard."

"Hey, cut it out," Shirley yelled back at them from behind the drive-thru window. "I think the guy outside heard that."

"Sorry, Shirl. Let me know if he complains," Sump called back. "I'll give his order personal attention."

"Now, Carmen, if it's not ten, then it must be ninety-nine, ninety-five. Izzat it?"

"It's seven, if you gotta know. Not even. Sixty-eight hundred actually."

"An' this is your second year?"

"Yes." She knew where he was going, but couldn't think of a way to stop him.

"How much you think you'll be down by the time you're all done?"

"I dunno."

"You dunno? You gotta have some idea."

"Prob'ly more than ten."

Sump grinned. He held his thumb up from his fist, pumping it upward. "I'd say at least fifteen, don'tcha think?" He raised both eyebrows, stretching out his face, nodding sympathetically. "Maybe twenty."

Carmen was thinking about the paper she'd gotten back from Dr. Harlan yesterday, with no grade, just a note to see him during his office hour. She didn't think it was likely to be good news.

"It's not gonna be twenty," she said to the bun warmer.

"Any way you cut it," Sump said, "that's one big Happy Meal."

Darcardt in harness

Darcardt was lecturing, eyebrows twisted around his headache.

"Economics has always been the reason for America. We could go back to the migration of Asian peoples across Beringia in search of animals to hunt, because that's economics if anything is, but let's begin with the growth of mercantilism within the rotting carcass of feudalism. Spices, silks were like money, but not really. You had to have gold and silver.

"The ties that bound together feudal Europe were untied by a landed nobility in search of greater wealth and power—or, to get straight to the real motivating factor behind all human activity—status. The fealty had provided status before, then things changed with the Crusades and Marco Polo.

"Feudalism's political units didn't have the resources to pursue sufficient new wealth, so they were absorbed into larger ones in the fifteenth century—nation-states. They had the power to explore, claim, dominate the peoples of the New World, and they soon developed the economic and religious ideologies to enslave them, to strip them of their material wealth."

This was what it said on the page, the way it had sounded in Darcardt's head until he woke up ill. By the time he had gotten to class it had come out kind of differently.

"The bitch-goddess property," he'd said at one point, describing why Southerners sacrificed their own civil liberties to keep slavery.

"His Royal Highness, Richard the First," was his response to a question about Watergate.

The class was very different from the way he had envisioned it. The students who normally were attentive stopped raising their hands about twenty minutes in, and sat red-faced through the rest of the period. One got up and left.

Those who had smirked or slept through the semester, though, were raising their hands and asking all kinds of questions. They seemed to be enjoying the class for the first time. If not for them, he wouldn't have been able to keep going when he felt those stabs of pain.

The concluding passage from his lecture notes was a paraphrasde from the conclusion of Marshall Berman's *The Politics of Authenticity*: "You may not be interested in politics, but politics is interested in you."

Somehow it had transformed into "Just do it."

Darcardt waved dismissively to the class, leaned back to sit on his desk, and practiced closing the right corner of his mouth with the fingers of his left hand.

Billy goes mad

Billy always hung back in the line so he could whisper to Mark and try to get a seat next to Jerinda during lunch. Jeremy used to sit with them until last month, when he'd tried to use Billy's reduced-price lunch number going through the line and he'd gotten yelled at by the lunch lady. Billy tried to explain to him why he got the reduced-price lunch, but Jeremy started making fun of him. He'd carried it on into arithmetic and out onto the playground during recess. "Yer-er poor-or, cuz your daddy's gaw-awn," he'd taunted, staying just out of Billy's reach until they lined up to go back inside. Billy tackled him, then bit him, leaving a bleeding imprint of his teeth on Jeremy's cheek.

Jeremy and his new friends called him Cujo after that. Billy didn't mind. He could take that better than being called poor.

The college meets

"Outcomes assessment," he heard, and giggled. "Are they making us assess outcomes now because we missed the boat on needs assessment?" Guppy whispered to Harlan.

Harlan suppressed a snort, pretended to concentrate on the rest of the Vice President's report. Guppy felt cheated.

"Curriculum redesign," Guppy said wistfully. "Whatever happened to curriculum redesign?"

Harlan rolled his eyes toward the amphitheater ceiling. "Curricular redesign, it was," he whispered.

"That's right. You're a genius, John."

"Oh thanks, just what I need, administrative potential."

"Well, let's not jump to any conclusions." They listened for another half-minute to see if there was anything new.

"Who do you suppose is behind this, anyway?" Harlan finally whispered.

"Why go beyond the usual suspects? System Administration. They're busywork machines. It's well beyond cottage-industry status."

"What is?"

"Educational-attainment measurement euphemisms."

"Yeah, but there's got to be a reason."

"Of course there is. It's state legislatures looking at us more closely these days, to make sure what's left of the middle class is getting a good bang for their buck." He lifted his eyebrows when he said bang.

Harlan was nodding slightly, the blush of his cheeks fading. Guppy could tell Harlan was turning inward, getting ready to dwell on his probationary status.

In grad school I had four teeth pulled instead of having them fixed, so I could afford to finish, Harlan thought. *Just so I could sit through this.*

"So, are you in the pool yet?" Guppy whispered.

"What pool?" Harlan said from the corner of his mouth.

"The euphemism pool." Guppy wore his poker face.

Harlan turned his head, looked him in the eye. "What?"

"You haven't heard about it? It's system-wide. The only disqualifier is that you can't have been engaged—in a formal way, you understand—in educational-attainment measurement beyond your own classroom."

Harlan smiled. "I've got that base covered."

"Oh, and . . . well, it should go without saying, that if your euphemism should actually prove useful, thereby freeing up instructional time, it's disqualified."

"What if my euphemism makes for a significant shift of resources from administration to teaching?"

"Then the State University and State Ed acquire an automatic co-patent, and bury it."

Harlan snorted again. Koemover, McAdam, and Assembly President Pernell glared in his direction.

". . . will prove to be an exciting innovation in the classification and measurement of the effectiveness of our existing objectives and practices."

"Ee-ee." The back door was opening. The college staff turned as one to observe the latecomer. Earhart looked directly back at them, huffed, and strolled to the first open seat near an aisle, eight rows up from the front, next to Koemover.

It was McAdam's turn to speak. He rose from his seat and walked, with head hunched down, to the lectern in front. His confidence was still back in his seat.

"Well, our friends in Albany are still trying to hammer out a budget." He tried to grin, but the flesh inside his lip caught on his teeth, making him appear nauseated. McAdam searched out a face to focus on. Koemover was too rapt, sitting too close to the aisle, and right next to Earhart. McAdam had learned she had a way of fixing her gaze on him that made him question himself. He couldn't risk eye contact with her.

He fluttered a transparency onto the overhead projector. It showed deadlines for the college's budget process, emphasizing with four question marks each stage where the lack of state funding figures made the budget impossible to project.

"As you can see, we're in a real gray area now." He chanced a look upward from his notes. A sea of blank expressions, except for

Darcardt, who looked like he was trying to smile, or at least most of his face was trying to smile. Up in the corner, Dr. Guppy was whispering to young Harlan.

This seems like the safest time to bring up the mill. He decided it would be best to look directly at Darcardt, his new ally.

"One positive thing that appears close to fruition is a research grant for the college, that some of us have been working on, to study local economic development."

Research? Koemover's eyes were shining now, his face a wash of appreciation. He resolved to bone up on economic development so he could help shape the study.

Wispen was frowning. *Some of us have been working on?* He peered around the amphitheater for signs of recognition. Aside from Koemover, no one seemed connected in any way to what McAdam was saying.

. . . the monkey chased the weasel. . . Darcardt thought. He couldn't get the nursery rhyme out of his head. What was worse, he had an awful fear that it might not only be inside his head. He did his best to grin as a cover, but he wasn't even sure he was doing that right.

". . . although nothing is finalized, the initial discussions went excellent."

"Went excellent," Guppy repeated to Harlan.

"This should prove to be a real boon for the college."

"Pop goes the weasel," Darcardt said out loud. Heads turned.

McAdam grabbed his state budget transparency and hurried, head down, to his seat.

Harrison Pernell, zoology professor and president of the college assembly, called on Wispen for his report.

"Thank you, President Pernell. I would have to ditto the remarks made by President McAdam regarding the State budget picture. We are hoping, of course, that we'll get the anticipated State funding transfers to carry out the next phase of our campus security-force expansion. Speaking of which, our people would like to have everyone's cooperation to begin facility lockdown at ten p.m. rather than eleven, so we can accommodate the transition of security shifts. We are asking that all office computers be shut down by nine forty-five."

"But what if we need to do research then?" Harlan asked. Everyone on the faculty turned to look at him, some hoping he would prevail, many disgusted that he was questioning Wispen's authority.

"Is this research college-related?" Wispen queried.

The specter of being discovered using photocopiers, telephones, the mail for unauthorized projects rippled through the room. Harlan recalled the interrogation he'd received about a satirical essay from *In These Times* that he'd once left on the photocopier. It had dealt with an issue in his friend Gene's doctoral work, so he had copied it to send as a thank-you for the help Gene had given him.

It was suggested he be more careful in the future.

"Of course it would be," Harlan said defensively, "college-related."

Wispen made his *sure it is* smile. He glanced in McAdam's direction and saw that he was looking down at the tabletop. An inspiration seized him.

"Well, considering that, as President McAdam just informed us, the college's revenue stream is likely to be based more and more upon research grants, it would be unwise of us to put up obstacles to people doing their work."

Barely perceptible nods of appreciation and smiles flickered through the amphitheater. Maybe this guy Harlan was all right.

"We can accommodate that," Wispen continued, "by asking that you simply call the security office to let us know if you are going to be in your office or in any one of the research facilities after dusk. Actually, we'll get to work right away on a form for documenting afterhours use of college facilities." Wispen grinned confidently, McAdam was still communing with Formica, and Pernell thanked Wispen for his report.

"Are there any items for the Good of the Order?" Pernell asked. The only upturned face was Darcardt's, who had been humming and gurgling off and on since his singing debut in the meeting. Everyone else seemed to have learned a lesson from Harlan's effort to affect policy.

Darcardt raised his hand, straight up like he was holding the string of a balloon pulling him into the air. Pernell and Wispen glanced at each other in silent agreement to ignore him.

"Bumblee, bumblee, bumblee," Darcardt hummed, eyes shining.

Guppy observed the way Harlan was trying not to look in Darcardt's direction. He knew how much Harlan admired, one could even say worshipped, Darcardt. It was obvious that something was wrong today, beyond the predictable oddness that Darcardt had cultivated in recent years, since the death of his wife Judy.

"Perhaps we can move on to committee reports," Pernell droned.

Darcardt inched up in his seat, waving his arm from side to side, hand fluttering like it was trying to fly away from his wrist.

"The first committee report is from . . ."

"Uh, uh, uh." Darcardt's smile was collapsing into a need to warn others of impending doom. He was raising up in his seat from his knees, legs tucked under him.

Throats were clearing all over the room, beginning with Guppy and Harlan. They grew into such a crescendo that Earhart was snapped back from the out-of-body experience she'd cultivated to get herself through the meeting.

"Dr. Darcardt would like to say something."

Once Earhart had tuned in and spoken up, it was impossible for Pernell to ignore Darcardt any longer.

"Uh, yes, Charles. You have something for the Good of the Order?"

"Yes. Yes, I do." He settled into his seat, put the heel of his right hand under his chin. "I had a dream last night, which I believe was prescient. The entire State University was operated out of one technician's room, where he fed videodisks into machines to be beamed out to campuses and workplaces and residences. Apparently the courses had all been designed by faculty who, by this time, were long since gone."

He labored for air, for coherence, for details that could knit the dream fragments.

"There was no need . . . no prospect, for independent thought."

Pernell rolled his eyes, began glaring at his watch.

"One history course for all, one introduction to philosophy . . ." Darcardt's throat ached, as if the words were being torn from him.

"I tried to stop it. . . but suddenly I had wheels and was being rolled, into a closet."

Hands were in the air, bored with the Cassandra impersonation, impatient to usher Darcardt into retirement.

He opened his mouth once more; at first no words came to reveal the images blazing inside his mind. Finally, "the horror, the horror" was all he could manage.

An uneasy silence fell. Wispen shook his head sadly. Harlan felt again a queasiness in his stomach, a familiar discomfort that suddenly had a name. After five full seconds, Pernell quietly suggested they begin the committee reports.

Grass futures

"Erly, erly, erl," Kenny's stomach protested. He'd had nothing to eat since midmorning, when he finished Tilia's bread and cheese from yesterday. He'd been toiling along the road through the southeastern section of the town of Greenland since midday. *Going to the college, going to the college.*

Chewing on the green shoots that shouldered up in sheaths above the June grass had eased his hunger for a while. Now it was adding to the churning in his stomach. He felt starved, but there was nothing else he knew to forage this early.

A cattle truck was gearing down for the curve before the climb up Mason Hill. Lurching and groaning up the grade, it passed Kenny at a pace he could have jogged. It wasn't the rank earthy odor of cow manure, or the stench of cheap oil exhaust, that doubled Kenny over. It was the cows inside the truck being sent off for beef, part of the federal herd buyout program, bellowing their terror. It made Kenny sit down in the gravel on the side of the road, gasping and holding his heart. He was still sitting there when the pickup truck coasted to a stop beside him.

"Where ya goin'?" the driver asked.

"Uh . . . that way," Kenny pointed down the road westward. "Into town."

"Onlius?"

Kenny nodded.

"I'm not goin' that far, only into Lowmarket, but I'll get ya part of the way."

Kenny said thanks, and tried to look out the window at the outline of green meeting blue on the horizon. Instead he found himself studying the man with *Dorsey* stitched in red letters in a white oval over the heart of his brown overalls. There was such a sadness, a loneliness about the man that Kenny couldn't look away. "So, uh, how ya doin', Dorsey?" he asked.

The man squinted, coughed, and blew his nose into a red handkerchief. He smelled like oats—and something else. Kenny didn't know the name of the stuff, but he could remember the aroma from when his dad had taken him to the Agway.

"These aren't my coveralls. They belonged to a guy who used to work there. My name's Gerry. Gerry Scott."

"Nice to meet ya. I'm Kenny." They settled into a heavy silence again, though Kenny had a feeling the guy had something else to say.

Johnny in the dark

Darkness comforted him. Johnny could travel without being noticed, awake and alert while everyone else was asleep, at rest. When the western horizon was awash in bruised shades of purple, Johnny could feel himself settling up into a heightened engagement with everything around him. In daylight people looked through or past him. At night, if he wanted to be noticed, they had no choice but to watch him, try to figure if he was trouble.

That's what had happened when he strolled into the Sugarcreek in Bent to get some cigarettes. Dolly Swegovia gave him the once-over as he searched the shelves for Mallomars. He could see her tracking his movements.

"Pack o' Marlboros," he told her when she was ringing him up.

"Regular or Lites?"

"Regulars."

She checked the slots above eye-level. "I'm all outta Regulars. You sure Lites wouldn't do it for ya?"

"Pansy-ass."

"What?"

"Pansy-ass. Lites are pansy-ass cigarettes."

"Well, I ain't got any regulars of the Marlboros. Lites are s'posed to be better for ya, with the filters." Dolly always talked more when she was nervous.

"Yeah? They're like fuckin' tofu, those Lites are."

"Hey, I was just sayin', ya know."

"Yeah." Johnny just stood there in front of her, head cocked back a little, feeling the edginess in her voice.

"We got other kinds o' Regulars, ya know, unfiltered cigarettes. How 'bout a pack of Camels?"

"My old man smokes Camels."

Though he said it tonelessly, as a statement of fact, like it's dark outside, or it's much warmer than usual this time of year, Dolly felt like she had done something he could not forgive.

"Ah . . . you want cigarettes, or not?" She tried to sigh as if she were bored instead of frightened.

Johnny had been about to ask for the Camels, until she sighed. Now he had to give her more grief. Why did people do that shit to him?

"Yeah I want some cigarettes. That's what I said, didn't I?"

"Yeah, an' I' been tellin' ya the cigarettes we got. So what kind's it gonna be?" Dolly was getting pissed.

"Marlboro," Johnny said, smiling. "Regulars."

Celeste sizes up

Sauteed onions are so hard to clean from the broiler pan. I'd better just let this soak. The thought was Celeste's. The voice behind the thought belonged to her mother. It made her look over her shoulder. It made her cover up whatever she was doing, close her book and put it in her desk drawer or slide it in between the box spring and mattress, tucked inside the fitted sheet.

Celeste had to walk away from the kitchen sink and look back at it from across the room. The sink was fine. So were the cabinets and the countertop, the stove, refrigerator, and stools at the counter. When she retreated from them they were still hers, still the right size.

From this chair at the dining table, each sink basin was the size of the nail on her little finger. From five steps closer they fit the palm of her hand.

Five steps farther away might make them invisible to the naked eye. That would be outside the dining-room window. That would be too far away.

Celeste walked back into the kitchen, found a Chore Boy scrub pad in the cabinet under the sink, and started working on the broiler pan.

Guppy raised the paper up from his lap and went back to reading.

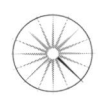

Casimirs, fueling up

"Chester, you pump the gas for me, honey, an' don't forget the cans."

"Aw, Mom, I wanted to go in, too."

"You can go in when yer done, darlin'. I need you to pump the gas first, though, like your father woulda done."

"All right, but I'm sittin' by the window goin' home."

"Sure thing, darlin'. Just remember the threads are gone on that one plastic cap, so you gotta make sure it won't fall over."

"I will."

"I'm comin' in." "Can I come in?" "I wanna go in," the other kids were saying.

"No you're not all comin' in," Mrs. Casimir said flatly. "You just all been in the store gettin' groceries. Besides, this place is too expensive for anything 'cept gas."

"Ain't I gettin' nothin' for pumpin' the gas?" Chester whined.

"I already bought y'all a treat with the groceries."

"Yeah, but I'm pumpin' the gas."

"Some things," Georgette said, reaching for the handle of the pump nozzle, "you oughtta do without gettin' somethin' for it. Get back in the car, Chet."

"Now I ain't gettin' a treat?"

"You heard the rest of 'em. If you get to go in, they'd all hafta go in."

"Move over, you baby," Chester said, pinching Carrie's arm as he pushed into the middle seat. "Ya spoiled it for me again."

Mrs. Casimir went about filling the station wagon and the gas cans methodically, feeling the heat slowly leave her cheeks.

Dolly kept track of her progress from inside the store. *C'mon, c'mon,* she prayed to herself, hoping she'd come inside to pay before this guy snapped.

"Look, I don't know what your problem is, but it isn't my fault. We're just sold out, is all."

"Yeah, you told me. But, hey, who knows, maybe you do know somethin'," Johnny said softly. "Listen, I'm lookin' for a guy . . ."

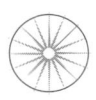

A meal deal

"Where ya headed?" Gerry asked.

"Nowhere," Kenny said, startled. He blinked and clutched at his backpack.

"You okay?"

"Yeah." Kenny worried that his stomach's growling was audible.

"I didn't mean to spook ya. I guess I asked you before about where you're headin', right?"

"Yuh."

Gerry downshifted to climb the next hill, so smoothly that you would swear it was an automatic transmission. The steering acted like power, although it wasn't.

He glanced over at Kenny, noticed how the overalls were a little too short and a little too tight, that the Dukes of Hazzard iron-on logo was almost completely worn off the T-shirt. This guy wasn't headed to a business meeting.

"Up here's where I turn off the state road," Gerry pointed. "You can head straight on in to Onlius from here."

"Er-erl. *Erl*," Kenny's stomach insisted.

"Wazzat you?"

"Uh, yeah."

"Ain't had nothin' to eat? Since when?"

"I dunno. This morning."

"Y'in a hurry to get to Onlius?"

Kenny wanted to get his errand over with, but realized he had no idea where to find his cousin once he got to the college. It was late, he might not even be there any more today. He thought he might be getting an invitation to eat.

"You wanna have supper?" Gerry asked.

"Sure." If it weren't for the sadness surrounding this guy, Kenny would've felt like grinning.

Instead, he reached inside the front pocket of his backpack, to touch his tuft of deer fur.

Tin can season

"Hey, Dolly. How are ya? Hello, young fella," Georgette said to Johnny on her way into the Kwik Fill. "Izzat your deer rifle outside?"

"Yeah it is. Like it?"

"Looks like a beauty, but ain't nothin' in season, is there?"

Johnny slid his eyes off Dolly. "Cans," he said in a funny way.

"Whatzat?"

"Cans. Y'know, tin cans?" His eyes creased into a smile.

"Oh yeah. Well, keep practicin', son," she called, as Johnny backed out the door carrying a brown paper bag.

"You don't look so good, Dolly, whatsamatter?"

Dolly held her breath, standing on tiptoe to see over the register through the glass door.

"Is he gone yet?" she whispered.

"Is who gone? That guy with the rifle?"

"Yes. Georgette, he was makin' my skin crawl, I tell ya."

Mrs. Casimir walked carefully to the door, cracked it open, peered out. The rifle was gone, her kids were arguing as usual.

"I'm not positive, but I think so."

"Shew," Dolly exhaled. "What a prick."

"Well, what'd he want?"

"He came in here lookin' for cigarettes, then he was askin' about some kid he's after."

"Kid, what kid?"

"Some kid named Kenny, he said. Some kid who's hitch-hikin' around. I guess I gotta call the police."

"Uh-uh, don't do that," Georgette said. She was afraid that would cause trouble for Kenny.

"Why not?"

"Well, the guy didn't actually do anything, did he? It'll make ya look bad, Dolly."

"Ya think?"

"Yeah, could. You'd need some kinda charges to bring."

"How 'bout harassment?"

"You could try, but d'you remember Lorna gettin' that harassment charge against Night Train?"

"No, never heard of it."

"Well, Night Train was hangin' around the store all the time, sayin' gross things about the X-rated videos and laughin'. She finally got a harassment charge on 'im. You know what the judge said?"

Dolly shrugged.

"The judge told him don't do that no more. That was it, just don't do that no more. And Night Train admitted it, is what I heard. Snickerin' the whole time."

Dolly sagged onto a stool behind the counter. She was still shaky. "I hate this job. I woulda been outta here a long time ago, but Stu says no, 'cause if the mill shuts down . . ."

"I know," Georgette said. "You ain't even gotta say it. Everybody's sayin' the same thing. So listen," she continued, patting Dolly's hand, "just forget about this jerk, he ain't worth the aggravation. Didn't look ta me like he was rowin' with both oars. I got a feelin' he won't be back."

"Goddamn. I hope not."

"Yeah, don't worry. So, lemme pay ya for the gas an' I'll get outta your hair. I think it was thirty-four all together, with the gas cans."

"Says here thirty-three." Dolly winked. "That's a lotta gas in them cans, Georgette, whatcha doin'? Goin' into business mowin' lawns?"

"Naw. Just somethin' Stosh needed, I dunno." Georgette was the one getting nervous now. "I think he said this is about all he needs."

"Aw, that's a shame, you been my best customer."

Georgette noticed that Dolly wasn't breathing so shallowly anymore. "Well, the kids're all out in the car."

"Yep. See ya later."

That was a close one, Georgette thought. *When this is gone, Stosh is gonna have to go someplace else to get the gas for the skidder.*

But first, I got a job for him and Prett.

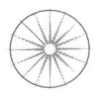

Taking Kenny out

Rough-barked maples, so large that it would take three people holding hands to stretch their way around, lined the east side of the road. Grown for shade and sap, no one had used them for years. Gerry and Kenny drove past a sagging barn, held upright by the memory of being upright. Gerry didn't seem to notice these things as he drove, but Kenny saw them as he stared across the seat of the cab, waiting for Gerry to speak up.

When they pulled into the circular driveway, Gerry took the left side of the loop, and parked the truck in front of the barn.

"We've gotta stop in here for a minute," he said.

Kenny lumbered out the passenger side and circled around behind the truck before following Gerry into the milk-house. It felt cold to him, even though it was so warm outside. The bulk tank had a film of dust on it, as if it hadn't been used in a while.

Gerry swung the barn door open and motioned for Kenny to go in. The smell of calf manure in his nostrils jerked Kenny's head back.

"Raising 'em for veal," Gerry said. Along the far wall were rings pounded into the upright two-by-six studs, each ring with a piece of twine tied to it; at the end of the twine, a calf.

Kenny didn't know a lot about dairy farms, but he thought the stalls near him once had been used for milking cows. "Nice calves," he said.

Gerry snorted. "Yeah, but I wish the price of veal was a little better. The herd buyout's knocked beef prices to shit."

"What's the herd buyout?"

"Federal government's pushing us to sell out milk cows 'cause they say we got too many."

"Zat true?"

"Guess it is, right now. But it ain't gonna do much, in the long run."

"Then why they doin' it?"

"I dunno." Gerry had a long stem of grass dangling from his teeth. "Haven't thought about it much. Prob'ly just another way to push the small boys out."

"Oh." *So this is why he's sad.*

"Better let the cows in," Gerry said, more to himself than Kenny. While the calves milled about, suckling, Gerry still watched, quietly. "Let's get ourselves somethin' to eat," he said, when they were done.

Gerry scuffed his work boots sideways along the edge of the porch steps to make sure he got all the manure off them, then groaned a little as he bent over and untied them. Kenny took his shoes off also, but was afraid his socks were probably pretty ripe after so many days on the road.

He put them back on after Gerry said it was okay.

Supper turned out to be just what Kenny wanted: five peanut butter and jelly sandwiches on white bread (Gerry had four), milk, Oreos, and vegetable-beef soup out of the can. Gerry disappeared for a few minutes after putting the dishes to soak, came back looking scrubbed and with a change of clothes for Kenny. He squinted toward Kenny. He needed glasses, but was afraid they wouldn't look good on him.

"Wanna go watch a baseball game?"

Kenny nodded, trying to match Gerry's look of sadness. He wondered why baseball was such a bad thing.

The Younger Brothers

"Hello, my name is Baxter," Wispen lied, supplying McAdam's first name. "I'm a younger brother."

The air in the hotel-basement conference room hung thick with a moldy smell from the carpet. All the other men in the circle, dressed neatly, most in suits, eyes nervous but focused on the floor at their feet, shifted a little in their chairs to help him feel more comfortable.

"It was a yellow print sundress," he continued, haltingly. "With a little, uh, lace on the sleeves and the, uh, bodice." The others nodded, slowly; a few clenched their teeth to steady their jaws.

"There were . . . are . . . two of them, Michelle and Amanda. It was usually . . . right after school, when my mother was cooking dinner. They wanted to dress me up to shame me in my father's eyes, because they thought he paid more attention to me. They were jealous . . ."

He went on, more steadily as he saw validation in the others' distant gazes: little frilled panties, curled hair, lipstick, rouge, perfume. Blue satin shoes with ribbons. Being forced into his father's study, the aroma of cheap perfume making his father look up from his paper, the humiliation of discovery. The talk of military school.

"When I think about it now, over forty years later, I still feel the shame."

He found himself even more bitter toward the end, not getting the relief he wanted. Still, he knew he'd come back, he felt it sharpening the edge he needed. It was worth the two-hour drive each way.

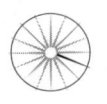

Celeste takes a step back

"I'm telling you, between Gary Hart and Oliver North, they don't know what to do. Celeste? I never got a chance to finish telling you yesterday. You were, you know, uh."

She looked puzzled. She remembered feeling just fine yesterday.

"I can't remember if I told you about Reagan's speech on Ellis Island. Did I?"

She shrugged.

"Well. He's still using that Freedom Fighter label for the Contras, heading right into the hearings."

What did you expect? Celeste couldn't muster the energy to ask.

"He said Nicaragua shouldn't become a partisan firefight. As if the Boland Amendment were partisan."

Celeste was trying to listen, but couldn't keep focused on Reagan. Her father's face kept flashing in front of her, first intermittently, then taking over.

"Wait, it gets worse. Carlucci, you know Carlucci, right? Reagan's National Security Advisor? Carlucci called the Contras 'innocent victims' of the Iranian arms-sales scandals. What a . . . what a . . . I don't know . . ."

Guppy peered over the top of his reading glasses at his wife. He didn't understand what was happening. Ever since the beginning, they'd been able to share moral outrage. Lately Celeste was so distant, he was afraid he had no way to talk to her. There was no safe ground.

"You are coming home," her father said. "You tried, you failed, you're sick now and getting worse, and you're coming home." He was stuffing her things into plastic trash bags, lining them in the hall by the door to her apartment.

Celeste could only see his fingers now, purposely taking apart the space she had tried to make for herself. She could not see his face any longer, nor herself at the time, tugging at her father's arms, pleading with him to stop, dumping some of the bags back out onto the floor.

She also couldn't see her mother, following behind her, methodically repacking them.

On the town

What was the most important thing? Kenny struggled with it, but was having trouble bringing it back. Something about the Happiest Man In the World, after the baseball game, and before the police came to break up the fight, when he and Gerry took off in the truck and went hiding at Blackberry Lake.

No, the hiding was the most frightening part, because Gerry was saying he was going to find that Rye guy and kick his ass, and then he'd laugh about something Jonesy had said; and when Kenny got laughing too and the beams from car headlights looked like they were slowing down and the police were maybe coming, then Gerry would shush him and say, "The cops are gonna bust your ass, Kenny." And then a couple of minutes later he was cursing the guy from Rye.

Maybe that was the most important thing. The guy from Rye whose son had played center field in the game. The father was big, with longish hair that was some brown color you got when you dyed it. And a big, loud mouth, his voice harsh and all up in his nose like he'd had too many orange sodas to drink and had all that snot in his throat. Yelling, *"We got a center fielder!"* every time his son made a play, like there wasn't even a center fielder on the team that Gerry liked from, where was it? He had to keep asking Gerry. Lowmarket, Lowmarket. That was it, that's what Gerry kept telling him.

Then when Gerry's team lost because their center fielder ran in on the ball that was hit over his head, Gerry got really angry. "I was the best center fielder that school ever had," he'd kept saying in the truck driving to the bar in town.

Wait. Maybe it was when Kenny was driving the truck because Gerry said he had to because if Gerry got stopped for another DWI, they'd take his license away. He remembered how to shift from when he'd driven his uncle's John Deere tractor, how you had to push in the clutch with your foot and pull the shift lever through the gears. But the tractor had a throttle you set by hand, and it would stay where you wanted it to, so you didn't have to use your other foot for the gas. He kept telling Gerry that every time he yelled at him. If it weren't for Gerry laughing every once in a while instead of yelling when Kenny hit a mailbox, he would have thrown up. Again.

As if the beers Gerry and Jonesy and his other friend Randall had bought him and made him drink, before they sent him over to ask that lady singer if she would dance, hadn't made him sick to his stomach. He thought he remembered saying to them, "You just wanna make fun of me."

Even after he'd helped get Gerry out of the truck and into the house, sitting up at the kitchen table, his face all flushed and puckered like he could barely keep from crying, picking at the gold flecks in the tabletop with his fingernails, telling about how he took over the farm but lost his family because of it, even then Kenny could barely pay attention to what he was saying, he was still so sick from the beer and the driving, and the hiding out, oh, and the bar fight. But he did remember that there was something important he had learned tonight, that he didn't want to forget. *But what was it?*

It seemed like it was before the fight that began when the Rye guy showed up at the bar with some buddies and started mouthing off again about the game. Jonesy was mimicking him and making Gerry laugh, but Randall looked nervous, peeling all the labels off the Labatts Blues and watching the bigmouth. The song the bigmouth played on the jukebox really got to Gerry. *What was it? Oh yeah, "All My Exes Live in Texas,"* but it wasn't until the guy yelled something about his kid that the fight started.

Kenny tried to roll onto his back on the sofa, hoping he could take his hand off the floor without the room spinning.

Boy, that was a sad story about Gerry running away from home, thinking he was gonna hafta go to Canada to get out of being drafted.

Kenny thought about Johnny Percy and shuddered.

It was nice that he was the kind of man to keep a bull calf around for so long just because his dad wanted him to, even though it cost so much to feed it. What had he called it? John Calvin maybe? Too bad Gerry's father never said why he changed so much while Gerry was gone. Too bad Gerry thought he was the one who made everything bad on the farm.

The Happiest Man In the World. That's what Jonesy'd called the other guy, the dancer. You just had to stare at him, out there on the floor spinning around and prancing. Randall had started to say something to make fun of the guy and Gerry'd laughed like he thought it was funny, but kinda quiet, too quiet for it to be real.

Kenny smiled all over again, thinking about the Happiest Man in the World dancing with his wife, them grinning so hard at each other that you just knew they were still crazy for each other, even though they were both heavy and his hair was thin and hers was gray in places. It looked like they were both in their forties, about the same age as Kenny's parents when his mom went to the Home.

Oh yeah, that was the most important thing. What Jonesy said that explained why Gerry was sad, about his wife leaving him and taking their kids because he was so moody. It was when they were watching the Happiest Man in the World. Jonesy said, "He's got his family, that's why he's happy."

The more he thought about it, the more he thought it was true, and the harder it was to sleep. He rolled back on his side and put his hand on the floor again to steady himself.

CIA Director William Casey* on Herman Wispen

What do I think of Dean Wispen's activities on behalf of the college? On balance he's okay, but something is missing.

He impresses me as a very diligent individual, well aware of the value of subterfuge, and absolute control of the operation.

Wispen knows what all good operatives know: certain people are expendable for the greater good. There are those who would undermine America by insisting we always play by the rules. Well, I can tell you it's not always possible to do that.

They complained about those eighty people who were killed by the car bomb, the one planted to assassinate the Hezbollah terrorist. Those kinds of things happen, they come with the territory. It's not my fault they were innocent.

If there's any weakness in Wispen, it's that he's not willing to take one for the team. I get the impression he lacks the essential virtue of total unquestioning loyalty to the directive, especially if it means he's got to be the expendable one.

I don't know. I can't see it with Wispen.

---

*William Casey was diagnosed with brain cancer in 1986 and died before the Iran-Contra hearings could uncover how much he knew about President Reagan's involvement with the scandal.

Chapter Six

Kenny Takes His Shot

Kenny and Madonna, sittin' in a tree

Kenny had to get up four times in the night to drink water, each time feeling drunk again and dropping back into fitful sleep. The last trip, Gerry passed him on the way back from the kitchen, heading toward the bathroom, in a hurry.

"You have just got to be the most cutest boy I've ever laid eyes on," the blonde lady in the red spangled jumpsuit said to Kenny.

"Yuh," Kenny replied.

"And the nicest."

"You're real nice, too."

"Why thank you. And the most sweetest."

Kenny smiled a casual smile and looked into her eyes. "You got eyes the same as a bird's egg, the ones in the spring that you find under trees, kinda broke on the ground."

"Oh, Kenny, you mean a robin's egg? Why they're so beautiful."

"Yuh." Kenny didn't know where to look at her. Her teeth sparkled white, her eyes sparkled blue, her shirt sparkled red. She had a voice that made him tremble, especially when she was saying she needed him.

"It's so lonely on the road, Kenny. A different town every night, and always men looking at me, wanting to dance and afterward, you know, trying to force me to be with them. It's awful."

"Yuh. I guess." Kenny leaned back in his chair, crossed his legs, smiling, he thought, like James Bond in a movie.

"And you are the first man to really appreciate me, who would never take advantage of me."

"Uh, yeah, no." Kenny tried to stop looking down the vee of her top. Her hand on his leg, just inside and above his knee, was driving him wild.

"Kenny, I've got a question for you." The sweet sadness in Madonna's voice turned him around, made him gaze deeply into her eyes. "Kenny, meeting you was the best thing that ever happened to me. The money, the fame, all those men, none of those things have made me happy. But finding you, that has made me happy."

"Madonna, honey, you're not the way people talk about you. You're really swell. What did you wanna ask me about?"

"Could I stay with you?"

Kenny's face twitched. He turned slightly away.

"I'm sorry, I've pushed you into something you're not ready for. It's just that I've been unhappy for so long." She watched Kenny, who was silent, looking down at the sawdust on the bar floor.

What would Aurelia say? he was thinking. There was probably enough room for Madonna in his bedroom, but if she didn't like tuna fish or stayed in the bathroom too long or used too much toilet paper, Aurelia would be on his case.

"Tap, tap, tap," he heard. "Tap, tap." Madonna disappeared from his dream, replaced by a voice saying "Mr. Scott? This is the sheriff. We'd like to talk with you please."

Kenny pulled on his clothes and fled past the front door before Gerry opened it. He listened behind the closed kitchen door just long enough to hear Gerry answering questions about where he was last night and when he got home, before he panicked and sneaked out the cellar door. By the time Gerry started calling him to talk with the police, Kenny was crouched behind the stone wall beyond the barn, hiding.

Darcardt in the open

Driving sheets of rain swept in off the lake, chasing people from doorway to doorway. Darcardt felt it deeper than dampness, like a chill settling into marrow. He gazed, sad-eyed, out from the eaves of the entrance to the Research Center across the Commons toward the Hayslee Building.

"Charles, would you like to share my umbrella?" Guppy asked. Harlan sighed audibly because he had not offered first.

You're going to have to get over this infatuation, Guppy thought. *He's not God. Besides, he's retiring.*

"Charles? Do you have an exam? Do you have to go to LaRue?" Darcardt nodded but did not speak.

"I have an umbrella as well, Dr. Darcardt. I'd be happy to share mine." Harlan angled his open umbrella out into the rain, feeling underestimated. Some raindrops spattered off the vinyl onto Darcardt.

"I didn't realize it was raining so hard," Harlan apologized. Darcardt wore the same look, unaffected by the raindrops dripping from his glasses onto his cheeks.

"Uh-hem. Uh, Charles? Are you all right?" Guppy asked.

"Let's go. We might as well. We can't stop it," Darcardt said. He stepped out into the rain quickly, both Harlan and Guppy lunging after to hold an umbrella for him.

"It's going to get you, too, you know," Darcardt said to Guppy.

"Pardon me, Charlie, but I've got this umbrella."

"You can try to protect yourself, but you can't really. You're only fooling yourselves."

Guppy and Harlan exchanged quizzical glances behind Darcardt's back.

"There's no use pretending, Ernest. There's nothing to be gained from it. Neither for you, John," he added, stopping and looking directly at Harlan, who reached his umbrella over to cover Darcardt, leaving the rain to splash on himself.

"That's right, John. I knew you'd understand."

Harlan's hair stuck matted to his scalp, rain running down inside the back of his shirt. Darcardt swiveled his head in Guppy's direction. "You see, it's no use, Ernest."

"Sorry, Charlie, but I'm not following you. Are you talking about the rain? The umbrella?"

Darcardt nodded. Harlan stepped in under his umbrella. Darcardt stepped out, turned and walked on toward Hayslee.

"Charlie! Charlie!" Guppy called. "There's no need for you to get soaked."

"I want to get used to it," Darcardt said, looking straight ahead.

"But why?"

"Because I want to be prepared. I want to know what it's going to be like."

"What are you talking about?"

Darcardt stopped, glared at Harlan. "Tell him, John."

Harlan looked back and forth from Guppy's puzzled expression to Darcardt.

"You don't know either, do you?" Darcardt said toward Harlan's cheek. "You two had better wake up."

Harlan lowered his umbrella and closed it. As the rain poured down over him, Darcardt smiled. "You're getting used to it." When he turned around again, Harlan shrugged his shoulders at Guppy, bewildered.

"Someone's got to tell them after I'm gone," Darcardt said. "They deserve to know."

"Know what? About the rain?"

Darcardt wheeled around. "It's the market, man. The market. Just like the rain. It'll get us all. By the time the bastards are done, no one will be safe. Well. Almost no one."

Harlan chewed on his lower lip, pondering. He was thinking he might understand. "Are you talking about the end of government regulation?"

"Smart lad," Darcardt replied.

"And how, one by one, groups of people are being turned back into the competition?"

"Labor . . . the poor . . . farmers . . . students. That's why you've got to tell them. They need to know."

"The elderly are losing it, too . . . small businesses," Harlan added.

Guppy held his umbrella in both hands over his head, glancing back and forth from Harlan to Darcardt in disbelief. *They both have water on the brain.*

"John understands. Let me show you, Ernest," Darcardt offered. He reached into his pants pocket, selecting a penknife from among the key chain and coins. Opening up the blade and motioning with it, he said, "This is supply-side economics."

He reached toward Guppy's umbrella with his left hand. "Ernest, let me borrow your New Deal for a moment." Darcardt tilted the umbrella down in front of him, and his face up into the rain. "This wet stuff is the market."

Guppy and Harlan stood with heads uncovered in the driving rain, watching Darcardt slit panels of fabric off the frame of Guppy's umbrella. "This is the cutbacks in student aid," he said. Then, "Social Security," as he carved off another piece. "Farm supports.

"Unemployment insurance.

"Health care."

By the time they reached the entrance to LaRue, only three panels were left. Darcardt pushed in the release and slid the knob down, shaking rainwater from what was left. "Use this umbrella when you're walking with Koemover, Wispen, or any of those lapdogs. You stay under the three panels that are left. If they ask, tell them they're for the military, the big corporations, and the science sellouts." Darcardt shook for an instant, water flying off him like from a cocker spaniel.

"Have a nice day," he said, before he walked away to his class.

Harlan snorted.

Guppy stood grinding his teeth.

Not the happiest man

"Where the hell did the kid go?" Gerry asked the empty house after the deputy sheriff left.

It was too quiet again. He turned on the radio while he ate a bowl of cereal.

Bono sang "and I still haven't found what I'm looking for."

Gerry turned the radio off, chewed in silence.

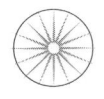

Kenny in the open

The gravel on the edges of the road was mushy, laced with puddles. He'd waited under a rotted fence-line elm for what seemed like hours after the police left, and after Gerry drove his truck off to work, before he thought it was safe to come out from behind the stone wall. Kenny had been thinking of how hungry he was when the rain hit. There was nothing he could do but keep moving, neck hunched into his shoulders, head bare beneath the storm.

Johnny on a parallel

"Fucking monsoon."

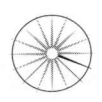

Celeste assesses

What to do with herself once she finished the last chore of the morning? The household detergents were all in their places on the contact paper under the sink, arrayed from violet to yellow, their bases perfectly aligned in their magic-marker circles and ovals. The vacuum-cleaner bag was dumped out, whisked clean. Celeste watched the dryer dial shudder toward zero, waiting for the buzzer. When she realized that ironing sheets would not carry her far past eleven, she felt the tightening of her ribcage around the lungs. She would have to tackle one of the big projects: the garage, the basement, or the attic. Each had an aspect of dread—the basement was chilly, the attic made her feel dizzy, and she would have to go outside to get to the garage. Maybe the rain would help. Maybe it could blur the lines between what was inside, hers, and outside, not hers.

Johnny's commie connections

Johnny was soaking wet, exhausted. Kenny's trail had been cold for over a day. He decided to stop at an army buddy's house for a while. Sometimes the only people he could talk to with any kind of control were other Vietnam vets.

"Hey, hey, Randall. Whatcha been up to?" Johnny called, catching him out in his garage grinding a car fender.

"Johnny P. What the hell you up to?"

"Bummin', Randall, just bummin'."

"Ya look burnt, man. Like ya been rode hard an' put away wet."

"Well, I got caught out in it this mornin'. Ya know how it is when it's rainin', won't nobody stop, an' the shits are even worse 'n usual."

"Had breakfast?"

"Cup o' coffee and some Little Debbies."

"Hungry?"

"Naw. Just need to dry out."

"Sure thing, man. Pull up by the stove."

Johnny pulled himself out of his poncho, squatted on a molded plastic lawn chair, unlaced his boots.

"You doin' okay with this business?" he asked.

"Yeah, pretty much."

"Still not payin' Uncle Sam?"

Randall grinned. "I pay him some."

"Yeah." Johnny pulled his pack of Camels out of his shirt pocket, teased one up to his lips. "Ya want one o' these?" he offered Randall.

"Camels? Whyn'tcha just light up one o' them oily rags over there?"

"I know. They didn't have none o' my Marlboros left at the store. These are my old man's brand."

"Your old man? How's he doin'?"

"Okay, I guess. Still got that farm down in the Southern Tier, over by Olean."

"Is it in Olean?"

"Naw, just east, outside a little town." Johnny's voice trailed off.

"What little town? I kinda know that area."

Johnny muttered something.

"What?"

"Cuba, I said. My old man lives just outside of Cuba."

Randall smiled a little. "He got a lotta commie friends?"

"Fuck you."

"Hey, relax." Randall glared at him. "You gotta chill, man. You're too wound." He worked in silence for a few minutes, letting Johnny soak up the heat.

"Your old man milkin' cows?" Randall asked disinterestedly.

"Yeah, some. Raisin' beans, too."

"Beans?"

"Somethin' new, I guess." Johnny was relaxing now, the warmth from the stove settling over him. He closed his eyes, trying to picture tiny green sprouts peeking up out of the earth.

"You been helping him?

"Naw, still hangin' around, collecting disability."

"D'you get much?"

"Me, naw. Don't need that much."

"Where ya livin'?"

"Here an' there."

Randall started to pull his mask back up over his nose and mouth, then sighed and pulled it completely off his head. "Hey, J.P., you wanna beer? I gotta try the hair o' the dog, man."

"You shittin' me? This early?"

"Yeah," Randall chuckled. "I was hangin' out late with a coupla buddies from around here down at this bar in Rye. We're buyin' beers for this kid that was with us. Hey, d'you know Gerry Scott?"

"Doesn't sound familiar. Is he the kid?"

"Uh-uh. He's a coupla years younger than us. Took over his old man's farm."

"He go to Nam?"

"Naw. But anyway," Randall laughed again, "this kid with Gerry was a real piece o' work. You shoulda seen him tryin' to put the moves on this singer. He almost puked on her."

"Who is this kid?"

"I dunno. Just some kid named Kenny that Gerry picked up hitchin'. Hey, you want that beer or not?"

Johnny had pulled his boots back on, started lacing them up. "Nope. I gotta get goin'. You think I could talk to your buddy Gerry about those beans?"

"Guess so, but I don't think he's growin' 'em. He's still got cows. But for veal."

"But still."

"Sure. He's over on the Sand Road, offa Route 932, back down by where they put those powerlines through. Only workin' farm on the road still, I think."

"Thanks, Randall. Catch ya later."

"Yeah, I hope ya find what ya need. You know, J.P.," Randall said gently, "it'd be good for you to raise something. Give you somethin' to do."

"Yeah, raisin' somethin', I'll think about that."

Prett and Stosh get deputized

"We c'n only do this lookin' around for the bad boy today," Stosh had insisted. "Me an' Prett're movin' the skidder pretty soon so they don't catch up to us."

"Well, it's raining, so it's a good day to stay out of the woods," Georgette had insisted.

"Som'times it's better for us to move the skidder when they's not a lotta people out."

Georgette didn't respond. She was sliding her thumbnail up and down between her front teeth, thinking. "Would you lose a lot if you just moved it now while it's raining?"

"Mebbe half a truckload." Now Stosh was weighing the odds, trying to get the rest of the trees out from this patch of state land as opposed to moving the equipment with less fear of being caught.

"They'll be harder to cut in the rain," Prett observed, always in favor of the cautious route.

"Okay, okay. We move the skidder, then we see if we can find Jettie's bad boy."

Georgette emptied the last of the coffeepot into Stosh's mug. "Just be real careful, he's carryin' a deer rifle."

Stosh grinned. "Prett, it's not deer season. If we catch him an' take the gun, an' we're leaving some trees behind, mebbe they make us D.E.C." Stosh laughed again and scratched his sideburns. "Mebbe," he wanted to hear his joke again, "we be D.E.C."

Zola loves Lloyd

"Zola May," Marie Earhart asked, "do you know anything about that party at Ernest Guppy's house after the retirement dinner?"

Zola jumped in her seat a little, startled because Marie's question was about something other than work. It took her a few seconds to respond.

"Um, yeah, I heard there was going to be a party this Thursday."

I wonder if Guppy's invited her, Marie thought. *He's so thoughtless.* "It is right after the dinner, isn't it?"

Didn't he invite her? Zola May was thinking. *What a dork.* "I think it is, Dr. Earhart, but I haven't heard much."

I knew it, Marie thought. *He didn't ask her.* "Well, I'll put a note in his mailbox. Thanks, Zola May."

"No problem." *Guppy, you pig.* "If I hear anything, I'll let you know."

"I'd appreciate that. So, is everything going okay for you?" Marie felt warmed to the conversation.

Kenny Takes His Shot / 147

Zola was worried. "Okay about what?"

Marie tucked a loose strand of hair behind her ear. "Oh, you know, your new life."

"Oh, you mean," Zola smiled, relieved, "being married?"

"Well, I don't mean to be intrusive."

Zola paused, reflecting. "It's going okay."

"Good. You looked so happy at the reception, dancing with Lloyd."

"Lyle," Zola suggested. "Well, I was happy . . . I mean I am happy. Being married has helped."

"Oh yeah. Really?" Marie was looking at Zola like she was seeing her for the first time, actually looking into her eyes as if she were expecting to find another person there.

"Yeah." Zola began to feel a warmth radiating from inside, the way she felt making love with Lyle. She started to drift on it.

"What's different?" Marie asked.

"What?" It looked to Zola like Earhart was studying her. There was a sadness in Earhart's eyes, as if she were seeing the light of a distant star dim. *What can I tell her?* "I, uh . . . feel more settled, I guess."

Marie's eyes widened, the way they would look if she were on the other side of a magnifying glass. "Great, Zola, good." She turned to go back to her office. "Maybe I'll see you, at Guppy's house?"

"Yeah, I hope so." The warm feeling returned. Zola smiled.

"And you are bringing Lloyd, right?" Earhart smiled back.

"Yeah. I'm bringing Lloyd."

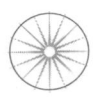

Kenny crosses the line

The pounding rain gradually eased to a steady drizzle, the grayness to the east swallowing the dark cumulus. Kenny kept glancing back through the trees for signs of clearing, and also for fear that the sheriff would circle back.

He needed to get to the state road heading west toward Pope Creek, then up to New Canada, and finally Onlius. Yesterday's scraps of memory from his ride with Gerry to the baseball game in Red Swamp weren't any help, mixed up with the scramble toward Blackberry Lake after the bar fight in Hamilton, not to mention that he was headed in the wrong direction.

Kenny had watched the county sheriff back out the driveway, start to head south, then do a three-point turn to get back onto pavement. He realized that the muddy back road, with the woods to retreat into, would be his best chance to avoid being caught.

Even louder than the rain rippling through new maple leaves and smacking onto the muddied dirt road, was the crackling sound overhead as Kenny walked under the power lines. It made him duck and wince, sounding over and over like the beginning note of a sky-ripping peal of thunder.

He thought he could smell something burning, like sulfur or plastic, the freshness in the air vanishing. The clear-cut beneath the power lines felt empty of life. Even the rain seemed dead. Kenny hurried across as quickly as he could.

Harlan attempts association

Guppy leaned back in his chair, casually glancing over the rectangle of uncluttered space that was his desk at Harlan frantically leafing through manila file folders that held pages of photocopied testimony of Vietnam veterans. *Looks like he's obsessing again.*

Where is it? I know I had it. One quote Harlan remembered reading months ago had haunted him since he'd first seen it, knowing it was significant but unsure at the time just why. Now that he knew the insight, he couldn't unearth the quote.

"A-hem." Guppy waited for Harlan to look up. "What're you doing for lunch?"

"Hadn't thought about it," Harlan muttered.

"Well, if you'd like to take a break, get out of here, let me know."

"Okay," Harlan sighed. "I'll let you know." He kept searching file folders.

Don't do me any favors, Guppy thought. Scanning down the roster of students for his last class, Public Administration, he realized the most it would take would be forty-five minutes. It was ten-thirty, and if Harlan wasn't in a mood to go to lunch he could end up with nothing to do, lost in his thoughts. The image of Celeste's raw, blistered hands surfaced.

"Well, I'm definitely going off-campus, so what's it going to be?"

Harlan heaved a sigh, said "What?," then, "Oh, yeah. I'll be done in about a half-hour, I guess."

"Good." *I hope he doesn't mind waiting if he finishes before me,* Guppy, the time-manager, thought.

Horace goes downstream

Horace held his cigarette an inch away from his lips, that odd way he had of smoking. The ash had burned almost back to his fingers—the middle and ring fingers—his smoking hand being the one without an index finger. The way he stood so close to the window, Cough swore Horace was only getting secondary smoke off the glass.

Brackish brown water stretched wide and almost calm into the northeast corner of Horace's window. The water that had reached the southeast corner roiled frothy on its path over the spillway and down onto the rocks at the base of the dam. Today it had a larger pulse because of the rain that had come in from the west, off the lake, adding to the Adirondack snowmelt pouring downriver from the east.

It was soothing to watch the water spill over the dam, just the way it had done for over a century, powering the mill. Every change Horace had witnessed in his forty-two years of work there—most for the worse, he thought—had not taken away the basic fact that it was waterpower that had built the mill, and the town. Horace wondered who owned that now that the mill was changing hands, being phased out and moved overseas.

"Ow." The cigarette had burned back to the scar tissue on his fingers, snapping Horace out of his thoughts. He couldn't put it off any longer, he might as well go to the office to pick up the new list of layoffs so he could post it on the board before he left. He hated getting the list, hated himself for posting it so that no one would see it until after he'd gone home. But he hated it even more when he had to look people in the eye when they'd just lost their jobs.

He did not sneak out when he was first given the duty of posting the list, because he'd thought it was important to let his workers know how bad he felt. But once the rumors started to fly about the mill closing down, Horace was told that he couldn't ask them about coming back any more. Recently he had become superstitious about even looking at the list, after seeing his best friend's name on it.

Something told him he needed to check it out this time, so he scanned down it, seeing NiClay, Edgar and just below it Pattell, Horace. What the hell? He read the heading again. Notice of Layoff in Two Weeks.

The sons of bitches. After all the dirty work I've done for them over the years, to leave me out in the cold.

There had to be something he could do to keep his job, but he couldn't figure out what. Horace decided to hold onto the list until the noon break and read it aloud. And he decided to go put a bug in Cough's ear right then and there about the water rights to the mill dam.

Johnny, strung along

There was no one at Gerry Scott's farm when Johnny got there. He nosed around in the house, finding only one sign that Kenny might have been there: a ball of string that looked like the one he remembered seeing in Kenny's backpack.

His guess that Kenny might still be on foot, and likely headed in the wrong direction, paid off when Johnny picked up some large sneaker tracks about a quarter mile down the wet gravel road. The prospect of catching up to Kenny ratcheted up his senses and his feverishness, and blunted his exhaustion.

He'd know soon which side Kenny was on.

Prett has the right-of-way

Stosh and Prett had moved the skidder home under cover of driving rain, and figured they might as well scout out more places to cut.

The power line right-of-way that started in New Canada and cut east toward Utica had been the bane of every property owner along the right-of-way, giving the power companies the right to spray herbicide, leaving brush, briars and anxiety in its wake. Roads built to service the line opened access for snowmobilers, all-terrain vehicles, poachers, and illicit garbage haulers to trespass and spoil what was left. Highschool beer parties in the summer under the lines always resulted in more trash as well as fear of the campfire not quite extinguished, the cigarette butt carelessly flicked away.

Security patrols along the road were much less frequent this year because the utilities were investing more in their aging nuclear plants, to help in the campaign to get a newer nuke on line, to get its growing cost overrun onto customers' bills rather than against stockholder dividends.

Stosh and Prett idled the half-ton onto the powerline road, peering through the fogged window for hardwoods, POSTED signs, and best of all—realtors' signs, near the edge of the right-of-way. They crossed the line from Maryston into Lowmarket without knowing it, Stosh scribbling down, on the back of a receipt from Halifax Lumber Company, promising locations.

"Prett, the roads're gettin' too close together, an' these maples are awful scrawny."

"Yeah, Stosh. I ain' seein' no ash or cherry no more."

"Well, we're goin' away from the big woods, y'know. Headin' toward the city."

"What city? Syr'cuse?"

"No, no. Don' you know where you are? Onlius. We're gettin' closer to Onlius."

"Let's go home, Stosh. I don' wanna go no farther." Prett had only been in Onlius once, taking care of a jury-duty notice that had come for Little Prett after he'd gotten his driver's license. Prett had passed out in the county building when two sheriffs got in the elevator with him on the second floor.

"One more stretch, Prett. Then we go look for Jettie's bad boy."

"I don' wanna, Stosh. Let's go home."

"What ya 'fraid of, Prett. Not the bad boy's rifle?"

Prett glared. He worked his mouth a few seconds before answering. "Ya oughtta know better, Stosh, than ta say somethin' like that. I want the rifle."

"What ya worried 'bout then?" Stosh already knew, but couldn't resist tormenting it out of him.

"Don' wanna run into no law." Prett squinted his eyes straight ahead, worked his jaw in a quick, mincing sulk.

"What's wrong with the law?"

Prett stuck his tongue in his cheek, staring straight ahead.

"You gotta problem with the law, Prett?" Stosh grinned at him.

Prett's eyes narrowed even more. He was thinking about that brief time when he'd been drafted and was in Army boot camp, and woke up once from a wet dream to see the drill sergeant and all the other guys in his barracks staring at him. They were all dressed in full uniform. Prett hadn't been able to even see someone in uniform on TV ever since.

Stosh was growing bored with bothering him. "We'll only go up ta the next road, crossin' the line. Okay."

Prett worked the truck over the construction road by straddling the left tire rut, rainwater sluicing up to the crankcase. Once they cleared the rise and started down the slope that crossed Sand Road, he was relieved. As soon as the truck tires reached the gravel, Prett turned left and gunned the truck, breathing easier that it wasn't paved, and that he was getting away from Onlius.

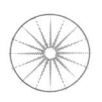

Kenny dodges dissociation

Kenny kept to the back road from Gerry's house, picking up the pace because he kept feeling he was being watched.

Who'd know where I am? I don't even know where I am.

He started to trot, looking back over his shoulder. Misjudging a mud puddle, Kenny's foot fell into the middle of it, sending him tripping and then rolling into the gravel.

Kenny jumped up, tried to sprint again, thought he saw a figure duck behind a roadside apple tree. He turned around and saw only the fresh blossoms, smelled their indescribably fresh sweetness. Then a familiar voice, one he had not heard in a long time, started shouting in his head, *You run side to side, Kenny! Run side to side!* He zig-zagged as he ran, like he'd seen on spy movies, with his dead father's voice in his head.

Johnny's takeout order

Everywhere it was green. And wet. Johnny, so tired, had been out on the road for days. He had lost track of where his base was, and his nerves were beyond frayed.

"What's that crazy bastard doing?" he said to himself, standing straight up with just the barrel leaning against the apple tree, to steady it, to steady him.

He thought about letting the gook get away, letting him run until he disappeared around the next bend in the road.

But he remembered Randall's story about the gook kid he'd let get away because he didn't want to shoot him in the back. The next thing they knew, they were in a firefight. The lieutenant told them never to let that happen again.

Where's the rest of my patrol?

Kenny had almost reached the bend that would take him out of sight, still weaving as he ran.

Johnny cleared all thoughts from his mind, squinted down the sight, and squeezed the trigger. As he watched the gook yelp, pitch forward and spill off the road into the ditch, he thought again how it never made him feel any better.

Kenny sees his father

"That's when it gets serious, son. That's when life gets real, in a hurry."

"Did that happen to you a lot, Dad?"

"What's that, Kenny?"

"You know, gettin' shot at?"

"More than once, Kenny, and once is too many. I hope you never have to worry about it."

Kenny was seven years old, getting a talking-to for poking a neighbor kid with a stick, pretend-playing it was a bayonet. The neighbor kid started it. The neighbor kids always did.

"Did you ever get shot, for real?"

"No." Wiley turned quiet, his eyes seeing something from a long time ago. "Not by a bullet. What would make you think that?"

"Mom said you got hurt when you were a soldier."

"I did, Kenny, but not in the war. I never got shot. I got hurt back in the States."

"Oh."

Kenny really couldn't tell the other kids any more that his dad was a hero in the war, since it wasn't even in Korea where he'd gotten so sick that now he probably was going to die.

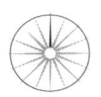

Harlan takes a drink

Harlan had no exams the rest of the day. He'd gone home late morning to settle in for the long haul. Already he was surrounded by piles of essay booklets and deli wrappers of food. The answering machine was on. Everything was set.

And Harlan was stuck.

He started out well, finishing the last late papers from the comparative politics class. Then he hit up against US foreign policy, and the sheer jingoism of the essays threw a chill on him. The Reagan presidency had taken its toll, it was clear, despite his efforts.

Harlan thought about Darcardt's articles, the ones he had read in graduate school, the kind of scholarship that made him want to teach at Onlius State. "The Periphery Within." "Caesar's Due: The Pacification Campaign in the Philippines in Imperial Perspective." And Harlan's favorite, "The Limits of the Stick: Military Buildup Backfires." That was the kind of work he had thought he'd be doing, not reading thinly researched essays that glossed over a shortsighted realpolitik.

Where do they get this stuff? Reflecting on his reading list, the discussions in class, what he knew about Guppy's and Earhart's methods, he couldn't figure it out. He slipped back into a graduate school conservation.

"It's the culture, man. You can't fight the culture. Don't even try," Cornelius said. *"Mythos over logos, every time, baby."*

"They can't be that gullible," Harlan replied. *"You make it sound like all they know is the last thing they saw on TV. My students think for themselves."*

Cornelius pulled from his backpack a photocopied picture of a blindfolded sheep. He waved it in front of Harlan. "I just handed this out to my class and told them it was the American voter." He grinned.

"Who's the shepherd, then?"

"What?" The grin wavered.

"Let's say you're right about the voters. So what? My question is, who's leading the flock?"

A third grad student, Alison Fargo, had been listening quietly, smiling affectionately. "Well, Cornelius, I think John's got you there. It's Marcuse. You've got to see not only the facts, but the factors behind the facts."

Cornelius scowled, sliding the photocopy into his backpack. John was glad Alison had said it, because her optimism was so infectious that Cornelius would have a hard time dismissing her and going off into a funk.

"Hey, don't put that away. I'd like a copy," John asked. "I can use it to get my class thinking about blindfolds."

Cornelius shook his head.

"Oh, come on now, Neal. Give John a copy so we can get back to studying." Samir was even more anxious about the comps than the rest. His student visa was riding on passing the exams, staying in the program. And since losing his visa would mean going back to Iraq, it could mean his life.

"Yes, Neal. Do give John a copy," Alison said. "But you know, Samir, John's question helps with studying for the comps. A well-thought-out discussion of the motive forces behind voter behavior could work in every sub-field."

"If it's couched in the literature of the sub-field. That's what we should be talking about," Samir insisted.

"Sounds good to me," Harlan said.

Cornelius leaned back in his chair, arcing his hand around the windowless study lounge. "I don't have a problem with it," he said, then looking directly at Samir, "in the context of the literature. However . . ." he tilted his head back and rolled his eyes to the ceiling, reflecting, "beyond preparing for the comps, it'll be a waste." He held the picture in front of Harlan again. "The best we can expect from teaching is to get them to recognize themselves, because even if they start to see what's behind it all, it'll only be dangerous for them."

Alison was confused. "Dangerous? How so?"

"Suppose they think they can study it, ask questions, maybe even teach it when they're ready to teach?"

"So what? Where are you going with this?"

Cornelius's eyes widened. "You're serious? You really think this is all about getting them to ask questions?"

"Well. Yes."

Cornelius frowned, then laughed, then shook his head. He dropped the picture on the conference table. "So what'll you do when they start questioning your authority?"

"I'll tell 'em they're on the right track."

"And you want to teach, right?"

"Right."

"So let me ask you this. When your students start to question the university, and you don't have tenure, or you're up for a promotion, you're going to applaud them?"

Harlan paused for a telling moment. "I hope so."

"You hope? You're not sure?"

Now Harlan was scowling. Alison and Samir were waiting for him to answer, embarrassed at how Cornelius was pressing him.

"I see myself encouraging my students to be critical, yes."

"Even if it screws their chance of getting jobs?"

"I'd tell them that could happen."

"And if that threatens your job?"

"I'd have to weigh the risks against the issue."

"Oh, so you might draw the line on some things?"

"Yes."

"And if you thought some information might get your students in trouble, would you keep it from them?"

"Like what?"

"Like, say, information that could adversely affect your chances for tenure?"

"Well, I'm not stupid."

"Right." Cornelius picked up the photocopy and studied it. "Okay, I'll let you have a copy, but you've got to promise me something."

"What's that?"

"Oh, no. Promise first."

"I'm not going to promise until I know what it is."

"Okay, then. You've got to tell your class you might be the one putting on their blindfolds. Okay?"

Harlan's mouth suddenly tasted bitter. He let his hand return to the tabletop, even though Cornelius was pushing the picture toward him. He thought about pointing out he'd answered that way because he'd grown up poor. But when he looked up from his fidgeting hands into Cornelius's sardonic eyes, he knew it would be useless to explain.

"Let's get back to the exams, huh?" Samir said softly.

Harlan kept his eyes on his notebook, until he was sure Cornelius had put the photocopy away. He wondered if hemlock tasted the same whether you were forced to drink it or not.

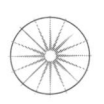

Kenny checks out

He stayed curled up in a ball in the ditch for a long time. After he heard footsteps sucking faintly in the mud on the road, after hearing the truck pull up and people arguing, and long after hearing the truck rumble by and fade off up the road. He listened to his heart pump, pump, pump and air moving into and out of his lungs.

Robins called to each other.

Kenny gently increased his breathing, tensed and released the muscles in his legs, arms and back, felt with his nerves for signs of where he'd taken a slug. Besides being sore, he didn't feel anything wrong.

He uncurled himself and sat up. He was drenched in sweat and rain, but he was all right. He had heard the gunshot, felt the sudden pressure against his spine, so sharp it had knocked him over, but no bullet had entered him.

Kenny slipped his backpack from his shoulders, dropped it to the ground, and pulled his jacket off. There wasn't a hole in it. Had he dreamed the whole thing?

He turned the backpack over and that was when he saw the gaping hole. He stuck two fingers through it into the front pocket. His head began to feel light. Inside the pocket he found the slug had pulled the deer fur through the main pouch, before it had gotten buried in his Cub Scout manual.

Kenny's eyelids fluttered back. He fainted.

Johnny in captivity

"Hey, stop that bangin' aroun'. I don' wanna hafta send Prett back there." It got quieter in the truck bed. Prett and Stosh giggled at each other.

"Squee-hee-heel, pig," Stosh chortled. "Squee-heel."

"Sh-hush, Stosh. Don' let him know we're funnin', from that movie."

"That's pretty good, Prett, from the banjo movie. How'd you remember that?"

Prett snorted chunks of laughter out his nostrils. "It's the best part, the funny part. I been always wantin' to fun with that."

Stosh's smile faded. He rode the rest of the way as quietly as Johnny Percy did, tied up in the back of the truck.

Kenny answers a question

"You're a dummy. Whatcha gonna do now, dummy?" It was a voice from years ago, elementary school, the body connected to the voice sitting atop him on the playground. Other voices calling him dummy were above him and behind his head.

He could feel the dampness of the earth against the back of his head, the weight across his hips, pinning him down.

"Whatcha gonna do now, dummy?"

This time the voice did not belong to the bully who'd knocked him down, Ronald McDoney. It was deeper, huskier, a larger part of his memory.

He saw Cough checking his progress without appearing to be watching him, the foreman shaking his head. Kenny had not lasted half a day at the mill.

The weight shifted to his shoulder, casket against his neck, dampness on his cheeks, chin and chest. It was the same voice, same question as he watched his father being lowered into the ground.

Wet leaves stirred from the ground as the wind grew. They slapped against Kenny's face. He opened his eyes, saw thin maples and birch and poplar reaching up to a retreating blue sky.

Now fully conscious, lying on his back in the woods on the edge of Sand Road, he heard the same question, same voice. When he realized why it was so familiar, he did not smile. Instead he rose to his feet to get back onto the road, to begin answering himself.

Harlan bites off more . . .

The first glass of wine was to take the edge off, the second because the first wasn't enough. Harlan got dreamy, sleepwalked through a batch of papers. He felt good reaching the end, celebrating with a sandwich and another glass of wine. The third essay into the next pile he drifted into sleep, leaning back in the recliner.

"Go ahead," Samir coaxed. "You can do more, I know you can."

"You're not even close to being done," Cornelius said. He held up a copy of Poulantzas.

Harlan was gagging, his mouth and throat were raw. He glanced over at Alison for support, or at least sympathy. She returned a look that said she knew exactly what he was feeling.

A library clerk arrived at the door of the study carrel with a fresh load of books. He tilted the cart sideways, dumping them onto the rest of the pile on the floor. Books and journals swam around Harlan's knees. He wasn't sure if he could pull his legs up out of them.

Cornelius was busy tearing apart the theory-of-the-state books, handing the pages to Samir at Harlan's elbow.

"Swallow, John. Just keep chewing and swallowing. Don't think about it, except remember the scholars and titles."

Harlan kept forcing himself to choke them down.

"It's what you have to do," Alison said, smiling weakly.

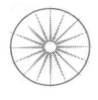

Kenny goes for cover

The wind picked up and shifted, so that it was in Kenny's face. He had turned right onto Colson Road, only because it looked from the tire tracks like the truck he'd heard had turned left.

A mile and a half down, just across Bullhead Creek, Colson teed with Route 45. Kenny squatted at the edge of the pavement watching for traffic. Four cars passed him going southeast, three in the opposite direction. When the next car sped by southeast, he took a right. The only thing that made sense to him now was going where there was the least traffic.

Kenny was guided by what his second-grade teacher, Miss Strathairn, had told him. You might not be able to see it, she'd said, but everything happens for a reason. Sometimes you've just got to keep going.

Then he remembered Mrs. Kelly teaching him to read. The letters came first, and he was able to recognize them after only a few months. They still danced and twirled, making the b and d, and p and q, and m and w, and n and u, always treacherous.

But he worked at it, with Mrs. Kelly at his side, after school every day for two years. Left to right bewitched him. She made up songs, danced with him, drew a leopard on one of his sneakers and a rhinoceros on the other, traced her finger across the page for him.

Kenny was one of many students in Mrs. Kelly's first grade class, and not the only one who received special help. Mrs. Kelly never thought about saying no; it was her job.

He found a dirt road branching off to the left from Route 45, jogged up it until there was some tree cover, then slowed to a deliberate walk. Tense and relax. Tense and relax. The muscles of his legs fell into a rhythm as he climbed the long grade of Quarter Road rising toward Ash Ridge.

Get this over with, he was thinking. Get to Onlius, find his second—maybe third—cousin, and tell him that Cough and everybody in Alta needed help keeping their jobs. Once it was done he could get a ride home. Alta would be saved and he'd never be in the line of fire again.

Gunnar Molshoc awaits the storm

More rain was on its way. Gunnar didn't need to look skyward for the advancing line of mottled gray and black, or hear bird flight in search of shelter. It was the way the air had tasted in his coffee.

Gunnar was working for Renora and Sean Sullivan, who had been wanting this house on Ash Ridge since before they were married, when they were still seeing in each other's eyes the children they would have. Taking care of Sean's folks had slowed them down in buying the property, as had the first of the kids when they came along as twins. It had taken the Sullivans nine years to scrape together the down payment for this piece of property, and three more to get the foundation set and frame built. When Renora was told there wasn't any water on their land, she cried for days. Friends had to stop Sean from burning down the frame, talking him into trying one more time for a witcher to find water. Gunnar was the person who could find water if it wanted to be found.

Gunnar had driven by the lot on Monday, observed the poplars, hemlocks, maples and the few ash left standing against the sundown horizon. Such a beautiful spot carved out from the forest would make you dream. It could carry you through twelve years of high-school hopes hitting up against walls. His heart had ached a little with the fear that he might not be able to find water for them, that the singed clapboards on the lee side of the house might be the destiny of the rest of the place.

He'd begun with the dried-out peach pit, clutching it so he could feel it turn when he was over a vein. The pit twitched Gunnar's hand only once, in the northwest corner of the Sullivan's land, up over the ridge and on the gently sloping hill beyond the back of the house. He'd walked every other square foot of the place twice more before driving in a pine stake as a marker. Besides driving the driller over today, he wanted to witch it again with a forked cherry branch, just to make sure. The problem was that rain could mess up the witching. Gunnar sipped his coffee, studied the whippoorwills and killdeers sounding their case against the building breeze.

Kenny could not see Gunnar from Quarter Road, but he did feel as if he were being pulled to where the horizon was highest against the darkening sky.

Zola bonds with Marie

"Zola May, the light's blinking on this thing. I think it's out of paper."

"Just a minute. I'll check it."

Earhart huffed an okay, adjusted her sandal straps, glanced around at the supply shelves, opened a file-cabinet drawer disinterestedly.

Whatever she had interrupted Zola from was taking longer than she had expected. Finally, Earhart opened the front of the photocopier, spotted a snagged piece of paper and worked it free. Checking the paper tray, she saw that the last few sheets were bent on the right corner.

"Sorry I took so long, Dr. Earhart." Zola May was wringing her hands as if she were in trouble.

"The paper was caught, Zola May, that's all. These last few sheets are bent."

"Oh." Zola May checked the rollers, saw nothing out of order there, then rapped the toner compartment. "Sometimes the problem is that the toner doesn't settle the way it's supposed to."

"Yes, I know," Earhart said matter-of-factly. "But now we just need to load it with some new paper. Isn't this bent paper a lighter weight? "

"You're right. Thanks." Zola was mildly panicked, more used to faculty being helpless with the office machines.

"No problem. You were busy."

Zola kneeled down to get a new ream of paper from the carton, noticing a manila folder hidden beneath it. She loaded the paper for Earhart, held her breath in hope while she finished using the copier, then picked up the folder as Earhart disappeared into her office.

I know I didn't hide it there, Zola worried, as she skimmed through the yellow legal pages of McAdam's Whitewater file. *Why all the secrecy about these waterpower rights, anyway? Why can't Marla type this for him?* She began to chew on a fingernail as she made a mental list of the people who could have taken it, then left it for her to find again. Having it back was making her more anxious now than when it was lost.

"Oh, Zola, don't do that," Earhart said, as she passed through the office suite again.

"I'm sorry, don't do what?"

"Don't . . . don't bite your nails." Marie laughed. "It's silly, it's just that I've always admired your nails. Especially since, you know, you have to do all that typing."

Zola blushed. "I'll try, Dr. Earhart."

"Marie," Earhart replied. "You should always call me Marie, Zola."

"Sure, okay. It's just that I admire you for working so hard and earning your title. You deserve to be called doctor."

"I won't argue with the work part." Earhart looked off into the middle distance. Zola thought she saw bitterness behind the smile.

"I guess the way I look at it, what we earn is the right to be called whatever we want to be called."

"Yeah, I can see that."

Earhart's smile was only a little self-conscious. Zola returned to worrying about McAdam's secret file. *Nice ass*, she thought toward Earhart, wondering why she'd never noticed before.

McAdam undercover

"Marla? This is Zola May. Would you let Dr. McAdam know I've located an item he's been looking for? I can bring it over right away."

"An item? What item?"

"Um, something he asked me to do for him. To help you out."

"Well, I'll buzz him, I guess."

Eighty-three seconds later, Zola was still holding the phone when McAdam burst into the suite, out of breath.

"Zola May, Ms. Axe told me you'd located the item?"

"Yes. Here it is, Dr. McAdam. It was hidden in the copier paper box."

"Copier paper?" His face was turning scarlet with anger. "You hid it in a box of copier paper? Then lost it for five days?"

"I don't think so."

"I don't think so? What do you mean you don't think so?"

"Dr. McAdam, I just found the papers in the box. I don't know how they got there."

His glare bore into her, his lips furling and unfurling. Zola's heart was pounding.

"Wait a minute! You're serious, aren't you?"

"I've been trying to tell you, I have no idea how it got there."

"Well, who could have taken it? Who could have known?"

"Only a few people. The security guys. Vice President Wispen. I've been trying to figure it out."

"Wispen?"

"Or Dr. Koemover. Someone, you know, who has the keys to get into everything."

"Wispen." McAdam sank into one of the plastic stacking chairs Zola May kept for students waiting to see their advisors. "Does anyone else know you found this folder?"

"Just Marla."

"Ms. Axe." Worry contorted his face. "Wispen."

How about taking it out of here? Zola wanted to say. She was so busy all the time, she couldn't understand why she had to be bothered with the intrigue and backbiting over in Admin. *Don't they have enough to do over there?*

McAdam combed his fingers through his slicked-down wavy hair, as if the answers he was looking for would soak into his fingertips. His eyes were red from fighting back tears of frustration. It gave Zola a sudden tenderness toward him.

"Doctor McAdam? What can I do to help?"

McAdam turned to look into Zola's eyes. "I do need help."

"I'd be happy." She almost touched his shoulder.

"Well, this is what I need." He told her how hard it was to get away from campus undetected, that he really had to get something from Gordon at the courthouse, and it would be wonderful if she went for him on her lunch break.

And could she not take any more time than usual, because of course it would be noticed. And, he knew she already knew this, but she wouldn't mind him telling her again that this had to be kept absolutely quiet, from everyone, including her husband.

And this was only something he needed help with at the moment, he added, because then she needn't have to worry about anything beyond her normal duties.

And he would remember her assistance with this matter when her next performance review came up, that is, of course once it had gone through the normal process on up through Wispen.

"It's almost your lunch time now, isn't it?"

She nodded grimly.

"I'll not slow you down. Zola May, thank you. I'll be back by, let's say, around five-thirty, to pick that up from you." He winked. "There won't be many people around by then."

"But Dr. McAdam, five-thirty is . . ."

"I know, maybe a little early. Let's say six."

"But I . . ."

"Thank you again. This means so much to the college."

Zola shut down her computer and pulled her purse from the desk drawer. She was doing her best not to show emotion.

"You know, I've just been thinking," McAdam said, brightening. "At six there's usually no one over by the maintenance sheds."

Cujo on the loose

Early morning rain on the tin roof of her apartment eased Janie to sleep after Billy left for school. She had no exams today, and let herself drift off. She woke up at noon with the trots, took some Pepto-Bismol, went back to bed.

"Cujo. Hey, Cujo. Wanna come over to my house?"

Billy had settled into the Cujo nickname, basking in the notoriety. He was getting phone calls from friends and invitations to their houses every day. This time it was Justin, whose parents bought any video game or accessory Justin wanted. Billy liked that.

Janie got up and fixed herself tea, lounged on the couch in front of the television watching General Hospital. When the show ended she jumped up, startled. Billy should have been home a half-hour ago.

Earl, you bastard. You better not have taken him. She hadn't seen Billy's father in weeks, but that didn't mean anything. One halfway-decent drunk, and he'd get an idea in his head. Barb might have told him that Janie'd been out all night, leaving out the part that she was working a double. Even though Barb rarely had a good word to say about her son, Janie was not foolish enough to believe that Barb sympathized with her. She often thought she should have listened when Barb warned her not to marry Earl. If she'd been certain the advice was more about Earl's untrustworthy qualities than Barb's dislike of Catholics—like Janie—Janie would have paid more attention.

She rang Earl's number, got no answer. That could mean anything, she reminded herself, but still felt sick. She had to figure out what to say to Barb before she could call her. There didn't seem to be any way to ask about Earl that wouldn't make Barb suspicious. And if Barb asked to talk to Billy, she'd be in deep shit.

I'm gonna kill him, Janie thought, when Justin's mother called and, in that self-righteous tone, told her that Billy had come home with Justin. She bit her lip when Justin's mother asked, "Hadn't you missed him?"

Speaking in forked stick

The sky was gray like crushed stone, beyond question bringing rain, forgotten hope. So beautiful Kenny could not stop himself from keeping his eyes on the horizon, the trembling of freshly-budded leaves, thinnest uppermost branches bent from the wind as if in prayer. Kenny saw a man framed against the sky, water falling on his broad shoulders as if he were a part of it, messenger and message.

It looked to Kenny like shards of rainbow were coming out of the man's hands. Splashes of spectrum floated like oil in water puddles in the turbulence. Without thinking about it, he crossed the road and crunched up the gravel drive past the house, climbing through the fringe of pines up to the ridge. The man didn't even turn when Kenny came to his side. Kenny stared at the driller, because the man was staring at it.

"Know anything about winches?" the man asked, as if Kenny had arrived on time.

"No."

"Well, this is what you have to keep in mind about 'em," he said, before explaining that when it was cold and rainy like today the return wouldn't work as clean as usual. "So you just have to be patient and listen, 'cause if you listen you can hear if it's slow because of the cold, or because of the rock it's into."

Kenny listened. He heard a rhythmic clanking within the splattering of raindrops on the truck fender, upon his head and through the branches of the pines.

"Can you hear it?"

Kenny nodded his head. He was sure he'd heard something else too; he just didn't know what it was.

Gunnar smiled at his new assistant. No matter how many people had come to watch him work, he was still amazed and pleased by it. This guy looked sort of fragile, though. Better not scare him away.

"Doesn't it sound beautiful?"

Kenny nodded.

"Do you know what it is?" Gunnar asked, in a whispery, childlike voice.

He shook his head.

"It's the water in the earth, looking for a way to come up to meet the water from the sky. It's a special thing to hear, isn't it? 'S why I drill sometimes when it's raining."

So that's what it is? They stood together getting soaked, smiling into each other's faces, until the rain let up. Kenny grew sad as the winch kept slamming the bit stalk deeper into solid ground, the sound fading away.

Celeste is garaged

Guppy called Celeste, wanting her to pick up, to talk to him about something normal. He let it ring seventeen times, hoping he wouldn't have to hang up worrying, wondering if he should drive home to find her.

Celeste could hear the phone ringing faintly, but she was in the garage and it had stopped raining. So there was no way she could get back.

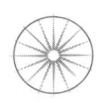

Other lost boys

She leafed through the photo album, tracing her finger over the edges of the plastic holding them in place. Her mother sitting on the picnic table with her arms around her father's neck, smiling, tossing her hair back. Herself twirling Kenny on the tire swing, he a blur of joy.

Aurelia reached down into the very bottom of the chest to retrieve the other album, the one her mother had stopped showing to Kenny years ago. At the time she could remember feeling angry with him for not remembering the baby, looking at the photos of their baby brother, who had died just past a year old. The baby had never been healthy.

It was the final blow for Martha. Her friend Grindel's answer was the same to Kenny's problems, the baby's death, and Wiley's deteriorating health. Martha was not close enough to God. That was why she had gone off to her thorned wilderness.

Aurelia remembered it differently now. Kenny had been as hurt as the rest of them by the baby's death, but lacked the means to mourn, quickly losing the memory of the loss.

She was waiting till the last minute to go see the people Cough had told her about. As more time passed, she was questioning whether Kenny wanted to come home, to give her someone to take care of, to give her life.

Later, Tilia opened the door at Aurelia's knock, as anxious to hear news of Kenny as Aurelia.

"Hello. Are you Sonny Boy's sister?"

"Sonny Boy?"

"Sonny Boy was Papa's name for him. You are the one who called? Papa's friend Cough tol' you?"

"Yes. Cough did."

"Come in. Eat with us." She led Aurelia into the kitchen. "We have supper now."

"Okay, but I can't stay long. I want to find him soon as I can."

"Yes, yes, we unnerstan'. We want to help. Papa! Come in to eat! We got company!"

Alfonzo scuffed his shoes on the mat inside the back door to the kitchen. He'd gone out to work in the vegetable garden, to keep occupied.

"Hello. Let me wash my han's. You Sonny Boy's sister, right?"

"Papa, his name is Kenny. She don' know no Sonny Boy." Tilia balled up a towel as she spoke, working it between her hands, waiting to hand it to Alfonzo.

"That's right, I know. I'm sorry, I just forget." He returned the towel to Tilia's worrying hands.

Aurelia clutched the edge of the table, sipping breaths to steady herself. She didn't know if the person these people had taken care of was her brother. Why would he let someone else adopt him just a few days after disappearing?

Tilia handed her a glass of water she had not asked for. Aurelia drank deeply, gasped, sat down.

"He's a good boy. We could tell." Tilia dished some green beans and a piece of chicken onto the plate in front of Aureila. "Eat an' tell us about him."

"He was always different," Aurelia began. "Momma said that even before he was born she didn't think he knew where he was going." She smiled mournfully.

They sat together at the kitchen table, ate and talked, drank coffee and tea and talked. Alfonzo showed Aurelia the gardens, while Tilia made fried dough. They had more coffee and talked. Aurelia said no thank you to Alfonzo's offer of wine. By the time she said she had to leave because she was riding to the college with a friend, she was remembering that her brother was a young man a few months away from his twenty-third birthday.

Back at home, Aurelia decided to look on her own for a few more days before calling the police. She fell asleep thinking that her mother was Kenny's age when she met her father, right after he came back on furlough from out west. Somewhere he said he was not supposed to tell anybody about.

When the rain comes

Rain angling in off the lake pounded on the driveway, turning it a slick dark. Celeste waited for the gray of the sky to merge with the slate roof in a seamlessness, the same empty shade. A puddle formed at her feet, uniting her with the rest of the outdoors. She walked into the evenness of the downpour and back into the house.

Guppy came hurrying in a few minutes later, calling, "Where were you?"

She was in the bathroom, toweling off, startled by the frantic tone in his voice. "I just came in from the garage."

"Oh."

Celeste looked at her husband matter-of-factly. "Why, what's wrong?"

"I just . . . uh, called from the college, didn't get any answer."

She peeled off her soaked t-shirt, draping it carefully on the edge of the tub. *I need to remember that this one will protect me.*

I panicked for no reason, Guppy thought. *Look at her. She's okay.*

Guppy stood in the doorway watching her towel her hair. Her stomach was still flat, breasts straining the wet nylon. She looked so much like when they were first living together, when he was a grad assistant finishing his dissertation. Sometimes he would come home to find her lounging in the bath, inviting him in to make love before dinner. Now he still admired her, but was more interested in getting right to dinner and his newspaper. He was sure that if he got around to thinking about it, he could figure out why he had lost interest.

He retreated to his study, giving Celeste room. Okay, then, he didn't need to call off the party tomorrow.

I wonder if she could make dinner early?

Celeste was cleaning the living room windows. It was the third time that day.

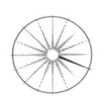

Guppy's bad news

"Dinner was great," Guppy said. He had been flattering Celeste extravagantly since he'd come home, thinking she wouldn't notice.

She noticed.

He was certain she'd be looking forward to the routine.

"Celeste, did you hear what happened?" he asked, around the clatter of clearing the dishes.

"I don't think so," she answered, looking to the ceiling for guidance. She tilted her head, as if listening to voices, thinking he wouldn't notice.

He didn't.

"Let me catch you up." She appeared to be disturbed. She kept staring at Guppy while he was ferrying dishes from the table to the kitchen counter. Her silence forced him to stop.

"Uh, something wrong, hon?"

"That's what I was wondering," she said drily.

"Come again?"

"What's with you? Why are you helping?"

At first he felt stung, caught doing something he should've been doing all along. But with a moment's reflection, he began to feel foolish. He'd been interfering with things that made her feel good about herself.

"Sorry, I guess I lost it for a minute." He laughed. "I've been messing you up here, haven't I?"

She sighed. "Look, Ernie, it's good of you to help, but let me decide how, okay?"

"Yeah, sure. So, what can I do?"

"Don't you have some exams?"

"Well, I'm all caught up. I just haven't finished the paper."

"Then go ahead, finish it."

"You'll be okay?"

She looked annoyed, like he was implying she was incapable of washing dishes by herself.

"All right, I get the picture." He retreated toward the den, paused. "Do you want to hear the news when I'm done? There's some great stuff."

Kenny Takes His Shot / 171

Celeste had been feeling okay. When she heard the word "news" her forehead and cheeks went clammy. Silvery white dots crept in from the outer corners of her eyes. She sank into a chair.

"I don't know if I'm up to it. Just let me finish the dishes."

"Well, let me know."

"Okay." The dots faded, her rib muscles un-tensed. She thought that she might be able to listen to him again once the dishes were washed, when she'd finished getting the house ready for the party, after everything in the basement and attic had been sorted, catalogued, disinfected.

Guppy was back in limbo about the party, about Celeste. The daily news was his last means of talking to her without having to communicate. Better to stick to important things beyond his reach, preferably things disgusting enough to make him feel something, yet not so horrible that he'd lose the desire to mock.

He settled into his high-backed leather chair in the den, unfolded the Times with care and reread the article about CIA Director William Casey's bout with brain cancer. He wondered to himself just how much of the truth about Iran-Contra went to Casey's grave with him.

Johnny plays a bad hand

Georgette hadn't told them what to do with Johnny Percy except to get him off Kenny's trail. The problem was how to keep him from coming after them.

Because they hadn't figured that out, he was still tied to a chair at the kitchen table.

"You gonna play or not?" Prett asked Johnny again. He'd dealt him a hand of cards, face up, every time it was his turn to shuffle. The first couple of times Stosh and Georgette had found it kind of funny, the last seven it had gotten to be annoying.

"I don' wanna play cards no more, Prett," Stosh finally said, tossing his cards onto the rest of the deck. "You're goin' ta win anyways."

"No, no. Don't quit again jus' when I'm gonna win. You never lemme win."

"I wanna go bullhead fishin'. The fishin's always better after a rain. Ya wanna go?"

"I wanna finish the game. Looka this. I got five trump an' the jack. Ya gotta finish it."

"Let the bad boy take my han'. Ya been wantin' him ta play anyway."

"I don't want him to play. I've just been kiddin'. C'mon, Stosh, ya never lemme win."

"Naw, I'm goin' fishin'."

"An' I gotta put the kids to bed," Georgette said. "Are you gonna be okay keepin' an eye on him?" She tossed her cards in front of Johnny.

"What? Ya think I can't watch him?" Prett leaned his chair back from the table, scratching his stubble with the edge of his cards. "G'wan," he waved them away.

Georgette was upstairs getting sticky kisses from the baby, and Stosh was loading worn tires into the bed of the pickup to burn in his fishing smudge fire, when Johnny ran out of the house into the night, leaving Prett on his back on the floor, coughing up blood from the fall.

Kenny and Gunnar go back

Gunnar saw a stubbornness in Kenny's face that he couldn't believe. "I'll help you get back home if that's what you want. Just give me time to see if I can get water for Nora and Sean. Until then, you can stay with me."

"Yuh, but you won't hafta put me up for long. I'm goin' home soon as I can."

"You wanna call your sister?"

Kenny wasn't sure about that. If he wasn't going to finish the mission, he at least didn't want to take the chance of messing everything up. "Uh, no. That's okay."

"That's up to you, Kenny, for sure. Gettin' shot at is more than you bargained for, I know. The only thing is, I'm wondering what you're goin' home to, 'cause if the mill's gone, there ain't no more Alta."

It had been sixteen years since he'd last seen him, but Gunnar hadn't forgotten the son of his mother's best friend, most of the time wandering around lost. It was the same for Kenny after his mother went to the Home as it had been before.

Just like Gunnar's life in his father's house hadn't changed at all when his mother hung herself from the rafters of the kitchen, her Bible in one hand.

Interior Secretary James Watt* on Gunnar Molshoc

Gunnar Molshoc is one of the two kinds of people we have in this country: liberals and Americans. I'll let you guess which.

What he thinks is Mother Nature he's hearing while he's out there hugging trees with his left-wing cult environmentalist friends is actually the voice of pure unadulterated evil. When Jesus Christ does come—and it will be soon—Gunnar Molshoc had better hope he hears His voice. He'd better hope he's not out talking to the willows and whippoorwills.

---

*Reagan's first Secretary of the Interior gained notoriety for testifying before Congress that while there was still the need to protect some of the public's resources from private development, "I do not know how many future generations we can count on before the Lord returns."

Chapter Seven

The Inside Track

Kenny goes inside

He heard the birds first. Still dark, the birds sang as if from memory of sunrise, as if to call it.

A cardinal, a pair of robins.

Kenny had not known the calls belonged to them until later, after Gunnar identified them. He was surprised that Gunnar also had been lying awake in bed before dawn. Although he'd asked Gunnar about the birdsong, most of the things he learned from Gunnar came from watching him.

Gunnar didn't like to talk very much. He said he preferred to listen, because that was how you could tell what was going on. That was fine with Kenny. It meant there was less chance of saying something stupid.

Breakfast was Eight O'Clock coffee percolated in a tin coffeepot, with eggs and homemade toast from the lady next door. It brought Kenny back to mornings when he was little and got up to eat with his dad before Wiley went to the mill. He'd be perched on Wiley's left knee, ankles locked together holding on, while his dad ate and sipped coffee, left arm wrapped around Kenny, squeezing him, occasionally tickling. The last thing they'd do was plant wet kisses on each other's cheeks before his dad left for work.

Wiley walked both Kenny and Aurelia to school once they were old enough, and sometimes they left early and sat together on the plank bench watching the river empty itself down the gorge.

Kenny loved to see the falling water turn from black to green to frothy white, but even more he remembered its torrential music. He used to stare down into the whiteness until it was all he could see, then close his eyes and listen to it falling white. Eventually he could feel the brightness inside filling him up, a calmness replacing his usual unease.

Sometimes he even lost the sensation of holding his father's hand, hearing his voice. After his dad died, Kenny regretted every word he had missed. It was why he was hanging onto everything Gunnar said now.

"You hear it?"

Kenny strained to pick up some sound, anything to stand out from the silence. He shook his head.

"Try again." They were standing at the base of three majestic pines, tall and graceful in their sweep up to the lightening sky. Gunnar called them his cathedral pines.

Again Kenny shook his head. He could not hear a thing, nothing other than Gunnar's voice asking the question. Gunnar held his hand up to his ear, like he was gathering something inside him, and said, "Try again."

Kenny raised his hand to his ear, closed his eyes, focused. Still, there was only silence, not even a whisper of wind. It did calm him, though, and he relaxed

When he opened his eyes, Gunnar was obviously pleased. Kenny broke into a full grin.

"You did hear it, didn't you?"

Kenny felt a tug of guilt. He didn't want to lie to Gunnar.

"I heard something that made me feel good."

Gunnar's smile broadened. "You've got a fine ear, Kenny. You should be able to find your way around without any problem."

Kenny's smile faded. He was confused. How could hearing nothing help him? His fingers began to twitch on his hands. He tried to hold them rigid at his side.

Gunnar could tell something was wrong. "You didn't really hear anything?" he asked quietly.

"No. I couldn't hear a sound."

"They why'd you smile?"

"I dunno. It made me feel good."

"Yeah it did. Do you know how unusual it is to hear silence?"

Kenny tried to think about that, could not get his mind around it.

"It's what some of the Vietnamese called the sound of one hand clapping. At least that's what it meant to me when I heard it."

Now Kenny looked really confused. He plucked at the pockets of his overalls, sidled from one foot to the other. "All I heard was nothing."

"And I'm telling you, that's good. Stay in that silence long enough, Kenny, and you can always find out where to go and what to do."

"How?"

"A voice will tell you."

"Whose voice?"

Gunnar had a little bit of the side of his lip between his teeth, gently squeezing it. He seemed to be weighing out whether it was right to answer the question. Suddenly he shook his hands and closed his eyes for a moment. When he opened them there was no hint of indecision. "It'll be your voice, Kenny. It'll say the right thing to do."

Harlan on defense

"Why did I make a special trip in for this?" Harlan leaned over his desk, scrutinizing Markbright's essay, trying to decide whether he'd seriously attempted to answer the question.

> The US policy toward Central America has always been motivated by anti-communism. Neo-dependency theory is an excuse for sympathizers to criticize our defense efforts and weaken American resolve. Guatemala is a good case in point.

"Don, have a seat. Let's go through this line by line."

"I prefer to stand." Markbright stood, feet shoulder-width apart, arms folded on his chest.

"O-kay. Let's start with your thesis here. To me, that reads like you're saying there's no other motivation for US foreign policy than anti-communism. Is that right?"

"Absolutely." Markbright shot a look over his shoulder at the students waiting to see Harlan, the closest ones eavesdropping for signs of weakness, clues for avenues of attack. Others were pacing, some sitting disconsolately in the stacking chairs, eyes downward as if counting flecks in the floor tiles. Markbright's friends returned his look with thrust-jaw nods.

"And you're saying that Guatemala is probably the best evidence you have?"

"Yup."

"What specific, uh, policy actions by the US are you looking at here?" Harlan asked, flipping through the essay booklet. He had been expecting references to the CIA coup of the Arbenz government in 1954, which had led to the emergence of a military dictatorship and, later, death squads.

"Didn't you read it?" Markbright shouted. "I thought so."

"That was rhetorical, Don. I was asking myself while I was looking through the essay again."

"I didn't think you read it," Markbright muttered from the side of his mouth closest to the clutch waiting at the door.

Harlan heaved a prolonged sigh. It was something he had picked up from Guppy as a means of self-defense. Irate students expected anger, in fact provoked it, but they were thrown off balance by boredom in the face of verbal attack.

"Pardon?" he asked.

"What?"

"I said, pardon? You just said something, didn't you?"

Markbright reddened slightly, then blustered. "How come you had to ask what examples I used? You oughtta know."

"Well, Don, I finished reading this paper of yours along with about seventy others a couple of days ago. Would you remember everything in here?"

"Yeah." His friends snickered out of Harlan's earshot.

"You would? That's great, Don. I wish you had been working with Ollie North at the National Security Council. It'd make things a lot easier for Congress right now." Harlan watched his comment fly over Markbright's head.

"Okay. What do you say we get to the essay. You've got support for the military now and as far back as the Ubico dictatorship in the 1930's. What was the biggest concern of the US in foreign policy in the thirties?"

"Communism." Markbright's eyes appeared hollow.

"Communism? Why communism?"

"Russian expansionism."

"You mean Soviet expansionism? Where was that happening in the 1930s?"

"Eastern Europe. You know, Poland, the Wall."

"You mean post-World War II, don't you, Don? After the 1930s?"

"Whatever."

"Well, if you're talking about the 1930s, you need to have examples from the 1930s, don't you think?"

Markbright said "yuh" under his breath and leaned in so Harlan could lower his voice.

"Are you having trouble remembering what our biggest concern was in the thirties?" Harlan asked quietly.

"It wasn't communism?"

"No. It was fascism. Don?"

"Yeah?"

"You haven't done all the reading, have you?"

"Yes, I read it all."

"Then why did you miss the material about the pre-Cold War?"

"I didn't miss it. I just didn't agree with it. That neo-dependency stuff is just one guy's opinion." Markbright's voice was rising, pulling his allies into the office door.

Harlan leaned back in his chair, studying Markbright's face. Eyes reflecting bitterness, a dogged determination to defend conventional wisdom. *What's the best way to get this guy to open his eyes?*

"Don, you know that if you disagree with anything from the reading or what's said in class, I want you to let me know."

"Yeah, that's what I did. Look what it got me."

"But in order to support your position you need to have some evidence. Look," Harlan said, leafing through the endnotes, "at all the evidence LaFeber has pulled together to support his position. You have to do more than just state your position."

Harlan could see there was more than a grade at stake for Don.

Markbright could feel his buddies looking at him. "Shit. What's this LaFeber book cost anyway? Twelve ninety-five? How much could it be worth? It's not the gospel."

Harlan considered telling him that if he was resistant to some idea it might be due to a flaw in his own logic, looking at issues too narrowly. Instead he said nothing, to let Markbright maintain an appearance of dignity.

Maybe he won't go to the dean behind my back now and add another letter to my file, Harlan thought, as Markbright left and the next student stepped up.

☼ Celeste slips away

"Celeste, it's time for us to go," Guppy was saying, and she just kept winking at the waiter and laughing, in that husky, throaty, sexy laugh she had when they first met. Guppy was looking at his watch, thinking it was awfully late and he had work to do, even though it was actually only eight-fifteen. The problem was that no matter what he did, he couldn't get Celeste's attention. The more she smiled and tossed her hair back, the more miserable Guppy became, the more it seemed too late for them to stay.

Finally, he skirted around the table and took her elbows to pull her up, to guide her away from the others. The closer he held her, the farther away she felt, as if she were gossamer flesh. It reminded him of the trick someone in the education department had shown him, where corn starch was supersaturated in water until it was silky liquid in a bowl. But when you worked it between your hands, it could be rolled into a firm ball the consistency of oatmeal cookie batter; only as soon as you stopped working it, it melted through your fingers.

"Celeste, you've got to come with me, now," he was saying, as she drifted away. He couldn't work fast enough to keep her solid and with him.

He was still calling to her when he woke up and found himself clutching his pillow.

Feeling foolish, hoping she had not heard him, he wandered through the house looking for her.

She was nowhere.

☼ Johnny gets a new m.o.

The buzzing wouldn't stop. In fact, it was speeding up, like everything else. He'd thought that once he'd taken the VC out, things would go back to a normal pace, but they hadn't. And then he figured it was because those clowns had caught him, tied him up. Once he got away, he'd kept telling himself, it would stop. As soon as he didn't have to hear any more of their shit about the guy not being VC.

But all the way on that run to the old house his mind kept racing, then through the night as he tried to sleep. Johnny didn't so much wake up as sit up, another surrender to insomnia. He thought he might as well hitchhike on over to the post office to pick up his disability check before he planned his next move.

It wasn't until after he'd been to the post office—where he was hassled by the woman because he'd lost the key—and gotten to the bank that he felt his brain slowing some. That's when he became really worried, because now his uncertainty would grow. The more calm he felt, the more doubt he had about what he had done the day before on that rainy back road.

That was when he overheard a conversation between an old Italian couple he knew about a woman who'd been to visit them the night before, looking for her lost brother. If he hadn't been able to slow down his thoughts, he might not have heard what they said. The lost brother sounded so much to him like that Kenny kid that Johnny stayed put, fiddling with the chained pen, listening for more.

Johnny had heard enough that he was sure he wanted to go to their house, to pay them a visit later, after dark.

Celeste, heal thyself

The unlit end of the attic was stacked with boxes full of her graduate school life. There were thick files of class notes, old rosters with names she no longer recognized, catalogs and brochures for outdated textbooks and films, evaluations of her teaching. She'd planned on throwing everything out. She just wanted to look one more time.

She found a folded piece of stationary paper, addressed to her, with acorns in the upper right hand corner. It started out Dear Dr. Oliver, which made her wince because it wasn't true, then went on to explain what an inspiration her class had been, especially with her message of how people found their own power—blacks, women, the poor. By the way the rest of the note read, Emily Kroeger—a name

Celeste could not bring back to memory—had not experienced any kind of empowerment before Celeste's class.

It made her feel good about this stranger, this Dr. Oliver, and stirred her regret that she had never brought her into being.

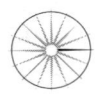

Koemover gets recruited

"Thank you for inviting me to breakfast, Vice President Wispen. This was a great idea." Koemover settled into the open seat across from Wispen. He tilted his head to the side to catch sight of any stray crumbs on the vinyl table top that may have escaped the waitress's damp cloth. After sniffing sharply, twice, to test the air, he felt safe enough to accept the glass of water she offered. This eatery had more to prove, though, before he would order anything.

"Dr. Koemover, or may I call you Stanley? I've been looking forward to this talk for some time."

"Stanley is okay if you prefer. Doctor is also fine."

Wispen looked mildly confused. "Uh, Doctor. I've been wanting to talk to you about the research project President McAdam mentioned the other day. I assume you're involved in the planning?"

"Actually, no. I . . ." Koemover stopped short. It bothered him that he'd had no idea. Research design was his specialty. Research had to have rules. He excelled in making rules, defining behaviors, collecting data, measuring outcomes. Without rules there could be no deviance, without deviance no norms, without norms no observation, no data, and so on and so on. No data would mean no measurement, no assessment. In short, life would lose all meaning.

Wispen leaned across the table. "Do you know who *is* designing the grant?" he whispered.

A shudder began in Koemover's loins when he heard the word "grant," traveling down past his knees and up his spine, out through his fingertips.

"No, I'm afraid I don't."

Wispen searched Koemover's face for signs of guile, as Koemover composed himself by imagining his parents having drunken sex, both passing out before finishing. He calmed himself in seconds.

What's all the shaking about? Wispen wondered, thinking it the key to unmasking Koemover's poker face. He had often thought that Koemover might be a first-class operative, but he hadn't detected sufficient avarice to feel comfortable with him, to trust in his potential for betrayal.

"So who is it?" Koemover asked.

"Who is what?"

"Who is designing the research grant?"

Wispen knocked his coffee cup over, leaned against the table enough, as he reached with his napkin, to send the spill into Koemover's lap. In the time it took Koemover to jump backward, for the two of them to sop at the spill and the waitress to come and finish cleaning up, Wispen had figured out how to respond.

"You were saying," he said.

"I, uh, believe I asked who was designing the grant."

"Oh yes, yes, that's right. Well," he pursed his lips, "I'm afraid I'm not at liberty to say. You see, based on your reputation, I assumed President McAdam had shared his thoughts with you. But if he hasn't," Wispen looked away, out the window into the distance, "I'm not sure I would know why. The best thing to do is trust that Dr. McAdam will let you in on whatever portion of this grant, if any, he feels is appropriate for you."

Wispen noted Koemover's pinched face when he said "portion" and "if any." He signaled the waitress for the check, accepted Koemover's hurried offer to pick it up, and rose quickly from his chair. "You know . . ." he said, shook his head and finished, "No, it probably wouldn't work."

"What? What were you going to say?"

Wispen looked straight into Koemover's face. "Doctor, you know how these research grants work, especially large ones like this, I don't have to tell you. Everything hinges on how they're initially set up, the definition of the problem, all that."

Koemover bobbed his head in agreement, blanching at the memory of how he'd once lost a subsequent phase of funding by honestly reporting all of the results too soon, an error he would never repeat.

"I'm just thinking, with all that President McAdam has to do, he might miss some opportunity of advantage to the college, inadvertently miss it. If he were approached the proper way, you might be able to provide a significant service with your expertise. How to do that, though?"

"I could ask him."

"Yes, yes, you cou-ould. But, since there are sensitive negotiations still ongoing with the sponsor," Wispen said knowingly, "it may be too delicate just now."

Koemover nodded more fervently.

"I know," Wispen added, as if the thought had just entered his mind. "Would it be all right with you if I asked President McAdam about the project, on your behalf? Sort of remind him, you understand, how great your contribution could be?"

"I could go with you."

"Yes, that's a great idea! Let's do . . ." Wispen frowned. "Those negotiations, Doctor. I'm concerned that President McAdam may feel, what's the word I'm looking for, skittish about bringing in someone else at this stage. But since I'm already apprised, my intervening for you wouldn't pose any threat. Of course, if you're uncomfortable with it, we can leave it up to the president."

Koemover leaned forward in his seat, plaintive eyes blinking back tears of frustration. "No, no. I appreciate your help on my behalf."

"On the college's behalf, Dr. Koemover. Your reputation is, well, you probably know. Listen, I'll see to it as soon as I can, then get back with you." He pumped Koemover's sweaty hand once, smiling. "I just know this will be a meeting we'll look back on some day and say, 'that's when it all began.' Well, back to work, Doctor."

As he paid Wispen's bill, Koemover had the strongest sensation he was inside a maze, and someone had just lifted a partition allowing him to get to the food reward.

He took it as a good omen.

Harlan is crushed

As soon as John Harlan saw the sallow tone of Robin's skin, circles like bruises beneath her eyes, he started thinking it. She'd been the best student in his Contemporary Political Thought class this semester, probably the brightest this year, maybe since he'd been teaching. *"Why is everyone spending so much time on theories of the state?*

Isn't civil society where it's at?" Robin had asked. He'd felt a swell of admiration for her.

The kindness in her smile when she told Potts he was wrong, and the way he was left speechless—but still not upset with her—made Harlan realize he had a crush on her, too.

She called him John, in a confiding, musical tone, even when they were in class. He'd decided he would ask her out as soon as the semester was over. Once she was no longer his student.

But she'd missed class the last three weeks, including the paper and the final exam, and he hoped she was coming in to ask for an incomplete. She'd waited for everyone else to finish lodging complaints, then came into his office, closing the door behind her. Harlan waved her to the chair next to his desk; she leaned tiredly against his bookshelf.

"I can't finish the class, John," she said.

Don't let it be cancer. Don't let it be cancer. I don't want to do another cancer talk.

"John, they tell me it's cancer."

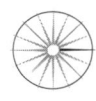

Dance of the veils

"Fellow Boosters, what a wonderful treat it is to speak to you about a glimpse into Onlius County's future," McAdam began.

"Thank you, Brother Gordon, for the introduction. Yes, I can say that my proudest accomplishment since becoming president of the college is bringing back an F with teeth."

The Boosters cheered, patted each other's backs.

McAdam beamed. "Brothers, I have to tell you, meeting with the new owners of the mill was an incredibly learnful experience. I don't have to tell you their plan for restructuring has raised serious eyebrows around here, but in the long run, rest assured they will be an integral part of this region's development. The negotiations on the sale are not complete, but so far we can feel good about the early indications, their willingness to work with our community leaders."

"Bax, they're going to lay people off, right?"

McAdam winced, then nodded. "The information they shared with us indicated it's for the best, Gordy. The union has simply been too active, too limiting for the mill. Besides," he winked, "as overall wage levels go down and people in this area begin to understand the new situation globally, lower-wages-and-benefits-wise, we'll be more competitive when we have fewer agitators complaining about the environment and work safety. So you see, it's a long-term win-win."

More backs were clapped, more cheers went up as McAdam wondered whether the college would get more students coming for workforce retraining.

Harlan against the tide

Darcardt was weary. If it were up to him, he would have skipped the department meeting and stayed home. He was having trouble staying focused.

Harlan came into the meeting last, straight from talking to Robin. While everyone else was trying to decide how to distribute the latest round of budget cuts, he was thinking about dropping everything and running off with her to Belize to make her last few months wonderful.

"We cannot proceed without day-tuh," Koemover was saying. He squeezed his thumb and forefinger together as he said it, as if pulling the plum from the pie, plucking the one ripened berry from the briar. Data to Koemover was its own universe, one parallel to our own, where gauging the floodwaters would take precedence over moving the family to higher ground.

Harlan was walking along the beach with Robin, holding her hand. She was golden from the sun, glowing in good health. The orchid serum the locals recommended left her with no trace of cancer. She squeezed his hand, leaned to him to take his lips inside her own soft mouth.

"Wait a minute! If we pool the Intro students into mass lectures and have recitation computer labs, won't we need fewer full-time lines?" Koemover offered.

Guppy glared at him.

"The computer-lab experience will be beneficial to our students in the job market," Koemover said.

"What about critical thinking?"

"Critical thinking, shmitical thinking. You're like a broken record. What do the employers want? They're our customers."

They want smart, creative people who will work for next to nothing, Harlan thought, before he drifted back. *He was telling Robin that they were needed most in Nicaragua, helping to spread the Sandinista literacy program peacefully throughout Central America. She was disagreeing, saying that the environmental breakdown in Africa was a greater threat.*

"Those aren't computers they're buying, they're pods," Guppy was shouting, snapping Harlan back. He knew he should be in this too, fighting to keep the money for teaching lines, against the onslaught of the technocrats. Yet part of him was tired of it all. The Koemovers and McAdams and Wispens of the world were on the rise.

It didn't help that at the moment he could still feel Robin's warm tears in his shirt, against his chest.

Gunnar on the rocks

The winch moved up and shuddered back, slamming the bit stalk into the rock. Gunnar listened to the bit striking the granite, waiting for the sound that it needed to be bailed out. Kenny listened for the winch to stop as the signal to help, the rest of the time watching a turkey vulture soar over the ridge to detect carrion.

Aside from the light wind through the trees and the kunk, kunk of the driller, there was no sound. Yesterday's memory of hearing underground water was lost to Kenny now, but he knew that something was wrong with Gunnar. He couldn't see the trouble on his weathered face. It was more in the way he moved a little too quickly, a little too awkwardly, too much without grace.

The turkey vulture glided in place overhead. Kenny stood up, head back, taking it in. He began to turn slowly beneath it as it soared in a narrow arc. After three turns, Kenny lost track of the bird, but kept spinning himself until he became dizzy and toppled over.

"Je-sus, Kenny. What's wrong with you?" Gunnar snapped. Kenny was instantly contrite. He sat up and brushed at the dirt on his pants, wanting to see Gunnar grinning back at him. Instead, Gunnar was shaking his head, kicking at a clump of dirt. The scorched corner of the Sullivans' house kept staring out at them, as if to say that fire was its destiny.

You are a stupid son-of-a-bitch, Gunnar heard in his head. That was his father's voice. Gunnar let it move through him without speaking it. Though it had come from inside him, it still wasn't his.

"You okay?" he asked Kenny, reaching out his hand to pull him up, like a fallen teammate.

Kenny looked up at him a little too long, and directly, before he put out his own hand. Until then, he had been forgetting about being shot at. But now he was reminded that it was dangerous for him everywhere, with everyone. He couldn't judge character well enough to keep from being hurt.

Gunnar saw the fear in Kenny's eyes and began to bristle. *This half-wit's problem isn't my fault.*

"Let's take a break, go for a walk," he muttered to Kenny.

Gunnar idled down the winch motor, then disengaged it. If the water was a lot deeper, he'd run out of cable in this reel. The possibility of not being able to bring water to the Sullivan's gnawed at him.

It's that kid's fault. He threw off my dowsing.

"Kenny," he called sharply. "KEN-ny." Gunnar sprinted up the short slope to the ridge. He couldn't see Kenny anywhere.

Why, that shit. Gunnar jerked the cap from his head and slapped it against his thigh. *He ditched on me, after I fed him and gave him a place to sleep.*

The turkey vulture's shadow draped over Gunnar for a moment. It made him look up and turn, just once, watching the bird watching him, waiting for him to cause something to be dead.

Gunnar knew now that his worst nightmare had become real. His father's thoughts were coming to him in his own voice. It would be even more difficult to keep him out of his head.

"Kenny," he called, this time plaintively. "Kenny."

Only the wind answered.

"Kenny," more urgently. Then he added something his father never could say, calling it out into the wind and the trees, to the highway and beyond. "Kenny, come back. I'm sorry."

He called it out over and over, until Kenny inched out from behind an ash tree.

The special gift

Harlan had poured himself a tall glass of wine, took a gulp, then another, and leaned back in his recliner. What a day he'd had. First the news of Robin's cancer, the mind-numbing department meeting, then the visit from the young woman whose brother was lost.

One of his students, Janie Nicmond, had brought her to talk to him. Even with Janie's introduction, and both of them doing their best to reassure her, she was so afraid to speak that he'd come close twice to calling the conversation quits. Finally he'd asked Janie to tell him the story about the mill closing, and Kenny being sent for help, while his sister stared out the window past Harlan's shoulder, with red watery eyes that reminded him of Robin.

Harlan was floored by the news that President McAdam was Kenny's cousin. 'Baxie,' Aurelia had called him.

Baxie? Harlan couldn't picture anyone calling McAdam Baxie, not even as a kid. Then again, he couldn't imagine McAdam as a kid. General manager of the pickup baseball team, CPA for the fifth-grade lunch money extortion ring.

He'd felt awful telling them Kenny's trip was all for naught, because McAdam had already come out in favor of the new owners.

It had put Aurelia over the edge. She'd started sobbing, then screaming about someone named Cough being at fault. This set Janie off, who announced she was going home to her kid (which Harlan had no idea about) and Aurelia could ride home with Zola May.

"Dr. Harlan, I need to talk with you some more about Kenny."

"First off, Aurelia, you need to stop calling me Dr. Harlan. I don't have the doctorate yet, for one thing, and I'm not very formal. Okay?"

"Sure," she said, having no idea now what to call him.

"Can you tell me something? Tell me when Kenny began to get lost."

She'd had to choke out that he had always been that way, and the doctors said they didn't know what caused it. Throughout, Harlan watched her brown eyes resist every attempt to fix on something.

"No one mentioned the possibility of a birth defect? Did your mother take Thalidomide?"

He could tell that Aurelia was hating Kenny. He had put her through more in the past week than in her entire life. Losing her father, her mother going away, was nothing compared to this.

"My mother never took any drugs," she'd said, tears spilling down her cheeks.

"You poor kid," Harlan had heard himself saying. It was as if he was outside himself, watching another person who looked like him comfort this woman.

She'd cried as rigidly as Harlan thought humanly possible, while he sat wanting to hold her, yet afraid of what Guppy called the campus touching police.

"I think it was Dad," she'd said in a whisper. She told him how she'd remembered him being sick. He had died young.

She'd painted a picture of her father at the end: hair coming out in clumps, sores on his hands and feet that wouldn't heal, how gaunt he was, like he had flu all the time.

The end of their conversation was burned into his brain.

"Aurelia, did he ever tell anyone what he thought caused it?"

"No. Mom only said he got it when he was in the service, after Korea."

"*After* Korea? Where was he then?"

"Back in the States. Somewhere out west."

"Out west, you mean the Southwest? And it was secret?"

"Yeah."

"That's it, Aurelia. I'll bet anything he was an atomic veteran. He was at the bomb tests."

"And that's why Kenny's . . . different?"

"There's no way to know for sure. Especially now. The important thing is, you can stop blaming yourself and your parents for what happened to Kenny. It wasn't your fault."

An atomic veteran, Harlan thought, as he sipped the last of the wine. *Maybe my dissertation is worth finishing. Maybe it can do someone some good.*

Gunnar close to the edge

Gunnar had kept the driller running as long as he could before shutting it down. The bit was dull, they were out of water for cooling, and the cable was all out. By now he would have given up if he was drilling for anyone else. He was planning, instead, to get a larger reel with more cable and keep going.

"He never actually hit her, Kenny. It was almost worse because he always had some scriptural quote to make it sound like what he was doing was okay." Gunnar paused, sipped black coffee from his thermos.

Kenny listened solemnly. He was really scared of Gunnar's father after hearing all this, and didn't want to hear more. But Gunnar had learned that whenever he was behaving like his father, it helped if he talked about his childhood to anyone who would listen.

"When he told my mom that after high school my sisters were all done—they'd have to find guys to marry them who would stay on the farm—that pushed her over the edge."

"What'd she do?"

"She, uh, she gave up."

Gunnar didn't remind Kenny how she had helped push Kenny's mother off the deep end.

Flight of the red-tailed hawk

"Yeah, I went to Vietnam," Gunnar said. "I enlisted. Told my father I was drafted. It was the only way I could figure to get outta there."

Kenny watched waves of anguish wash over Gunnar's face. With the last one he closed his eyes and held out his hands palm upward. After a few moments passed Gunnar opened his eyes, waited for them to become unseeing before he continued with the story.

"Kenny, when I saw my mother hanging from that kitchen crossbeam, when my father forced us all to look and said she did it because she was unclean, unforgiveable, my first thought was to join her." Gunnar began to rock, squatting on his heels.

"There was something else in that room, some evil . . . I don't know . . . presence. It was like I was hearing something in the way the flies were buzzing. It's the only sound I really remember. My sister told me later my father was preaching about blasphemy, and I know we were all standing there and his mouth was moving, but all I could hear was the flies, and then I smelled what a body does when it's given up on living. I cut her down and set her on the kitchen bench and walked out, all the while he was cursing me. That's what she told me, I couldn't tell you for sure myself.

"I do remember what happened after I got outside, though. A red-tailed hawk was flying over the barn and I watched it. It flew in bigger and bigger circles until it turned away. I got on the Farm-All and followed it across the lot toward the Old Woods, next to the Scotts' farm. I had to get off and follow it on foot up the side of this ravine into the hemlocks.

"This hawk was still circling, but it got tighter and tighter until it lit at the top of this yellow birch. I was crazy out of my head, wanting to hurt myself, so I climbed the tree thinking I would jump, ya know?

"I didn't get up as high as the bird was perched, but that hawk watched me the whole time and didn't make a move to fly away. It was like he wanted me to look right at him. Ever had an animal do that?"

Kenny nodded, said "Yeah."

"I couldn't climb any higher because the branches were too thin, and the bird keeps staring me dead in the eye. Then he looks out, like there's something more important out in the ravine. So I looked.

"And I saw how he sees it all, from up above. The river that had carved away that ravine had been gone for who knows how long, but from that perch you could still tell. The meadow had been lake floor and some of the hills probably islands. I realized that bird hadn't seen any of those things, yet at the same time knew they were there."

"What did you do? I mean, what happened with your mother?"

Gunnar squinted. "She was dead, Kenny. There wasn't anything anybody could do."

"I . . . I know. I meant, you know, was your father right? Do you think she, uh . . . went to . . . hell?"

"She'd already spent enough time in hell."

Kenny said quietly, "My mother's friend said my father was going to hell."

Gunnar winced. "You want to know what I think about hell? Just understand, your hell will be different. Everyone's is."

Kenny didn't really want to know what hell was like. He wanted to believe there was no such place. What he wanted most was to be in a place where his mom and dad were together and happy.

Gunnar told Kenny he thought his mother's hell was pretty close to the biblical one, something she had fought so hard that it finally got her. His own had already been partly lived, trying to be his father's son, and then later in Vietnam. He said that if it hadn't been for the red-tailed hawk, and the Buddhist girl he'd met overseas, he'd never have found his way back. Now he believed that hell was whatever path of self-punishment a person decided they deserved.

"I've seen people try all kinds of ways of killing themselves. I had buddies in Nam who kept re-upping just for the rush. Kenny, you could see the death in their eyes."

Kenny was sitting quietly, twisting the bark off a maple twig.

The more Gunnar said about people trying to kill themselves while it looked like they were still alive, the more he thought about his mother.

Darcardt defends his life

It had fallen to Koemover as the incoming department chair to introduce Darcardt after the dinner. He'd already spoken about his years of service to the college and touched briefly on his scholarship, which was distasteful to Koemover since it was grounded in critical theory.

All through the introduction Darcardt's forehead was clammy, his chest tight. He had been looking forward for weeks to this chance to speak. Now that it had arrived, he was considering scrapping the whole thing.

"Thank you, Dr. Koemover. Now we've arrived at the part of the program where the fossils get to speak." Laughter sprinkled through the hall.

"This is often the occasion to reminisce about what was wonderful, and I was tempted to follow in that tradition. However, it's a temptation I intend to resist.

"And, in case you were looking forward to a real bonus, forget it. I will not be brief." More laughter helped him loosen his lectern grip.

"I've had the pleasure to work with many people dedicated to the essence of education—that is, passing along an appreciation for the culture of freedom. Always ridden with conflict, the torment of doubt, but unfailingly rewarding because only through the teaching of freedom can we ever hope to live it."

Couldn't resist the grand gesture, Koemover thought. *What a crock.*

"It is fashionable today to focus on the shortcomings of public education. I'd like to suggest it may actually be our last best hope.

"Because of federal and state funding cuts, property taxes and tuition have gone up. Middle-class families are strapped, so they can't give their kids money for college. So they take out more loans and criticize the schools, and all the while the banks are in the trough.

"Yet because we are public," he jabbed the air with his finger for emphasis, "we have a responsibility to be accessible. So we strive to do the same job the private colleges do—with less money—for everyone.

"And every day public education gets more responsibilities. Teachers as social workers, counselors, in some places prayer leaders, in others expected to teach value neutrality, as if that were even possible.

"Public schools do cultivate values. They always have. They are supposed to do so.

"However, the kind of values they cultivate are dangerous to commercialism. Critical thinking, respect for diversity and equality, threaten the dominant culture.

"In a word, the problem of public education is that it is public. And the myth of our time is that nothing that comes from the public is good, so any visible benefit of public institutions scares the yachting shoes off of them."

The absence of laughter bolstered his resolve.

"So let's cut to the chase. Can a degree from a public college or university guarantee anyone a job? No. But neither can a degree from a private college or university.

"Do our students want a guarantee? They do, but we can't deliver. That's the private sector's job, but they're not delivering either.

"So we're blamed for not providing things that were never in our power to provide. Meanwhile, to use our potential to help solve these problems of the economy would be too threatening to the ones who currently benefit.

"This prejudice against the public sector leaves us with fewer and fewer spaces for democratic experience, until we have only the anti-culture of consumerism. How could consumerism be the hallmark of a civilization? We have nothing to pass on, nothing to teach but skills for jobs that may feed us, but leave us unfulfilled.

"Those skills are necessary, but not sufficient.

"Ladies and gentlemen, the irony of public education in our time is that it is precisely because we aren't broken that we are being fixed.

"Thank you all again for listening to me defend what we hold dear. Those of you who will continue the fight know who you are. Keep it up."

McAdam wore an uneasy expression through the applause for Darcardt, as if he had just finished eating salmon loaf that was off. He'd believed after the non-conversation about Harlan that he knew where Darcardt stood, that he was an ally. Now he'd have to rethink the whole picture.

He wished there weren't so many of the faculty in the standing ovation. He'd have a tough time remembering them all.

Musical mill owners

"Cough, what're you doing" Janie asked, "hanging around after your shift? Something up?"

"I was kinda hopin' you'd have somethin' up. Didja find out anything over to the college?"

"Only that Aurelia's still going nuts about Kenny being lost. From the sound of it their cousin's as far as you can get up the ass of the new owners." Janie stepped off the walkway inside the mill gate, because Horace was eyeing them. "What's he starin' at us for? I thought he was on our side."

"Damn fool! T'day he wants the deal ta go through. There's a new rumor, y'know."

"What is it now? Is Horace the buyer?"

"Nope. Japanese, they say."

"So why's Horace happy about it?"

"He heard from one of the higher-ups that we're gonna stay runnin'. Horace says the whole operation'll be a tax write-off. 'It's even better, he says, 'cause now it don't make no difference if we run at a loss, it's better for the Japanese."

"Whatcha think, Cough?"

"Don't believe a word of it. The only thing it tells me is they're nervous, too. The deal must not be done yet. Besides, with the new taxes they don't need write-offs."

"Yeah, so what's the story on that waterpower deal?" Janie lowered her voice to a mutter as she saw Horace taking an interest in their conversation.

"It was s'posed to be kept quiet," Cough answered, in a husky whisper. "The water rights belong to the town. The board's meeting tomorrow night for the vote on turning 'em over to the new owners. Boy, has someone put the fear in them. None of 'em are talkin', but they're convinced it's gotta go to the Germans, or Japanese or Arabs, whoever they are."

"They don't know either? How could they not know?"

"They gotta know, but everybody's got a different story. Whole deal's rotten."

"Uh oh. He's heading this way, I better go in for my shift. So, what're we doing?"

"We're tryin' to figure out how to pressure 'em to vote no on the water rights. I'll let you know during your break tonight if we come up with something. Anyway, thanks, Janie, for tryin' to help with Aurelia and Kenny. Him wanderin' around lost is just another thing on my mind. There's too many sick people out there." Now Cough's back was almost to Janie. She patted him on the arm before he went out the gate, and she went in to work her shift at Alta Paper.

Kenny grows young

His overalls chafed his crotch as he walked. He was noticing how the nurses and orderlies in the hallway were watching him funny.

Gunnar had taken Kenny in the pickup to his mother's nursing home in Hostos. He'd offered to wait in the lobby to take Kenny back afterward, but Kenny asked Gunnar if he could come inside.

Gunnar smiled a little when Kenny told him he had a plan.

The tile floors were worn slick in the hallway center; eddies of wax dulled the edges along the walls. Fingernail scratches showed on the vinyl wallpaper. Disinfectant battled the odor of decay.

Martha's room was on the second floor in the back. From her window she could see the short strip of lawn before the parking lot, the dumpster, and beyond it the hillside running down to the bank of Onlius River.

Gunnar hung back in the doorway to her room, hoping Kenny would be okay on his own. If he could help it, he didn't want to stay, because he was afraid of what Martha might do when she recognized him. One look into the blankness of her eyes convinced him he need not worry.

Kenny gazed at her, surprised at how thin and gray her hair had become, and how under her eyes there were bags the color of cinnamon.

"Wiley? Honey, it's so good to see you. Are we going home?"

Kenny glanced over his shoulder. Did Gunnar look like his father? He hadn't noticed.

"Wiley, who's that with you? Is that Cough?" Martha blinked her eyes, as if coming out of ether.

Kenny took a couple of steps into the room.

"Wiley, you look so young, like when we met."

He drew to her like a magnet, reached down and enveloped her with his arms. Her face was in his neck, she ran her fingers through his hair, kissing his cheek and jaw.

Gunnar twitched, sniffed, looked at the floor. Kenny held on for the emptiness left in him, because of all the years she was gone. Martha was holding on just as tightly, believing her son was her dead husband returned.

She was trying to kiss his mouth as Kenny was pulling back. "Mom, it's me, Kenny."

"What, honey?"

"It's Kenny, your son, Ma. It's me."

"Kenny, oh Kenny, my baby. No, it can't be, you're all grown up. Where's Aurelia?"

"Uh, she's home, Mom."

"How'd you get here, Kissy Ears?"

"I got a ride from a friend."

"A friend? What friend? Where's Aurelia" She was trying to climb out of bed, tugging away the napkin stained with squash and mashed potatoes.

"It's okay, Mom. He's right here. It's Gun . . ."

"How are you doing, Mrs. Hopewell?" Gunnar jumped in.

"The Lord provides. Who are you? Kenny?" she called. "Is this Cough with you? I haven't seen Cough in so long."

"Naw, Ma, this isn't Cough. It's Gunnar . . ."

"Kenny, I'm goin' down the hall, give you a chance to talk with your mother alone," Gunnar said, interrupting again.

"Okay," Kenny answered, and Gunnar ducked out.

"My baby boy."

Kenny sat on the mattress beside her. She pointed to his sneakers, her signal that he should take them off.

By the time Gunnar had finished his cup of vending-machine coffee in the waiting room and come back to check on him, Martha had gotten Kenny to strip down to his underwear beneath the bedcovers, and was stroking his hair, singing.

> Baby's gone, he's in the wood
> Baby's gone, he's in the sea
> Baby's gone, he's in the river
> Baby's gone, away from me

Kenny was curled on his side, snoring gently. Gunnar pulled the door closed, and stood guard.

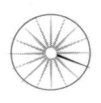

. . . she'll cry if she wants to

"Sure you're up to this?" Guppy's eyes shone with the excitement of entertaining, the look that told Celeste she couldn't say no. He was looking out the front hallway window.

"As long as I can go upstairs. You can handle things alone if you need to, right?"

"But you're not feeling bad now, are you?"

"I just needed the rest. It was the right thing for me to stay home instead of going to the dinner."

"Well, you missed a great speech. Charlie went out with a bang. Oh, look. Marie Earhart is here already."

"You get her, Ernie. I'm going to the kitchen for a drink." Celeste still hadn't decided what she felt about Earhart.

Returning from the kitchen, Celeste discovered that Zola May had arrived with her new husband, and John Harlan had shown up with some young woman she'd never seen before, apparently a student. *Just what I need,* she thought. *More people to ignore me.*

The guests had been there long enough to settle into an awkward silence, or else they had brought an awkward silence with them from the retirement dinner.

Earhart was trying to talk with Zola May, while she and Lyle eyed each other suspiciously. Guppy was fawning over the young woman holding Harlan's elbow.

Celeste named to herself the other guests she knew were invited—Darcardt, of course, Koemover, Bobo, some other faculty and students—and thought about her likely role. She saw herself going upstairs with a headache early on.

"Yes, it's very busy this time of year. It always is," Zola was saying.

Earhart was nodding agreement. "Yes. I'd noticed that."

"Normally, we'd be real busy at the mill, too," Lyle added defiantly, "but they keep talking about closing it down." Though he meant it to insult Earhart, in some way she couldn't fathom, everyone heard Lyle's outburst.

Harlan left Robin to the effusive attention of Guppy and went over to talk to Lyle about the mill closing.

"It's the damn Japanese. That's what we heard today," Lyle said. "You don't know what to believe. Some idiot was even saying they won't close the mill once it's bought out, they'll just run it at a loss for taxes."

Harlan reflected on that for a moment, shook his head and said, "I don't think it's very likely, Lyle. Sorry."

"Yeah, well. Sorry don't bait the hook."

"You look unusually tired, Zola May," Earhart said.

Zola May shrugged. "I guess so." She glanced worriedly at Lyle twisting the cap off another bottle of beer. "Lots of stress."

Stress was the first topic to which Celeste thought she could relate. "Would either of you want something to drink? White wine?"

"White wine would be super," Earhart said cheerily, "but you don't have to go away to get any for me. Zola?"

Zola May knew what to drink now, but had been thinking she wanted a drink right then. Now she thought she must have been wrong.

"I'll wait, too."

The doorbell rang, prompting Guppy to look over at Celeste. She left him in animated conversation with Robin and went to the door, thinking she was feeling that lightness at the top of her head, the one that told her she was going to have to go off by herself.

a glance in the mirror

"Good evening, Celeste, how are you?" Darcardt asked.

"Fine, Charlie. Come in. Congratulations." She extended her hand, his arms spread out for a hug. She pulled her hand back, stepped forward as he outstretched his hand. Laughing, she hugged him, for the first time seeing in his eyes a look of struggle, with sadness or fear, that she recognized. He saw it, too, thought he knew where he'd seen it—in his mirror the past few days.

The hug ended with a nod of mutual understanding.

"You'll be okay," he said.

"Yeah. And retirement will be good for you."

"Sure it will." Most of his face smiled reassuringly.

Johnny finds a ghost

This young man had something up his sleeve. Tilia didn't believe he was really interested in talking to her about roses. He had that look like he was talking to an old person, someone not quite there. And why had he come to the back door?

By the time she got Alfonzo away from the *Evening News*, this John was in the kitchen vestibule.

"Whaddaya want?" Alfonzo demanded.

"I was just talkin' to your missus about the roses you got out front," Johnny said. "They're very, uh, beautiful and I wanted to know how you got 'em so nice."

Alfonzo eyed him up and down, taking long enough to make sure the guy knew how suspicious he was.

This ain't workin'. Maybe I should just scare 'em and make 'em tell me what they know.

"I can't say anyting about the roses, anyway," Tilia said nervously. "My son Michael grew them a long time ago, an' I just keep them. So you see I can't tell you."

Michael. "Uh," Johnny pressed past Alfonzo, "your son Michael, he wouldn't have been a soldier in Vietnam, would he?"

"Yes, he was."

"Huh. There was a Michael in my unit. Great guy."

"Our Michael never came back," Tilia said softly. "They said he was missing."

Johnny's mouth instantly cottoned, he was sinking along with Tilia. "Oh Jesus," he managed.

"Why don't you get outta here, mister?" Alfonzo said from the side of his mouth. He was holding Tilia up, hugging her sobs into his shoulder.

"I knew a Michael over there, is all." Johnny turned to leave.

"Don't go then," Alfonzo said over his shoulder. "You know what happened to him? The Michael you knew."

"Yeah," Johnny said. His head was swimming. He was regretting having come.

"Don' ask no more," Tilia pleaded.

"Mother, I wanna know this," Alfonzo insisted.

Johnny started to feel sick to his stomach, thinking about Michael. He didn't care any more about finding Kenny.

"Would you tell us about Michael? What happened to him?"

Johnny struggled to breathe. The buzzing filled his head. "He saved my life," he said.

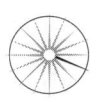

Guppy in party mode

I wonder why I'm here? Robin thought as she watched Harlan from her stakeout near the refrigerator. He was deep in conversation with some mill-hand who had come with the poli-sci department secretary, his eyes light and fiery. John had told her he only wanted to stop in for a little while, then go someplace to talk. He had something important to say.

Guppy spied Robin standing there as he was looking for a new distraction, right after Bobo and his friends took off. She was leaning back against the counter, in the same way Celeste did, or used to. Robin's expression was less bemused, sadder in a haunting way, but just as exciting as Celeste's party face. It made him curious. The thought of flirting hadn't even crossed his mind.

As she watched his eyes brighten in conversation with Robin, Celeste emptied. Once she was only a puddle, she managed to seep from the room.

Johnny above, Michael below

"I was crazy about going into tunnels. Tunnels was the way the VC operated, you know. Moving all over the place, us not being able to find them. Motherfuckers."

Johnny saw Tilia shrink and Alfonzo bristle. "Sorry. Sometimes it's like I'm back there.

"So, Mike wouldn't let me do this one tunnel. Said I'd already done 'em too much, especially without blowin' 'em first, which the captain wouldn't let us do. Mike, he was always arguin' with the captain about how at least with some of the tunnels we should blow 'em first.

"Captain says no, so Mike tells him he won't let me go down, and the captain says fine, then you go.

"An' I said, 'Shit man, let me go,' I didn't care at that point." His voice lowered. "I still don't get why he didn't say, yeah I could.

"Mike goes down into the tunnel and we don't hear anythin'. Not a sound for, like, minutes. Long enough that you started to hope you wouldn't find none of the enemy, then there's one pop like a gunshot, then the shit hits the fan. We're gettin' fired at from ten an' three o'clock at the same time, with no cover. Captain went down first and so quick, we lost the radio before we could call for support.

"I jumped inside the tunnel, outta the fire, with my rifle pointed down it. I didn't move, ya know, till it got quiet up there. Don't even know how I got away, 'cept they must've thought there were more of us an' went lookin' for 'em.

"Took me three days to hike back to base.

"I told 'em what happened, but they never got Mikey's body.

"He prob'ly didn't suffer," Johnny offered. "It was prob'ly real quick."

Alfonzo had tears welling in his eyes. He was wishing he hadn't asked.

The three sat without speaking at the kitchen table. "Overalls," Johnny said after a while.

"What's that, Johnny?"

"Overalls, that's what he used to talk about—what he was waitin' to get home for. Yeah. They were what he was goin' to wear. He said he was goin' to work at the mill, get married, have kids, live out in the country, grow, like, vegetables an' flowers. An' he was gonna wear his old man's overalls at work."

Alfonzo held his face in his hands. Tilia told Johnny about Kenny's visit, and the overalls. When she finished, Alfonzo was still hunched over the table.

Johnny hadn't said a word about shooting Kenny, but he went over it in his head as he lay in Michael's bed trying to sleep, listening for sounds of threat, guarding Alfonzo and Tilia from unfriendlies.

Celeste goes up with Earhart

Bobo blew in with a carload of buddies, mostly other lacrosse players. They had come straight from a party where they shot-gunned draft beer from a spare section of rain gutter. Guppy had invited Bobo for his sense of abandon, fueled it by pushing as much beer on him and his friends as they wanted. They rampaged through like locusts, then left for a beer blast at a frat house. Guppy beamed through the entire episode, because Koemover disappeared as he'd thought he would. Now Guppy was ready to settle in for a serious bull session.

Harlan was still quizzing Lyle about the mill. Zola May was staying away, afraid of Lyle's darkening mood and the amount of beer he was drinking. She went to find Earhart, who had gone upstairs looking for Celeste. Finding no one, she went into the bathroom to sit by herself.

"So don't you think we should let the trapdoor down? We've been up here quite a while." Marie and Celeste had taken refuge up in the attic.

Celeste leaned to pour more wine into Earhart's glass. She held it upside down a few seconds for the last drops to come out. "Don't worry, we still have another bottle."

Marie giggled. "It's not that. We've just been up here so long. Aren't you worried about Ernie and everybody?"

"They'll be fine. Besides, I want to hear more about grad school. And teaching."

"Oh, it's depressing to realize there are still such incredible sexists guarding the gates. One jerk told me I could never be a serious scholar because of my 'childbirth potential.' Can you believe that?"

"I'll see your sexism and raise you one," Celeste said. "My methods teacher hated kids. He and his wife had themselves fixed so they wouldn't suffer with offspring." She laughed, drained her wine glass.

"Oh, and he was so pompous. One day Horne was into his most passionate lecture, and he stopped short in front of this woman knitting in the front row. He's building to this fever pitch about variances or something, when all of a sudden he points at her, and says, "You know, they say knitting is a form of masturbation.""

"What an asshole. What did she do?"

"It was beautiful. She didn't even look up, just said sweetly, 'You get off your way, I'll get off mine.'"

Earhart roared, and Celeste marveled at how beautiful she looked, how rare it was to see her laugh.

"Great story, Celeste. You've told Ernie that one, haven't you?"

Celeste couldn't remember ever telling her husband the things she was now telling Marie.

She hoped she hadn't, because if he had heard all this from her and still ignored her, she wasn't sure she could take it any longer.

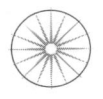

Kenny goes back in

"Kenny, it's time to go, kid. Calling hours are over." Gunnar had to shake Kenny's shoulder hard, several times. He could not have been more disoriented.

"Oh, Kenny, are you leaving?" Martha cried. "I've just gotten you back."

He blinked over and over, hugged the sheet to him. "Didn't I have supper? Why do I have to get up?"

Larry Pendleton watched from the doorway. "He's gotta be her son, right?" he asked Gunnar. "There's a nut that didn't fall far from the tree."

"Is that part of your job?"

"What's that?"

"Being an asshole."

"Hey!"

"I'm just getting my friend out of here. Listen, you take good care of this woman, or I'll come back and have your job."

Outside in the air, Gunnar leaned against his pickup while he questioned Kenny. "Are you sure you wanna stay?"

"Yeah, I'm gonna try to get her outta there."

"You want me to help you?"

"I'm kinda scared, but it says I'm s'posed to do this by myself."

"You mean you saw this in your mind?"

"An' I just checked it again, you know, the feelin' in my hands."

"So it's workin' for you. That's great." Gunnar studied Kenny. He looked as resolute as it was possible for him to look. No matter how it turned out, the important thing for Kenny now was to try this, on his own.

"Okay, I'll be right here," Gunnar said, "to get you outta here. Good luck."

Celeste goes down with Earhart

"Celeste, what do you say we rescue Zola?"

"From the party, you mean, or from Lyle? Or from herself?" Earhart just looked at her, so Celeste kept talking. "What makes you think she wants to be saved?"

"Solidarity. Sisterhood."

The clarity in Marie's eyes made Celeste feel wobbly. "Have you talked to Zola since the wedding?"

"Briefly. I think she's lonely."

Celeste thought so, too. She felt like everyone was lonely. "Well, okay, but as long as we're at it, I want to get a fresh bottle."

"Well, sure. That's self-evident."

Celeste wobbled from the seat she'd fashioned out of boxes to the trapdoor. She put her ear to the floor for a moment, whispering to Earhart, "Coast is clear."

Marie helped her lower the door and fold out the ladder. By the time they made it down, Celeste had barked her shin on a step and they were both giggling helplessly.

"Zola?" Celeste whispered. "Zola? Where are you?" she rasped hoarsely as they tiptoed down the hall.

Marie got down on all fours, peering around the landing at the remains of the party. "Do you want me to hold onto your legs, to make sure you don't get sucked in by the gravity down there?" Celeste whispered. Her face was bright red from laughter. Before Marie could answer, she grabbed onto her ankles. Marie leaned forward on her hands, exaggerating the periscope effect.

"Zola? Where have they taken you?" Celeste whispered.

"Zola, we seek to free you," Earhart intoned softly.

Celeste collapsed on her back, laughing hysterically, suppressing it to keep from being discovered.

"You are the essence of woman," Earhart said, to Celeste as she leaned back to kiss her.

Celeste breathed through her surprise, then returned the kiss. They sat back, regarding each other for a while before climbing back up to the attic.

From where she was hiding behind the bathroom door, Zola was more relieved than angry when she heard them go upstairs. She had always suspected it would be like this at one of these faculty parties.

I'm proud of my husband, she thought. *He's a strong man.* She felt it. Why couldn't she say it out loud?

She went downstairs to collect Lyle, to get out of there as soon as she could.

"I thought it should be called the Long Petition," Darcardt was telling Harlan and Lyle, "because you would do it on one continuous roll of paper. That would have more heart than a bunch of ordinary petitions."

"There you are, Zola. We've just been talking to your husband here about some action that could save the mill."

That should be interesting. Like he needs another reason to obsess.

"Can we leave?" she asked Lyle.

"I s'pose." He lurched to his feet and they started toward the door.

"Don't forget that Long Petition," Darcardt called after them. "That might do the trick."

"I won't, Doc. Thanks. I'll pass that along."

Harlan and Darcardt looked at each other as they left. "You think they're okay?" Harlan asked.

"I don't know. Could be something's really wrong."

Outside in the car, Lyle was complaining to Zola about how she'd left him talking to the egghead professors. He'd thought it was supposed to be a party.

"I know what you're saying, babe. I'm sorry, let's get home and see if we can't help each other get over it, whaddaya say?"

Joys in the attic

The attic was alive with arcane pleasures. They had kissed, touched, talked, kissed longer, deeper, talked again. Celeste kept saying this was new for her and Earhart kept answering that, nevertheless, she was good at it.

Yet they still were fully clothed. The tension for Celeste was unbearable. Finally, she asked Earheart if they should move from the boxes to fold out one of the lawn lounge chairs.

Earhart looked at her with pure lust. "I wish I could."

This is it? Celeste said nothing.

"I can tell you're hurt. But I can't."

Celeste pulled in a deep breath of dusty attic, held the wine bottle upside-down above her glass. It did not so much as drip. She would not look at Earhart.

"You don't understand. Everything was happening for me just a minute ago, too. I let it go too far."

Celeste pulled her hand back, looked down.

"It's just that I can't, not completely. I want to, but I can't."

Celeste started toward the trapdoor. She was getting out.

"If I could I would! There's nothing wrong with you. It's me. I don't have any props with me. I've got . . . I'm HIV-positive. It's too dangerous. Any little cut . . ."

Celeste pulled the ladder cord back up. She rushed to hold Earhart.

Darcardt's last call

Darcardt swirled the last of his Scotch and ice and then gazed down into the glass, as if he were reading messages there. "John, there's more fear out there than you know."

"Out where? In the world?" Harlan was clinging to every word.

"Everyone is running is what I'm saying. The last two generations. It's the age of addiction. Don't let anyone tell you otherwise. I don't care whether you're talking about drugs or alcohol or sex or TV. It's the same."

"How about religion?" Harlan said. "Fundamentalists coming out the wazoo." He was in heaven, having the chance to talk with Darcardt alone, on the back steps of Guppy's house.

"Sure. That too. It's almost too obvious, because the born-againers still have the same trappings. Clergy, doctrine, collection plates—they're just telegenic, music video, direct mail these days. It's hard to tell where Disney leaves off and the PTL begins."

"You think that PTL is worse than North and Poindexter?"

"In its own way, but PTL's just a symptom. Are you saying that if the public could see through Jim and Tammy Faye, they wouldn't also see Reagan for what he is?"

"Okay. I get your point. It's the culture."

"John, it's always the culture. Mythos over logos. Image is everything. My kingdom for a photo op."

"But why are the last two generations any worse?"

"You could be right. It should probably go back at least three. Mass media are a large part of it, and television has a more pervasive influence than radio, I think, with the possible exception of Hitler's radio." Darcardt took a long pull on his Scotch.

"But you know, Goebbels thought Hitler started the war too soon. He really wanted television first."

Harlan thought he could feel his face redden. Darcardt's expression said, *yes, you need to remember that.*

"The main reason I said the last two generations," he continued, "is because that's about how long we've been scratching and clawing to stay on top. It's the same for every empire, but it's especially troublesome to keep everyone on the same page when you call yourself a democracy."

"But we saw through that in the sixties."

"We did?"

"I know, not everyone did. But enough to stop the war. And segregation."

"Before the movements got sidetracked, yes." Darcardt lifted his non-Scotch hand, palm up, and made a sweeping gesture. His eyes said pity to Harlan.

"I've got one more addiction for your list, Charlie. It's the fastest-growing religious sect in the world. It's called cynicism, and it appeals to everyone who doesn't want to sacrifice some material comfort for a better deal. And it's a self-fulfilling prophecy. If I don't give up my lifestyle, there won't be enough left to go around. It's more Augustinian than Augustine, because at least he saw salvation somewhere. For those believers who aren't connected, it's because they're afraid of losing the handle on the one little bit of security they have left."

"Like I said to begin with. It's fear."

Harlan screwed up his face, but nodded and said "yes," softly.

"You know, John. That's what I like about you. You're not a brawler, but you don't back down. I hope you can stay that way."

A spasm rippled across Darcardt's face. The glass of Scotch teetered in his hand. Harlan was just about to reach over to catch it when Darcardt stiffened and spoke to the ice in his glass.

"Fear times fear. They've got reason for it. They just don't have the right reason."

Minutes passed while Harlan tried to figure out how to respond. His head was heavy with all the drinks.

Once he understood there wasn't anything more to say, he went off, too late, to find Robin.

Celeste in flight

"Would you like another drink, sir? Or perhaps a pillow?"

The man's face was ruddy, as if he'd already had too many drinks in his last several incarnations. But the woman next to him said, "Go ahead, Frank. One more would be just perfect for you. Just right." She was beautiful in a cultivated, attended way, wrinkles surgically banished to the perimeter of her face.

"I'll have a martini, dear. Extra, extra dry. As bones, dear. Just whisper the word vermouth, darling, back in coach, ever so softly."

The way that Mrs. Obnoxious looked at her husband as he made the remark—as if it were the very definition of wit—made Celeste feel creepy. Or was it that her flight attendant uniform looked like it belonged to a chambermaid in a porn flick?

She brought the gin and vermouth in their little bottles, poured the gin into the glass and, without thinking, added the vermouth.

"Look at her. Did you see that?" The ruddy face gained composure with the wife's nod of validation, the smile that said she knew all along Celeste would screw up.

Celeste needed to see the eyes inside the smile to know that the woman was her mother, the man her father.

Falling out of the plane was anticlimactic, much less startling than snapping awake with her head in Earhart's lap.

"It's okay, Celeste. It's okay. Shh. Relax." Marie had been stroking her hair along her temples. Now she kissed the back of Celeste's head.

"My father," Celeste cried. "He was always such a bully."

"It's okay."

"No. It was terrible."

"How did your mother handle him?" Marie wondered.

"She never disagreed with him. Or even argued. Do you think I might have had a chance if she had done something?"

Marie's gaze unfastened from the Celeste in her arms to the Celeste in her childhood. "What choices did she have? Did she have anyone's faith in her when she needed it?" Her voice had taken on a cooler, clinical tone.

Celeste pulled away. "Jesus Christ! You don't have any idea what it's been like for me, all my life. Do you think this was easy for me to figure out?"

"You know I didn't mean it like that."

Do I? Celeste thought. *What do I know?* She knew she didn't like the feeling of being under a microscope. She knew she was feeling hopeless.

She started to climb down the ladder.

"Celeste. Don't go. I only meant it was something I learned from what happened to me. I'm sorry."

Celeste kept going down, almost falling out of the attic.

"It's just that with your family, you can't expect to make that clean a connection. Or break," Marie said, too softly for Celeste to hear. She followed Celeste down from the attic.

"I guess I'll go home. If you need to talk . . . " Marie said to the emptiness.

Celeste nodded, to acknowledge without responding that she had heard. Her mind was already racing in search of a place to go, a friend to talk to, some way to find herself.

becoming a climber

Kenny circled back to the river side of the home, sneaking around the building to the ivy trestle that ran up to Martha's window.

Gauging that it might not be sturdy enough to hold him, Kenny looked down at his bulging belly, then felt the lath crisscrossed into a trellis. He sucked in his stomach, was surprised by seeing his toes for the first time in a while, standing up. Now that he felt slimmer, he thought he'd chance it. Only three laths snapped on the way to the second floor and in through the window he'd left unlocked.

His mother lay flat on her back, eyes wide open as if studying the ceiling. Kenny couldn't tell if she was still awake. He crept over to her bedside. She smiled at him.

"I knew you'd come back. Here, get in," she invited, pulling back the covers and patting the mattress beside her. Kenny climbed into the bed and her arms. "I missed you," she said.

"Me too."

"Don't leave me again. Promise?"

"I promise. Can we go for a ride? Would you like that?"

"Oh yes, in just a little while. Can't we rest first? I'm so tired, Wiley."

Kenny only pulled back a little. He leaned into her warmth as she fell asleep, until he forgot about Gunnar idling his getaway truck on the street, and fell asleep himself.

They both dreamed of Wiley.

Jerry Falwell* on Marie Earhart

The Lord wants us to know all love the way we know His love. The Lord God created nature as a gift to us, and that's all we need. Think about the bounty of that gift, its richness, its beauty, and you know why it's wrong for any man, or woman, to go beyond it.

God created Marie Earhart as part of His gift. She came into this world as the result of a natural act. Her disease is what comes of an unnatural act, an act of her own choosing.

Her fate does not have to be yours. The love of Jesus Christ can be yours, and I can help you, every one of you, man and woman and child, to know it.

And you can help me spread it to others. Just give me a call.

---

*Reverend Jerry Falwell, head of the Moral Majority, "sometime after 1970" recalled "all copies of his earlier sermons warning against integration and the evils of the black race." Chris Hedges, *American Fascists*, p.28

Chapter Eight

Burning Love

In the closet

Gunnar shut off the truck engine after idling twenty minutes. He'd tipped his tractor cap down over his eyes to block out the light from the mercury street lamps. Dampness had long settled into him before he woke up and decided to go after Kenny.

All the service-entrance doors were locked. Gunnar circled the home twice before noticing the broken slats of the trellis. He climbed up carefully, crawled through the window and felt his way to the bed. The covers were scattered, the mattress cool, as if no one had been there for hours.

Okay, Kenny, where'd you go?

Inching the door open, Gunnar scanned the hallway in both directions. Nothing moved in the flickering fluorescent light. He slipped out the door, headed toward the elevator, passing several rooms. He pushed the right double door just as Larry, coming from the other direction, was pushing open the left.

"Hey! What the hell you doin'?"

Gunnar sprinted down the hall, into the stairwell, and up a flight before he found a place to hide. He listened to Larry run past the door, hoping to hear the footsteps disappear. Instead they faded, then came pounding back. He had no choice but to stay under cover.

Kenny was thinking the same thing one floor down in the storage closet where he was hiding with his mother.

The difference was that while Gunnar had been trying to find Kenny, in his sleep Kenny had lost all memory of Gunnar.

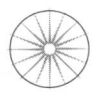

Kenny comes out

"Do you want me to sing you a song, baby?" Martha asked. "So you can sleep."

Kenny shifted his weight to the other foot, brushing against a plastic spray bottle of disinfectant, catching it before it could clatter to the floor. "Ma, shhh," he whispered. "I don't wanna sleep in here. We're hiding."

"Hiding from what, baby?" She was sitting on the floor of the closet, her nightgown tucked between her knees. The light shone dimly under the closet door.

"Everybody, Mom. We're hidin' from everybody. All them guards an' nurses."

"I don't understand, Kenny. Nobody's keeping me here."

Kenny turned this over in his mind, the thought that his mother had wanted all along, all this time, to be away from him and Aurelia.

She was pulling at a loose thread in her nightgown, turning it against the weave and then smoothing it back. Sideways and back, sideways and back. The look in her eyes seemed to suggest that thread was the most important thing, not only in her life, but in the fabric of the universe.

"I thought you wanted to go, Mom. I thought you'd wanna go home an' be with me and Aurelia."

"I was a burden. I've been a burden to Aurelia. She's got enough to do, taking care of you, taking care of your father."

"Dad is d-dead. He's been dead for years." Kenny could barely get the words out.

"I knew that," Martha said. "I knew it. I've known it." The thread was smoothed straight.

Kenny was empty. He had not been allowed to see his mother in years. Aurelia had thought that best. She believed Kenny could not handle his mother's questions about how Wiley was doing. She never told him how much of it was because Martha couldn't handle her guilt that Kenny wasn't normal.

"It's okay, Ma, he's fine," Aurelia always said, never agreeing that her mother caused Kenny's problems, never disagreeing. Martha would rend a thread, smooth it back. Aurelia would let her drift to another topic, they'd read the Bible together. Like talk-show hosts they'd keep the worry alive, to save it for another episode.

Footfalls were sounding up the hallway. Kenny shrank back against the wall, hushing Martha as he pulled hanging smocks around his shoulders.

"Kenny, what are you doing? Where are you going?"

He thought he could see her shivering. "I can't let 'em find me, Ma. Don't let them know I'm here."

"What're you saying, baby?"

"Shh, Mom. Don't let 'em know I'm here."

"You're not going away from me again?"

"Mom. I want you to come home with me," he whispered. "But I gotta do somethin' first. I can't get caught in here."

Kenny wasn't sure if his mother's silence was in heed of his warning. When the second-floor orderly stuck his flashlight in the closet, she yelped and came right out, so quickly he didn't even need to turn on the light. She told him she was in there looking for Jesus.

Kenny sneaked out, waiting until he was down the bank by the river's edge before he let go, sitting on the ground with his knees pulled up to his chest, rocking on his haunches, sobbing.

Gunnar was on his eleventh lap around the block, his next-to-last un-chewed fingernail.

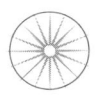

building a memory

Kenny walked south along the river's edge because it was downhill. The walkway opened out at Eastview Park. He crossed the ball field to the sidewalk paralleling East First, still moving south. When he got to Seneca Street he turned right onto the bridge, because he wanted to get out over the water, darker than the night that had not yet touched bottom.

Midway between the fourth and the dimming fifth street lamps he found a spot dark enough and still high enough to do what he knew he had to do. He climbed up onto the whitewashed stone abutment, balancing on it.

Kenny stared directly beneath him, gradually raising his gaze upward toward the northeast. He never stopped to ask himself why he, who had barely known the concept of south enough to find his own feet, now could do this. When he was certain he had spied the nursing home, he almost lost his balance.

He looked a good long time at where his mother lived across the river, fixing it into what might be a memory, before he climbed down.

Kenny shadowed

The cop who shouted Kenny down from the railing idled alongside him the rest of the way across the bridge. Kenny slowed until the car was just past the intersection, then turned right onto Station Street. He was so nervous that he crossed the parking lot and started hiking up the railroad tracks so he could get away from the street.

A quarter-mile up from the Seneca Street Bridge was the rail station, unoccupied since 1963. The windows were plywood nailed over shattered glass. The WPA mural on the south end of the clapboard building, a collage of immigrant workers in factory settings, was faded almost beyond recognition, where it wasn't covered with graffiti. As Kenny passed it in the three a.m. darkness, it sounded like it talked to him.

"Long time passin'," it sang.

Kenny jumped, and circled wide around the building.

"Don't you like me? Why don't you like me?"

Kenny stopped still. He would have run if he had any idea which direction was safe.

"Nobody likes me. I don' know why."

A figure pivoted on its center from the horizontal, then stretched itself upright from a stone bench at the front of the stationhouse.

"Ooooouhhhh," exhaled from it, along with a thick stream of urine.

"That'll make some flowers," it said in Kenny's direction.

"I didn't do nothin'," Kenny said. "I was just walkin' by."

It jumped as if startled.

Kenny took one tentative step back, the loose pavement stone crunching beneath his sneaker. It hunched down and sidestepped with him. Kenny trotted, it kept pace.

"Get off of my land."

"I'm goin'."

"You aren't gonna tell nobody where you found me!"

"I don't even know where this is," Kenny called back.

A laugh escaped from it, stabbing Kenny. "This is my home," it said.

"Are you gonna shoot me?" Kenny could no longer stand the suspense.

"Shoot you? Why should I shoot you?"

"For bein' on your land? I don't know."

This time the laughter bubbled warmly, then cooled. "It won't matter, you know. There's no place you can go that's not my home." It stepped from the deep shadows of the eaves of the stationhouse into the mere darkness of the parking lot, becoming a young man not too much older than Kenny, bundled in layers of shirts and jackets and pants and socks in oversized work shoes.

Kenny's hands fell to his sides in disbelief. "I'm so tired." He closed his eyes. "I don't know where I am, or where I'm goin'." The young man listened, squatting on his haunches. "I've been away from home longer than I can remember, and I don't know my way back."

The young man rose to his feet, gestured toward the run-down stationhouse. "You can come to my place. There's an extra bench out back."

"You mean it's okay?" Kenny felt like crying.

"Sure. This is just one of my places, y'know. I got places all over."

"You do?"

"Yeah. Until the cops come by. Then it's theirs for a while."

Lyle goes Long

The answering-machine light was blinking when Zola climbed out of bed. Lyle was still sulking. She thought about waiting until he got up before pushing the play button.

"Hey, Lyle, this is Cough. We're tryin' to figure out somethin' for tomorrow night's board meeting. We gotta get 'em to hold onto the water rights. Gimme a call quick as you can."

She ran down the hall to get Lyle, wouldn't let him shake her off or lie in bed ignoring her. "You've been bitching about the mill so much, go get on that phone."

But it surprised her when he did.

"'Lo, Cough. You called 'bout the mill . . .

"Uh huh. Yeah, that makes sense. How you gonna get everybody there?

"No ideas, 'cept for callin' everybody like you already been doin' . . .

"Sure I can be there." Lyle made a face at Zola, as if to say, *see, it's your fault I have to go to this thing.*

"Can't everybody on second shift sign something?"

"Yeah, a petition. Wait a minute, Cough, there was somethin' one of those college guys told me last night. Some kinda petition." He cupped his hand over the receiver. "Zola, what was that petition that guy was talkin' about last night?"

"What?"

"Yup, the long petition. That's it. Everybody signs the thing, Cough, everybody.

"Uh huh. They can use my truck. Sure thing, Cough. Maybe."

The tension was visibly draining from Lyle's face. Zola sank into the chair by the window, Zola folding every part of her body into her Zola At Work, Immune At Her Desk pose. "So what did he say?"

"He said it sounded like a good idea. I told him we needed a lotta paper an' he laughed. 'Paper we got', he said."

Zola could see Lyle trying on hope. He reached for her and she went to him.

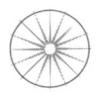

Sizing up the shadow

Gray merged into gray. The rail yard still was without color as Kenny woke. These days, trains that were supposed to carry freight ran just often enough to keep the tracks from surrendering to weeds and rust. Emilio rode them occasionally, he'd told Kenny as he showed him the bench in back. Kenny was interested to see Emilio in daylight.

Flames from the campfire were the first color to emerge from the gray. Something about the place was sapping Kenny of energy, of his will even to sit up.

Emilio squatted over the fire with his jackets and outer shirts undone, soaking in the warmth. Occasionally he glanced over at the bench, waiting for this guy to do more than open his eyes. He didn't know whether Kenny was scared or just slow.

Kenny could not remember seeing a darker-skinned man in his life; he could see in the light that the man was even thinner than his mother, and his close-cropped hair was so uneven—there were nicks in his scalp—that Kenny wondered if this guy's sister cut his hair too.

He was having a hard time figuring out anything about where he was or why he was there. His moment of clarity on the bridge might as well have happened to someone else. He was certain, though, that his name was Kenny.

"Hey, man. You gonna get up?"

Kenny lay still for a few seconds to make sure there wasn't anyone besides Emilio around before he sat up. Stiff from the hard bench and early morning chill, he stretched as he rose to his feet, wondering whether he should make a break for it.

"I'm not prejudiced, you know that Kenny. I was in the Army with plenty of colored guys, and I worked with some. There's good ones and bad ones, just like everybody else. But, they're different from us, I can tell you that. Yessir, different."

Wiley was trying to explain to Kenny the television coverage of the riots after the Martin Luther King assassination, when Kenny was very young. He had begun to cry because of the sirens, fires and smashing of windows.

"It's wrong to do that, Kenny. They are stealing things and hurting people."

"Are they bad people, Dad?"

"They're doing bad things, son, but they're really angry. Someone they love has been killed."

"So they're not bad people?"

"Some of them probably are."

Squinting his eyes into a new focus, the twisting of his mouth belied Kenny's confusion. "You're a good boy, Kenny. I wish it was easier to figure this stuff, but it's not."

"How do I know who's good, Dad?"

Burning Love / 219

"Well, it's just like with everything else, Kenny. You got to see what they do, and go from there."

"See what they do. See what they do." Kenny kept whispering it to himself to keep from bolting.

Emilio sighed. Although he was used to people being scared, he was really hoping this kid was just slow.

what fathers want for their sons

Tilia poured Johnny another warm-up. He thanked her again, then tuned in to Alfonzo's story about his father fighting scabs back in the strike of '37.

"The worst part was them bringing in those boys from de old country, he said. They didn't have no English hardly, right off de boat, he said. Made him sick havin' to swing de bats at 'em, but whatcha gonna do? Man who got chased outta plenty of jobs when he first come over, havin' to do that, you 'magine?"

Johnny shook his head, tapped his cigarette ashes into the mason-jar lid Tilia had set out for an ashtray.

"I remember your father comin' in to work once. Didn' stay long, maybe a year. Guess he started de farm back up again."

"Yeah, you got that right," Johnny said. "The only thing he hated worse than farmin' was doin' anything else." He saw Alfonzo stiffen and frown.

"But he always came back to the farm," he added. "Guess that's what really turned 'im on."

"Your mama loved the farm," Tilia said. She came around the table to sit across from Johnny, so he would be sure to catch her expression. "It very hard when she died. Very hard."

He averted his eyes and tucked his tongue in his cheek. She got up again to finish washing the breakfast dishes.

"The thing about my old man was he seemed to care more 'bout us workin' than anything else. Didn't give a shit about whether any of us did good in school. It was all work."

Alfonzo shifted in his seat, sucked the last of his coffee from the saucer. Tilia took it from him before he could set it back on the table.

"Was Michael good in school?" Alfonzo asked.

Johnny shrugged. "Can't really remember. He wasn't bad."

"He coulda gone to college," Tilia said over her shoulder. She waved her hands in the dishwater like there were some dishes she was still washing.

Alfonzo closed his eyes. "He took a test," Tilia continued. She collected Johnny's coffee cup and saucer, swiping the dishrag beneath it. "They tol' him at the college he could go there, they tol' him he was smart enough."

Alfonzo ducked, as if the statement were a missile, with a time-delayed fuse. "Why didn't I know that?" he said finally.

"It wouldn' make no difference." She spoke quietly, calmly.

"It woulda been a difference, if I'da known."

"Michael, he only tried coss I wanted. All he wanted was to work at the mill, like his papa. After."

Alfonzo's anger boomeranged. He turned ashen. "What?"

"He wanted go fight first, like his Papa. It was goin' to be a surprise. When you got mad, we didn' know what to do. We thought you'd get over it."

Johnny could tell, in the aimless working of Tilia's blue-veined hands, what the problem was. "They didn't mean no harm, Alfonzo. No disrespect."

Tilia slowly shook her head no, in agreement.

"They just didn't think he was gonna die."

McAdam checks for plants

The dandelion mocked him. It was taller than it had been the day before yesterday, the last time he'd dug it up. McAdam checked for clues that this was an entirely different dandelion in the same spot, perhaps planted by Wispen or one of his associates. Then he panicked, thinking that Wispen was using the dandelion for a distraction while doing something even more heinous, somewhere else in his house.

Johnny on active duty

"Hey, Alfonzo, who you got there with you?" Janie asked, eyeing the man tilting the rifle out the truck window.

"Johnny's his name. You know him, don' you? His papa owned the farm on the Corners."

"Percy Corners? That's not Young Johnny, is it?"

"Yeah. He's a good boy. Don' worry. He knew Michael."

She whistled softly, shook her head. "Man, I wish Cough was here, or Lyle or somebody. It's Lyle's truck. I don't know if he'd want somebody he doesn't know riding around with a rifle going off half-cocked."

"I thought you needed somebody to help drivin' this thing aroun'? Johnny wants to help me soon as I told him, now you don' want him?"

"Alfonzo, you know it isn't up to me. Cough's the one who set this up, an' he's on shift. Plus it's Lyle's truck and he's on shift, too."

Alfonzo turned on his heel, stomped back toward his truck.

"Hey, Alfonzo, don't get mad! Where ya goin'?"

"Maybe you don' want an old man's help."

"Don't start on that, Alfonzo. You know better. I'm just making sure we don't screw this up. This is the mill, y'know."

"You think you got to tell me 'bout the mill? You a college girl. You think you gonna stay aroun' here, college girl? Don' tell me about the mill." He was pacing between Janie and the pickup.

Janie was more surprised than Alfonzo and Artie Furlong to find her face so red, choking for words to shout back. She'd never put it together before, that just because she was going to college, everyone would feel she wasn't as afraid of the mill closing.

Her eyes narrowed into fierce slits. "I know all about the mill from guys like you." She punctuated with her finger in Alfonzo's chest. "I've been hearin' it for years, so don't try to tell me what's up. That mill's what's raised my boy so far, and I don't have any other job, and Artie and I have been followed around and threatened, so just lay off."

A rifle shot tore through the air. They both jumped, then spun around to see Johnny grinning. "Missed it. Biggest damn paper hawk I ever saw," he said. "Surprised you didn't see it, swoopin' in to pluck up this here roll."

Janie glared at him. "He'll scare people away."

"Wasn't that the idea?"

"Not everybody. We wanna get people to sign this, Alfonzo. That's what it's about."

Alfonzo considered it, rubbing his stubble with his gnarled fingers. "Johnny," he called.

"Alfonzo."

"How 'bout you follow wid my truck?"

"Then who's gonna ride with you and the petition?"

"I wanna pick up Benjie an' Nick. They know a lotta people who'll sign."

"Sure thing, man. I'll keep the hawks off your tail."

Alfonzo raised his eyebrows at Janie; she nodded back grimly.

Johnny leaned farther out to prop the rifle against the side of Lyle's truck, pulling himself through the window. He held the butt of it against his hip as he walked.

Janie burned, but spoke calmly to Alfonzo. "You sure he's gonna be okay?"

Alfonzo nodded defiantly. "He knew Michael. He's a good boy. He wants to help."

"Be careful, Alfonzo," Janie said in a low voice. "Give me a holler at home if you need me."

"I'm gettin' Benjie an' Nick. It's gonna be okay, Janie." He paused, worked his jaw back and forth to bring out some difficult words. "I'm sorry, you're a good girl."

Janie smiled, touched him on the cheek.

C'mon, c'mon, Johnny said, anxious to begin his redemption.

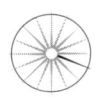

Guppy in a happy place

Dark, jet-black hair in loose curls fell across her eyes, pulling his gaze into the warm brown richness of hers. Whenever he tried to trace the lines of her face—high cheekbones framing a straight profile nose, gently flaring nostrils and pouting, full sensuous lips, glistening moist, swollen blood-red, panting so slightly, trembling—the eyes called him back, tugging at him like an invitation to dance, revealing glimpses of her other lives, the color changing from green to hazel to brown to gray to chestnut to blue and pale blue, to brown, ever more trusting and wanting, asking, asking.

She eased toward him until the toes of each open sandal, held onto her flawlessly bronzed feet by the sheerest of red satin straps, were on either side of his right shoe, then leaned in to whisper "That's better," warm sweet breath, lips brushing his ear, scented hair caressing his cheek. Each nerve on the right side of his body could feel her. His left was the dark side of the moon.

"I want more," she breathed, leaning back only enough for him to turn his eyes directly into hers again, to see that his answer was yes, before coming closer, his nerves and flesh rewarded with touch. "Let's," she teased into his ear, her tongue's tip reaching past her lips to taste him, leaving behind a memory of the wetness inside her mouth.

There were so many people at the party that they needed to press closer, their cheeks brushing as he turned to find her ear. "We could find a quiet place," he whispered, suddenly sinking, unsure. He needed to lean away for her to respond, did not wish to.

It seemed she understood him in the gentle pressure of her bosom against his sleeve, but she mouthed, "I'm sorry, I can't hear you," her lips lingering in the rounded gesture of the "oo."

Now knowing, he reached his arm around her. She stretched her arms upward, back, gliding his fingers with hers, and arched her muscles from her arm, then her ribs, past the curve of her waist till his thumb found the valley inside her hip, the length of his fingers stretching across the rounded firmness beneath the sheer layer of silk. He felt her tense invitingly to keep him there before giving his lips once more the softness of her ear, somehow making his palm cup even farther under the curve of her. She leaned into him this time, the threads of the fabric of her dress clinging to him.

Guppy searched the room fleetingly for Celeste, did not find her, did not in fact see anyone noticing them, and abandoned himself. "Let's go up to the bedroom," he invited. She smiled yes.

He held her hand, leading her through the crowd downstairs up toward the room, the sound of his beating heart filling his head. Letting go of her hand to fall back upon the bed, he awoke as he bounced on it, alone. There was no dream woman, no Robin, and no Celeste, only his blood pounding.

Guppy reflected for a moment about the party and all the people who had been there and now, apparently, were gone. *I'm in trouble all the way around,* he thought, before he began to call out for his wife.

Earhart feeling lost

She paced, she drank coffee, she felt herself craving a cigarette, which she hadn't done since grad school. Marie had only started smoking in college as a way of staying awake to study or work delivering pizzas. It was something to do when she was bored and fidgety, like right now.

How did I get myself into this? Yesterday morning she wasn't thinking about Celeste, wondering whether she was going to call or come over. Before the party Marie had been planning her summer, research and visits to friends on Cape Cod.

She sucked the last coffee from her cup, chewed on a few specks of grounds until the bitterness filled her mouth. She hated herself for her logic. There were too many times when it failed her, by being so unwavering.

Marie paced quickly, with even, resolute steps, as if she were a race-walker, as if there were a finish line at the end.

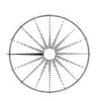

The shadow named

"My name is Emilio Aguinaldo, man. I got it handed down from him, from the Spanish-American War."

"Which side was he on?"

"Actually, both. Or maybe I should say neither."

Kenny's mouth dropped open. "Was he a good guy?"

"The best. It's not that tough to understand. First he fought with the Americans against the Spanish, then after the Spanish left the Philippines, he fought against the Americans because they wouldn't let the Philippines be independent." Emilio guessed by Kenny's expression there was no point in explaining further. "So what's your story?" he asked.

Storm clouds crossed Kenny's eyes, darkening and thickening. He felt his forehead warm and slick with sweat. So many faces were rushing forward into his mind's eye, it made him woozy.

"Hey, kid, you look sick."

Kenny tried to answer, could only gasp.

"Forget it. Forget I asked anything, okay? Just breathe."

Kenny gasped for a few minutes and then held his head in his hands. Emilio got him a drink of water from the cut-out plastic milk jug he kept under the eaves of the station house.

"How's that? It helping?"

Kenny nodded as he gurgled, not stopping until he'd drained the jug. Emilio made a face and then sighed, returning the jug to its place.

"Wish I had some food to give you. You wouldn't happen to have some money?"

Kenny shook his head. "I don't think so."

"Nothing in that backpack of yours?"

Kenny's face said it was news to him that he had a backpack.

"Kid, it's right over there under the bench you were sleeping on."

"Oh. Yeah."

His expression was just as puzzled with the first few items from the backpack. A Cub Scout manual with a bullet embedded in it, waxpaper wrappers with ants scurrying away the crumbs. Kenny held them up for Emilio to see. "Sorry," he said.

Emilio shrugged.

Pieces of what appeared to be a dead frog fell from the front pouch as soon as he unzipped it. Emilio sniffed. "It's okay, kid. Uh, I'm not really hungry, y'know."

"All right." Kenny reached into the pouch, anyway. The hawk feather stung him. *Gunnar.* In the bottom corner, almost indistinguishable from the last of the deer tail, was some pink fuzz. Kenny sniffed them, the only contents that smelled like they'd never been alive, a dusty fragrance of floor wax on synthetic fibers.

Tears rolled down his cheeks. "Mom," he said to Emilio, suddenly remembering everything.

Harlan gets the message

Should I call her or leave her alone? If I call her, what could I say, after last night?

Harlan had fretted about it from the moment he woke up. Still he tried to gather his thoughts to write more of the dissertation.

> Witness the Grenada invasion as a case in point of the use of the traditional reward structure of the military to encourage loyalty to the performance of the mission, where over 7,000 medals were awarded for an action involving 5,000 combat personnel.

Why am I such an idiot? Robin is so wonderful, and she's so sick right now.

He paced from the desk in his office to the kitchen sink, staring into the stacks of dirty dishes for a clue about why he had come in there.

Am I hungry? He decided he wasn't. *Am I thirsty? Oh, yeah, I came in to make more coffee.* Harlan rinsed out the pot, scooped in fresh coffee with the grounds that were stuck to the basket, and filled the pot to seven. He knew if he drank that much he'd get a headache, yet he was hoping the caffeine would force him through the restlessness. While he worked on the coffee, the insight came.

Overkill is not a chance result of Cold War politics, but rather a guiding principle of the budgeting process for military spending.

"God, this is awful," he said aloud, the coffee boiling over the stove. He wanted to punish himself for not calling Robin, yet not wanting to call.

Overkill, he thought, then whispered, each time jotting down insights, until it became a mantra. With the last chant, on his third page of notes, Harlan surrendered to the guilt and took a break, deciding he could no longer hold off.

"Hello," she said after the fourth ring and two clicking sounds. "If I was home you'd be talking to me right now, but I'm not, so you aren't. I'll get back to you as soon as I can, if you let me know how to get through to you." A long beep followed instantly, during which he wondered if she'd recorded that message just for him. He said "I don't know" into the receiver and hung up the phone.

Koemover uses DDT

It was quiet, blessedly quiet, around the office, making Zola smile, the first time this week she hadn't felt stressed to the max. McAdam was leaving her alone, which was making her kind of nervous, since it must mean they were close to shutting down the mill. She had been quietly angry all the while McAdam's file was missing, suspecting it was just a setup to test her loyalty, as if this gambit of his were a college policy.

Lyle was buoyant this morning after talking to Cough. He'd never before lent his truck to Rastin, or his father, but he couldn't wait to get it over to Cough's so they could start the Long Petition.

Zola got herself into a zone, typing Spring 1988 memos that Koemover was anticipating the need for, her fingers a direct live connection to the letters a-s-d-f-j-k-l-;, her eyes an electronic scanner identifying letter patterns to trigger her fingers.

There were more immediate projects, but her years of experience in the ego triage at work told her that Koemover's hypothetical future memos were the most important for maintaining emotional health today. He was the only one around, relishing his new office now that Darcardt had vacated it.

What a prize, a job everyone else refused to accept, Zola thought.

To: Vice President Wispen
From: Department Chair Koemover
Date: (February?) (March?) 1988
Re: A New Efficiency Measurement System—Proposed

Proposal—Routinize jobs via subtasks necessary for job completion, as determined by review of actual work performance recorded by surveillance cameras. Suggest random sampling for surveillance, rotating on a periodic basis (2 mos.?) Calculate high-end average of job performance, utilizing the (proposed) Deduct Dead Time (DDT) formula. DDT is determined by totaling non-essential work activity (e.g. pleasantries exchanged @ reception tasks, laughter in person-to-person information exchange, excessive grooming, undergarment adjustments, etc.), for comparison against essential work activity. DDT can provide all future job description, work scheduling and merit recognition criteria. Estimated installment time 6 mos. Budget needs minimal re benefits. Will require surveillance cameras and security personnel increase and upgrade w/ DDT training.

The phone rang, startling Zola.
"Hello, Political Science Department. May I help you?"
"Uh, yeah . . . yeah. Who is this?"

"Zola May Lester. Is . . . this . . . Dr. Darcardt?"

The person on the other end coughed, cleared his throat. A long silence followed.

"Hello? Dr. Darcardt, is that you? Are you all right?"

"Yeah, hello? Who is this?"

"This is Zola May Lester, at the department office. At the college."

Silence.

"So what did you want?" Darcardt asked.

"Uh, Dr. Darcardt, you called me, remember?"

"Oh, I did? I'm sorry, Zola, I can't seem to remember what I was calling about. I'll see you later, okay?"

"Sure thing. Goodbye."

"Goodbye."

She hung up the phone, stretched and swiveled back into typing position. The phone rang again.

"Hello, Zola?"

"Yes, Dr. Darcardt?"

"I just called you, didn't I?"

"Yes."

"I think I need some help finding my way in today."

Zola swallowed down a lump.

"I'll see what I can do, Dr. Darcardt."

"Okay, Mom. I'll wait for your call."

It was almost time for her lunch. She could probably skip eating and drive out instead to pick up Darcardt. She really didn't mind. He was retiring, after all. It wasn't like taking care of her father while he was lying on the couch complaining about his injured back for seventeen years. Still, she thought she could feel her eye sockets sweating.

Wispen making policy

McAdam was in conference with the college attorney about an alumni malpractice suit against the college, enough to keep him busy for awhile. Wispen strode the campus walks and hallways on his rounds, secure in the knowledge that he was at least two moves ahead of

McAdam again, with a two piece advantage in the endgame. There was only one more play he needed to make, in fact, and that didn't even involve McAdam.

He was feeling so good about the way everything was falling into place that Wispen didn't even bother to order the work done through the usual process of forms, but instead borrowed a screwdriver himself to tighten the spring on the Admissions Office door, after he'd concluded it opened much too easily.

Darcardt's close shave

On the last morning Charles Darcardt had to go in to the college, most of the hour he spent making breakfast went for trying to find the percolator. He hadn't recognized the Mr. Coffee on the counter.

Zola's was the first name on the card by the wall phone under the heading WORK. Darcardt had not remembered putting the card up, could not seem to place any of the names. He recognized his daughter Bonnie's name on another card, dialed her number, listened to it ring fourteen times, and hung up.

"Dr. Darcardt? Hello? Dr. Darcardt?" Zola was rapping on the front door. "I'm here to give you a ride?"

"The door's open." He had just finished shaving, putting little pieces of toilet paper on the razor nicks. When he met Zola in the hall, ready to go, he whistled softly. She blushed a deep red.

"Frances, you look beautiful."

Zola tried to shrink away, fade into the doorway.

"You shouldn't be here, Frances, you know that. What is it? Is something wrong?" He was trying to hold Zola's hand.

"Uh, Dr. Darcardt. It's me, Zola May. From the college." She spoke slowly, deliberately. "You called and said you needed a ride in, to the college."

Shock chased off the concern, followed by shame, in Darcardt's face.

"I'm so sorry. Forgive me. Please."

"It's okay." She wished she could look at him. "Are you ready?"

"I'm . . . I'm ready." He held his left hand against his chest, tried to breathe. "Zola? Promise me something?"

"What, Dr. Darcardt?"

"Can you promise me first?"

"Sure," she said, leading him by the arm to her car. "I promise. What is it?"

"Please don't tell Judy, okay? Please don't tell her."

Tilia in spring

The men had been gone for hours before Tilia gave in, went up to Michael's room.

Kenny had left it the same as before, as if he had not even slept there. Johnny had peeled the mattress and bedding from the springs and slept on them sandwiched between the bed-frame and the dresser.

She got down on hands and knees to crawl onto the mattress, favoring the left hip she expected it was her destiny to break, then sat up again. There was a new feeling about the room that was more than Johnny's presence, more than the Kenny effect. It was as if there were something she was supposed to see that had been hidden.

It could not be another paperback bawdy book under the mattress, because she had checked thoroughly after she'd found the first one. That was when she'd first gone in to put fresh sheets on the bed, the day after the MIA letter arrived.

Tilia climbed onto the springs, wobbled from side to side before she lost her balance and rolled over. Gray hairs that had escaped her bun caught in the coils near the footboard. By the time she got free she was stretched out on her stomach staring at the base of the footboard, below the mattress line.

> Michael was here
>
> I am an American
>
> Michael
> -n-
> Janet

She ran her fingertips across the gouges in the grain, letting them linger in the curves of the heart. *I am an American.* Why would he write such things? She searched her memory for Janet and could find no place for her. Michael had always said he was going out with friends, usually Bobby Conerale and Jim Ostrum. He never mentioned a girl's name.

Michael's yearbook was downstairs on the bureau. Tilia knew that it would probably contain enough clues to solve the mystery, but she did not want to go just yet.

These uncovered messages were the strongest signs of life she had felt in Michael's room for years.

She was going to savor them.

Prett's dental plan

Prett tried to chew the sandwich, smooth peanut butter with raspberry jam, but the crust was too tough for his inflamed gums. He soaked the edge of it in his coffee, dropped it between his gums and squeezed them together, wincing as the sugar from the coffee and the raspberry seeds attacked the nerves in his mouth. He whimpered.

"Why don' you go get your teeth fixed?" Stosh asked, without sympathy.

"Damn butchers. You know I ain't got no more teef."

"Yeah, but you got false teeth, aintcha? What the hell is the matter with 'em? Get 'em fixed!"

Prett turned away from Stosh on his ash stump and tried to gobble the rest of the sandwich down. He tasted putrid blood in among the raspberry, bleached wheat and peanut butter. As he tried to move the butter with his tongue, away from the frayed flesh that had once held his teeth in place, unwilled tears spilled from his eyes. The blood in his throat made him gag. He coughed against it, tried to clamp his jaws shut, but instead retched onto the ground.

"Jesus, Prett! Quit it, willya? I'm tryin' ta eat over here." Stosh inserted the least grease-stained finger into his mouth for moisture then pointed it up in the air, sniffing for confirmation that he was upwind, and went back to gnawing on his beef sandwich.

After retching and groaning until he was empty, Prett stumbled to the truck and climbed into the back, rifling through Stosh's toolbox. He snatched up a pair of side-cutters, bent out the side truck mirror so he could peer into his mouth, and cut away the stinking edges of his gums.

As he finished scuffing the rotted flesh into the dirt, he thought of how it had been when his teeth were okay, when he had insurance and could afford to go to the dentist.

Even though he had hated the work, there were times he wished he had not quit the mill.

Aurelia holds the fort

The clothes dried quickly, it was so warm with a crisp light breeze. Aurelia took them down in the usual way, folding everything, matching the socks, clothespins secured in their own pouch on a clothes hanger. She was thinking she could iron Kenny's things, too, although he never went anyplace where he needed pressed clothes.

It wouldn't hurt to mow the lawn today. It was only the 8th of May, but the grass was high enough for her to kill a half hour.

She was mad that Janie wasn't going to the college today. Janie had told Aurelia so late that she missed the chance to ride with Zola May. And then the look that Janie gave her when Aurelia said she couldn't drive herself. Didn't Janie know she already felt guilty enough? Aurelia knew her limits, and driving all the way across the city with two lanes of traffic each way and parked cars and who knows how many stoplights, not to mention college kids walking around all over the place. No thank you. She'd end up in the hospital with nobody to visit her, and Kenny with no home to come home to.

No sir, she was going to sit tight today. And Janie better know she was taking her along tomorrow, to graduation, she better know it.

Once she'd mowed the lawn, Aurelia was running out of things to do that could take her mind off of Kenny. She could put the clothes away or maybe start some big project like cleaning the windows or mopping all the floors in the house.

She decided to take Kenny's clothes upstairs to his room, to bring the crisp, clean spring air inside. She reached the top of the stairs, made the turn into Kenny's room and held her breath for a moment as she saw the made bed, felt no signs of life.

Four and a half steps from the bed to the dresser. She stuffed his underwear in the top right drawer, gathered his socks to put in the top left. They were all white, or actually, had been white. Kenny would only wear white socks, and he refused to wear slippers, so the soles of his socks were always soiled gray or brown, depending on what he had walked through. Aurelia had done her best to get them clean and white again.

She pushed them into the sock drawer, began to pull her hands back, when the snakes began to writhe up around her wrists and arms. She screamed, shook them off her, and they wriggled across the floor toward the stairs and freedom.

For a moment, Aurelia could not move.

Prom night. She hadn't been sure about it. Her father had told Cough he'd wanted her to go, that if Martha were able to say, she would have wanted her to go. Aurelia had not been sure.

The boy had been fine during the prom, dancing a few slow dances with her, only showing off for his friends part of the time. Afterward they'd gone parking in his father's Buick, down by the river on the maintenance road near the sewage treatment plant.

They made out, or rather he made out with her, as she wrestled first with her need to make him stop, then with her need to let go of her fear.

Aurelia had been so caught up in her head that by the time she'd decided to embrace her desire he had already stopped. Then she wasn't even sure how far he had gone, until on the ride home he told her he was sorry about not kissing very well, that he wasn't used to it. She had been his first.

The memory of the snakes was beginning to fade. At some point it would be submerged, just like the fact that she had once been asked to the prom.

Robin makes the grade

He stared at the blank space next to her name, unable to fill it in with an Incomplete that would eventually convert to an "F". He thought of her insights in class, the notes in her class journal, the quality of the rest of her work, and marked down an "A" for the semester. After taking her to the party last night, if anyone questioned Robin's grade he'd really be in trouble. Harlan decided he just didn't care.

Celeste crash-lands

She kept an eye on the traffic behind her with the side mirror, using the rear view to spot blemishes to squeeze between the nails of her right thumb and index finger. Celeste's face was a landscape of red puffy swells against ashen skin.

She had driven south to Syracuse, to watch the huge passenger planes fly overhead. There was a small, mostly abandoned park nearby, where she liked to go to make light of her mother's suggestions that she really should have become an airline stewardess. Once she had told Guppy about it. He had laughed, teased her, and made her question why she had ever trusted him enough to reveal her secret.

"I'm sorry," he'd said, and had never brought it up again. She felt better. But from that point on, she also worried that he might have been right.

She listened to the planes sear through the sky and cried until she was empty. When she was dry and numb, she got in the car and headed back to Onlius. The young man on the side of the road didn't look particularly dangerous, but she picked him up anyway, hoping his innocent looks were deceptive.

Kenny talks small

The woman was white, so Kenny was hesitant about getting a ride from her. But Emilio hadn't told him it was wrong to trust all white people, just to be extra careful, so he decided to give her a chance. Besides, she had something wrong with her face and she seemed really upset.

"Yes, ma'am. Onlius."

"Where in Onlius? I might be able to take you there."

"I'm not sure."

He could really be dangerous. Celeste felt fear, and at the same time, excitement. This might be the last drive of her life.

Tensing her breath to keep it even, she braved a steady stream of small talk, punctuated by quick occasional attempts at direct eye contact. The guy was wearing too-small overalls over a lavender T-shirt whose logo was faded beyond recognition. His face had seen an unusual amount of sun already for the second week of May. Celeste wasn't sure of the exact source of the disagreeable odor, but she suspected it was coming through the rips in his sneakers. She pushed the button for the floor vent to off.

Kenny was pleased with himself for keeping up with the conversation. Yes, it had been awfully sunny, except for that one rain on Wednesday. Warm May. Sunny. Yes, he was kind of tired from walking. No, it's not really all that bad. Visiting a relative, yes. In Onlius. He grinned at that one, feeling very sharp. Visiting a relative. He'd have to try to remember that one.

Why's she so jumpy? "*Chatter is what they do when they're really scared, Kenny. The faster they talk, the more nervous they feel about you.*" He thought Emilio had been right about that. *What's wrong with me?*

Kenny shifted on his seat to study her.

"You said Onlius, right? Where in Onlius?"

"I dunno."

"You mean you don't even know how to get there, right?" Her voice was rising. She filled every lapse in the conversation.

"Right."

"But you've got to have some idea."

"He's at the college."

"The college? You're sure?" It was the last place she would have guessed.

"Do ya know how to get there?"

She knew the way to the college. She also knew that going there made her feel sick and weak.

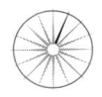

Janie, where Billy is not

". . . An estranged husband and father, dead from shooting himself after shooting and killing his former wife and three children."

Janie twisted the radio dial off and shivered. Billy's father was such an asshole, but he'd never do anything like that, she'd once

236 / The Middle of Everywhere

thought. Then he'd taken off on a drunken tear for three days when she was pregnant with Billy, ending up with Jessica Fillmore. She'd wondered how she could have been so naive about him.

He was so cute, and troubled, and dangerous, at least according to her mother. She had left home to be with him, even though by that time she knew it was a mistake.

She was tired of her parents trying to tell her who she should see and how late she should stay out. Earl reminded her that she was old enough to decide on her own. It was obvious who would get her out of that old folk's home and free.

Billy should be home by now, shouldn't he? What's the number of that kid he went home with yesterday?

Janie had to work second shift again, and needed to get Billy supper, then take him over to Barb's house for the overnight. She was supposed to check on how the guys were doing with the petition, too. Billy was going to get it if he got home late.

Where Billy is

"Here, Billy, try some of this pie," Justin said.

"Tt-ppuh, tt-ppuh. Okay. Gimme it."

Justin handed Billy a fresh handful of dirt. He sprinkled some on his tongue, closed his mouth and considered it.

"Well, whaddaya think? Purty good?"

"Yuh, yuh. Tay-stee."

"Hey, Billy, weren'tcha s'posed to go home right after school?"

He let the mud drip from his tongue back onto the dirt pile in Justin's backyard. He didn't answer.

Kenny closes in

"Is that the college?" Kenny asked, pointing to the tallest buildings in Onlius.

"Where? Oh, those tall buildings?"

He nodded. "Uh-huh."

"No, they're high-rise apartments for, you know, low-income people."

"But we're near the college, right? This is Onlius?"

"Yes, this is Onlius."

She watched him squeeze his hands into fists, leaning forward in his seat, looking around excitedly.

"It's not that much farther."

"Can you take us right there? Right to the college? Please?"

Celeste didn't answer him. She wasn't sure if she could handle running into her husband.

"I'm sorry," Kenny said, close to tears. "It was so hard for me to get this far and I . . . I could get lost again." He clutched his backpack, struggling not to plead.

"It's not out of my way," Celeste said around the arid lump that was her tongue. *I'll tell Ernie everything when I see him. Maybe it'll be better anyway if it's not at home.*

"I'll take you to the college, Kenny, you just relax."

"Thanks," he replied, trying to remember now what he was supposed to do when he got there.

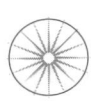

Kenny at a normal school

"Where is she?" Celeste whispered, spotting Zola's vacant office chair.

Kenny glanced quickly from the tile floor to study Celeste. She had led him into the department suite from the side hallway, which weaved through the Research Center to a little-used back entrance opening to a path to the student lot. They hadn't spoken to anyone on their way in, Celeste fearing she might run into Marie.

"She must be at lunch," Celeste whispered again.

Kenny hugged his backpack.

"I guess we could try calling from here," she said as she paced. On the third pass she suddenly climbed into Zola's chair. "McAdam was who you wanted, right?"

"Yes, ma'am."

"All right, then." Celeste dialed, Kenny watched her wait as it rang and rang. "Nobody's picking up, not even Axe."

He slid his back down the wall, squeezing his knees.

"We'll call back later, all right? Just relax, Kenny."

He rocked back and forth on his haunches.

"Calm down, Kenny, you've got to get a grip."

"I'm trying."

Celeste returned to pacing. Going over to the Admin building was out of the question. Waiting around so close to Marie's and Ernie's offices, she felt vulnerable.

"Kenny, I've got to get out of here right now. Do you want to come with me?"

"You promise I'll get a chance to talk to him?"

"Yes. I just need to go right now."

She watched as he held his hands palm up, eyes closed, an expression of calm beginning to spread across his face.

"Okay, I'll go," he said dreamily.

"Let's get out of here, then. The same way we came in." She decided to take him home. If that made it tough for Guppy, too bad.

The way Kenny was hugging his backpack and petting his little pieces of fur made her want to see Ernie's expression.

~

Celeste hadn't noticed he was missing in action until she was almost out the exit door. She'd been thinking about what had gone wrong with her and Guppy.

By the time she found Kenny in the psych lab he was sitting on the floor with his sneaker laces triple-knotted, his nails chewed down to bleeding.

The only thing Kenny could tell her was that something from the classroom they passed by, maybe the smell of chalk dust, triggered the flashback.

Mrs. Porter never listened to him, not after he'd lost his pencils, scissors, crayons, and ruler on the first day of school. Kenny had told her the older kids took his school supplies while he was walking home, but she told him she'd been warned about his antics and wasn't about to let him get away with that kind of monkey business, thank you.

So when he was trying to tie his shoes for the fourth time today, and she reminded him, and all the aglets were gone so he couldn't get them laced, he got kind of frustrated.

He had jerked them off his feet, at her suggestion, got the hush puppies turned around so that some of the laces got jammed into the wrong eyelets and had to start again. Meanwhile he looked up from his sock feet to see everyone else waiting for him, the bigger kids especially annoyed because he was slowing them down from extorting lunch money on the way to the cafeteria.

"Are you quite finished, Mr. Hopewell?" Mrs. Porter asked, the same way she had when Ted was in tears finishing his math test.

He could tell she was about to tie them herself, or worse yet, have someone else do it. He couldn't get his fingers to work right. The faster he was trying to lace them, the more unlaced they got.

Mrs. Porter's kielbasa breath was bearing down on him. Kenny could hear the crackling from her knees and ankles, 1940s perfume struggling to overcome the odor of chafed thighs.

He worked his hands faster, then brought the shoes up to his face to try to catch the frayed ends of the laces in his teeth.

"You'd think that a boy your age, a normal boy, would be able to do this," she hissed. "Perhaps we'll have to assign a normal child to this pair of shoes." She peered over her shoulder at the rest of the class. "Is there some normal child who could do this?"

Melissa Barriston, Karen Cohan and Angela Costraros shot their hands up into the air instantly, the rest of the girls and the obedient boys following in short order.

Kenny tore into the shoes with his teeth, shredding the left one before Mrs. Porter could get the teacher in the other first-grade class next door to come in and pull it away from him. It was he who brought in the pair of loafers they made Kenny wear for the rest of the year, even after Wiley got him some new sneakers with laces he could tie just fine. Mrs. Porter ignored the notes from home, although both Wiley and Martha had gone in to tell her how bothered Kenny was. If he wasn't allowed to do things he had learned, why should he learn new things?

Carrie's Friday night

Fingers of blue and yellow and orange, waving and reaching, dancing and stretching, hungering to eat all the way to the ceiling. They caught Carrie's eyes, always. She looked up from her book. They made her afraid, excited.

She was gazing at the burner flames as her mother made supper.

"Carrie, honey, don't stare like that. It gives me the creeps."

"Okay. Sorry." She put down her book, set the table, and plopped back down on her chair. She slid a butter knife blade back and forth down the cracks between two leaves of the table to dislodge crumbs that had dried like glue.

"I thought you just started a new book," Georgette said.

"I did, Ma."

"Isn't it good?"

"I guess so." Carrie stopped scraping out the crumbs. She used the knife blade to unearth some grit from beneath her fingernails. "It's just Friday night."

Georgette let the words hang in the air. Carrie was always like this on Friday nights since the fire.

"Oh, my God, Carrie. You've got a Ouija board. Where did you get a Ouija board?"

"My cousin lent it to me. We could try later."

"Sure. After we do all the other stuff we planned to do, all right?"

"Okay."

They had braided each other's hair, made up stories about what happened in that shed, ate pop tarts, crackers and chips they'd sneaked out of each other's houses, talked about what they were going to do when they grew up, listened to tapes on Joanie's Walkman, read passages from Georgette's latest trashy paperback romance, decided which boys were cute, lit candles and tried to smoke some of Mrs. Prwanzas' Ultra Lite cigarettes, compared erroneous information on how girls got pregnant.

The fire started before they got around to the Ouija board. Joanie got trapped in the shed going back in for her Walkman and the rest of her mother's cigarettes. Not all of the shed burned down, but the oily rags went up fast. The fire chief said it was either one of the candles or the cigarette butt. If it had not been for the half-burned Ouija board, Joanie's mother may have accepted the cigarette-butt explanation.

Stosh drove Joanie to the hospital, a wet towel wrapped around her head. Carrie'd wanted to go, but there wasn't enough room in the truck, so she stayed home in shock.

Chester was relieved that Joanie wasn't hanging around his sister any more. He was sick of being the only one to point out how queer they acted, even at school.

A bridge is burned

Through the bandages that still covered her ears and eyes: "If I ever catch you around that Casimir girl again, I'll have her put in prison, you understand me?"

At the company town meeting

Johnny Percy recognized the look in their eyes. It was clear they'd already gotten to the town board. You could tell them you were going to dump raw sewage in the water tower, put radioactive waste in the school basement and do biological warfare tests in their garages and it would be fine with them, as long as somebody from Mid-Northern Lakeland Inc. told them so.

Johnny wished they'd let him bring his rifle into the town office for the meeting. Glaring at them wasn't doing much good. These people needed to get a healthy respect. He'd told Alfonzo and Cough the rifle would be just a visual aid, like the guns people brought to enforce the penny auctions at Midwestern farm foreclosures.

"Where's the petition?" Johnny whispered harshly. Cough turned around and got in Johnny's face. "Young Johnny, we're real grateful for your help today. We couldn'ta done it without ya." He didn't blink. "But let me tell you somethin' just between us." Cough motioned for Johnny's ear.

"We don't wanna tip our hands too soon," he whispered. "The timing has to be just right. Besides, it isn't here just yet."

"*What?*" Cough caught Johnny's arm to keep him from launching out of his folding chair. He led him out of the room to the hallway by the town clerk's office. Johnny's eyes were narrowing, like he was looking for a fight. Cough had to hush him all the way.

"What'd you say?" he demanded, as soon as Cough stopped.

"You heard me. The petition's not here yet."

"Whaddaya mean it's not here? It was here an hour ago."

"Yeah, I know, but it's still in Lyle's trunk, remember? He drove it home for supper, then he's comin' right back for the meeting."

"But who's with him? Who's keeping an eye on the petition while he's eatin'?"

Cough's pause was too long for Johnny.

"Don't know, do ya? Might be nobody's guardin' it, and the meeting's already started."

"Now you listen, Young Johnny. You ain't the only one who's been workin' on this, y'know."

"This isn't even my fight. I don't work at the mill. I wanted to help Alfonzo is all, an' now I'm into it. I'm sick of losin' fights that aren't even mine."

Cough put a hand on his shoulder. "I know it, son. You been a big help today, chasin' off them Mid-Northern boys." He frowned. "Listen, I'm kinda worried myself. You wanna take my car out there an' see what's goin' on, kinda hustle them along if they ain't on their way?"

"Just gimme the keys."

"Here ya go. He's out on Martin's Creek Road, on the right past the tire-retread place. Y'know where I'm talkin' about?"

"I'm there, Mister Niclay. You get back in there and stall 'em if you need to."

Cough answered with his resolute stride down the hallway back to the meeting room. "Shit, Lyle," he cursed under his breath. "Where the hell are ya?"

Lyle on the job

"There's gotta be thousands of 'em, babe. Thousands."

"I know, honey," Zola puffed. "You said that before. Great."

Lyle was wrapped around her, in a fever, pulsing with excitement. Zola was overwhelmed.

"Thousands, thousands, thousands." Lyle repeated, each time a little faster.

"Honey, honey, honey."

"Thousands . . ."

"Honey!" Zola braced herself still, grabbed the sides of Lyle's face in her hands.

"I know it, babe.

"Lyle! No!"

"What?!"

"It's time for the meeting, Lyle. You've got to get the truck to town."

"Inna minute, babe. Only one more minute."

She knew there was nothing she could do but let him finish.

"Thousands. . ."

Horace takes the silver

"There's the fucker. We finally caught up to it," Wade said, pointing down the driveway to Lyle's truck.

"Whatcha gonna do?" Horace asked.

"Whaddaya think?"

"Well, you're just gonna get rid o' the petition, right? Keep the mill goin', without the troublemakers?"

Wade's mouth hung slightly open, like he'd just heard the most ridiculous thing. Teddy grinned at him admiringly. "Oh yeah, I'm sure they're gonna keep the mill open for ya. O' course," Teddy said. He pushed past Horace.

"How ya wanna do this?" he asked Wade.

"Torch it."

Teddy nodded. "Get it outta the truck first?"

"Uh, uh. Not enough time."

"Ya sure?" Horace asked, as loudly as he dared, the sound carrying halfway down the driveway.

"This is when you go back an' sit in the truck, Horace, an' let us finish the job. Might be some stuff you don't wanna see."

"Wait. You're not gonna hurt anybody?"

"Truck's kinda close to the trailer," Teddy observed.

Wade ignored Horace. "That's why it's gotta be quick. Just do it, now, right in the back of the truck."

"I ain't . . ."

"Shut up, Teddy. Don't say nothin' more." Wade's eyes shifted to Horace, bore into him. "It's time this old man went back to the truck."

"An' what if I don't?" Horace had no idea he'd gotten the courage to ask.

"It's simple. You hold us up, we don't get the job done. Or . . ." Wade hissed, "you stay an' become a witness. Maybe an accessory."

Horace was ten paces back toward the truck before Wade said "maybe."

"Hey, Horace?" Teddy called softly. "If you walk back to town yourself, we never even seen you before."

Wade chortled at Horace's heavy frame crackling through the brush past their truck.

"We'll do it on three," he said, as he lit the kerosene-soaked rags.

"One . . . two . . . three . . . ," Wade whispered, so quietly that Teddy could hear voices in the trailer before the roll of paper went up.

Flames reflected dark and watery in Wade's sunglasses. They shot up past the tops of the frames with a loud "crack" as the gallon can of chain-saw fuel mix exploded.

"What're we waitin' for?" Teddy said nervously.

"We gotta make sure."

"That thing's gotta be gone by now."

"Shh . . . Just one more minute."

The side of the truck bed that Teddy could see was scorched. Something more than the roll of paper was on fire.

"Look at that thing, Wade! Let's get outta here!"

"Just a second."

"Wade! The whole fuckin' truck's goin' up! We gotta get them outta the trailer!"

The more the flames filled his lenses, the broader they made Wade's smile.

A scream escaped the trailer. "Wade, they're gonna burn up in there!"

Wade turned the ignition switch calmly. "Don't worry, Teddy. It's a dry heat."

The Judge makes his move

"The mystery's over now," Cough said, spotting the man sitting just inside the doorway to the town justice's office. He pointed his index finger in that direction and tapped it on his knee until everyone from the mill was looking.

"Izzat who I think it is?" Artie Furlong asked.

"Yeah, it is. Sumner Hayslee," Cough said ominously.

"Who?" They all looked at Cough.

"Hayslee. You know," Cough added, "the Judge."

"Not *the* Judge?" Alfonzo asked.

"The one and only."

"The Judge who's wanted dis mill for a long time?"

"Yeah, Alfonzo." As if on cue the three rows of mill people shifted in their seats to catch a better look.

"He don' look so big," Alfonzo muttered.

"It ain't his size, Alfonzo," Artie whispered.

"I know it. If he's so important, then why is he here? He must not be such a big shot."

There ain't any Arabs, or Germans, or Japanese, or whatever. It's been the Judge all the time. Cough studied him, his detached air with the mill people and the town board. The way his face was a veneer of composure all the time, barely covering an irritability with every facet of his life. Watching his face redden when some common person made eye contact, Cough realized just how addicted the Judge was to power.

It wasn't enough to Sumner that he already held so many people's lives in his hands with the businesses he owned. The fact that this was the only paper mill he didn't have was so galling to him that he wasn't about to tolerate it any longer, and the only thing standing in his way was the franchise for the hydroelectric plant. Once they turned it over to the mill, it would be his.

Tommy Fergus was town supervisor, a job he'd wanted more for the health insurance and the feeling of importance than for serving the public. He was a glad-hander, and there were more drinking buddies in the crowd of mill workers than he wanted to see. In fact, there were more people at this meeting than at any other he could remember.

Bucky Fresh, the member of the board with the longest tenure, was the most anxious man facing the vote. Arguably the most influential elected official in town, he chafed at the knowledge of how far he was from being a bona fide member of the power elite. The Judge was certainly first due to all his statewide connections, and the current mill owner, C. Oliver Dorman, second. The owner-editor of the Alta *Weekly Reporter*, Fear Staunton, might think he was third, but everyone knew it was a small-town rag and the dailies in Onlius and Syracuse and Watertown were the only ones that carried real news.

The sale of the mill could put Bucky up a rung, or maybe two, depending on who ended up in the owner's seat. For Bucky, a shut-down mill would be preferable to one owned by Sumner Hayslee.

Sumner had inherited the title Judge from his father, who'd inherited it from his father, the only person in the Hayslee line who had in fact been a magistrate. It was his grandfather Rudolph's ruling, in fact, that had ensured the Town of Alta would retain the riparian rights for the hydroelectric plant, back in the days before Niagara Hudson had merged with Mohawk Electric and began to gobble up hydropower franchises. That same ruling also set up the quest for the mill, because it was the one thing, the only thing, Rudolph had not gotten for Sumner the First at his mother's insistence. The more Sumner whined about it, the more Jacqueline Candleston Hayslee had pushed her husband to somehow get it for him. Rudolph reluctantly began working on C. Oliver to sell him the mill.

"Bullshit" was C. Oliver's standard response to Rudolph, then Sumner One and later Sumner Two. By the time it had come to Sumner Two to follow in the tradition, the principle of the flawed inheritance was no longer the object. The publicly-owned power plant ran on falling water, such an embarrassingly appealing alternative to the steam generation business into which the family had conglomerated. Sumner Two needed to have it so he could shut it down.

"It's not the production, but the power that counts," Sumner One had always said. Sumner Two agreed. Nuclear power added so much more to the rate base, was so exotic, not like the abundant waterpower in the area. That was the fact that really bugged Sumner Two—waterpower and wind power were so common.

He cringed every time he drove by a windmill rusting next to a silo or barn. If that idea caught on again, people might get interested in solar power and biomass and who knows what else. People might start thinking about the quality of their lives, how much time they spent with their kids, *what they did with their kids.* Video-game sales would drop, families would turn off their TVs. *They might read more.*

Sumner Two had to push all these fears from his mind before he could come to this meeting. So he'd ordered Francoise to let no one disturb him, and to prepare some cucumber slices.

When he awoke, every particle of his being was the Judge.

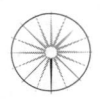

Johnny on the spot

"Bastards! Sonsabitches!" Lyle kicked the side of his scorched truck each time he screamed.

"Hey! You all right?" Johnny shouted out Cough's car window as he skidded down the driveway.

"Yeah. Sonsabitches!"

"Okay, I'm goin' after 'em!"

"After who? Who ya mean?"

"I gotta get goin'!" Johnny yelled as he backed the car around. "Two guys in a Ranger Club Cab! I think they torched ya!"

"I'm goin' with ya!" Lyle yelled back, running alongside the Chevy.

"No! Get to the meetin'! Tell 'em what happened! I'll bring 'em in if I can!" Johnny gunned it, kicking gravel stones in Lyle's direction as he ran through the gears.

"Bastards!"

The college cavalry

"The third resolution on the agenda this evening," Fergus said as evenly as he could, "deals with the disposition of the town property at Whitewater Ridge to Alta Paper."

"What'd he say?" Alfonzo asked.

"Shh, it's the one about the mill," Cough answered.

"But what'd he say?"

"Shh. I didn't hear it either. Pipe down," Artie said.

"The town will receive a guarantee of power for its offices at cost of production plus cost of billing from Alta Paper providing that sufficient flow is available . . ."

"What're they sayin'?"

"They are explaining the terms for the giveaway of the community's birthright," one of the new arrivals said.

"Who're you?" Cough asked.

"We're friends. We've come to help," the younger one whispered. "Aurelia Hopewell and Janie Nicmond told us what's happening."

"Shh," Artie insisted. "I can't follow all this."

"The very first thing you need to realize," Darcardt announced, "is that the details are irrelevant. Don't let them even bring it up for a vote."

The mill people looked at him approvingly.

". . . operation of the hydroelectric station shall conform to all municipal, state and federal regulations, appertaining to, including environmental, work safety. . ."

All eyes in the back of the room were on Harlan and Darcardt, all ears waiting to hear how to keep the measure from coming up for a vote. Darcardt's temples began to throb. He leaned back against the wall, and his shirt stuck to it. Harlan helped ease him down into a folding chair vacated by Artie. Artie's wife Gloria pressed her cheek up against Darcardt's forehead, and declared that he was feverish. Then everyone was looking at Harlan with the same sense of expectation. He swallowed and thought up his angle of attack. This was the moment he'd been begging for all his life, and now that it was upon him, he was desperate to be somewhere else, anywhere else.

He opened his mouth, but nothing would come out.

Cough looked him in the face to gauge whether his panic was real, concluding to himself that it was probably worse than it looked.

"You guys from the college?" he asked Harlan.

"Uh, yes. Janie told us what was going on, and Zola May Lester. Uh, where's Janie?"

Can't know her too well, if he has to ask. "Second shift," he replied. "Everybody here's on other shifts."

God, I don't know any of these people and they're hostile on top of it. "Oh, yeah. I should have known."

Cough regarded him for another moment, then sat back down to listen to Tommy Fergus drone on about the resolution. Harlan sat in silence, resentful. He might have said or done something, but at the moment he wasn't able to think.

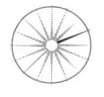

Lyle loses his love

Lyle had jumped up from their bed and run naked out the back, kicking in the clutch in time to coast the truck away from the trailer. Zola

May put butter on the blistering burns from his calves to his shoulder blades, peeling away as much of the burnt blue vinyl as she dared, leaving the patches that looked like they had fused with his flesh.

"It still hurts like hell. Can't you get any more o' that on them burns?" He whined in a higher tone than usual, full of resentment at the loss of his truck. Lyle had so many speeding tickets, including the ones he'd pleaded down, that he could only afford basic liability insurance.

"I'm afraid to do any more of it. I think you'll be all right, though. Shouldn't we get going to the meeting?"

"The meeting? The meeting? Ain't I done enough? You think I'm gonna be able to drive that truck?"

"That truck is ours," Zola began quietly. "Just like my car is ours. Whatever we need to do, we'll do."

"Yeah, and it'll cost *us* a lotta money."

"So you don't think we oughtta try to save your job?"

"I ain't goin' to no meeting. That's enough." He tried to cross his arms, winced.

"I don't get it," Zola yelled. "At least tell them what happened."

Lyle harrumphed and scratched. "What time is it?" he finally asked.

"Almost a quarter to eight."

"When did the meeting start?"

"Seven. You know that."

"I guess it's okay." Lyle's frown metamorphosed into a smirk. "Well, maybe it was worth it."

"You guess? What does that mean? They're waiting over at the town hall for our truck, and it's supposed to have a huge roll of paper in back with thousands of signatures on it. Am I right?"

"Well, sorta."

"Sorta?" She was out of patience. "Whatever it is you haven't told me, you better say right now."

"It's okay, hon, it's gotta be all right by now. Ya see, the petition was in another truck."

"*Another* truck?"

"Cough wanted it switched, so they couldn't do anythin' to it, y'know, before the meetin'."

"So that roll in our truck was just a . . ."

"Yup. A decoy."

"And somebody burned up the back of our truck, and almost killed us, for a decoy?"

"Yeah."

"Bastards. Sonsabitches."

Celeste, lost and found

Celeste planned on driving until she found a place where her forehead felt cool, where her mind would stop grinding about what to do. It wasn't that she knew what it would feel like, more what it wouldn't feel like.

It wouldn't be a place with vertical blinds, or guilt, or the Op-Ed page of the *New York Times*. There would be no faculty parties or exams of any kind; time would not be measured in semesters.

Getting lost seemed to be what she wanted, so as long as she knew where she was, she kept driving. It didn't really surprise her that when she found herself totally lost, she was at Marie Earhart's.

There goes the Judge

Artie lent them a couple of hydraulic jacks on coasters so the Long Petition could be brought into the Town Hall as an exhibit. At first Tommy Fergus insisted that they roll it out to confirm the three thousand, four hundred thirteen signatures of voters they managed to get in less than a day. But after a full minute of rolling and rolling, the signatures becoming a steady blur—and each time he yelled "stop" to verify, seeing names of people he knew—voters—Fergus regretted it.

"Michael Berry," Marian Younis, the town clerk read aloud. "Beverly Berry. Tilia Aligheri."

Alfonzo sat up straighter, the curve of his back less of a question mark.

"Alfonzo Aligheri. Michael Aligheri."

Some of the mill workers shuddered, a few glared at Alfonzo. He sat even straighter, set his jaw.

"I think we get the picture," Fergus interrupted.

"Georgette Casimir," Marian read.

Fergus shouted, "We don't need to hear the whole thing."

Bucky Fresh had been watching the anger rising in the Judge's face, red blotches on his cheeks and neck, fingers drumming faster on the armrest of his chair. "I'd like to hear more of it," he said quietly.

"Arthur Furlong, Jeremy Dates," Marian continued. Marian's brother Ray and her sister-in-law Eunice both worked at the mill.

"I said . . ." Tommy Fergus began, before he felt the eyes of scores of mill workers and their families.

He's spitting the bit, the Judge thought. That would leave only Oscar Van Pelt on the town board who might have the guts to stand up to the mob. Sumner made a little wave with his left hand that Oscar saw, but which the mill workers could not. Oscar rose to speak.

"Even if we are to assume that these are valid signatures," Oscar said flatly, "we have to consider the economic impact studies . . ."

The double doors at the back of the meeting hall burst open from the force of Teddy and Wade being pushed through. They tripped and fell in the aisle at the foot of the jack stand holding the Long Petition. Johnny Percy stepped inside the doorway, his rifle cradled across his arm, grinning fiercely at the town board in the front of the room.

"Who the hell are you?" Oscar shouted.

Johnny pointed toward Wade and Teddy with the rifle barrel. "I just caught these boys destroying the petition." He looked confused by the paper roll on its stand. "They just burned up Lyle Lester's truck."

Marian sprinted to her office to call the county sheriffs. Everyone stared at Wade and Teddy except Johnny Percy, who looked from the Long Petition over to Cough, twice. Cough couldn't meet Johnny's eyes.

Oscar cleared his throat and said to the floor, "I make a motion to approve the resolution to turn over the town's hydroelectric franchise to Mid-Northern Lakeland Inc." When he finished he glanced in Sumner's direction, expecting to see the okay sign. He saw the Judge's recently vacated chair. All other eyes looked to the empty chair as well.

"I tol' you he's not so big," Alfonzo said out loud. Bucky Fresh's question, "Is there a second?" echoed back to him. The only sound was tires spinning gravel from the parking lot by the rear entrance.

Lyle and Zola May showed up just in time to look Wade and Teddy in the eye before they were read their rights, handcuffed, and taken away. In the commotion, Oscar Van Pelt and Tommy Fergus held a whispered caucus on how to salvage the resolution.

"I don' like this," Alfonzo said to Cough.

"I don't neither, Alfonzo. But whadda we do?"

"Motion to table," Harlan heard. He looked at Darcardt next to him, his eyes now open and clear.

"John, suggest a motion to table."

"To table?" Harlan puzzled. "Won't the company just come back next meeting and push it through?"

"Of course they'd try, but take a look around you."

Johnny Percy paced in the back of the meeting hall, too pumped up to sit down. The only mill people not in animated debate were gathered around the Long Petition, gently rolling it out to study the names of neighbors and friends who had signed to save Alta Paper.

"You think tabling it will keep them together longer," Harlan said.

"Looks that way, don't you think?" Darcardt sat up more and surveyed the hall. "That's what they'll need the most in the long run, John, to stick together."

No one was happy with the outcome, because it meant the fight wasn't over. But Harlan had enough of his wits about him by then to tell them they'd had a victory, which they already knew, and that the powers-that-be would come after them again, which they already suspected. But they loved what he told them about the worker-owned steel mill in West Virginia, and the community-owned paper company in Canada.

It was obvious they would not let themselves be stuck again.

The Judge delivers a ruling

The Judge took the call only after Francoise assured him that it was Young Dorman—C. Oliver's son, Mark—on the line.

Yes, he suspected the vote would go that way. That's why he didn't hang around. He said it with the same dull conviction he'd practiced over and over.

Well, perhaps it was best to let them win this one. No, he wasn't crazy, and he planned on forgetting that Young Dorman had said that.

"It only looks like giving up if you don't have the big picture. It's best to wear them down so much in some battles that eventually they let you win the war."

"Should I arrange bail and legal help for Wade and Teddy?" Dorman asked him.

"Shut up, and don't ever say that again."

After a stunned pause, Dorman asked, "You mean leave them high and dry?"

Idiots I have to deal with! "That is not your concern. Are you following me?"

"I think so."

"Then just sit tight, and relax. Can you do that?"

"Yeah, sure."

The Judge said okay, and to wait for word from him. After he said goodbye and hung up, the Judge called Gordon to talk over Plan B, setting up Young Dorman for the fall.

Kenny chez Guppy

"Kenny, don't worry. I know you felt better with Celeste, but you're going to be okay. Really."

Kenny was still flinching every time Celeste's husband said something to him. He felt uneasy about this guy. Maybe it was because the guy corrected him so much, about the way he talked, the way he sat, how he ate his dinner. Or was it because the guy couldn't look Celeste in the eye, or maybe how Celeste couldn't look him in the eye? And why hadn't she come back?

Why won't he listen to me? Kenny kept wondering as Guppy drilled him about what to do tomorrow at graduation. Kenny wasn't sure how many times he nodded off before Celeste's husband finally sent him up to bed.

Remember all this stuff, he kept telling himself. But he didn't have a lot of confidence that he would.

Senator J. Danforth Quayle* on Johnny Percy

The defense of America is a terrible thing not to do. It's terrible not to be defensive of one's country.

That is, the defenders of one's country are terrible if they are wasted.

When called to defend my country, from communism, I chose to do what many American sons and daughters did, which was to ask my father to get me into the National Guard, which I did join, and did defend.

So whether the fight is in the fields of Vietnam or Central America, or in the jungles of Lebanon, I know Johnny Percy would join me in defending every son's right to have his father get him into the Indiana National Guard.

---

*Senator Quayle, who became George H.W. Bush's vice president and impeachment insurance, once corrected a sixth grader's spelling of potato by insisting he add an *e* at the end.

Chapter Nine

True North

☼ Kenny's big day

"Kenny! Time to get up!"

The voice sounded from above, as if from God. Kenny sat up, quickly scanned for clues. He was wearing maroon pajamas patterned in paisley, the pants of which stopped three inches above his ankles, the shirt revealing diamond-shaped patches of stomach and chest between each button.

Sets of clothes were laid out about the room, ranging from casual chinos slacks matched with an Onlius State football jersey to a dark pinstripe suit and white dress shirt with pearl buttons. It looked like a bunch of people were getting dressed up.

"Kenny! Are you up?"

"Yeah."

"You don't need to get dressed right away. Just put on the robe that's on the bedpost."

"Okay."

The robe felt like his grandmother's silk pillowcase, the one that was supposed to keep her hairdo in. It was the color of heavy cream as it is just poured into coffee, as it rolls and swims toward the surface. Its sleeves were a good deal longer than those of the pajamas shirt, so they fell a thumb's-length short of his wrist-bone.

He tied the robe together gently, hearing the fabric rend as he tried to straighten his shoulders.

"Kenny! Are you coming?"

"Oh yeah, I forgot."

The expression on the face of the man he found in the kitchen was at once hopeful and lonely, amused and anxious.

"You need some breakfast and a briefing," Guppy said. "Today's your big day."

Kenny smiled at him, reassured. He was really hungry, and happy to hear it was his birthday.

Harlan's breakthrough

His third cup of coffee sent Harlan running to the bathroom, where he sat with a legal pad on his lap scribbling ideas for after the graduation ceremony. Something had been nagging him all night, disturbing his sleep, about this sea change in the military. Harlan had found a lot of evidence to support his thesis, but still something was missing: the dynamic.

Why had the US changed the way it treated its soldiers during the Cold War? It was becoming more like its major opponent over time. Maybe the peacetime draft—begun in 1940 and maintained through Vietnam—had something to do with it.

Harlan ranged back to his office, paced to the kitchen for more coffee, into the living room, back. If he didn't feel close to a breakthrough, he would have been getting ready for the graduation. It was the last chance to test the waters with Robin without calling her at home.

He plopped into his easy chair and cruised through the channels. Saturday morning junk. When he saw the huge boulder on the Acme catapult and the tiny roadrunner, it slammed into his head again.

Overkill. Then another insight. Who still wins even if the coyote always loses?

Janie comes clean

Aurelia was at the door an hour early, dressed in a gray plaid skirt and white high-collared blouse, both of which she had bought at the

Salvation Army. Janie asked her to wait at the kitchen table. It wasn't nearly as cluttered as usual, only cereal bowls and Magic Stars cereal, the gallon of two-percent milk approaching room temperature.

"I'll do this for you," Aurelia offered, as Janie retreated down the hallway for a shower.

"I don't care." She didn't rush the shower, embarrassed at the clutter.

The milk and cereal were put away, the dishes done and the table wiped up when Janie finished. Aurelia was collecting all the toys Billy had left out, into one organized pile in the corner of the living room, the matchbox cars lined in a row like bumper-to-bumper rush hour traffic.

"You do miss him," Janie observed as she looked over Aurelia's shoulder. Aurelia returned a wounded, resentful look.

"Um," Janie said. "I'll be ready in a couple more minutes. As soon as I check on Billy." She called Barb and pleaded with her one more time to come along and bring Billy, but Barb was most concerned that he not miss any of his favorite cartoons.

"Okay, Aurelia, let's go," she said, wishing someone cared that she was graduating.

Darcardt sees the light

White light poured in through Darcardt's bedroom window, one ray illuminating the suspended dust. He kicked the covers to make it swirl. Light and dust. He'd been thinking about it since first opening his eyes this morning. Dust to dust.

Such a relief that his head felt clear today. That was where the light came in. He hadn't been able to make things stop rushng through his mind the last few days. They were the kind of meaningless, obsessive thoughts one gets in a fever, or when a job won't let go, even in sleep.

The light was a sign he'd made the right decision. *Better do it while I can still move.* Every part of his body below his brain ached. He thought he could feel his marrow throb. *Goddamn bomb!* Whenever he had the throbs, he blamed it on being too close to the Nagasaki fallout. *The plutonium one,* he thought bitterly, the one Truman dropped to see if it would work as well as the uranium one. The one that was supposed to end the war before the Soviets could start on Asia, but was too late to prevent the war in Korea.

He worked himself upright on the edge of his bed, though he couldn't keep enough breath to stay there. Darcardt swung his elbows back and forth three times for momentum, then slid off the bed in a lurch for the door. It kept him going to know it was all he had left to do, while the carpet gained gravity.

The manuscript cascaded from the roll-top desk to the floor as he opened it. He thought for a moment before finding a pen and sitting down. He had to oval the pen a few times to loosen up the ball for the ink to flow, an added agony.

Darcardt wrote as carefully as his fingers would let him, printing Harlan's name below the title, *The Spiritual Basis of American Democracy*. He couldn't see the last three letters because the light was blazing in his eyes. *Wow! I guess Plato was right,* he thought as he curled up on his side to sleep, feeling fine just now.

Prett pulls the cord

One half pint oil, the rest gas. A gallon of gas has one half pint of oil. Three quarts, one and a half pints gas, one half pint oil. The formula looped through Prett's mind as they loaded the truck.

Four feet high by eight feet long by four feet wide's a full cord, four feet high by eight feet long by stove length's a face cord.

Normally Prett would be pleased with himself to remember that much, especially since they didn't cut firewood very often anymore. It would be like Prett to quiz Stosh on facts like that, giving him only a little time to answer after he'd puzzled on it for maybe an hour.

Today Prett couldn't stop the onslaught of facts, he was so feverish.

Last night he'd used cloves and comfrey on his inflamed gums to get twitchy snatches of sleep.

"Y'sure ya wanna go to th' woods?" Stosh asked.

"Yessh, I wanna go. Shomethin'sh gotta take my mind offa thish."

So Stosh drove them in the pickup on Route 38, just east of the county line, as Prett read through every road sign, scrambling the letters non-stop.

Johnny got his gun

Cough had been lying awake, watching the sun through the cracked window glass and plastic he hadn't yet bothered to take down from the winter. He'd slept fitfully since the town board meeting, partly due to the excitement, more from anxiety and guilt.

The sky was aluminum gray when he wrestled from the covers and got up to use the toilet. Coffee usually came next, so he wandered to the kitchen to put the kettle on, took a mug from the cupboard, scooped in the instant granules. He thought they might have to get a pool going to pay for Lyle's truck.

That would settle one problem, but there was a bigger one.

Kenny was still missing.

The sky's paleness was draining to the horizon, replaced by an iridescent blue.

He lit his third cigarette, feeling the smoke drift down into his deadened lungs. In a couple of hours he was planning to go to the college with Aurelia and Janie. To look for him.

What possessed me?

We were desperate, he answered himself, *an' Kenny'd been getting around so well in town for so long, I forgot how he is.*

His cheeks burned with the lie. Why hadn't he let Janie and Aurelia in on his plan?

Cough closed his eyes and his ex-wife's face came into focus. He opened his eyes again. Ashes crumbled onto his work shirt, the cigarette burning down between his fingers.

He lit a fresh cigarette, let the smoke curl up to his nostrils and into his eyes. That brought back the image of it, the burned-out back of Lyle's truck, Lyle's fury at the loss, Zola May's hurt with how much less important that made her. That was bad but an easier thing to dwell on than thoughts of Kenny lost.

"Cough? Are ya up yet?" he heard someone calling through the screen door in front.

"Just a second." It turned out to be Johnny Percy.

"Cough. I wanted to tell ya somethin'."

"You wanna come in, have some coffee?"

Johnny toed a nail head on the bottom step of the porch. "Naw. I just got to tell you something. Couldn't wait any longer."

"Uh, okay. What is it?"

Johnny sniffed. "You're not gonna like it."

"Well, then, why don'tcha just tell me straight out, so I can get back to my coffee."

"Y' know that kid," Johnny said, taking in a breath. "That I guess you're lookin' for? That Kenny?" He didn't wait for Cough to answer. "I think he might be dead."

Cough fell back against the door frame. "How?"

"I took a shot at him a few days ago. I thought he was bad news. Thought he was a gook."

"Shot him? What the Christ?"

"I didn't know, man. I d been on the road a coupla days. It was raining real hard. He spooked me bad."

"Jesus Christ!"

"I dunno for sure, I only saw him go down."

"Show me where you were. I wanna see Kenny." Cough grabbed his car keys.

Okay, Johnny thought. *But I wasn't shootin' at Kenny.*

They drove in wary silence. Johnny kept the butt of his rifle on the floor, tucked between his feet, the barrel up past his left shoulder.

Johnny was as calm and focused as a person could be. Cough hadn't even thought of bringing a gun. He had a .22 rifle and a twelve-gauge shotgun he'd used for hunting partridge and pheasant, years back. Right now he was training on Johnny's muttered directions to Kenny's body.

Later he'd worry about why Johnny had brought his rifle.

Celeste on her own

He has no idea who I am, oh, God, how long have I been going through this?

Celeste sat on the floor in Earhart's living room, running her hand back and forth across the carpet, assembling a heap of lint fibers from out of the chocolate, orange and beige pile.

Why have I stayed there?

Images of her husband flooded her, sitting in his office chair reading; pontificating with students; watching her pick up after him; falling asleep slumped over a book; having food brought to him in his chair. Why had she been attracted to him?

Marie had committed herself to going to graduation, as a cheerleader for several young women for whom her attention and support were critical. She asked Celeste to go too.

Celeste said she'd be okay, Marie should go alone. When she said it she believed it. But she hadn't thought Earhart would actually leave. She realized now that she was alone.

An earnest ambush

McAdam emerged from the air-conditioned conference room with the commencement stage party, in full graduation regalia. He was trying to stay behind Wispen, to keep an eye on him.

Guppy had stationed himself with Kenny in the foyer of the Du Pont Science Building, where the processional would pass in full view of the graduates and the local television cameras.

"What're we doing here, Mr. Guppy?"

"Waiting for the right moment, Kenny. Don't worry, it should be any second now." He peered around the corner.

"Mr. Guppy?"

"Yes." Guppy was gritting his teeth, anxious to send Kenny into the fray and be rid of him as soon as possible.

"You sure this is the best time to talk to him?" Kenny's heart was pounding so hard his chest hurt.

"All the people who could help will be with him, Kenny. You just make sure they hear what I told you to say."

"O-kay." Kenny could barely breathe. He sat down on the stairs, head hanging down, panting.

"Kenny? You're not going to pass out on me, are you?"

"I don't know, it hurts." He pressed the palm of his right hand to his chest.

"Take it easy, Kenny. Breathe. Breathe." Kenny's eyes were rolling back white. He slumped against the stairs.

"Christ!" Guppy whispered. "The bastard's having a seizure."

Guppy tucked his mortarboard between Kenny's head and the edge of the step, to keep him from hurting himself if he thrashed around. His arms and legs were already moving like a dog chasing a rabbit in its dream.

Do I confront McAdam myself? What evidence do I have?

Kenny was so still now that Guppy wasn't sure he was breathing. "Oh, Judas Priest! He's dead! I'll lose the sabbatical for sure now." Then Guppy heard footsteps on the concrete path, getting louder near the Science building.

McAdam! They're here! Guppy shot glances back and forth between Kenny and the processional, until the party had passed the open stretch of Commons.

"This could be evidence if he's dead," he hissed, jerking the mortarboard from behind Kenny's head.

It's not my fight, anyway, he rationalized. *If McAdam wants to do this and it screws the community, he'll just have to live with it.* He hesitated, realizing that abandoning Kenny would likely destroy his last best chance to turn it around with Celeste.

After one look back at Kenny's motionless body, Guppy jogged out the back of the building, to join the other faculty in the processional line.

Out into the real world

"Thank you, President McAdam, trustees, administrators, faculty, families, customers . . ." Boomer Hall, 1987 commencement speaker at Onlius State, used *customers* rather than *students* intentionally.

Bobo was slumped over in his folding chair, still hung over.

"I say customers, *consumers,* not because I want all you young people to buy the products of my corporation—although that would be a good idea—but no, I call you customers because you've been involved in the greatest of all enterprises."

McAdam sat up straight, flushed with pride.

"Yes, I'm talking about the system of learning you've been the consumers of, for these critical years . . ."

Guppy leaned over to whisper to Harlan. "Have you noticed that your F customers paid the same as your A customers? I wonder how they feel about that?"

Panic seized Harlan. He began to note mentally which of his failing students would be most likely to complain behind his back. Then he realized the list also could include those who had gotten D's, C's, B's and even A's, if they felt their egos hadn't been stroked enough. His insides tightened.

Bobo's friends let him slump completely in his chair, head tilted back, mortarboard hanging precariously from bobby pins fastened in his hair.

Harlan leaned over to whisper to Guppy. "Where's Darcardt? He'd really like this, don't you think?"

Guppy said yes—not sarcastically enough, Harlan worried. Guppy seemed preoccupied.

"I mean the Old Man." Harlan usually resisted using Guppy's phrase. "Where do you suppose he is?"

"It's his last time around. Maybe he decided to phone this one in."

Yes, that's probably it. Last night was pretty taxing on him, Harlan thought. *I can't wait to tell Guppy about the mill fight, as soon as this is over.*

"How many of you have thought of the importance of your parents' role as consumers?" Boomer asked.

Harlan caught a glimpse of one of the graduates mugging along with Boomer's speech, trying to make the person next to her laugh. Her friend seemed more annoyed than amused, staring straight ahead.

He wished he could see who the mocker was. It was making him wish he could go sit with her. Once he'd seen her well enough to know for sure it was Robin, he burned for wanting her, and from shame.

". . . and of course, the most important customers of the education product are the employers, most of which will come from the largest corporations, our globe-spanning ambassadors to the world."

Koemover, Wispen, McAdam, and the entire stage party were nodding their heads, leaning forward in their seats.

Bobo was sitting as an island of hangover. His belly rumbles and moaning had pushed his compatriots to the perimeter of the Bobo experience.

"So you see, your time here has not been an escape or avoidance of the real world, just not a wholly mature version of it. If you turn your attention to the projector screen behind me, the slide presentation I've prepared will illustrate."

Then the State University of New York College at Onlius Class of 1987, their families and friends, the college faculty and staff were treated to a lesson in how to make good through luck and pluck—Boomer Hall's life in slides.

Mission Accomplished

Everything was calm and clear and quiet when Kenny's panic passed, but he felt shaky as he puzzled out a route to the ceremony. The placards on stands with arrows pointing to the Field House helped.

When Kenny got within hearing, the man on the stage was going on about some special school he'd gone to. They had uniforms, and extra classes on things like classics, the man was saying, and they didn't go home to their families every night. Kenny felt sorry for the guy, wondered what he'd done wrong so he couldn't go to a regular school.

He was standing in the middle of the carpet they'd put down for a center aisle, just a few paces from the back wall, among the SRO crowd of families and well-wishers.

". . . as we made this pyramid, you can see by the looks on our faces how valuable an experience this was . . ."

Kenny thought this slide must be upside down because everyone around him was making those faces and laughing like that time his fly was open during the fourth-grade assembly, but he guessed the man didn't know it because he kept talking.

I prob'ly oughtta try to see this, so I can figure it out. He moved a few steps onto the carpet, turned his back to the projection screen, bent over and peered through his legs.

McAdam was on his way to the podium, frantically searching for a diplomatic way to tell Boomer his slide was upside down, when he spied a person in the far reaches of the field house nearly standing on his head in the center of the grand aisle.

Where had he seen someone do that before? He couldn't place it exactly, only some vague recollection of a family gathering maybe fifteen years ago with a goofy kid cousin.

The puzzle slowed McAdam's attempted rescue of Boomer. Some overexcited graduates had gone out into the aisles and assumed the same posture as Kenny. This, Boomer had noticed.

"Have you ever realized that if you look at human faces upside down long enough, they're really grotesque?" Guppy observed.

Harlan shot him a look. *Have you always been this strange?*

Boomer's composure was under siege. He tried to right the offending slide, but didn't know how. "Well, as I have just demonstrated by deliberately putting this slide in upside down, the problem with people schooled in the public sector is they lack the discipline to get the great tasks done that need to be performed."

Properly chagrined, three graduates left the aisle to get back to their seats; a dozen more replaced them.

"It's the higher standards for excellence in the private sector that make for higher performance" introduced the next slide, which showed a twenty-five percent improvement over the previous one. One of Boomer's prep-school buddies was falling feet-first past a high bar suspended sideways on poles from a ninety-degree inclined track.

Kenny stood up, tilted his head to the side to see this one, facing the screen. The growing army of Kenny-ites followed his lead, as they would any good aerobics instructor.

The slide was jammed beyond Boomer's ability to affect an electronic advance or retreat. McAdam searched the assembled faculty and staff for an AV technician. Wispen set the timer on his watch for thirty seconds, after which he was going to signal security to come put these kids in their seats.

"What's the hidden meaning of this slide?" Guppy asked. "Maybe it's a meditation on the relative difficulty of achievement. Something about varying social class advantages."

Boomer finally wrenched the locking ring off the slide tray, and ripped the offending slide from its cage. It had been a temporary disability. Replacing the locking ring, he clicked forward to the next slide with confidence and ease. Kenny rolled his neck around to loosen the muscles; too much blood had rushed to his head.

:26, :27, :28. Wispen swept his gaze around the field house, sensed the rabble was settling down, and gave up on calling in the troops.

Alone in the aisle, Kenny blinked away the last spots before his eyes. The slide man was done talking now, replaced by a voice that was somehow familiar. He moved up the aisle toward the podium, first cautiously, then with a growing sense that his mission was nearing its end.

McAdam had just finished thanking Boomer, and was setting the conferral of degrees in motion. Watching Kenny approach, he looked in alarm at Wispen, motioning for him to get security.

Wispen studied the effect of Kenny's approach. He saw Kenny's eyes locked on McAdam, judging correctly that this young man posed no threat to anyone else. His limp smile back to McAdam suggested he had no idea what to do.

"Oh, there he is," Aurelia whooped out loud before she realized it. She was trapped four rows from the top of the bleachers, rows filled with strangers blocking her path to the aisle. She would just have to watch Kenny, she decided, never let him out of her sight, until she could collar him.

"Where are you going?" the marshal of the processional hissed as Kenny passed.

"To talk to my cousin," he whispered back, hoarsely.

Cousin? McAdam thought, shrinking back in horror. Reflexively, he looked for television cameras and newspaper photographers, gauging how to proceed with damage control.

Relief shot through Guppy as he watched Kenny approach the platform. He thought about bolting from his seat for a moment to take him aside, then gave up on it. When he realized Kenny might deviate from the plan and tell McAdam it was Guppy's idea, he began to look for a quick exit route.

Kenny climbed the steps next to Isabel Agajanian, kept going when she stopped to get her diploma from the academic vice president, and went straight up to McAdam. "You've gotta help us in Alta keep the mill open."

"I've got to what?"

"You're Baxie McAdam, aren'tcha? You're my cousin, your mother came from my mother's people. I'm Kenny Hopewell, from Alta. We need the college to help with the mill."

McAdam reached past Kenny to shake Isabel's hand, scanning the stage party nervously. Boomer's arms were still crossed in a huff. Wispen feigned attention with one of the SUNY trustees seated next to him.

"I'm afraid I can't."

"You gotta. Everybody's countin' on you." Kenny had grabbed McAdam's hand, pumping it for emphasis.

"This is not the time."

"After this you'll help?"

"Look, I didn't say that. You've got to get out of here."

Kenny focused on his face, then suddenly remembered exactly what he wanted to say. "Baxie, I know you lied." McAdam was hearing it in his mother's voice, Kenny's mouth even twisting in her way. "You ought to have gone to Vietnam like your brother, you never had heart trouble."

McAdam used his other hand to pull free from Kenny's grip. Wispen waved once briskly and nodded, sending four security guards scampering to the front platform where they pulled Kenny down behind the scaffolding. The television cameras had already captured Boomer's sound bites and moved on, but hundreds of parents were snapping pictures, filming and videotaping Kenny's detention.

"I just wanna talk to the president. He's my cousin," Kenny pleaded.

"Right. Mine, too," said the guard twisting his arm.

"No, I mean it. I'm s'posed to talk to him, about the mill."

"Look, kid. You better pipe down right now. In case you hadn't noticed, there's a graduation going on." He tugged Kenny's bent arm upward.

"Oww. Cut it out."

"Sure, sure." Dan the security guard put his knee in Kenny's back.

"Hey. Easy, boys," Wispen snapped as he came on the scene. "I want him now, alone. Let's not get rough yet." *Maybe he'll come in handy.*

Dan waved the rest of them off. At the side of the platform, they twitched and made threatening gestures at Kenny behind Wispen's back.

"I won't let them do anything bad to you," Wispen soothed. "Just trust me."

Kenny was near-delirious from fear. One of the guards had whispered something fierce and sexual that he wanted to do to Kenny if he got him all alone.

"I didn't do nothing wrong, mister."

"I know, I know. Calm down. Start with your name."

"I'm Kenny Hopewell. I'm Baxie McAdam's cousin. That's why I wanted to talk to him."

Baxie? "About what?"

"I'm not s'posed to tell." Kenny worried his lip. Mr. Guppy had just said that morning not to trust anyone else at the college, especially not Wispen.

Security was beginning to have its hands full. A small but growing crowd was trying to get past them to Kenny, including Harlan, Janie and his fans from the slideshow.

Someone broke through, a woman. Kenny saw two of the guards turning to give chase to her before he heard, "Kenny, Kenny, you okay?"

"Aurelia, oh, Reel." She looked far too young for the Salvation Army clothes she was wearing. She was more like a young woman pumped up with adrenaline and lifting a car off her infant child than his cautious older sister.

Wispen turned around to look at her: scared, defiant, straining to get free of Dan.

"Who's that?"

"My sister."

"Careful, boys, let her go." He nodded in the direction of the crowd. "If she's here, too, can you tell me what you're doing?"

"I guess it'd be okay. Lemme talk to her quick first."

Wispen turned his back momentarily and stood just beneath the edge of the platform.

"Aurelia," Kenny whispered, "gosh, I'm glad to see you."

She hugged him awkwardly. "You had me worried sick."

"How didja find me?"

"I talked to Cough. He told me everything."

"Then it's okay to tell? This man wants to know."

"Sure it's okay. I've been talkin' about it to everybody. They have this big petition thing since you've been gone."

"Okay, mister, I'm ready to tell ya."

Wispen turned and smiled ingratiatingly. "So what is it?"

"'Bout the mill, in Alta, how they've been tryin' to close it down. We need him to get the college to help us keep it open."

A range of possibilities whirred through Wispen's brain. He could make these people look really bad and ingratiate himself even more with the mill owners, or let them embarrass McAdam. Or—he could not suppress a smile—he could suggest that McAdam was in league with them in a secret attempt to undermine the sale of the plant.

"Well, let's see what we can do." Wispen took Aurelia's hand and led her and Kenny out from beneath the platform, told the security guards to get them chairs near the stage exit stairs. The crowd slowly broke up and went back to their seats, except for Janie and Harlan.

Wispen climbed back up on stage, after he whispered to Dan the guard, flashing McAdam the okay sign. McAdam's blood froze. His hands failed him for the congratulatory handshakes, especially as he seemed to be fondling Susan Fermi's breast when she received her diploma. It didn't help whenever he looked at Kenny, who was beaming at him.

"So congratulations, and good luck to the 1987 Class of Onlius State College." Recessional music blared from loudspeakers, the stage party rose and began their march toward the rear of the arena. By the time they had looped back toward the front exit and picked up a good stream of faculty and graduates, Kenny and Aurelia had been swallowed by a sea of professional media and concerned people with filmed evidence of his mistreatment. McAdam was swept out of the field house, made quick excuses to the trustees and Boomer, before sprinting to a delivery entrance on the other side of the building.

As he reached the growing throng around Kenny, who was now standing on his folding chair, it became absolutely clear what was happening. *The bastard's holding a press conference!*

"Mr. Hopewell, can you confirm that Dr. McAdam is on the side of the workers in the mill dispute?" asked Carol Pedanza from the *Onlius Record*.

"It's what I was told. Yeah." He furrowed his brow. "Sure I'm sure."

"Mr. Hopewell, can you tell us more about the beating you received?"

"The beating," McAdam whimpered. *The sonofabitch interrupted a commencement ceremony.*

"Well, nobody really hit me that I can remember." Carol's disappointment was visible. "Somebody did twist my arm behind my back, though, and put me down with his knee." Kenny smiled back when he saw her face brighten again.

"Why were you given this beating?"

"I dunno." Kenny's mouth hung open as he reflected on the question. "All I can tell you is they stopped being mean when I told 'em I'm here for the mill, and that my cousin the president said he was gonna help."

The reporters turned away as a herd from Kenny. Most of them missed McAdam squatting on his heels, moaning. The few who did spot him and approached for a comment began the chase when he bolted away.

"Baxie seems awful upset," Kenny said.

"Well, congratulations, Janie!" Harlan told her. "And congratulations to you, Aurelia. You found him."

"Had enough of an education, Kenny? Ready to go home?" Janie asked.

"Yeah, for sure. Can we eat first? It's a long way."

Gunnar hits a vein

A red hawk circled over the fringe of pines, sun warming the air that lifted it in the drafts. Gunnar noted it, sensed the omen.

The Sullivan's were there with the kids, wandering up and down, finding ways to be nearby.

Gunnar had gotten a longer spool of cable, and set it up so he could send the bit and stalk slamming deeper into the earth.

Renora brought him tuna sandwiches and coffee with cream and sugar, fixed the way Zane liked it. Gunnar didn't use sugar at all, but drank the coffee and smiled, knowing it meant a lot to her.

He looked into the blue sky at the hawk and back at the kids, to see if they were watching. They were playing in the gravel that had been opened up in the side of the hill near the driveway, conducting elaborate marriage rituals of pairs of ants before they squashed them with the ball-peen hammer of sudden judgment. He knew it would be useless to call them.

At first it was just a different sound from the bit slamming into the stone, a softer, duller report. Gunnar watched, wondered if anyone else picked it up.

The kids were engrossed in the ants, the hawk circled, Zane and Renora knelt together to inspect the scorched clapboards. Gunnar had told them today would be their last chance because they were well over two hundred feet, and there wasn't much cable left on the new reel. He thought he saw the beginning of a smile un-tensing the muscles of Zane's face as he gazed at his wife, just before he heard the unmistakable sound of water meeting the bit and climbing up around it.

He was noticing just then how sweet and fresh the air smelled.

Guppy runs, Guppy hides

There was no place he could think of that was safe. His office was far too obvious, and at home he would be especially vulnerable, because he had lost any sense of Celeste's feelings.

Guppy drove for a while trying to figure out how to avoid being drawn into whatever trouble Kenny had caused. The McIntosh town sign jolted his memory. Charlie Darcardt would be the perfect person to hide out with until the heat was off.

∼

After calling the police to Darcardt's house, Guppy sat on the front steps disgusted with himself that he had waited so long, worried he might have put his foot in it by calling.

Celeste will never come back. I've lost her because I'm so selfish. The sudden terror of being alone made him vomit onto the ground by his feet. Tears soaked into his beard.

When they first began going out, Celeste was still shaken from her breakdown. He was so important to her, she told him constantly, because of his stability. Guppy didn't know when she'd begun to feel trapped, but he knew it was long before he'd let himself be aware of it. Her insecurities had not been as big a threat to their marriage as her recovery was appearing to be.

The Onlius County sheriff's deputy asked him the standard questions, wearing the standard-issue emotionless expression. *Who is John Harlan?*

"Someone Dr. Darcardt worked with at the college. Yes, actually someone I work with, also. My officemate."

Why is his name on the manuscript?

"I have no idea. He was at graduation, sitting next to me this morning. Yes, of course other people saw him there. You could probably get him at home.

"I don't know. He could be anywhere. I'm sure if you left a message, he'd get back to you."

Guppy noticed the growing tension in the deputy's questions. He thought he might have to vomit again, then considered how that might fit into the scenario the deputy was building in his head.

"I should be going, officer. My wife will be wondering where I am," he managed.

After the paramedic said that the early indications pointed to death by stroke and cerebral hemorrhage, the deputy said thanks for your help and we'll call you if we have any more questions.

He drove straight home hoping Celeste was there, wondering if he'd be able to handle it if she got healed without him.

Celeste in her new skin

Celeste was sitting in the living room, in Ernie's chair, reading *Community is Possible*.

He wanted to say something about his feelings, to touch her. But his arms hung at his sides, his mouth could only release the words "Charlie's dead."

She recoiled. "That's terrible," Celeste said slowly. "What happened?"

"They said a stroke." His eyes, searching for an angle of connection, could find none.

The terrible logic of it washed over her in the aftershock. She wanted Marie, but couldn't really have her. She was reclaiming her home, and wasn't sure she wanted it any more. Her bond of the wounded with Darcardt the night of the party had been the beginning of her climb back into herself. Now, just like that, he was gone, unreachable.

Even while the Celeste who was newly herself mourned wildly, what was left of Guppy's wife remembered the language of their relationship, the bitter, dry abstraction.

It made her sick, but just now it was useful, helping her get through this loss that crowned the others.

She met his eyes, seeing herself there. She wondered, when he looked into hers, if he saw anything.

"That's too bad," she said to Guppy. "He had such integrity, and he's done some fine work." She shoved a bookmark between the pages and set the book atop a journal on the end table next to her.

"Things will have to change, Ernie."

He'd forgotten how intense her eyes could be.

"I know."

"I won't make any guarantees. I don't even know if I'm going to stay here." Her gaze was almost fierce.

"I understand."

"I noticed the guest room upstairs looks like you had a slumber party last night."

Kenny, he thought.

"He did okay, you know." She smiled briefly. "At least that's what I was told. You should be proud."

He smiled back, relaxing. "Thanks. Any chance I'll catch a break for helping him?"

"It's good to dream, Ernie. Hold onto that dream." She picked up the book again so matter-of-factly, he wasn't sure if she'd been joking.

So, he realized, *I'm not going to get any sympathy for going through this.*

He watched her read and stop every few moments to underline a passage. It made him strangely excited.

He had no idea how unsettled she felt inside, how close to running.

When he cleaned the guest room, Guppy could not get himself to throw away the one tuft of deer fur that Kenny had left behind. He left it on the top of the dresser, a good luck charm for himself.

How ants are like Alta

"Something's wrong. I know he dropped right here." Johnny kicked at dead leaves, paced up the road bank.

"Are ya sure?" Cough's voice was low and steady, breath shallow in his chest. He felt numb.

"I know he went down here," Johnny insisted.

"Kenny?"

"Yeah," Johnny said softly. "I would have walked point for Kenny."

"You didn't even know who you were shootin' at?"

Johnny nodded, cradling the rifle across his wrist.

Cough kept himself upright leaning against a shag hickory, feeling the ants climb out from their bark shelters and crawl across his fingers. He'd never thought before how some ants sacrificed themselves for the rest, how they knew that with sacrifice and patience everything would be all right for the rest of the colony.

Celeste leaves an impression

Marie Earhart read Celeste's note, the words carefully noncommittal.

So she's back there with him. She touched her left breast, remembered Celeste's mouth there this morning, and lay back. Strange, she didn't feel jealous, or alone.

Stosh is downed

"Goddammit, I tol' ya to wassh out for the limb. I tol' ya," Prett shouted to Stosh as he lay trapped beneath the fallen cherry tree. They had decided to chance getting a load of logs from the woods off the power line right-of-way.

Prett hacked at the tree with his McCulloch. Stosh was absolutely still. The little bit of his face that Prett could see through the leaves was birch white.

"You gonna be all right, Shtosh. I promish," he said over and over.

The last of the tree twisted Stosh's elbow back as Prett rolled it off him. "I gotta getcha home, getcha to Georgette. You jusht hold on."

Stosh lay motionless, eyes closed from shock.

Prett heaved him onto his shoulder and propped him up in the passenger side of the truck cab. Stosh's lips were purple, his eyes open now, dull and glassy.

Prett never let go of Stosh's hand while he sped home.

Touching the dream

His letter of resignation was drafted and ready for McAdam.

Wispen thought it would be smart to clean everything out of his office first, in case someone got the idea to seize his files.

He pulled a manila folder labeled Christian Anti-Communism Crusade to pack in his cardboard box, flipping through the pages, recalling the times he had used these materials to bait people into exposing their un-American proclivities.

Wispen smiled at the betrayals, broken promises, baits-and-switches and deceptions recorded in back of a thick file with the innocuous label, *Accounts Paid and Balanced,* in his neat, tight script on a bank-ledger form. It had given him strength with every new challenge to his authority.

He made one final entry before packing the file away. MCADAM, he wrote proudly in the account-name column. Finally getting the upper hand over McAdam in the same moment that he was getting his dream job—streamlining the workforce at the Mid-Northern Lakeland Paper Mill in Alta—was the ultimate.

I really am blessed.

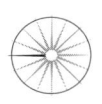

Emilio remains a patriot

A flyer from P&C supermarket, an invisible hearing aid special offer, and two discount life insurance come-ons were the mail in the post-office box Emilio kept as the one connection with those who had a home. One of the life insurance letters was routed through a local agent who had added the sweetener of a one-hour retirement planning consultation.

"Retirement planning? Have I done that yet?" He thought about it the whole time as he walked back to the abandoned train station. Should he make an appointment so he could pull the guy's chain, or just recycle the postage-paid reply card with the rest of the stuff?

Planning? he thought as he picked through the weeds along the riverbank for bottles and cans to return for deposit. *Sounds like socialism. That's not the American way.*

. . . meet me tonight in Atlantic City

"Certainly took ya long enough. Billy Boy's been waitin' for ya since eleven-thirty." Barb was drying the dishes from lunch and, Janie suspected, breakfast, having hurried to rinse them when she saw Janie drive into the yard.

"Eleven-thirty? I said eleven-thirty would be the earliest the ceremony would be over," Janie said. She looked on the rack where another dry dish towel normally hung, seeking an avenue to ease the guilt. Barb noticed.

"Is that what you said? I wasn't sure, you were in such a hurry, ya know. Billy's the one who said you'd be back." She spoke it over her shoulder, the edge of guilt softened as her voice broke.

Janie moved next to her, Barb turned her head away.

"Is something wrong? Are you sick? Is something wrong with Billy?"

Barb's shoulders shook under the weight of it. Tears streamed down her cheeks, plunking into the sink.

"Naw, naw. It's not your precious Billy." She snuffed, and wiped her cheeks and nose with the dish towel.

"Then what is it?" She patted her shoulder, feeling Barb stiffen and brace against her touch.

"You don't care about him. Don't pretend you care!"

"Wouldja please tell me what you're talking about?"

"She'll hurt him. She doesn't care anything about him. She just wants to use him."

"Use who?"

"Earl. Your husband, remember? Billy's father."

"Who's gonna hurt him?"

"Melissa. She's run off with him. That tramp."

"Ya mean Melissa Ogden, from the mill?"

"Yes."

"That bitch. I've been fillin' in for her at work."

Barb turned quietly from the sink to face Janie. "He called me, from Atlantic City."

"Atlantic City, huh. He always said he would take me there."

"Yeah, I remember." Barb said it so softly Janie wasn't sure she had actually heard it.

"Barb, Atlantic City's no big deal. What is it, really?"

"He said they're not comin' back, and . . ."

"An' what?"

Barb walked across the kitchen, through to the back door. She stared out the window at Billy spinning on her tree swing. Janie followed her.

"They wanted me to send him down there," Barb said. "On a bus."

Janie could not catch her breath.

"And I thought about it, too. Even after I offered to bring him there and they said no way, they didn't want me to."

Janie watched Billy lean back in delight, his sandy hair almost brushing the ground as he spun. Her heart was slamming inside her chest.

"Look how happy he is. And they wanted me to put him on a bus, all alone."

The spinning swing slowed, swiveling to a standstill. "Mom!" Billy called as soon as he caught sight of her. "Mom, c'mere."

Barb stepped to the side so Janie could open the door.

"He's been a real good boy, Janie, but I think he wants to go home."

Janie ran to give him a hug, carrying him back into the house with his arms around her neck and legs scissored over her hips.

"Say goodbye to grandma."

"Okay." The circles around Barb's eyes grew brighter red and shiny through his hug.

"You be grandma's good boy, Billy," she called as he and Janie were climbing into her car. "An' come back again soon."

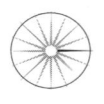

Together to stay

He was holding Wispen's letter, wondering if this meant he was done for, when the phone rang.

"Baxter? It's all over," Gordon blurted angrily. "I just got the call from the Judge. He said the whole deal's dead. The hydro vote last night killed it."

Last night? It was over last night!

"Baxter? Are you still there?"

"Yes, Henry. I'm just trying to handle my disappointment." *Yes! Yes! Yes! It was over last night!*

"Well, I thought you'd want to know, as soon as possible, so you could make the adjustments at your end."

I'm holding Wispen's letter of resignation in my hand. I'm off the hook, and he doesn't know the job he thinks he's going to is gone. McAdam said, "Thank you, Michael, I appreciate the gesture. We'll be able to take it from here." He struggled to keep his voice grave.

"Are you sure you're okay, Baxter? I thought you'd be crushed about losing the grant."

"The grant? I'm afraid I'm not following . . ."

"Bax, the grant was predicated on the deal. The grant's dead."

Dead! The grant! How are we going to make up for that? McAdam clutched at the hair on the side of his head. "Ye-yes, I knew that, Michael," he gasped. "We'll take it from here. Goodbye."

President McAdam sat slumped at his desk, folding into ever-smaller sections the letter of resignation that had been the answer to his prayers, but which now he couldn't afford to accept.

To the source

Such a warm, sunny May had left the river lower than normal, thicker and sluggish like the day last fall when the air had hung heavy with the aroma of last ripening.

It was Zola's idea to come to the river, for Lyle to forget about his truck for a while and try to be happy about the mill.

"Son-of-a-bitchin' Mercury piece of shit." Zola's car was too compact for Lyle, its automatic transmission slipping too often, its four cylinders lacking in power and acceleration.

"This is stupid, a total waste of time." Lyle walked the river path two paces ahead of Zola. "Ya know that Rastin wanted me to come over today, don'tcha? Said we could fix the truck over to his house. Have a few beers."

Zola heard it in her father's voice. *A few beers.* Words she associated with loneliness and abandonment.

"You're right," she said. "This is a waste of time. I don't know why I thought I could help you." She turned back toward the car.

"Oh, so ya don't wanna go now." The hurt in Lyle's voice sounded genuine.

"I never said that."

"Then why are ya goin' back?"

"I'm sick of feeling like this. I'm doing my best, but if you decide you need to go off with your brother, I'm not going to fight."

"Ya don't mind?"

"Lyle, some people just tried to burn us out, but we came through it, alive. You've still got a job. I think I'll be able to handle it if you go over to your brother's house."

"So you're okay bein' alone?"

"You ought to know how I feel. But I'm not gonna be alone. I don't have to anymore."

280 / The Middle of Everywhere

"I could be with my brother and still be alone."

That's when it hit her. *He's not proud of himself. He's trying to get out from under being a Lester.* "I thought you liked being with your family," she tested.

"Then you're the only one who thought that." Her surprised expression made him continue. "Do you have any idea what it's like? Having everybody expect you to be just like Rastin? Or my old man?"

"Then what makes you want to go over there?"

"Well, at least one thing, they'll stick by me. They won't have their noses up in the air like at the college."

"If you want, you can be a Brooks now." She looked him squarely in the eye.

At first he was angry, until her fierceness changed to a smile.

"It's up to you, babe," Zola said. "Y'know, I always liked the name Elizabeth. I just might change my name to Elizabeth Brooks-Lester."

Lyle smiled back at her. "You will, huh."

"Yes. And I may change my hair color, too."

His eyebrows lifted in surprise. "Don't do that. I love your hair. I think it's pretty."

Zola's smile swelled. "You mean beautiful, don't you?"

"Yeah, beautiful." He touched her cheek. "Beautiful Mrs. Brooks-Lester. Uh, Zola," he asked, after admiring her for another moment. "You still wanna go to the river?"

"Yeah, I do. But you have to want to go, too."

"Then let's go."

It was his turn to be surprised, in the glade of birch and maple saplings, when she kissed him, the way she tucked her shoe behind his knee and pressed herself to him, one great merger of warm electricity surging through them.

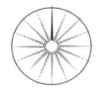

Darcardt's special gift

For reasons beyond the obvious, the backbone of American democracy has always been a spiritual one, centered on a belief that it is part of the natural order for people to govern themselves.

Harlan wasn't sure if he felt greater guilt or embarrassment. The guilt was because every fiber of his being told him that, once again, he would fail someone. Darcardt's manuscript would never go further, and *that* was because of the embarrassment.

How could he be the one to spread the news that Charles Darcardt was exploring spirituality at the end of his life? Even if it seemed like Darcardt wanted him to do it?

The embarrassment about Robin was even stronger, the latest and most needy person he'd made promises to, knowing as he made them he would break them.

Harlan thought that, yes, it was probably the embarrassment.

The need to write his dissertation nagged, more powerfully than Charlie Darcardt's legacy or Robin's living death. It made him sick with himself, but it was a sick he was used to, one he had learned to live with, after all.

Besides, he still was struggling to figure out the last thing Darcardt had told him, after the board meeting, when Harlan had asked how the Judge could so completely have underestimated the millworkers.

"Don't be too hard on him," he'd said. "It's not his fault he lacked the advantages of a public education."

Martha in the parlor

Yesterday had been confusing. Martha had seen Wiley, and then someone who said he was Kenny, but Kenny was nowhere near that big. She was haunted by the thought that Helmut Molshoc had come back, and maybe he was coming after her.

The new orderly's breath was sickening and he had bothered her too many times last night, taking her from the closet she had been in with Wiley, or Kenny. *Why did he have to do that?*

She recalled her sense of peace in the closet, seeing the cobweb way up in the corner. If you didn't know better—if you hadn't been sitting on the floor talking to your dead husband, or your son—looking up past the light, you'd swear it was just a shadow.

But a tiny brown spider kept the web, up in that scrubbed and airless corner of the world. Martha couldn't get the web out of her mind—the symmetry of it, a home left invisible by the way the inside darkness met the inside light.

She kept that image in her mind when she felt anxious, about the orderly with the frightening breath, about seeing Helmut Molshoc again, or about seeing Wiley, or about not seeing Wiley.

Johnny gets the call

The crow's cawing distracted Johnny when he was beyond tight. He started to look up into the trees.

Cough closed his eyes, to get lost in the feel of the ants on his hand. If Johnny was going to do something, Cough wished he'd get it over with.

Something about the crow's call was pulling Johnny's attention away.

"You killed people before?" Cough couldn't believe it was such a matter-of-fact question, or that he had asked it.

"Yeah. Of course I did." Johnny couldn't locate the crow for the freshly budded leaves.

"Why? Why'dja do it?" It seemed to be an important question at the time, something Cough thought he deserved to know.

"Whaddaya mean? I had to."

"Had to?"

"It was them or me. To survive."

"So it was only when you were in the service?'

"Of course. Wha'dja think?"

Cough was silent. He closed his eyes again.

"I was taught to kill," Johnny continued. "We all were. It's what bein' a soldier's all about."

Cough opened his eyes and pointed straight up into the trees to the crow. Johnny followed with his eyes, then raised the rifle and sighted the bird.

"Whatever you did over there wasn't your fault. They didn't give you a choice, did they?"

"No, but I did it. I killed people, people I don't even know for sure were the enemy."

"I understand that. But didja have a choice?"

"Don't ask me that! Why're you asking me that?"

"Because you helped us, and it looks to me like you don't know any more, when you got choices and when you don't."

The crow lifted from the tree limb and dropped down toward them, as if offering itself to Johnny, before it arced away. The afternoon sun left a rainbow against the crow's feathers, like oil floating on a dark puddle.

"You don't need that guilt no more, John. It's just keepin' the old fight around. You don't want it no more."

Cough drove the back way to catch the road home, after Johnny said he wanted to walk to his buddy Randall's house. The afternoon sun angled down through mackerel clouds, bronzing the light in his rearview mirror. On the corner where he turned right onto the state road, a flight of swallows dipped and rose and turned as one, lighting on telephone wires at the finale of the aerial display. A late flock of Canadian geese pushed their V across the sky where the blue edged into white.

"What a lucky sonofabitch I am."

Kenny, given some room

"Are you sure you don't want to come? Alfonzo and Tilia'd love to see you." Aurelia noticed the tinge of guilt in her voice, wondered where it was coming from.

Kenny's smile startled her.

"I'm okay, Reel. I just wanna stay home for awhile, y'know. I miss it. I miss my room."

"If you're sure you'll be all right."

"I'll be fine. I'll go the next time. Tell them, okay?"

"Yeah. Definitely."

"And, uh, Reel? Aurelia?"

Her eyebrows raised.

"From now on, I'm goin' with you to see Mom."

She nodded and tried to swallow. She'd never noticed how much he looked like the pictures of their father when he was in the Army.

"I'll leave the porch light on for ya, Reel. Have fun, okay?"

She passed him on her way to the door, touching his arm lightly before wrapping her arms around him, warm sobs into his shoulder.

"I love you, Kenny. You know that?"

"Yeah, Reel. I love you, too."

She looked back at him watching her through the screen door as she climbed into the Rambler. She waved. He flicked the lights on and off, their secret signal.

She couldn't believe how much he looked like a grown man.

Kenny strolled through the house, sat in each room for a few minutes, taking in the familiarity. In the kitchen he made three peanut butter and jelly sandwiches for himself and ate them, washed down with a quart of milk. Afterward he climbed the stairs to his room, to look again at the fragile husks of skin the baby snakes had left behind when they left his dresser drawer, while he was on his mission.

Johnny's last hitch

Tilia had made special desserts and coffee for Aurelia and their other guest. After Johnny left in the morning, she and Alfonzo had talked for the rest of the day about how they could get him together with Aurelia. He'd told them he'd be back as soon as he finished with a little errand. They had no way of knowing that he had given up his rifle, and was hiking on the road, trying to hitch a ride to his fathers' farm on the Southern Tier, now that he'd burned down what was left of the old place.

Gerry Scott, looking for love

Even before she took off the leather vest, Gerry was feeling squeamish about watching her act. The C-section scar was only the clincher.

"Look at her move," Randall laughed. The stripper was clomping around in a circle, motioning with her hands for them to get closer.

"She has the gift of music," Jonesey said.

Gerry laughed and peeled the label off his bottle of Molson Golden, and tried to avoid eye contact with the stripper. He'd really wanted to be at the bar in Red Swamp, watching the Happiest Man in the World with his wife, gazing into each other's eyes. Gerry wanted another chance to see what that was like.

Robin's last stand

John,

Fear is what's mostly ahead, even if I survive the cancer. I don't really have a family, not the way it matters. They don't know who I am. Neither do I.

I know they would get doctors and everything. Then I'd die from suffocation.

I'd rather die crawling under barbed wire someplace leading people to freedom, and I would do that with you.

Just don't ask me to waste my time waiting around for you at faculty parties, while you're impressing a few academic snobs.

Let's go away together.

Who am I kidding?

Robin read the letter again, folded it, and thought again about whether she should send it to Harlan.

Harlan on his mission

Harlan whistled softly, picked at his teeth with his thumbnail, reread the opening paragraph from Carmen's paper. It was better than he'd expected, maybe too good, a source for worry.

The citations were right this time, APA format, with page numbers. The time he'd spent helping her might have paid off.

He checked one reference against his own copy, then settled in to read Carmen's paper for substance. By the third page, he'd seen two interesting insights not mentioned in class or in the assigned reading. She had thought it through on her own.

Somehow it reminded him of Robin, and Conrad, and Conrad's sense of humor made him think of Everett Winslow, who had managed to work a classmate's attack of gas into a mnemonic device about Teapot Dome.

It was a good paper, very good even, not great, but enough to bring a smile of admiration. Harlan felt so pleased with it that he read through eight more before realizing he really did need to pee.

It might not last, but for that moment he was happy being a teacher.

The Casimirs, staying alive

Georgette had coaxed Stosh back from near death and rigged a sling for his arm after Prett snapped it back in place. She was sure he'd live, was far from sure that he'd ever be able to do much with it again.

Prett started to moan about the pain in his gums as soon as she told him Stosh would be okay. The comfrey she gave him worked well enough to calm him down.

"What we gonna do, Georgette? Ain't none of ush got anyting comin' for retirement. Never paid into no Shocial Shecurity. An' Shtosh is bad, ain't he?"

"I won't lie to ya, Prett. His arm is real bad. You might have to start takin' Claude out with ya."

He held his jaw in both hands and sucked gently on his gums, circulating the comfrey around inside his mouth, while she watched, feigning unconcern.

"Shouldn't be thish way, Jet. Ain't right."

"Well, you can never figure, that's for sure. Wouldja' have ever thought that Johnny Percy would come over here this afternoon and leave his rifle, sayin' he wouldn't need it no more?"

"It'sh a damn good rifle. Don't mind havin' it. Jusht hope we don't need it."

"I know what ya mean, but it don't seem so. Life is hard. No matter what ya do, you can't expect to have a great life. That's not what it's for."

She left Prett putting more comfrey on what was left of his gums, and went down the hall to tuck the kids in.

Georgette hugged and kissed the baby, crossed the room to pat Claude's foot under the thin cover. Down the hall Carrie was setting out her clothes for church tomorrow morning, picking the shoes Joanie thought were cute, praying again that she'd come and sit in the pew beside her, so they could whisper to each other during the service.

After her mother's footsteps receded down the hall, Carrie tiptoed to the kitchen and stared at the new rifle leaning in the corner behind the door. It was drawing her. She wished she didn't have that hard hurt from being lonely, the hurt you could live in for the rest of your life. She wished her heart wasn't racing so fast, that her finger didn't feel good on the trigger.

The baby started crying down the hall. Carrie put the rifle back in the corner and went to her, picked her up and cradled her until she fell asleep again, all the while thinking about Joanie, all the while feeling her way down the dark hallway.

True North

The room seemed strangely familiar, like it belonged to someone else he knew.

The quiet of the empty house made him lonely for a while, before the smell of his bed and pillow made him settle to sleep.

Then fierce winds buffeted Kenny, lifting him off the bed. He was four feet above his body, watching himself lie on his bed in peaceful sleep.

The storm picked up, rocking him harder. Clouds appeared with his father's face, with Cough scowling, with Johnny Percy sighting down a rifle barrel.

Kenny had never felt chaos like this before. If there had been a way to end it, he would have, even going back on the road again.

This will be okay, this will be okay, he kept repeating, as if the mantra would protect him.

He began to cry, suspended above himself in a storm of all his fear and confusion. Kenny hung on, fixing on something he'd seen on the road, early one morning as the sun glittered on light dew. He was walking by a golf course, and at that moment could see thousands of spider webs splayed across the course, all the way to where a tree line cut off the light. It looked like part of a pattern he should recognize.

Kenny closed his eyes and rode the storm.

The wind spun him like a needle dial on a Twister board. He came to rest, aligned with his body below, head above head, feet above feet, settling back into himself.

He looked around his room, the way a newborn would. The wicker chair in the corner was still peeling its white paint, but now it was a reminder of how old it was, of how many people who loved him had sat in it. The top of his dresser, littered with the treasure of his adventure, seemed less like it belonged to a confused, sloppy kid. And the oval mirror mounted on top reflected a face that might still not be sure of where it was going, but definitely knew where it had been.

Kenny smiled, content to drift back asleep—where he always knew where he was—and stay there until Aurelia called him downstairs in the morning for breakfast.

Oliver North* on Baxter McAdam

His father knew my father, in military school. They learned to shred together. In fact, that's Baxter's problem. You've got to have a good shredder. Plus, of course, you need Fawn Hall. Marla Axe is not right for him. She doesn't understand the work.

Look at Wiley Hopewell. An unfortunate consequence of the Big Game. At the mill they would know that if they could see the Big Picture. You need the courage to go outside the law if you want to preserve it.

Back to McAdam. I only wish I could have helped. He's a good soldier. We need more good soldiers if we're going to have freedom.

My only other advice is, don't let the card carriers get you down. Remember what we learned from the Watergate patriots.

There's always another day.

---

*Before becoming the darling of the right-wing media, Oliver North admitted to committing the crimes central to the Iran-Contra scandal, and then sued the Reagan Administration for making him the fall guy.